"What . . . what's the matter?" she managed to ask, her voice sounding like a faulty pipe organ. She flushed slightly. He was still staring at her, not taking the hand she held out. She allowed it to drop to her side and struggled to regain control.

"I don't need this," Nick rasped, and his hands flashed out to grab her wrists and jerk her back to him. "I don't need this kind of complication."

She wanted to ask what he meant, but he was kissing her again, his mouth urgent and greedy, devouring her as if she could be consumed in that embrace. Her head tilted back and she felt her hair fall loose from the ribbons that held it up. Nick's hands were on her, his touch searing through the thin muslin of her gown. She was aching everywhere, an insistent throbbing that demanded she ease it, but she wasn't certain how. At the moment, she had lost all sense of what was right and wrong. All she wanted to do was satisfy the burning need. . . .

BECAUSE of YOU

MICKI BROWN

ST. MARTIN'S PAPERBACKS

BECAUSE OF YOU

Copyright © 1993 by Micki Brown.
Excerpt from *The Island Harp* copyright © 1991 by Jeanne Williams.

Cover illustration by Judy York.

ISBN: 0-312-92960-9

Printed in the United States of America

St. Martin's Paperbacks edition/February 1993

10 9 8 7 6 5 4 3 2 1

To the real Amber Jenné—my second "daughter"

CHAPTER
1

Memphis, Tennessee—February, 1865

"HERE'S another one," Celia announced, and Amber Jenné turned with a groan. She crossed the parlor to the window, pushing impatiently at an errant strand of tawny hair that had escaped from its neat coil on the nape of her neck.

"No. Not another one, for heaven's sake."

"Oui. They come out of the woodwork, it seems, just like the rats in the alley, no?"

"Just like rats, *yes,"* Amber said, pushing aside the lace curtains to peer out. A carriage had rolled to a halt at the end of the paved walkway, and the driver was opening the door. Amber bit back a sigh of dismay. Then she frowned. It was a girl, young, with clouds of ash-blond hair that had escaped the hood of her cloak. Amber's gold eyes narrowed slightly as she inspected the visitor who stood on the sidewalk and looked at the house as if afraid to come in.

Sighing, Amber knew that her aunt would not refuse whatever it was the girl wanted. Leala Jenné rarely did. If it was within her power to help someone, she did. While commending her aunt for her openhearted generosity, Amber found it increasingly difficult to walk without stumbling over some poor Union soldier just released from the hospital. Leala also tended the wounded from both sides. She played no favorites.

Neither did Henri Jenné, Amber's father. Henri had amassed a fortune before the War Between the States had begun, and he'd managed to keep it during the long years, even increase it. He was almost, in Amber's opinion, as bad as her aunt in giving away his money. Not that she really minded, but it was just so tiresome trying to live in a house filled with so many strangers. She wished she could go back to New Orleans, but that was impossible. For a while longer, anyway, her father had said.

"It's safer in Memphis," Henri had commented, smiling at his only child fondly. "Here, General Washburn extended his promise to me that we will not be bothered. I cannot count on such a promise in New Orleans. There are too many undisciplined troops raging about in New Orleans for us to return yet. Linger a while, *chère*. It's pleasant here."

"I know, but—" Amber had stopped, knowing there was no way to explain to her father that she resented the constant influx of unfortunate people. How did she admit to being less than generous when her family was so wonderful? It would be too shameful.

She glanced back out the window at the girl approaching the house and sighed.

"At least this one isn't a former prisoner with lice and bedbugs," Amber said aloud.

"No," Celia said, "but I think she will want us to find one for her."

"Assuming you mean find a released prisoner and not a louse or bedbug," Amber said wryly, "I agree."

The knock on the door was firm, and Celia opened it, inviting the girl inside. "Come in," she said in her charming French accent, "it ees too cold to be outside today, no?"

"Yes, yes it is." The girl glanced from Celia to Amber,

who waited in the hallway. "Are you Mademoiselle Jenné?"

"Yes, but not the right one. You're looking for my aunt, I imagine, and she has stepped out. Won't you wait by the fire in the parlor where it's warm?"

Observing the girl as she smiled gratefully and crossed the hallway to the small parlor where a warm fire burned in the grate, Amber decided she was very pretty. And very worried. Most of the people who came to Memphis looking for loved ones in the past few weeks fell in the same category. Everyone wanted to find husbands, brothers, fathers, sons—men who'd been released from prison since Grant had finally agreed to an exchange. Many of those came to Memphis, hiding if they were southerners, waiting for a train or steamer upriver if they were not.

"May I get you some hot tea?" Amber asked as the girl shivered, holding out small hands to the fire that looked delicate and work-worn. In spite of her frail appearance, there was a definite strength about her; maybe a strong will, Amber decided. The girl's chin was willful, and she had arrived in Memphis alone, without even a maid to attend her. Yes, there was determination in the soft blue-gray gaze she turned on Amber, mixed with a guarded courtesy.

"Hot tea?" The girl smiled suddenly. "*Real* tea?"

Amber laughed. "Yes, *real* tea. And not the fifth or sixth dregs of it, either. My father is a merchant, and he ran across a shipment last month."

"Thank you. I'd like that. It's been months—years— since I've had any tea that isn't sassafras or so thin it looks like water. One learns to appreciate small luxuries too well, I'm afraid."

"Don't we? There have been times when even warm feet are an inexpressible luxury." Turning, Amber rang for Celia, who had been one step ahead of her as usual, having brought a tea tray. She had even placed some small pastries on the tray, and Amber saw the girl's eyes light eagerly.

"Voilà," Celia said with a flourish, placing the silver tray on a low table and arranging it artfully. "Tea, petit fours, and . . ." She paused, frowned, lifted the cover off a small covered dish, and continued, "Ah. Croissants. Not fresh, but still good."

Amber suppressed a smile at the visitor's obvious delight and effort to remain composed, but said only, "Please, Miss—oh dear, I'm afraid I did not ask your name. Aunt Leala will be cross with me. She always insists that I get names first, because so often people leave before I can."

"Steele," the girl responded, eyeing the pastries and hot tea, "Jessamy Windsor Steele. I'm here to find my brother."

"Of course. Celia, please bring me the book, so that I can enter her name. Croissant, Miss Steele?"

"*Mrs.* Steele." Jessamy flashed her a quick smile. "Sorry. I should have said so."

"Quite all right." Amber poured the tea, and thought of how many people she'd seen sit across from her in this small, cozy parlor and try not to appear greedy as they ate whatever Celia had prepared on the tea tray. Most of the South was hungry, and those who came to Adams Street were no exception. Rather, the southerners who sat in this parlor and had swallowed their pride enough to ask for help were almost invariably thin and gaunt.

Amber eyed this girl's frayed garments for a moment before she asked gently, "Would you like to tell me about your brother? So I can write it in my aunt's ledger."

Swallowing the last of her croissant, Jessamy used her napkin and folded it in her lap, placing her hands over the fine linen. "His name is Nicholas Windsor, and he was taken by the Yankees at the Battle of Nashville in December. I thought he might have been sent here to

Memphis, to Irving Block Prison, but he wasn't. Thank God."

A delicate shudder trembled through her, and she steadied her voice and continued, "Then, through friends, I heard Nick was sent to Johnson's Island, but I also heard he was being held upriver at Rock Island. Truthfully, I don't know where he is. Lieutenant Conrad —his fellow officer—could not tell us much, but we did manage to find out that he was exchanged last week for a Union captain." Her lips twisted slightly. "There are not a great many ways to find out about released prisoners, even those who have only been imprisoned a month or two."

"That's true." Amber pushed the plate of petit fours closer to Jessamy Steele. "Did he take the Oath of Allegiance?"

Jessamy shrugged helplessly. "I have no idea. We've not heard from Nick in quite a while. My mother has received one or two letters from him in the past year, but that's all. He was riding with General Forrest the last we heard, and now—"

"General Forrest." Amber's delicate eyebrows lifted, and she tried not to show her concern. It was well known that Nathan Bedford Forrest was hunted by most of the Federal army, and had so far managed to outwit them at every turn. Memphis had become the main supply depot for the Rebel army since the town had fallen. Smuggling kept the Confederate army well-provisioned, much to the chagrin of the Union. Yankee medicine and supplies were regularly routed through Memphis by steamers, running the blockades set up on the Mississippi. All too often, General Forrest managed to waylay those supplies and confiscate them for his own struggling army. The daring general had even led a raid into Federal-held Memphis to attempt a rescue of southerners in Irving Block Prison the year before, but it had failed. Orders had been given to Union patrols to "Shoot on sight any man considered to be a member of

Forrest's brigade." If that was so, this girl might be in for heartbreak.

"I know what you're thinking," Jessamy Steele said with a sharp edge to her tone that surprised Amber. "But he's not dead. I know he's not."

Not bothering to offer a protest, Amber asked, "How do you know?"

Inhaling deeply, the girl looked at her with haunted eyes and whispered, "Because we haven't made up yet. He can't be dead if we are still angry with one another."

Startled, Amber couldn't form a reply. There did not seem to be anything to say, not with Mrs. Steele glaring at her so defiantly, as if daring her to voice the thought that he might be dead.

From the doorway, she heard her aunt's cheerful voice say, "Of course he is not dead, *petite*. My niece would not suggest such a thing. I am certain that she is merely thinking of the difficulties involved in finding released prisoners of any type, eh, *chérie?*"

"Yes, Aunt Leala, that is quite correct." Amber felt a wave of relief that her aunt had returned. She stood, smiling as her aunt breezed across the room and enveloped Jessamy Steele in a smiling embrace.

Leala Jenné smelled of gardenias and generosity, and left behind intangible reminders of it wherever she went. Charm and graciousness were distributed as easily as sunshine, and with as little effort. Now she was charming Mrs. Steele from her tense apprehension, patting her cheek and telling her how lovely she was and that of course they would find her brother.

"We have an extensive network set up, and it never fails me," Leala said blithely, apparently ignoring the few—and devastating—failures she had endured. "You shall see. We shall find this angry brother before the week is out."

Amber sighed with resignation. She hoped that her aunt did not speak too hastily. It would be dreadful if she did.

* * *

Wind whipped off the Mississippi River in icy blasts that made Amber shiver. The high bluffs were pale with a thin hoarfrost. She glanced at the girl beside her, noting that Jessamy didn't even seem to feel the cold. She strained to look for her brother. They had met every riverboat and steam packet that had come down the Mississippi in the past two weeks, and Nicholas Windsor had not been on any of them. Leala had managed to discover that he had, indeed, been released from Rock Island prison upriver, and he should be arriving in Memphis soon. No word had been forthcoming about his condition, if he was wounded or sick, or able to travel. All that could be discovered was that he was alive.

For Jessamy Steele, it seemed to be enough.

"He'll be here. today," she said strongly. "I feel it."

"I hope you're right," Amber murmured, clutching at her cloak and wishing there weren't so many rough men at the river. The roustabouts and stevedores seemed a bit too interested in the unescorted females, but when Roger joined them after tying the carriage up on Front Row, the stares grew less insolent.

Standing at nearly six feet five inches, Roger's ebony face was as broad as an anvil, and about as inviting. Few would have guessed that beneath that fierce-looking exterior beat the heart of a gentle giant. Animals and children loved Roger as much as grown men feared his ham-size hands and barrel chest.

"You all right, Miss Amber?" Roger asked in a voice that was curiously soft for so large a man. "Nobody bother you?"

"No one bothered us, Roger. And I'm certain they won't dream of it now." Amber smiled at him, wondering how they had ever managed without Roger. He'd come to them three years before, sick and hungry and needing a place to stay. He'd more than made up for

any efforts to care for him, by making himself indispens-
able. Even Henri trusted Roger's opinion of people.

"Do you think he'll show up, Roger?" Amber whispered.

"Yes, Miss Amber. Miss Jessamy is a fine young lady,
and her brother must be just as fine."

Fine was not the word that came to mind when Amber Jenné saw Nicholas Windsor come down the gang-
plank of a riverboat. He moved with a predatory grace
that radiated danger and confidence, which made her
feel safe and threatened at the same time. He was wearing military pants, a rough gray jacket, and men parted
to make way for him to move through the crowd, almost
as if they were afraid of him.

He was dark-skinned, with that rich color that came
from heritage more than the sun, and his hair was a
gleaming black that reflected blue highlights under the
winter sunshine. Strong features dominated his face,
with a square jaw, slash of cheekbones, and dark shadowed eyes that were carefully remote.

Amber realized she was holding her breath when her
lungs began to ache for air, and she gulped. She would
not have connected the tall, lean man with dark hair and
eyes and the look of a hungry hawk with the petite
blonde at her side at all. Jessamy had an underlying
steel core beneath her soft surface, but her brother was
solid granite.

Amber followed close behind as Jessamy fought her
way through the crowd to her brother.

"Nick!" Jessamy shouted impatiently, waving at him
and calling his name until he finally heard her. "Nick!"

When Nick Windsor turned, brows lifting in surprise
as he saw his sister, Amber felt as if she had been hit
with a twenty-pound hammer. *Lord,* she thought with a
mixture of amusement and dismay, *this has never happened to me before!* She hoped her reaction didn't show
on her face as he moved toward them in a graceful
stride.

"Jess," he said when he reached his sister, and that one word carried an entire range of emotion. There was disbelief, relief, and anger in the husky rasp of his voice, a voice that penetrated to Amber's core with the intensity of its vibrant tone.

Nick was frowning, the black hawk's brows dipping low over unfathomable dark eyes. His jaw tightened, and the dark beard stubble did not hide the slight quiver of a muscle as he held his sister at arm's length.

Amber stood quietly just behind Jessamy, trying to sort through the unfamiliar tangle of her reaction to this man. It was difficult, and she wondered wildly just why he had such an impact on her senses.

When Nicholas Windsor glanced up and their eyes met over his sister's head, Amber's knees weakened and her pulses raced alarmingly. There was an odd warmth in the pit of her stomach, and she felt so suddenly foolish that if someone had boxed her ears, she wouldn't have had to ask why. She must have looked as silly as she felt.

The black velvet eyes widened slightly, then narrowed to a bold scrutiny that made her wonder if she had soot on her nose. She took an instinctive step back and felt Roger's safe bulk behind her.

Roger murmured under his breath, "Now there's a man to watch out for, Miss Amber."

"What do you mean by that?" she whispered, but Roger shook his head and lapsed into silence. Amber's gaze shot back to Nick, who was holding his sister at arm's length and scowling fiercely. His voice was rough.

"I don't know what you're doing here, Jess, but you should not have come."

Her chin lifted in surprise. "I came to fetch you home."

"Home?" The hard mouth slanted in a humorless smile. "The last I saw of *home*, it was still smoldering from the fire your Yankee husband set."

Flushing, Jessamy glared up at her brother. "Alex did

not set the fire, Nick, and you know it. He was under orders, and he had nothing to do with the actual—"

"Save it, Jess. I'm not interested. Sorry you came so far, but you can go home the same way you came." He set her firmly back and away from him, and Amber saw the pain in Jessamy's eyes as she looked up at her brother.

"I don't know you anymore," she whispered. "You've changed so much . . . so much. You're not the same, Nick. You're—hard."

"Yeah? Well, if I hadn't learned to be hard, I wouldn't have survived. A man doesn't stay alive by being soft."

Jessamy's wide eyes flashed as she quavered, "How do you think I survived, then? I had to do things I never thought I'd do, and I'm not as . . . . as *cold* as you are. A person can survive and still keep a sense of decency, Nick."

Amber could feel the anger emanating from him, and she stepped closer to Jessamy as if to protect her. Nick obviously saw the move and interpreted it correctly, for his mouth curled into a mocking smile that made her flush. Then his gaze shifted to his sister, night-dark and burning with some sort of emotion Amber couldn't interpret.

"Decency, Jess?" he said softly. "Maybe we have different definitions of the word. I don't call it *decent* to crawl in bed with the same enemy who destroyed everything we have, so it's possible that you and I don't see eye to eye on that subject."

Appalled, Amber felt Jessamy's shudder of pain vibrate through her slender frame. Ignoring Roger's cautious hand on her shoulder, Amber took several steps forward. She forced a smile, but anyone who knew her would have been warned by the deceptively sweet tone of her voice.

"Mr. Windsor, your sister has come a long way to find you, and has been worried sick about you. I suggest that—"

"Who the devil are you, and why do you think you have any right to interfere?" Nick broke in coolly, eyeing Amber with such an intent gaze that she suddenly felt exposed.

The sugary sweetness in her voice never faltered. "I am Amber Jenné, and your sister asked my aunt to help her find out when you would be released. We have worked for two weeks, Mr. Windsor, so perhaps you could—"

"Miss Jenné, you were not asked by *me* to find out anything, and I feel no responsibility toward you at all. I'm tired, and I want to find a room for the night. Jess, tell Mother that I'll write later."

Staring up at her brother with disbelieving eyes, Jessamy dug a fist against her lips and said around it, her voice catching, "Go tell her yourself, Nick. I won't deliver any message like that."

Shrugging, he said, "Fine."

Furious now, Amber's voice took on a sharp edge as she said, "You are not at all the southern gentleman I have been led to expect, Mr. Windsor. I think your sister deserves more than rudeness from you."

"Do you?" He shrugged again, lifting broad shoulders beneath the worn, threadbare gray coat. The black eyes raked her with a dispassionate gaze. "It's really none of your business."

"It is when I'm involved in it, and I *am* involved, Mr. Windsor." By now Amber's eyes were flashing hotly and the sugary tone of voice had altered to a sharp crack that made his eyes narrow. She was almost quivering with her anger, and had opened her mouth to give him a more detailed opinion of his lack of character when he caught her gaze with such a chilly stare that her words died unspoken. Her heart thudded, and she recognized in that instant that this was not a man who would respond to a woman's irritation or efforts to cajole.

She was right. The raspy voice didn't rise, but was no less menacing. "I don't think I'd say anything else if I were you, Miss Jenné. You are quite right when you say I'm no gentleman. Don't provoke me into proving it."

Stunned by his blunt warning, Amber felt Roger stiffen beside her, but to her surprise the man said nothing in her defense. To cover her sudden confusion, Amber put a hand on Jessamy's arm, drawing the girl away from her brother.

"Come back home with me, Mrs. Steele. It's obvious that your brother wishes to be left alone."

Anger flashed in the blue-gray eyes awash with tears, and Jessamy straightened, glaring at Nick. "If you come to your senses and want to stop acting like a child, Nick, I'll be at the Henri Jenné residence on Adams for the next two days. After that, you can damn well do what you please."

Spinning on her heel, Jessamy stalked away, and Amber felt a wave of admiration for her. She glanced back at Nick Windsor, and her breath caught in her throat.

He was staring at her with that intent gaze that made her heart lurch and her pulses race erratically. There was something in his dark eyes that made her think of hot summer nights when there was no breeze and the air was so thick with sultry restlessness that no one could sleep. She shivered suddenly, in spite of the images conjured up by the direction of her thoughts, and Nick Windsor noticed.

Something sprang alive in the depths of his eyes, and was quickly hidden by the lowering drift of those spiky lashes. To a casual observer, he looked almost sleepy, but it was a contradiction and Amber knew it. There was nothing relaxed or sleepy about this man, nothing at all. He was like a coiled spring, every movement suggestive of power and a raw sexuality.

He saw her instinctive reflex and smiled slightly, one side of his mouth tilting up at the corner.

"It was a pleasure meeting you, Miss Jenné," he drawled in an amused tone that made her cheeks flush hotly. He brushed a finger against the brim of the battered hat he'd pulled on, then pivoted on his boot heel and walked away, each stride as controlled as a dancer's.

Amber cleared her throat and looked up at Roger. "Well. This was certainly unexpected."

Roger looked faintly amused, and there was a glimmer of wry understanding in his dark eyes when he nodded. "I'd say so, Miss Amber. But don't you fret none. I think Mrs. Steele will do just fine."

Not bothering to admit that she'd been thinking of her own reaction to Nick Windsor and not at all of Jessamy Steele, Amber followed behind as Roger parted a path through the crowd for the two women.

Nick Windsor strode angrily up the steep slope of the cobbled riverbank. When he reached the top of the levee, he ignored offers of rides being tendered by small black boys with scruffy-looking carts hitched to even scruffier horses. He didn't have the money to ride, not when he could walk. And anyway, he was too damned mad to do anything but try to walk off his temper. What in the hell had Jess been thinking when she'd come to Memphis to wait for him? Didn't she remember the circumstances of their disagreement?

One hand clenched into a fist; Nick stuck it deep into the pocket of his pants and concentrated on crossing the busy street that ran parallel to the broad Mississippi River. Federal gunboats still patrolled with casual arrogance, moving in and out of the harbor and cruising the tree-lined river. Drovers and boatmen swarmed the area, and everywhere he looked, Federal soldiers lounged, talking as if the world belonged to them.

At this point, Nick thought bitterly, most of the South did, anyway. He'd had to swear an oath to lay down his weapons for the rest of the war and not take them up again against the Federal army of the United States. Though it had galled him, he'd seen the futility in refusing. The war was about over anyway; anyone with a

grain of sense could see that, and he had to admit to a
feeling of relief.

Life wouldn't be the same after it was all ended, but it
would go on, and he couldn't deny that. It just wouldn't
go on for all the boys he'd known and lost. And it
wouldn't go on for his father and twin brothers either,
who had died at Shiloh when the entire world had
seemed to explode into senseless slaughter.

After Shiloh—God, after Shiloh, when he'd stumbled
across his youngest brother Bryce, almost half dead
from wounds that he should not have had—he'd found
that hatred was an emotion much more powerful than
love. Hatred had fueled his fight from then on, and it
kept him going now.

Hatred for the enemy was impersonal, but for one
particular enemy, it was a brilliant, burning desire for
vengeance.

Alexander Steele, a Kentucky cousin by way of his
mother marrying into the family, had earned Nick's hatred by joining the enemy at the beginning of this war,
and the hatred was no less intense for the fact that
Steele had married his sister. It had been Alex Steele
who'd carried out the order to burn Clover Hill, and the
gracious house had been nothing but charred ruins by
the time Nick saw it again. Odd, to become so attached
to a collection of brick and wood, but he had. It had
hurt him to see the blackened bricks scattered around
the hilltop, almost as much as it hurt him when Jess had
confessed her love for the enemy.

Nick stood on the top of the bluff overlooking the
river, kicking at a loose cobblestone. Maybe he'd see
what work he could find in Memphis for a while. He had
to have money. The fourteen dollars in his pocket
wouldn't last long, not with eggs twenty dollars a dozen
and fresh bread almost that high.

As he threaded his way through teams of wagons and
the chaos of the riverfront, Nick thought about the
young woman who'd helped Jessamy track him down.

She must be ingenious at getting her own way, because she'd sure looked madder than a wet cat when he'd cut her short. A faint smile tugged at the corners of his mouth again.

Cat was a good description for Miss Amber Jenné, he decided, because with her gold cat eyes and tawny mane, she looked as feline as any cat he'd ever seen. There was a lazy quality to the wide-eyed innocence of her smile that didn't fool him for a moment, though, and he knew she'd been aware of his appraisal. Miss Butter-won't-melt-in-my-mouth had better be glad his mother's training had prevented him from being just as rude as he'd felt like being, because another minute of the condemnation she'd focused on him, and he'd have kissed it from her eyes, bodyguard or not.

There was an air of latent sensuality in Amber Jenné that intrigued him, because most well-brought-up young ladies of the South knew better than to let too much of it show. A flirtatious little smile, a toss of her head, a few hints that she *might* let her beau kiss her good night if he was *real* attentive, and any self-respecting southern belle would have gone as far as she dared. Or usually wanted to go. His experience with the women of his class had been disappointing in the extreme.

His class.

Nick almost laughed aloud. There was no social class in the South anymore, unless one specified between damn Yankee and arrogant Yankee. Now his world consisted of Federal soldiers, merchants, freed slaves, and defeated Rebels. Everything was coming to an end, and the South would be slowly ground under the heel of oppression in spite of President Lincoln's fine promises.

On Vance Avenue, Nick finally found a boarding-house that wasn't too expensive or too dirty, and paid for a week in advance. If he hadn't found work in a week, he would move on. Texas, he'd heard, was a land of opportunity, offering a man freedom and wide open spaces. He could use that. After the two months spent in a Yankee prison under conditions so filthy hogs would have refused to linger, he needed fresh air and freedom.

There certainly wasn't anything in Tennessee to keep him, though he knew he would have to go back to Clover Hill and see his mother before long. He couldn't hurt her, or Celine, who had practically raised him from infancy. No, he'd go back, but just for a short visit. Then he was leaving it all behind.

CHAPTER
2

"I don't know," Amber said hesitantly, and saw Jessamy's face fall a bit. "I mean, your mother won't be expecting me, and to just arrive uninvited—"

"You aren't uninvited. *I* invited you." Jessamy's smile was hopeful. "Besides, Maribelle and Celine would die to see your clothes. No one has had anything new since before the war, and you always dress so exquisitely."

Amber felt embarrassed. Her wardrobe had been a bone of contention between her father and herself, because Henri Jenné felt that as his daughter, she should dress the part, while Amber had felt it was a slap in the face to those who suffered serious deprivations to see her garbed nicely. They had compromised by her only wearing a few new gowns during the year, and donating those to the less fortunate after she'd worn them a few times.

"And since you're insisting that Roger accompany me back to Clover Hill," Jessamy was saying, "you might as well go along for the ride. Come on. The weather's been clear, and spring will be here soon. The country is much nicer than the city."

Amber laughed. "You said you love the city."

Blue-gray eyes danced with mischief. "I do, but I love Clover Hill better than anywhere. You'll see why."

"You're assuming I've said yes."

"Haven't you?"

Smiling, Amber nodded. "You're a very persistent young lady. I can't imagine anyone ever refusing you anything."

Some of the laughter faded from Jessamy's eyes, and she glanced out the parlor window at the empty sidewalk. No tall, lean figure strode up the paved walk to the front door, and there had been no message from her brother. Amber felt a wave of irritation. Nick was so stubborn, when all it would have taken to make Jessamy feel better was for him to come and visit. Even if he had no intention of returning to Clover Hill with her, he could have at least forgotten his anger long enough to visit.

But he hadn't, and now Jessamy was returning home. During the past days with Jessamy Steele in Memphis, Amber had found her to be a lively companion, and had listened with interest to the story of how she'd met her husband.

"Oh, Alex and I knew each other as children," Jessamy had said with a laugh, "but we detested one another. I thought he was a sour old grump because we never could get him to join into our games, and he thought I was a scatterbrained hellion."

"I can't imagine why." Amber had to laugh when Jessamy gave her a quick glance, saw her amusement, and grinned impudently.

"I suppose it's obvious that I've always been the rebel in the family. Well, besides Nick. Only, now that he hates me, I guess he's no longer in the family."

"I'm sure your brother doesn't hate you."

"He gives a wonderful imitation of it then." Taking a sip of hot tea, Jessamy had lapsed into silence again, leaving Amber to wonder how war managed to destroy families so completely. Bullets didn't have to do the job; emotions could wreak more havoc than any piece of lead.

"If my father doesn't object," Amber said now, "I'll go with you to Clover Hill."

Henri Jenné not only did not object, but he asked Amber to take a look at the fields while there. When Memphis had fallen to the Union army in June of '62, warehouses of cotton had been destroyed along with other supplies to keep them from landing in Yankee hands. Cotton would be worth a fortune by the end of the year.

"Have Roger drive you in the carriage, though," he said with a faintly worried frown. "The trains are not safe for two young ladies to ride, even with Roger as a deterrent."

"I agree. Only last week, the depot at La Grange was fired upon by hidden soldiers. No one was hurt, but plenty of people were frightened out of their wits. This war can't be over too soon, if you ask me."

Henri smiled. "You're not alone in that sentiment. I predict that it will be over before the summer mosquitoes swarm."

"Do you know something I don't?"

"No." Henri glanced at a copy of the *Memphis Appeal* on his desk. Though the staff and presses of the Memphis newspaper had fled the city the day the Union captured it, and now operated from railroad cars throughout the South, the smuggled copies gave a fair indication of how the Confederates were faring. Henri sighed heavily and shook his head. "No, *chère,* I know nothing definite. Only that the poor South is floundering beneath the weight of her woes. It won't be long now. The boys are suffering in the February cold, and can't hold out much longer."

"You sound almost like a Secesh," Amber teased, and her father laughed.

"I'm not. If I were, I'd be in as bad a shape as they are. Well, perhaps I can help some of them. See if there are still some tillable fields, and if the owners are interested in leasing them out for me to plant, *chère.*" He

jotted down a few notes in his journal. "I will pay we
of course." Lamplight fell softly across his study ar
caught in the silvery strands of his hair as he concer
trated on the figures he was writing.

"You might ask Mrs. Steele," Amber suggested. "He
family still owns their land, though the house is gon
No one has taken it away yet, not even the Federal go
ernment."

Henri lifted his aristocratic head at her last remark
eyeing her with a smile. "Do I detect a note of souther
sympathy?"

"More than a note. An entire symphony. It's hard no
to be loyal when you live in the South. Maybe I ca
understand Nick Windsor's hatred for Jessamy's hus
band when I think of it in that light."

Sliding a pen thoughtfully through his spread finger
Henri was silent a moment before saying, "*Chère,* yo
should not become too involved. The war is almost ove
and rebuilding will be hard enough for these peopl
without muddying the waters with useless emotion."

Amber perched on the edge of his wide mahogan
desk and crossed her arms over her chest. "What do yo
mean by that? I hate it when you talk in riddles."

He shrugged. "No riddle, *ma petite.* I've stayed neu
tral for more than the obvious reasons, and thought yo
understood them. It is important in my business not t
offend either side, and misplaced loyalty can be misun
derstood by both."

"Ah, do you mean that I am not supposed to have an
patriotism in me at all, then? I see. No loyalty, no—"

"Amber Elizabeth." Henri's voice was stern. "You
know that I meant no such thing. Speaking out of tur
can only harm those you wish to help. Try and remem
ber that. Do I not give what I can to widows and or
phans, and soldiers from either side? *Oui,* I do, and
feel no guilt when I sleep at night. I know I have don
my best to help others during the day, no matter thei
loyalties."

"There's sense in what you say, Papa, but there are people who don't understand why we haven't chosen one side or the other."

Shrugging again, Henri stood up and put an arm round his daughter. "There will always be people who don't understand. And I will stick by my decision, because I have helped people, not shot them."

Amber toyed with the gold watch chain draped over his chest and gave a sigh. "You're right, Papa. Everyone can't be the same, and I'm glad you were able to help all these people."

"Good. Now, think of pleasant things. Perhaps we shall return to New Orleans soon, and I know you would like that, hmm?"

"Yes, of course." She stood on her tiptoes to press a quick kiss to his cheek. "And I'll find out about the fields while I'm in Cloverport. Cotton should be worth more than gold this time next year."

Henri's eyes twinkled. "You may yet grow into a merchant, *ma petite*. Be careful. A social butterfly such as yourself does not think of profit and margin."

Laughing, Amber teased, "Social butterfly? More like a candle moth, you mean. I've been burned too many times to consider myself social, Papa."

"You should have more fun. All you do is sit in the house and watch your Aunt Leala fill it with wounded soldiers and homeless boarders."

"She does an excellent job."

"Yes," Henri said wryly, "she does. But you have not been given the life I would want you to have. You are almost twenty, and I have not heard a single word of approval about any of the suitable men I have sent for your inspection."

"Inspection is right," Amber retorted. "What did you tell them, anyway? That I was a toothless old crone with no hope of finding a husband? The last man you dared send me sat with his mouth hanging open and his eyes glued to my bosom. I wanted to box his ears."

Chuckling, Henri said, "Pierrepont was not the mo
apt young man, I admit, but I'm getting desperate."

"Tired of supporting an old maid daughter?" Ambe
teased fondly, and saw her father's eyes curve into cre
cents of amusement.

"Much too tired. You are disobedient and willful, an
I pity the man who weds you. Perhaps I should send m
enemies to you instead of my friends, eh?"

Amber laughed as she crossed to the study door an
opened it, saying as she went out, "Only if you dislik
them *very* much."

"Yonder's the sentries, Miss Amber," Roger saic
drawing back on the reins. The carriage slowed, an
Amber peered out at the blue-uniformed men blockin
the road ahead. She'd known they would be stopped, c
course—any traffic into or out of Memphis was force
to halt and was subject to search for contraband. Th
reality made her mouth dry and her hands shake, an
she glanced at Jessamy.

Jessamy Windsor Steele stared straight ahead; onl
the slight quiver of her folded hands gave away her ner
vousness. Amber looked back at the uniformed mei
spread across the road.

"Are you certain you don't mind?" Jessamy aske
softly, and Amber shrugged.

"What's a little contraband between friends?"

A nervous giggle escaped Jessamy, and she quickl
covered her mouth with both hands. "Oh dear—if we'r
caught, even your Papa might not be able to help you.'

"Nonsense. Papa is known to be neutral, and beside:
he has more money than God. Well, he's close, anyway
Don't look so scared. It's a dead giveaway."

Aware of the Windsors' plight, Amber had insistec
upon carrying food supplies and some other necessities
As the smuggling of such goods would be dangerous
she'd not mentioned it to Henri, knowing he would dis
approve. Roger had helped, and there was a false bot

om beneath the carriage that held such things as flour,
ugar, meal, and dried fruits. Inside her voluminous
gown, Amber had pinned buttons, thread, yarn, and
even two pairs of shoes for the children. Jessamy was
similarly equipped, and Roger had muttered that they
dare not walk, or the clanking of their petticoats would
tell all.

As the carriage neared the pickets, Amber handed up
their passes to Roger, and he held them out to the soldier who stopped them.

"Where yew going?" the man asked, reading the
passes and barely glancing at the carriage occupants.

"Cloverport," Amber replied. When the soldier
looked up in surprise at her unfamiliar accent, she managed a smile. "I've friends there who need my nursing
skills."

"Friends?" The young man looked from Amber to
Jessamy, who was staring down at her lap. "Yew don't
talk like you're from Tennessee."

"I'm not. I was born in upstate New York."

Some of the soldier's suspicions eased, and he
grinned. "What are you doing in Memphis, then?"

"My father has a business here. You'll find our papers
are in order, sir, so if we could pass, I would be greatly
relieved."

After an instant's hesitation, the soldier handed
Roger the passes. "All right. We have to be careful, you
know. Too many of those Rebel gals try to sneak contraband through the lines. Took two of them just this
morning."

"Took them?"

"Arrested them. 'Course, General Hurlburt won't do
nothing much except ship 'em out on the next boat,
more's the pity, and there'll be another at it in their
place. If Hurlburt would shoot a smuggler or two, some
of this would stop."

"I agree that it would certainly make one pause,"
Amber said icily, and nodded to Roger. "Good day, sir."

With the sentries behind them, Amber took a deep breath and glanced at Jessamy. Then both young women began to laugh, and collapsed in each other' arms with relief.

"Thank God," Amber said, sitting back against the cushions and wiping at her streaming eyes, "he didn' ask us to climb down from the carriage. There's a pair of shoes dangling between my knees that would have tangled me up and sent me to the ground, I am sure.'

Jessamy nodded. "I have that length of fine wool wrapped so tightly around me that I'm not certain could move freely if I had to. And there's a hat for John Mullen, who's riding with Forrest . . . oh my, we would have been in trouble if he'd searched us, wouldn't we?'

"Yes, but he didn't."

"Thanks to you. And thanks to you, my family will have some decent food to eat. Salt meat and poke salad are better than nothing, but not nearly as good as real bread."

"And real tea."

They both laughed, and settled back into the cushions to watch the rolling hills pass outside the windows. Though the trip would take two days by carriage, riding the train was still dangerous. Confederate sharpshooters fired at the passengers of the Memphis and Charleston line as the trains sped through the countryside toward its destinations, and they intended to take no chances. The war might have been winding down, but it wasn't over.

Clover Hill was a pleasant surprise. After hearing how it had been burned during the war and the fences torn up for firewood by the Union army, Amber had expected a desolate waste. But the gentle rolling hills that met her eyes were beginning to turn green and soft, and bright patches of wildflowers blossomed along the roadside in straggling clumps.

Occasionally, a squad of Federal soldiers passed, sometimes stopping them to ask questions, sometimes ust eyeing them as they rode along. Here and there hey saw ample evidence of the passing of armies hrough the area, with burned-out houses and black, utted fields. Between some of the charred furrows, sprigs of green thrust skyward, a sign of hope. All in all, Amber observed, the land was renewing itself. If only people could do the same, renew themselves each spring by a total rebirth of spirit. She shifted position on the seat of the closed carriage and glanced at Jessamy, who was gazing across the fields with a sad expression.

"Are you all right, Jessamy?"

She turned to look at Amber and smiled slowly. "Yes. I was just thinking of some of the people who used to live here, people who have died. They're gone, but everything just goes right on. I wonder what I'd do if Alex —if Alex doesn't come home. I don't think I could go on as if the world hadn't ended."

"Have you heard any news of him?"

"Yes. Just before we left Memphis, Mr. Harper came by and told me that he'd heard Alex's regiment was being called to join Sherman in the Carolinas." She shuddered delicately and her voice dropped to a whisper. "I hate this war. It's taken so many, and ruined so much that was fine. . . ."

Impulsively, Amber put her hand over Jessamy's and gave it a comforting squeeze. "Perhaps, when it's over, things will be fine again."

"Perhaps. But there are those who won't forgive and forget, and there's been so much hostility on both sides."

Amber had seen evidence of the hostility Jessamy meant in Memphis, when the Federal soldiers harassed the citizens. And she had seen evidence of it when some of the whites oppressed the freed Negroes. She had been angry with both sides on occasion.

Yet she didn't truly understand the extent of the hostility left behind until later that day, when they happened upon a confrontation between former slaves and their white owners. The former slaves were dressed in new finery and drove a fine carriage pulled by horses the white men were claiming were theirs.

"You stole 'em, by God!" a man grated, his face flushing red and his eyes glaring with hatred at the bland countenance of the black man staring back at him. "You came to my stables with those damn Yankee thieves and took them for the army, but I don't see you in any blue uniform!"

"These here hosses was conf'scated, Mistuh Overton," the black man returned shortly. "I bought 'em at a sale, an' they's mine."

"Lying nig—"

"Doan call me that no mo', Mistuh Overton," came the soft warning, and Amber felt a spurt of apprehension that bordered on terror.

"Pass them quickly, Roger," she leaned forward to say softly, but he reluctantly pulled the carriage to a halt at the side of the road. The horses pranced nervously, sensing trouble.

"Don't dare, Miss Amber. They've got the road blocked. I don't want to risk any shooting."

Twisting her hands tightly in her lap, Amber sat in tense silence as the men's quarrel escalated into fury. Blows were struck, and then a shot rang out, shattering the still afternoon with terrifying swiftness. Amber couldn't help a scream, but Jessamy sat forward and asked if Roger had a gun.

"Yes, ma'am, I sure do."

"Then pull it out. Between the two of us, we ought to be able to get out of here before the trouble starts."

"Starts?" Amber gasped as Roger pulled out a huge pistol from his coat pocket and took up the reins again. "It looks as if it has already started."

"No, not yet," Jessamy disagreed, and to Amber's shock, she took a small five-shot pistol that was square and ugly from her purse. "When folks hear that shot and come running, I don't want to be anywhere near.

I've been around enough shooting to last me the rest of my life."

Recalling that Jessamy had said she'd been caught in the battle of Shiloh's Church, Amber lapsed into silence, holding tensely to the side of the carriage as Roger clucked at the horses and slapped the reins against their gleaming rumps.

It looked as if both of them had been right. Within moments men came running, black and white, and a full-scale brawl began. She could hear the noise of it even after Roger got the carriage moving and passed the men in the middle of the road, leaving them behind as swiftly as he could. A pistol was fired at them, but the ball went wide, and they were soon out of range.

It occurred to Amber as she was righting herself on the seat once the brawl was far behind that even when the war was over, the hostilities would linger.

March—1865

A strong wind tugged at the open edges of Nick's coat. He glanced up at the gray clouds boiling across the sky, and heard the low rumble of thunder in the distance. Late March was a notoriously wet and unpredictable month, and he still had a couple of miles to go before he reached home.

He'd left the train only a few miles away, jumping off at what had once been a station. Now it was a burned-out shell, a Yankee retaliation against the Confederate guerrillas who shot at the coaches when Federal officers were aboard. Forrest's men had managed to make a dent in the ranks until the Yankees had come up with the idea to put southern hostages in the crowded cars, leaving them as unwilling targets for the sharpshooters.

Yankee ingenuity. Nick's mouth twisted into a sardonic smile. At least the tracks weren't torn up on this section. He'd been lucky, and not encountered any Yankee troops during the ride. He wasn't certain what he would have done if he had. Though he'd given an oath not to bear arms against the United States, just the sight of a blue uniform made his hand itch for a pistol.

Nick continued the last of his trek over gently rolling hills and down to the crossroads. The town of Mercer was behind him, Toone not far ahead. Between lay the crossroads and what was left of his family home. They now lived in the small overseer's house behind the ruins. For the present they might still own Clover Hill, but with high taxes being levied to reduce the owners to selling, it probably wouldn't be in the Windsor family very much longer.

When he reached the drive that curved past the sooty remains of the once elegant house, Nick didn't even glance in that direction. He kept walking down the dirt road that led to the small, whitewashed house tucked in a grove of sharp-scented cedar trees and honeysuckle vines. Plowed fields stretched on each side of the road.

Surprised at the cleared land, where it was evident some sort of planting was being done, Nick paused to look over fields newly green with tiny buds of cotton. Cotton. This early? And where in the name of God had his mother gotten the money to plant cotton? How did she intend to work it? The slaves were gone, had been gone the year before when he'd come back for a short visit. Only Old Billy and Dempsey had stayed, both too old to go anywhere else. Not that they were still slaves. His father's will had specified that all the slaves be freed upon his death.

Scraping his boot over a long furrow, Nick bent, picked up a clod of earth, and crumbled it in his hands. Clover Hill dirt. Funny, how it felt different now than it once had. He'd always thought it would be his forever, that nothing would really change. Not the major things in his life, anyway. How young he'd been, and how foolish.

Nick shook his head, then stood and went back to the

rutted road. When he rounded the small crook, he paused again, seeing the neat little house with its white picket fence cutting the front yard off from marauding goats. A far cry from the days when Clover Hill had put several small boys to work with switches to keep animals from munching the front lawn alone, but there it was. Home.

As he approached, the front door to the house flew open and his mother came out onto the porch, her hand at her throat. New lines creased her normally smooth face, and her neat dark hair bore heavy wings of gray. She stumbled toward him.

"Nick . . ."

He broke into a run, and not bothering to swing open the gate to the fence, cleared it in a single bound and was up on the porch, swinging his mother off her feet and around in a circle. In an instant the porch was crowded with females, all crying and laughing at the same time, assaulting him with questions and demanding to know why he hadn't written to say he was coming.

Releasing his mother, Nick kept one arm around her slender waist as he fished for a handkerchief. Handing it to Abigail Windsor, he grinned at the assembled family and said cockily, "Well, you can kill the fatted calf, 'cause the prodigal son has finally returned."

Celine, her coffee-colored face severe if one didn't look too closely to see the joyous tears in her eyes, remonstrated, "I should take a switch to your backside, Master Nick, for being too busy to write your maman. I taught you better."

"Yes," Nick agreed, "you did." He reached out to ruffle his youngest brother's hair, thinking with a pang that he and Bryce were the only men in the family now. "So, Bryce, what have you been doing since I last saw you?"

Grinning, the boy took a few steps forward, showing only a trace of the limp he'd received as a legacy of Shiloh. "Dancin', mostly. And kissin' a few girls."

Nick's brows rose. "Trying to take over my duties?"

"If I can. Figured you weren't never coming back, and there has to be a man of the house."

Abigail Windsor looked up at her son with a slight frown, and he ignored it, knowing what she was thinking. He didn't want to spoil his homecoming, not yet. Not with the disappointment he knew she'd feel when she heard he wasn't staying.

Instead, he hugged his mother more tightly, glanced at his cousin Maribelle and Aunt Pretense, and noticed that his sister was absent from the group. He wondered if her Yankee husband had come to claim her already, then shrugged the thought away. He hoped so. If he ran into Alex Steele, there would be a fight for certain.

"What's for dinner?" he asked, laughing when Celine said she should have known that would be one of his first questions.

Throwing her hands into the air, the Creole maid exclaimed, "Always the stomach with you, Master Nick! Don't you ever get full?"

"I haven't had a full meal in more months than I can count," Nick said so soberly that Celine put a hand over her mouth.

"*Sacre bleu!* I am so foolish—forgive an old woman whose tongue wags at both ends. Tonight, we shall eat a lot, if not well. If not for the new lease, though, you might find yourself eating poke salad and wild turnips."

"New lease?" Nick asked as he followed his mother inside. Familiar pieces of furniture were scattered here and there, few but precious. An old oak sideboard gleamed in the pale light streaming through cracked glass windowpanes, and there was the smell of lemon oil in the air. The interior of the small house was immaculate as always, despite the fact that so many people had to live in the small dwelling. With his mother, Bryce, Jessamy, and Celine as permanent residents, it was crowded. For a while his Aunt Pretense and her three daughters had stayed, but had finally found a Tennessee relative who could give them spacious shelter.

Maryland, their home, was being torn apart by battles. Tennessee, it seemed, had seen the end of pitched battles.

Nick found a comfortable rocking chair made of bent hickory limbs and cushioned with a feather bolster, while his mother took the one beside him, folding her hands in her lap. She gazed at her son for a moment before replying, "Yes, Nick, I have leased our land to a well-to-do merchant from Memphis. As you have noticed, he has planted cotton. For the first time in years we were able to pay our bills last month. Soon, we'll have money to— Nick!"

He'd shot to his feet and grated through clenched teeth, "You leased out our land?"

Frowning, Abigail said, "Sit down, Nick. You look absolutely fierce when you scowl like that. Yes, I leased out our land. What would you have me do—let everyone starve for the sake of pride? You know me better than that."

Nick relaxed slowly, though his hands stayed curled into fists of impotent rage. Damn. Strangers plowing Clover Hill land, digging into the rich soil. It was a form of rape, as far as he was concerned, and one more reason to hate the Yankees who had brought his family to this end.

Eyes bleak, he sat down again and managed to regain control of his unruly temper. He met his mother's shocked gaze and shrugged.

"Guess there's not much I can do."

"No, Nick, there's not. Except stay to help us."

There it was, what he'd been dreading. He should have seen it coming, but he'd walked right into it.

"We can always talk about that later," he said evasively. "I want to hear the rest of the news first."

Abigail Windsor smiled faintly, and when her dark eyes met her son's, he knew she was already aware of what he intended. It was an odd feeling, but neither of them mentioned it. Instead, Abigail began telling him about the people of Hardeman County, friends, neighbors, relatives, those who had suffered the most, and those who had managed to escape lightly.

"The Jordans were hit hard, as were the Andersons. Do you remember the Leathers? Their father died, leaving the three girls alone."

"Girls? Not a one of them is younger than thirty."

"No, but none of them married. They've worked hard, and it's been so difficult lately, with all the men gone."

Nick didn't answer. He curled his hands around the bent arms of the rocker and gazed into the fireplace, a muscle leaping in his jaw as he clenched his teeth. Coming home to this, the desolation and desperation of friends and family, was almost as bad as lying in frozen ditches. Or languishing in a Yankee prison camp while strangers decided his fate.

"Are you all right, Nick?" Abigail asked, and he turned to look at her, nodding when she asked if he was ready to tell her about it.

"Yes. I got separated from my command with Forrest and ended up with Hood. I wasn't supposed to stay, but somehow, I got caught up in the movements and there I was. Hood needed me, and I agreed to stay with him until we'd beaten the Yanks at Franklin. Then I was captured. I was one of the lucky ones. We lost thirteen officers in that battle, seven killed and six wounded or captured. God, the men killed that day . . ." He paused, swallowing the bile that rose in his throat. "I wasn't badly hurt, but ended up at some field hospital, then prison camp. I got out in only two months. Some of our men had been there for over a year, some two. Few lived longer than that. Conditions were—are—deplorable."

Abigail's knuckles whitened as she listened. Aware of her distress, Nick tried once to stop talking about the war but found he couldn't. He didn't talk about the things that had hurt the most, but told instead of troop movements and the foibles of generals, how a battle had been won or lost on a whim of fate or a single mistake.

"And at Franklin," he said with a bitter laugh, "we could have whipped the Yankees and ended this for good, but Hood didn't give the orders to bivouac the men in orderly fashion. They were spread out so far, the Union army slipped right through our lines and dug in deep. If we'd been able to draw Sherman from Atlanta, or beat the Yanks at Franklin, we could have resupplied in Nashville and gone on up to Kentucky, then Ohio. We could have done it, but we didn't." Shrugging, Nick closed his eyes for a moment, seeing the carnage again, the blasted bodies and screaming men. . . .

"It's all so pointless," Abigail murmured. "We've lost much more than the war."

She was right. Nick didn't say anything, and they sat in sad silence until Celine called them for dinner.

It was almost dusk as they sat down at the table, and Nick felt a pang of guilt that his sister wasn't there. He hadn't yet asked about her, and his family had pointedly left her out of their conversation. That in itself was odd, because Celine would certainly have berated him for ignoring her. Yet no one had. For the first time he began to feel uneasy.

"Is Jess well?" he asked when his plate was filled with generous helpings of sweet potatoes, fried corn, hot biscuits, gravy, and thick slabs of salted meat. Not elegant fare, but filling and plenty.

"Yes," Abigail said simply, and didn't elaborate.

Nick stifled a wave of apprehension. Damn her, Jess had made her own bed, hadn't she? Why should he care if she was happy or not? He kept remembering her shocked, hurt face when he'd last seen her in Memphis, and how the tears had made her blue-gray eyes as shiny as silver.

"Is she . . ." He paused to clear his throat. "Is she happy?"

"As happy as anyone can be these days." Abigail gave him a steady look that seared him to the core. "She was very hurt by your actions last month."

Nick looked down at his plate, his appetite fading. "I know. I can't help how I feel."

"Neither can she."

There wasn't much he could say to that, but Nick was well aware of the meaning behind his mother's calm statement. No, maybe Jess couldn't help how she felt about Alexander Steele, but neither could he. Steele was the enemy, dammit, and she'd chosen him over her own family.

He wanted to ask where she was, but didn't. There was no point in it. He had no intention of going to see her.

After dinner, Nick went outside on the porch to smoke, and Bryce tagged along, his boyish face full of eager curiosity.

"Tell me about it, Nick," he said softly. "Tell me how it's going."

Nick scratched a lucifer along the porch post and lit his last cigar with it, looking at Bryce through the curls of smoke that coiled up in fragrant wisps. He blew out the flaming match and shrugged.

"We're done for, Bryce. It's only a matter of time now. Maybe a few weeks, at the most a month or two. That's it. The army's out of food, ammunition, and men. They're out of everything but fight. That's all that's carrying them now."

Unshed tears welled in the boy's eyes. "I wanted to hear you say different, say that we still had a chance."

"We don't, and it'd be cruel to pretend otherwise."

"Is that why you're home? Because you've given up?"

"No," Nick said gently. "I'm home because I was paroled and I gave my oath not to fight."

"Lots of men have given their word not to fight. Most

of the Confederate army is made up of men who promised not to fight but went back. Why not you?"

Swearing softly, Nick said, "Because I gave my word, Bryce. That means something to me. If I hadn't intended to keep it, I would not have given it."

"Giving your word to a Yankee isn't the same thing as giving it to a gentleman, and you know it." Bryce's young face was creased with lines of disillusionment. "You just don't want to fight anymore."

Angry, but understanding Bryce's disillusion too, Nick tried to find a way to explain something that he'd been struggling to understand himself. Finally, looking off over the rolling fields planted with someone else's cotton, he said, "No, I don't want to fight, Bryce. I want to rebuild. The time for fighting is almost over. It's stupid to keep fighting when you've lost. That doesn't mean I have to like it, but I've got to think about tomorrow. Life doesn't end until they throw dirt in your face."

For a long moment Bryce was quiet. Then he said, "Celine says you won't stay here. She says you intend to leave Tennessee. Is she right?"

"Yes."

The silence stretched. Smoke drifted lazily from Nick's cigar, shifting on the chill breeze that whispered around them. March was still a month prone to erratic frosts, and it felt as if there would be one this night. A bird chirruped, and Nick realized suddenly that it had been a long time since he'd heard one. Few birds lingered near a battlefield, and in Memphis he hadn't taken the time to notice if there were any birds. The sound was oddly comforting, as if the world still retained some of what it had once held for him. He turned, pressing his back against the porch post to look at Bryce.

In the fading light Bryce looked very young and very sad. Nick felt the same sadness, but didn't feel the same freedom to let it show.

"You all right?" he asked, and Bryce bolted from the porch and out into the night without replying. Nick watched him go, and it was a long time before he went back into the small house for the night.

CHAPTER
3

AMBER had the weary thought that she'd rarely been so glad to see any house in her life. She was bone-tired, and the rude jouncing of the buggy had made every muscle in her body sore. It reminded her of her first trip to Clover Hill and how exhausted she'd been then. This time, she had taken the train to Mercer, where Jessamy met her with the family buggy, only to go back with her the very next day.

Alex had sent word that he would be able to come to Cloverport for a short visit, and the two women set off at once to meet him in Mercer. Amber immediately liked the tall, handsome Union soldier, though several local ladies sniffed disapprovingly when Jessamy greeted him. There were bound to be hard feelings from those who'd suffered, and Jessamy ignored them.

Captain Steele favored the women with an icy glare that sent them scurrying away, threadbare cloaks flapping around their ankles. For that gallantry on behalf of his wife, he received a resounding kiss from Jessamy as he handed her up into the buggy.

"I don't mind them, you know," she said softly. "I do understand how they feel."

Alex grinned. "Fiery little Rebel. It wasn't too long ago that you would have shot me rather than kiss me."

"Don't be too sure that I won't now," came the swift

37

retort, and Amber laughed at them as the buggy lurched forward. A brisk wind blew, and she huddled deeper into her warm cloak as she settled back for the long ride to Clover Hill. Jess and Alex talked softly, and she noticed that there were frequent lingering glances between them, as well as furtive touches.

Amber felt like an outsider. It was obvious they could barely wait to be alone. There were times she wondered if she would ever find that kind of love. She'd felt no inclinations in the past, and little beyond a passing interest in any man. Perhaps she'd be like her Aunt Leala, and spend her life unmarried. Leala didn't seem to miss a man in her life, but Amber frequently felt an odd, restless yearning.

It was dusk when they turned into the rutted drive that led to the small house in the cedar grove. Long shadows fell over the road and fields, and the earth smelled damp and rich. Amber smiled. Her father would be well pleased with the cotton he received from the Windsor fields.

"You ladies all right?" Alex asked in his husky voice, and Amber felt Jessamy move at her side, reaching for her husband.

"We're fine, Alex. It's late, so why don't you go ahead to the barn? Dempsey will help you unhitch the horse and buggy. I'll tell Mother we're back."

"Sounds fine. Here. Let me help you down." He lifted both of them from the carriage, Amber first, then Jessamy.

Amber turned discreetly away and started for the house to give them their privacy as Alex Steele held Jessamy in a close embrace. She heard Jess's soft laughter and Alex's murmured comment, and felt a pang of what could only be described as loneliness. Odd. She'd never felt lonely before, had never missed the arms of a man. Lately, she spent a great deal of her time wondering what it would be like to love one man, to spend the rest of her life with him.

When the soft murmur of their conversation grew louder, Amber smiled. Alex's tone was husky, urgent, and she sensed Jessamy's agreement to his suggestion. Without turning to look, she knew they were walking back toward the barn together. They were obviously seeking more privacy than they would find in the house, and she didn't blame them. She would explain to Mrs. Windsor that Jessamy was delayed.

Soft shadows shrouded the house beneath the cedars, and inside, a single lamp glowed a welcome through the smoky glass window. Porch boards protested as she crossed and pushed gently on the door. It creaked softly on its hinges as she opened it, and when she stepped inside, Celine loomed out of the shadows.

"Mon Dieu," Celine muttered in surprise, "you have returned earlier than we thought."

"Yes. The roads were good and passable. Jessamy went up to the barn, but—"

"And Mr. Steele? Is he with you?" Celine broke in, her voice so agitated Amber sensed trouble. She frowned.

"Of course. He and Jessamy went directly to the barn —is there a problem?"

Celine's face was gray in the dim light thrown by a single candle she held, and she nodded. *"Oui,* there is a big problem if he goes out to the barn to sleep. Master Nick came back unexpectedly, and no one has told him yet that we were expecting Mr. Steele for a visit."

Amber's heart did a flip, and she turned back swiftly, recognizing the ramifications even as she fought a surge of anticipation at seeing Nick Windsor again.

"I'll try to catch Alex before he goes out there . . . dear Lord, what we don't need is a fight right now."

But even as she stepped outside and across the small yard, she knew that she was too late. Alex and Jessamy were just nearing the barn on the slope above the house. To call out a warning would be just as dangerous as what awaited in the barn, and so she said nothing as she ran toward them.

The barn door creaked softly, but sounded so loud in the still dusk that Amber shivered. Lifting her long skirts in one hand, she was almost at the door when she heard Jessamy scream.

Amber's breath came in short pants as she shoved open the door and paused in the opening. Her eyes adjusted slowly to the gloomy light inside. A single lantern glowed, swaying violently as Nick Windsor knocked Steele up against the upright post where it hung.

"You bastard," Nick was snarling, "what are you doing here?"

Steele blocked Nick's punch, stepping just far enough away as he shot back, "Visiting my wife, Windsor. I don't want to fight you. If you'd calm down a minute, we could settle this like gentlemen."

"Nick!" Jessamy screamed as her brother ignored Steele's suggestion and launched another attack. This one didn't catch Steele by surprise, and he managed to parry Nick's furious blows, though hindered by his long blue coat. There was the dull, brutal sound of fists striking flesh and men grunting with effort, primitive and frightening.

Clamping a hand over her mouth to stifle her own scream, Amber had the wild thought that she'd never dreamed men could fight like that, with raw power and vicious force, intent upon nothing but the combat. They were evenly matched, both tall, lean, and angry. They could do a lot of damage before someone managed to get them apart, and Amber wished frantically that Roger had not gone to Cloverport to purchase more goods. Roger would have been able to separate them easily.

Amber glanced around and caught a glimpse of a Navy Colt in the straw where Nick had been lying; she lunged toward it with a desperation born of fear. She snatched it up, prayed that she was holding it correctly, and pointed it at the two men as they slashed viciously at one another. Steele already had a gash over one eye that was dripping blood, and Nick—clad in his undershirt and trousers—had the advantage as he fended off the Union captain's brutal blows.

"I'll shoot the next man who moves," Amber called out in a voice that barely shook. "And I'm not really good with pistols, so it might be either one of you who gets shot. . . ."

Her words carried such a ring of conviction that both men turned in surprise. Jessamy was shaking with reaction, her hands over her mouth as she watched. She looked frozen, eyes wide with apprehension. Amber's hands tightened on the handle of the pistol as Nick Windsor took a furious step toward her.

"Give me my goddam pistol," he snapped, but she shook her head.

"No. Not until you promise not to fight Alex anymore."

"St. Peter couldn't get that kind of promise from me, and if you don't hand me my pistol, I might have to hurt you."

Alex Steele gave a harsh bark of laughter. "Is that how you Rebs are fighting now, Windsor? Against helpless women?"

Without turning his head to look at Steele, Nick said, "Keep out of this, Yank. It's my pistol."

"Do you think I'll stand here and let you hurt a woman?" came the angry retort. Nick took another step toward Amber.

"I don't think you dare move. If she doesn't shoot you, I might."

Later, Amber could never remember the sequence of events that followed. All she could recall was Nick's sudden move, as swift as a striking snake, then a numbing blow to her wrist that sent the pistol flying into the straw. At the same time, Nick caught her around the waist and propelled them both to the hard floor of

the barn, his weight holding her down as she instinctively began to struggle.

His face was only inches from hers, his expression
hard and fierce when she looked up at him.

"Don't ever point a pistol at me again," he warned
softly, blocking her reflexive slap at his face with an ease
that was as infuriating as it was frightening. His fingers
coiled around her wrist in a biting grip.

Chaff rose around her as Amber heaved against him
and found he was immovable. His grip tightened painfully and he pulled her arms up and over her head,
pressing them into the straw beneath them, a move that
thrust her breasts up against his chest with an alarming
closeness. Nick's dark, saturnine gaze dropped to her
chest, and she was aware that her cloak had fallen open
and her breasts pressed against the too-thin material of
her gown.

Amber's heart thudded painfully in her chest, and her
mouth was suddenly dry. "Let go of me at once," she
managed to say in a voice that was much cooler than she
felt.

A black brow rose, and Nick's weight grew heavier,
one of his long legs shifting to hold her down as she
bucked beneath him in furious retaliation. The struggle
had shifted direction, becoming a sexual one in spite of
the fact that Jessamy and Alex stood only a few feet
away.

It all happened so quickly, in the space of a few sec-
onds, yet it seemed like long minutes ticked past. Amber felt Nick's reaction to her, felt the settling of his
body into the notch of her legs, and his breath quick-
ened. She grew abruptly still, and he tensed. Then he
swore softly and jerked to his feet, pulling her with him.

Swinging her toward his sister, Nick gave Amber a
fierce glance as he said, "You're lucky I didn't break
your arm. Next time you pull a pistol, you'd damn well
better be prepared to pull the trigger as well."

Stunned as much by her sudden reaction to his body

against hers as she was by his harsh words, Amber couldn't find a sensible response. She stared at him silently, rubbing at her wrist, her breathing labored.

Alex Steele said quietly, "Look, Windsor, I know you've got a grudge against me, but this is my only night with Jess. I don't want to spend it fighting with you."

Flicking Steele a contemptuous glance, Nick bent and scooped up his pistol from the straw, sticking it into the waistband of his pants. Without saying a word, he snatched up the blankets he'd been sleeping in, grabbed his boots, and stalked from the barn into the crisp twilight. Jessamy gave a soft sob, and Alex put an arm around her shoulders.

"He's still full of hate, Jess. I promised you I wouldn't fight him unless necessary, but it looks like it's going to be necessary before long."

Burying her face in her husband's coat, Jessamy grasped the rough material with both hands, her words muffled by the wool. "I don't want you two to fight. I love you both. Why can't he see that?"

Amber took a deep breath and met Alex Steele's strained gaze across the space that separated them; she felt some of his pain at the situation. He loved his wife, but he had no intention of backing down from a fight with her brother if forced. And it did not seem as if Nick Windsor was inclined to declare a truce.

A noise behind her alerted Amber, and she turned to see Dempsey, the manservant who had been with the Windsor family since before William Windsor had married the beauteous Abigail Fontaine and begun his family. Dempsey was frowning, his aged face tucked into worried wrinkles.

"I saw Mr. Nick, Miss Jess, and he looks like he's been in a fight."

"You're very observant," Jessamy turned and said with a wry smile. She glanced up at Alex's bleeding face and shook her head. "I think you can guess the cause."

"I think I can." Dempsey paused, then said, "I'll bring

in the horse and buggy while you tend to Captain Steele's face. If you don't mind, after that I'll look for Nick. He might need me to help him."

"Of course, Dempsey. There are some medical things in the tack room, and I'll fetch them. Then you take them with you to tend to Nick."

Alex's mouth turned down in a mocking twist and he raked a hand through his dark hair as he gave his wife a quick glance. "Didn't look to me like your brother needs any medical attention. He caught me by surprise, and I don't think I laid a hand on him."

"No," Amber spoke up, remembering a thin trickle of blood from the corner of Nick's mouth, "you managed to cut his lip, anyway."

"Lucky punch," Alex muttered, then caught Jessamy's frowning stare and shrugged.

As the manservant led the horse into the barn, Amber released a long breath she hadn't realized she'd been holding. She turned to Jessamy and Alex. "I think I'll go back to the house. If you need me, I'm not far away."

Amber didn't expect to be called for any help, not if the light she'd seen in Alex Steele's eyes as Jessamy dabbed at the cut over his eye was any indication of the kind of treatment he wanted for the night. Dempsey would leave them alone in the barn, and hopefully, no one else would bother them. As for Nick, Amber wondered fretfully where he'd gone. There weren't a great many shelters left, only half-burned shells.

As she picked her way back across the yard again, Amber glanced up and saw a faint glow coming from one of the cabins that must have once belonged to the slaves. Roger had stayed in one of them, and she knew they'd been kept up for those few servants remaining. It occurred to her to wonder why Nick had preferred the barn to a slave cabin, until she yielded to impulse and crossed the yard to peer in the door.

It was in sad repair, obviously one of the vacant cabins. Of course. He would not have put anyone out, and had taken the barn instead of displacing Dempsey or Old Billy. Amber stood in the doorway indecisively, seeing the way the wood hung from its hinges in a drunken swing. It would not be as comfortable as the snug, warm barn with beds of straw and a tight roof.

Glancing up, she saw Nick looking at her, his back to the fire he'd begun in the old grate, his blankets tossed to the hearth. Smoke curled into the drafty cabin, whisking across bare planked floors, seeking the chinks in the walls as an outlet. Amber felt suddenly awkward, and cleared her throat.

"Are you hurt?"

Nick stared at her coldly. "No."

"Well . . ." Her voice trailed into silence, and she curled her fingers around the edges of her cloak to draw it more tightly around her. "I'm sorry I drew your pistol on you. I just didn't want—"

"Miss Jenné," he interrupted, rising from his crouch to fill the small cabin with his intimidating frame, "did you come here out of curiosity? Because if you did, I can tell you right now that I'm in no mood to answer any damned questions."

Her chin lifted angrily, and a sudden spurt of rage made her incautious. "You are the rudest, most infuriating man I have ever met," she said in that silky, sweet tone that usually presaged temper. "I wonder how you stand your own company."

"Tolerably well. It's the company of brash women with more mouth than manners that irritates me the most."

"Really?" Amber lifted a brow delicately, knowing full well that it would only make him madder. "It'd be most interesting to see what you classify as manners, since I've not noticed a surplus of that virtue in you."

Nick took a step closer; his mouth flattened into a thin line. "I don't have any virtues, ma'am, if that's what you're wondering. So, if you expect me to act like some

drawing room gentleman, you can forget it. My manners
got lost somewhere in Missouri, when a sweet-talking
little lady just like you tried to shoot me for bringing
home her dead husband. No, don't expect any hand-
kissing and compliments, because I'm all out of 'em."

"Are you? I doubt you ever knew how." Amber
stared back at him, seeing the hot flare in his eyes at her
cool response. "You don't strike me as a man who ever
cared about flattery or sweet words."

"Don't I?" he asked softly, moving with that swift
grace that took Amber off guard and made her realize
that she was provoking a dangerous man. His hand shot
out to grab her wrist and drag her to him, ignoring her
furious sputtering and attempt to pull back. "Let me
show you just how unmannerly I can be, Miss Jenné,"
he muttered, and crushed his mouth down over hers
before she could do more than inhale sharply.

His lips seared across her half-open mouth in a punishing kiss that made her breath catch in her throat.
With his hands curled over her wrists, he used his body
to shove her up against the cabin wall, leaning into her
as he ravaged her mouth. Amber made a halfhearted
attempt at pushing away, and quickly realized the futility of it. He was immovable, iron-hard and determined.
If she hadn't been so shocked by his actions, she might
have been able to control her response, but the initial
attraction she'd felt for Nick Windsor rose in a pressing
need that made her helpless in his embrace.

Despite insistent warnings thrumming in the back of
her brain, Amber yielded to his warmth and the fierce
urgency of his mouth and body as he leaned into her. It
was like kissing liquid fire, and she burned beneath his
touch as he skimmed her body with a bold caress. Her
cloak hung awry and her breath came in fast, hard gulps
of air when he briefly released her mouth and looked
down at her.

What he saw in her face must have encouraged him,
because his dark head lowered again and he captured

her trembling, swollen lips in a hungry kiss that made her moan. The cut on his lip certainly didn't seem to bother him any. She was shaking all over, quivering with a need she didn't understand and had never felt before. Every nerve in her body shuddered at his touch, was tautened to a piercing tension that left her as tightly strung as a violin, and she closed her eyes and kissed Nick back with a searing urgency that must have transferred itself to him.

Shifting slightly, Nick stepped away from the wall, taking Amber with him, his arms moving around her as he backed toward the fire. In a swift motion that held all the elements of a dream, he was lowering her to his blankets, following with his lean body. He bent over her, a hand on each side of her head, his gaze hot and intent.

Flames warmed the side of her nearest the fire, but Amber shivered as the glow threw Nick's dark, hard face into stark light and shadow.

Her breath came even more rapidly now, uneven and shallow as she stared up at him. The ridge of his brows lifted slightly, and the gleam in his black, velvety eyes flared. Deliberately moving his hand over the curve of her jaw to her throat, Nick watched her reaction with a predatory, guarded gaze. It was as if he expected her to stop him, and she knew she should. What made her slow was the unexpected response he'd sparked in her traitorous flesh, the aching need that throbbed inside her and made her want to surrender all. His hand moved aside the soft wool of her cloak and rested on the swell of her bosom, toying with the buttons of her dress. Amber jerked.

Nick's head lowered and he covered the peak of her breast with his mouth, sucking gently, wetting the thin cotton and making arrows of heat shoot through her body. She moaned, and curled her fingers into his hair to pull him away. But instead of pulling his head away, she was holding it still, her body arching closer as if seeking the source of the sweet pleasure that knifed through her. A deep, aching throb escalated inside her, and she cried out when his hand moved to her other breast. It wasn't until his fingers teased her breast, his thumb grazing across the tightly beaded nipple visible through the thin cotton bodice, that Amber knew she had to stop him before it was too late.

Summoning a strength she hadn't known she possessed, she whispered, "Nick—I can't."

His thumb rotated with a touch that made her writhe, and his head lifted, a taut set to his mouth.

"Can't, or won't?"

"Does it matter?"

"To you, maybe." His mouth twisted. "Either way, you're saying no, so I can't say that your reasons are worth a damn to me." He took his hand away from her breast and pushed to a sitting position, staring down at her with an unfathomable gaze. "I knew you were trouble the first time I saw you," he said calmly, his eyes narrowing when she sat up with a jerk. "You look like a cat, all graceful and soft and silky, and you've got the same perverse nature."

Ashamed that she had led him on when she knew better, Amber let his last remark pass, except to say, "I like cats."

"You would."

She pulled her cloak around her again, feeling suddenly chilled in spite of the fire Nick had started. Clearing her throat, she flashed him a quick glance.

"I'd better go back to the house."

"Sweetheart, the next time you offer me an invitation like the one you just did, I intend to take you up on it. So be damned good and certain you want to go through with it."

Nick's soft warning made her shiver with reaction, and she could tell that he meant every word of it. "Really, Mr. Windsor—" she began, halting when he gave a short laugh. His hand shot out to cup her chin, and she took a deep breath at the heated glow in his eyes.

"Mister Windsor? Kinda formal, isn't it, after what you just let me do?"

Her cheeks flamed. "I suppose so. It's very ungallant of you to remind me, however."

His laughter filled the small cabin. "Ungallant, Miss Jenné? How prim and proper." He leaned close, his voice lowering to a husky purr. "I'll bet you can be mighty improper when you're in bed with a man, your hair all spread out on a pillow and that sweet body open for him. . . ."

She gasped. Embarrassed, angry, and filled with a hot emotion she'd never experienced, Amber leaped to her feet, her voice losing all hint of sugary sweetness. "You are a rogue and a rascal, Nick Windsor, and I regret I ever felt sorry for you."

"Felt sorry for *me*? What a waste." He rose in a lithe motion that made Amber think of the cats he'd mentioned earlier, and she clutched her cloak more tightly around her. A faint, mocking smile still curved the hard line of his mouth as he gazed down at her and said, "You'd better run fast, Miss Amber Jenné, because if you don't, I'm going to lay you back down on this floor and show you exactly what I want to do to you."

For a heartbeat Amber stood looking up at him uncertainly, but when he shifted slightly, she whirled and ran, yanking open the cabin door and disappearing into the soft night.

Nick watched her go with real regret. He wanted her, and for a brief instant had been inclined to ignore her refusal. In spite of himself, he'd let her go, and he ached with the need to bury himself inside her. Damn her, the golden little cat, with those wide amber eyes and that thick, tawny mane that urged a man to bury his face in it at the same time he buried himself in her lush body.

Swearing, Nick leaned against the doorjamb and stared into the dark shadows that shrouded the house. Damn. He knew he shouldn't have come home. He hadn't expected this complication, nor had he expected

Alex Steele to show up, but here he was. It wasn't going to be easy for him, he saw that now. There would always be reminders of what was gone, what he'd never have again, and as long as his sister was married to the man who'd burned his home and fought against him, he would never feel at ease in the place where he'd been born.

Nick grazed the unrelenting wood of the door frame with his fist, not even noticing the splinters digging into his skin as he fought the urge to take up his pistol and go after Alexander Steele. He glanced up at the barn, saw the thread of light between the double doors, and clenched his teeth. They were in there, Alex and Jess, man and wife.

A groan escaped him, and Nick shoved away from the door. He stalked to the pile of blankets he'd tossed to the floor. First thing in the morning, he was leaving. He'd go back to Memphis, make enough money to leave Tennessee behind forever. If he stayed, he'd end up either killing his sister's husband or getting killed himself.

And if he stayed one more night, he'd end up doing what every cell in his body was urging him to do—find Amber Jenné and give her what she'd so prettily asked for earlier with her heated kisses and golden eyes.

Nick spent one of the longest nights in recent memory as he tried to get comfortable on the hard wooden floor. He was still awake when the first gray fingers of dawn filtered through the chinks in the walls.

CHAPTER
4

Memphis, Tennessee—May 1865

IT was raining again. Amber sighed and let the parlor curtains fall shut over the window. The streets were wet and shiny, and in the distance the boom of thunder sounded like small cannon. Until a short time before, she would have cringed at the sound and wondered if the Confederates were trying to fire on a Yankee steamer puffing into the Memphis harbor. No more.

The war was over, had ended the month before, with General Robert E. Lee's surrender at a place called Appomattox. No one was surprised. She was relieved, maybe, or saddened, but not surprised. The South had been limping toward the inevitable for too long.

Lincoln's assassination had been devastating, however. Not only to the grieving North, but to those of the South who could recognize the far-reaching implications caused by his death. The President's legacy of mercy had died with him. Reconstruction of the torn South and tattered Union would be slow and painful.

Amber wondered if Alex Steele had lived through the final battles in North and South Carolina, and if he'd gotten word to Jessamy. She hoped so. The last time she'd seen Jessamy, her friend had been weeping and distraught.

The same morning that Nick Windsor had left Clover Hill with the barest of farewells, Captain Steele had been summoned back to his regiment. His visit had been far too short, but infinitely precious to his wife. Poor Jessamy. She'd already been raw from weeping at her brother's abrupt departure and barely civil good-bye, when the messenger had come for her husband.

Amber felt a spasm of pain. After leaving Clover Hill, she'd tried to find Nick, but no one in Memphis seemed to know anything about him. She told herself she was trying to find him for her friend, but part of her acknowledged the fact that it was just as much for herself.

Nick had frightened her that night in the cabin, because he had introduced her to a depth of sensory emotion she hadn't known she could feel. It had frightened and exhilarated her, because at long last she understood so much that had always eluded her.

Passion, with all its inherent responsibilities, had never beckoned to her. She'd never felt the slightest inclination to allow a man such liberties, until Nick Windsor. Then, to her own shock and bewilderment, she'd not only allowed him to touch her, but she'd reveled in it. No, she could not ignore his existence now, not until she knew if the emotions he'd aroused in her were only a result of the situation or were real.

She turned away from the window as she heard the front door open, and smiled when Henri Jenné swept into the entry hall with a muffled curse.

"Damn this weather," he was grumbling when he looked up and saw Amber in the doorway. Henri's handsome face broke into a welcoming smile. "*Chérie*, you are—as always—a beautiful sight."

"So says my doting father," Amber replied, coming forward to help him remove his drenched hat and topcoat. Celia appeared from the back of the house, scolding in French as she helped Amber.

"You would like tea, monsieur?" Celia asked when

she held the wet garment at arm's length, her head tilted to one side like a bright bird.

"Yes, with a large dollop of brandy in it," Henri Jenné muttered. He brushed away the few drops of rain that still clung stubbornly to his dress jacket. "It's a miserable day, despite the warmer temperatures."

"Memphis is always wet in May," Amber said soothingly, taking her father's arm to accompany him to the parlor. "It prepares us for the heat of the summer. And gives us lots of mosquitoes to look forward to."

Henri gave a distracted smile as he seated himself in a chair near the fire. He glanced around. "Where is your aunt Leala? I thought to find her here moping because the house is too full to fit in one more displaced Rebel or Yankee."

Amber seated herself in a wing-backed chair near her father and laughed. "Who told you the house was too full? Aunt Leala has not seemed to notice. A new batch arrived this morning. I think she is putting them in the basement."

Henri leaned back in his chair and closed his eyes, muttering a French phrase that made Amber hide a smile. After a moment he said softly, "Memphis is filled with angry soldiers. There was an altercation on Poplar Road today, and another one near the Exchange Building."

"Near Federal hospital?" Amber frowned. A hospital had been set up in the Exchange Building, and her aunt went there almost daily. "That must be the reason Aunt Leala came back so out of sorts. I wondered, but she only said she was too busy to talk."

A wry smile twisted Henri's mouth. "She is probably afraid I will forbid her to go out until the city settles down. Even with Roger, it is dangerous. Lincoln's assassination has hit the country hard, *petite*. There will be vicious repercussions, mark my words. If not for the fact that the new man we hired is working out so well, I do believe I would move the business back to New York now."

"You finally found someone capable of running the warehouses?" Amber inquired, nodding at Celia when she arrived with the tea tray and Henri's decanter of brandy. "When?"

"Actually, Norman found him, thank God. I was so sick of interviewing unsuitable applicants that I swore I'd run the warehouses myself before I faced another scruffy man across my desk." His voice lowered. "They all seem so desperate. Times are hard, *petite,* very hard for men these days. With food prices so high and the glut of released soldiers—ah, but I ramble when I know you wish to hear good news." Henri opened an eye and peered at his daughter. "I don't even know the name of this new man, but Norman swears he's a marvel. I intend to go down to the warehouse tomorrow and see him for myself. According to Norman—a genial liar at times, but not stupid—the man has managed to whip those lazy workers into shape with only a few words and threats, and has taken a detailed inventory in just a week. Of course, only on two floors, but it's been so long overdue that— I'm sorry, *chère.* I'm talking business again. How was your day?"

"Boring, as usual."

Henri chuckled. "Boring, was it? You ought to tag along with me, then. I'll show you a day that can be anything but boring."

Amber fiddled with the braided trim on the wing chair, and thought of how useless her life seemed lately. Leala was caught up in her work with the wounded of both sides, as well as those homeless men left adrift in the city. Roger was kept busy escorting Leala, even to Irving Block Prison to take what medicine and food she could to the unfortunates incarcerated there. It was an exhausting routine. And she was left at loose ends all day.

In an effort to be helpful, Amber had taken on charity

work, but that had left her so depressed she had not been able to force herself to go back in three days. A pang of guilt struck her when she thought of all the pinched, hungry faces that looked to her for help at St. Mary's Church on the corner of Exchange and Second.

God, she felt so selfish. If she was as noble as her aunt, she would ignore her own feelings and do what she could for those poor victims of war.

She glanced back at her father and said suddenly, "I think I would like that, Papa. To go to the warehouses with you one day, I mean. Perhaps there is something I can do that will suit me."

Henri looked surprised, but nodded. "Of course, *chère*. You are welcome anytime. Tomorrow, we shall visit the warehouse and meet this marvel that has made Norman Martin swear he was sent by good fairies, eh?"

"I'd like that. And maybe I can find a way to help out, if you won't be so hard-headed and let me."

"You know I don't like the notion of my daughter working in a warehouse or business," Henri began with a frown, and Amber gave him a cup of tea liberally laced with brandy.

"It's not as if I would be actually *working*, Papa, so I don't know why you fuss so. I'd feel less useless if you wouldn't be so stubborn."

"Useless?" Gray brows rose indignantly. "You are the most beautiful of ornaments, *ma petite*, and not at all useless. I will not hear such nonsense, and—"

"All right, all right," Amber said with a laugh, "I give up! But if you will allow me to tag along with you a day or two, I would feel much better."

"That is agreeable to me," Henri said, sitting back and sipping at his tea. "You may go with me, and you will see that it is no place for a young lady like yourself to be."

Southern Warehouses & Company stretched along an entire city block, comprising a good portion of downtown Memphis. The vast buildings housed a variety of goods, such as cotton and other raw materials, spices, sacked grains, and almost every conceivable household item. New York–born Henri Jenné had inherited the business along with his wife, and since her death when Amber was a small child, had thrown himself headlong into making it grow. He'd succeeded admirably, and with offices in New York as well as the South, he'd managed to keep his business during the long years of the war when other businesses failed.

Ideally situated on the Mississippi River, where barges could transport goods from the Ohio River to the Cumberland and down the Mississippi to New Orleans, and from there on to Europe, Southern Warehouses supplied the entire South with goods. Many products were manufactured in the Ohio valley, some even farther away. Now that the war was over, business would grow by leaps and bounds as the South tried to rebuild.

When his carriage rolled to a halt on South Main, Henri climbed down and turned to help Amber. She lifted her dimity skirts in one gloved hand, putting her other hand in her father's outstretched palm as she accepted his assistance. Feathers bobbed in her elegant bonnet, and when she stood on the sidewalk outside the front doors of Southern Warehouses & Company, she adjusted the tilt of her hat by the wide satin ribbons that held it atop her head.

"Ready, *chère*?" Henri asked with an indulgent smile, and Amber flashed him an answering smile.

"Of course. I just had to straighten my new hat so I wouldn't embarrass you."

"As if you ever could," Henri replied, laughing down at her as he curved an arm around her slender waist and escorted her into the bricked building that housed offices and warehouses. It had recently been redone, and boasted new furniture and potted plants that the decorator had insisted made it much more elegant. Rich Persian rugs were scattered over the floor, and there was an air of affluence in the gleaming brass and sumptuous stretches of mahogany paneling.

A clerk waited at a small cherry desk, and looked up as they entered, then rose to his feet with immediate attention.

"Mr. Jenné. How good to see you, sir. Is there something I can do?"

"I certainly hope so, Mr. Dyer." Henri smiled. "Before I go to my office, my daughter wishes to view the warehouses. Are there any messages?"

While her father took his messages, Amber ambled to the far end of the wide corridor that served as a main vein to the offices as well as a reception area. Paintings hung on the brick walls, some of them new, and she inspected a few of them while she waited.

Thick leaded-glass windows soared from floor to ceiling at the far end of the wide corridor, with offices on each side. A door led from the hallway down a flight of stairs to the next building, where the warehouses stretched at angles. Amber paused at the windows overlooking the river and watched idly as barges cruised down the brown ribbon of water that was the main highway for transporting goods.

Behind her she could hear her father asking for Norman Martin, then his voice rising a little bit with exasperation.

"He's always down at the river," Henri grumbled. "Well, no matter. Tell our new supervisor—what is his name? Hmmm. Why does that sound familiar? Where will I find him?"

Amber turned away from the window to wait for her father by the door to the exit, and when he joined her, he was frowning.

"Is everything all right, Papa?"

"Of course, *chère*. It's just that I hate it when I can't recall things that seem important." His gray eyes twinkled. "You will find out one day when you get as ancient as I, that the memory is the first faculty to go."

"Old? You, Papa? I've seen twenty-year-olds who can't keep up with you."

Laughing, Henri Jenné was in an excellent mood as he escorted Amber to the stocked warehouses. She'd been there before, but not often, and could not recall them being so vast. Or so filled with goods.

"All this belongs to Southern Warehouse and Company?" she asked in amazement, and smiled at Henri's nod of satisfaction.

"Oui," he said, reverting to his native tongue, as he often did when thinking of something else. Amber stopped his swift spate of words with an uplifted hand, laughing.

"Papa, you know I don't follow French as well as you speak it. I'm an American. Please go more slowly."

Henri gave her a hug and switched to English, saying, "One day, all this will be yours. I only hope that you marry a man capable of running the business."

"Not much chance of that, when I haven't yet found a man willing to marry me," Amber teased, and thought immediately of Nick Windsor. A faint flush warmed her cheeks, and she wondered irritably why she thought of him. He should be the furthest thing from her mind right now. She'd made up her mind to forget him, and hoped that Jessamy would manage to do the same.

"Don't try to fool an old man," her father said, reaching to open a door for her. "When you find the right man, you will pursue him to Hell if you have to. I know that, though I doubt there is any man who'll be foolish enough to try to get away."

A faint smile curved her generous mouth as Amber entered the next building just ahead of her father. Halfway down the row of shelves that held various household items, she saw two men, one with a ledger, the other halfway up a ladder.

"Ah, that must be our new supervisor," Henri said

with a satisfied note in his voice. "I must congratulate him for his hard work. Look how he does not delegate responsibility but performs duties himself. I tell you, *chère,* we may have finally found a man capable of . . ." Henri turned in surprise to stare at his daughter.

Amber jerked to such a sudden halt that the feather in her new bonnet bobbed wildly. The man on the ladder was turning, and there was no mistaking the lean grace and build, the self-assured movements. Nicholas Windsor.

Her heart thudded wildly, and as she met his startled gaze, she knew that he was just as unaware of her place in the company as she had been of his. The quick wariness in the look he gave her told her a lot more than he realized, she was certain. It took her a moment to regain her composure, but by the time Nick had climbed down from the ladder and approached them, she was in command of herself.

"You must be Mr. Windsor," Henri was saying. "I have heard a great deal about you, young man. In the short time you have been here, you have managed to replace chaos with order. I am well-pleased with your efforts on behalf of my company, and—"

"This is your company?" Nick broke in, his dark eyes narrowed as he looked from Henri to Amber.

"Why, yes. Did you not know? I realize we have not been introduced, but I am Henri Jenné, owner of Southern Warehouse and Company. Norman Martin is president, and takes care of all the most crucial details . . ."

While her father went on, explaining the hierarchy of the board of directors, Amber met Nick's steady stare with her own. She refused to let him intimidate her, especially on home ground. If he didn't like the fact that she was the owner's daughter, then he could quit. Her chin lifted, and when her father paused to introduce them, Amber's voice was as sugary sweet as if she had never met Nick before.

"How do you do, Mr. Windsor?"

There was a telling pause, and when Henri began to frown, Nick said shortly, "Very well, ma'am. It's a pleasure to see you again."

"Is it?" Amber smiled. "I wouldn't have thought you would say that, but of course, you're only being polite."

"You're absolutely right." Nick met her lifted brow with a mocking smile.

By now Henri's brows were knit in a scowl, and Amber turned to him. "Papa, this is Mrs. Steele's brother. Perhaps you recall my telling you about him?"

Recognition quickly hid the surprise on the older man's face, and he nodded. "Of course. I trust you and your sister have made up your quarrel by now, Mr. Windsor?"

"Is that a prerequisite for working here?" Nick asked curtly, and Henri's frown deepened.

"No. Of course not. I merely wish for all families to be on speaking terms, but your personal life has nothing to do with your work."

"Good. I'd like to keep it that way."

Obviously at a loss, Henri looked from Nick to Amber, then gave a very Gallic shrug. "I am not at all certain what is at fault here, but I'm willing to ignore it if you are. I am concerned with my business, Mr. Windsor, and have been told that you are an excellent employee."

Nick's dark gaze shifted back to Henri. "That's true, sir. I am."

"Then we shall deal well together. *Chère*, why don't you wait for me at the end of this aisle, and I will be with you in a moment or two. I have some business matters to discuss."

"I thought that was the purpose of my visit today, so that I could see how the business is run," Amber said coolly, and felt rather than saw Nick's quick frown. "Wasn't it, Papa? I am, after all, fairly intelligent, and I think I can grasp the concept of buying and selling wholesale merchandise."

After a pause, Henri nodded slowly, and Nick sucked

in a deep breath. His mouth thinned to a straight line and the thick brush of his lashes lowered slightly in a lazy drift.

"Mr. Jenné, while I won't presume to tell you your business, I'd like to point out that I have absolutely no intention of working with a woman. It's nothing personal against your daughter, sir, but I'm accustomed to working with men. I'm afraid that I would not be able to take orders from a female."

Amber felt a wave of fury shake her from head to foot, and she glared at Nick. He refused to even glance at her, but kept his hooded gaze on her father. After a moment Henri said reluctantly, "She is not going to give you orders, Mr. Windsor, but she is a part of the business. I would appreciate your consideration and courtesy, and expect it from you. Amber is the light of my life, and I would not allow anyone to insult her."

"I have no intention of insulting her. Just as I have no intention of working for her."

Anger made her voice quiver when she asked sharply, "Are you afraid of being shown up, Mr. Windsor?"

His glance shifted again, the dark velvet gaze pinioning her with a sharpness that she could almost feel. "No, Miss Jenné. I just dislike working for a woman. As I said, this is nothing personal. Unless you wish for it to be."

There wasn't anything she could say to that without revealing her reasons, and she didn't want her father to know the liberties she'd allowed Nick Windsor. Not only would Henri be hurt, he'd be so outraged that he might call Nick out. Henri was from the old school, where such an insult to one's daughter called for drastic measures. That he was willing to keep Nick Windsor as an employee after his refusal to accept her was a sign of how desperate he was for a man he could trust in the company.

Knowing that, Amber decided to call a truce before her father was forced to fire Nick. Since it seemed as if

Nick had no intention of backing down, she swallowed her pride and injected what she hoped was just the right note of amused condescension into her tone.

"I have no intention of interfering, Mr. Windsor. And I won't let our personal differences affect any business decisions. I trust you feel the same."

His dark brow lifted. "Of course."

Henri gave an almost inaudible sigh of relief, and Amber knew she had made the right decision, though it galled her to allow Nick Windsor even that small victory. Turning away, she moved to the end of the aisle, deliberately presenting her back to him. Let him make of it what he would. At the moment, she was holding tightly to her self-control to keep from telling him exactly how she felt. She'd have her chance to say what was on her mind soon enough.

As he watched her walk away, Nick found it difficult to keep his mind on the questions Jenné was asking. His shock at seeing Amber had quickly degenerated into irritation, as usual. Of all the rotten luck. Curse it, why hadn't he checked into the company more thoroughly before he took the job?

The answer to that was plain enough. He'd needed it too badly, and it had seemed the perfect opportunity for him. Now it seemed that his luck was still bad. Amber Jenné. And her father owned the company. Nick felt like hitting something, and he fought the urge to swear aloud and announce his decision to quit. Lord knew, pride had become a cold bedfellow. But to work for Amber's father . . .

What was it about that woman that got to him so fast? He wished he knew. She could make him madder quicker than anyone he'd ever met before. Even Jess, who knew just how to prick his temper into raging fury with a few short words, couldn't match this woman.

With an effort, Nick jerked his attention from Amber's alluring curves to her father, and tried to remember the question he'd asked. He hoped he was in the general neighborhood when he replied, "Three shipments of last year's cotton have already gone downriver on barges, sir. They should be in New Orleans within the week."

"Excellent. I am well-pleased with how swiftly you've managed to whip my crew into line. It's amazing how lading bills and orders were so confused before you came. You have a future with Southern Warehouse and Company if you want it, you know."

Startled, Nick thought for a moment before replying, "I appreciate that, sir. When I took this job, I told Mr. Martin that I didn't know how long I'd be staying. My intentions are to earn enough to move on to Texas and buy my own place."

"I see." Jenné stared at him thoughtfully, then smiled. "I intend to offer you a permanent position if you keep working as you are now, Mr. Windsor. You might consider that before making any further plans."

"I'll keep it in mind."

After Henri Jenné had joined his daughter and they'd left the warehouse, Nick leaned back against a row of shelves. Damn. Not that he didn't appreciate Jenné's offer, but it wasn't exactly what he had in mind. Texas beckoned—Texas with hundreds of other dissatisfied, disillusioned southerners. He'd run into Lieutenant Conrad, who was on his way to Texas to join his cousin. His cousin had gone the week after Lee's surrender. Conrad said there was more land than a man could see in a month, and that it was free. Men lived by their own rules out there. Why didn't Nick come with him? Conrad had asked.

Nick wanted to go, wanted to leave Tennessee and its bitter memories far behind. This job was, as he'd said, temporary. He didn't want to get to Texas with empty pockets. But now—since Jenné had mentioned a future—the thought of staying did seem a bit more attractive.

With his past destroyed, the future seemed infinitely more important.

Levering his lean body away from the shelves, Nick glanced at Hopkins, who awaited his instructions. Stifling a sigh that the man couldn't seem to do anything on his own, Nick said, "Now let's count the next row, George."

"Yessir. Do I start at the top again?"

"The top is fine." Impatience edged his curt words as he grabbed a rung of the ladder and stepped up. "I'll do the counting, George. You write."

It would have been a hell of a lot easier, Nick reflected as he counted crates of iron kettles, if he hadn't seen Amber Jenné again. That tiger-eyed woman had a way of haunting him at night, and he'd only recently been able to banish the image of her lying under him, her lips parted and her lush breasts pressing against his bare chest. It ought to be another two months before he managed to sleep through a night again, dammit.

CHAPTER
5

NICK Windsor was shocked to find that he would not be pardoned under the new general amnesty policy announced by President Johnson on May 29, 1865. He was furious.

President Johnson adopted the fundamentals of Lincoln's Reconstruction plan. His first proclamation on May 9 was to declare all "Rebel" authority in the state of Virginia null, and he directed the reestablishment of national authority, and pledged Federal aid in restoring peace and state authority.

His second proclamation affected the entire South—pardon, amnesty, and the Reconstruction procedure.

Pardon was designated as a preliminary to restoration. In the past, the traditional policy had been to extend oblivion and forgiveness to former "Rebels" on condition of renewed allegiance. Formerly, there had been a limited pardon that did not restore rights as to slaves or confiscated property where third parties had intervened, even once the oath of allegiance had been taken. Johnson's proclamation of May 29, 1865, again offered pardon with conditions similar to Lincoln's, except that general amnesty did not automatically include those whose taxable property exceeded $20,000. To those excepted from this general pardon, however, there remained the possibility that a special pardon by petition would be granted.

Nick Windsor found this galling and insulting.

As the male heir to Clover Hill, he was one of those excepted from a general pardon. To ease the situation for his mother, he signed over all rights to the lands he'd inherited. While he hadn't wanted to remain in Hardeman County, it was still a devastating personal blow, and left him bitter. He found it a relief to throw himself into the growing business at the warehouse.

With the war over and the shock fading from Lincoln's assassination, business began to escalate again in the South. Southern Warehouses & Company's business increased as the northern industrial centers began to pick up production. More and more barges chugged downriver, many of them disgorging their cargo at the SW&C wharves.

Nick had little time to think of anything but business. In one way, it was a blessing, keeping his mind off his problems.

But he could not stave off the nightmares that came when he was asleep.

Those were the worst. Smoke filled the air, and the screams of wounded and dying echoed in his head until he woke up in a sweat, sitting up in his darkened room, slowly realizing it was only a dream. Perspiration would trickle down his naked chest in the stuffy room, and sometimes he got up and walked down to the brush-tangled bluffs to stare out across the rolling waters of the river which went on unceasingly. The Big Muddy, he'd heard it called, the treacherous river that was the end of the South and the beginning of the West.

There were times he regretted his decision to stay in Memphis and work for Jenné. But mostly he was glad for the steady work and good pay, the feeling that what he was doing was worthwhile. He regularly sent money to his mother, and the rest he put into a bank account for his future.

Cattle and land. That was what he'd decided to invest in for himself. It was the future, that elusive dream of security. Only the bleak realization that nothing in life was guaranteed kept him from quitting his job and leaving Tennessee. He wanted to be sure, wanted to have money in hand. SW&C had given him a small measure of security, but it wasn't enough. There was a burning need in Nick to have something solid to rely on, something that he knew wouldn't disappear at the drop of a hat or shift of wind.

Nick hadn't seen Amber since she'd visited the warehouse a month before. Now it was July, and there she stood, all cool and crisp in muslin and lace, and looking like a satisfied cat.

Pausing in the doorway of Norman Martin's office, Nick felt her gaze on him and turned. Cursing silently at his reaction to her, he raked her with a quick survey.

"Miss Jenné," he said, because he had to acknowledge her and couldn't think of anything else to say. He walked into the hall with an indifference he didn't feel.

Amber's brow lifted, and her mouth held a hint of laughter. "Yes, I *am* Miss Jenné. How are you, Mr. Windsor?"

"Fine," he said shortly.

Damn her, with that exquisite face that looked as if it belonged to a porcelain doll, the lush promise of a body that made a man want to pull her to him and take off all her clothes to explore satin skin and fragrant hollows. His gaze shifted abruptly back to her face when he realized she was talking to him.

Sensuous lips had curved into a soft bow. "I'm doing well, though a little warm," she volunteered. "Don't you think it particularly humid this year?"

Damn, Nick thought, *the weather*. Aloud he said, "Yes." His hands curled into fists, which he shoved into his pockets, rocking back on his heels and devouring her with his eyes. She was one fine woman, he had to admit that. If she'd only keep her mouth shut, she'd be near perfect.

As if reading his mind, Amber came closer, her tawny eyes gilded with soft lights and her heavy mane of luxurious hair shining like muted gold. A wave of perfume—French and expensive, no doubt—wafted toward him, and Nick's body reacted with a tight surge.

"Are you attending the Fourth of July celebration Papa has planned, Mr. Windsor?"

"Hadn't thought about it," he answered honestly. "What with pig-iron production all but ended and your father trying to buy up all the stuff for some unknown reason, we've had more than we can handle taking care of shipments and invoices and the tidy little details that go along with a business like this."

"Do I detect sarcasm, Mr. Windsor?"

He shrugged, aware of the fact that Mr. Dyer, the clerk, was doing his best to pretend he wasn't paying attention to their conversation.

"I don't know, Miss Jenné. *Do* you detect sarcasm?"

Amber's mouth curved upward, and her laugh was throaty. "Yes. I'm certain I do."

"Far be it for me to contradict a . . ." He paused, let the delay drag out just long enough, then finished, ". . . lady."

"Ouch. It really hurt you to say that, didn't it?"

His lips twitched. "You noticed."

Tilting her head to one side, Amber surveyed him for a long moment, her smile lingering. "You'd be surprised at the things I notice, Mr. Windsor."

"Bet not."

Her eyes widened slightly, and her tongue wet her lips in a uniquely feminine motion that made him want to jerk her to him and taste what she'd just moistened. Long lashes like moth wings fluttered in confusion, and she looked as if she wanted to run. Nick felt a wave of satisfaction. Good. He had her feeling at least *some* of what he felt.

Making a curiously graceful motion with one hand, Amber said in a soft voice, "You should take some time to play, Mr. Windsor. Come to the picnic. Papa has planned lots of food, and even fireworks."

Nick deliberately looked away from her and shrugged. She was too potent, and she had to know it.

"I've seen enough *real* fireworks to last a lifetime, and I don't really feel like celebrating Yankee holidays," he said shortly, and heard her laugh.

"You are an American, aren't you? It's got nothing to do with being Yankee or Rebel. The war's over, Mr. Windsor."

His gaze shot back to her, and through clenched teeth he ground out, "Not for me. Not for a hell of a lot of us."

Pivoting on his heel, he stalked away, almost shaking with the fury her light words had provoked. No, the war was definitely not over for him, or for a lot of men who'd fought.

The Fourth of July started out cloudy, but turned into a hot, humid day. On the riverbank by the row of warehouses, Jenné had set up tables and tents for his employees, and for any who wanted to participate. It was, Leala said, another form of charity, but one that would at least feed those too proud to ask for it. A picnic was different from the lines at the churches in town.

Sitting under the shade of a tent, Amber waved an ivory and lace fan back and forth, stirring up a cooling breeze. The humidity made her dress cling to her damply, and she had her hair piled atop her head in an intricate braid to keep it off her neck. She surveyed the crowd idly.

Blue coats still dotted the throng. Union soldiers were being slowly recalled, but there were those still in service. Amber wondered if the presence of the Federals would keep Nick from coming, or if he was just being stubborn. Probably the latter, she told herself as the day wore on and he didn't show up.

Baskets of food were constantly replenished. Fried chicken, biscuits, fruit, pastries, and other delectables lined the tables. Amber had eaten very little, but when her aunt brought her another cup of lemonade, she drank it gratefully.

"It's hot," Leala said bluntly. "Much too hot for a picnic. I told Henri that, but he didn't listen." She turned to look at her niece. "Are you all right? You seem awfully quiet today."

"I'm fine," Amber lied without a qualm. "Just a bit warm, as you said."

"I told Henri it was too hot," Leala repeated, waving a fan to cool her flushed face. "Never listens."

Music played in the bandstand set up on the green lawn, and Amber felt a moment's admiration that her father had been able to arrange all the details in a land ravaged by war. Of course, Memphis had fallen early. It had been in Federal hands since July of 1862, so there wasn't the widespread destruction here as in other cities. Atlanta had suffered a great deal, she'd heard, and was only ruins now. Charleston had also been burned. New Orleans had cringed under the rule of a tyrant, and was still under a form of martial law, though that was denied by the government. All in all, Henri said, the South could be suffering worse. In civil conflicts, the losers were usually devastated. So far, no southern officers had been hanged for war crimes, though Jefferson Davis was being held, as was Stephens and Campbell.

Amber wondered if Nick thought of that, then doubted it. He was too busy hating the North, hating Yankees, hating the ruined life he'd once led. Her fan waved faster and she frowned. Didn't he see what he was doing to himself with his hatred? And to those who cared about him?

"You look lost in thought, m'dear," a voice said beside her, and Amber glanced up in surprise.

"Mr. Martin," she said, greeting her father's partner warmly. "How are you?"

"Sweating like a pig," he returned cheerfully, then paused. "I forgot. I'm supposed to be polite and gallant and not mention such things to a lady, aren't I?"

"Yes," Amber said gravely, and couldn't resist adding, "I didn't know pigs could sweat."

Martin looked thoughtful. "Can't. Horses sweat. Sweating like a horse, then." His ready smile returned. "How are you, in spite of this heat? You look as cool as ice, m'dear. Always do. Don't know how you do it." He seated himself in a chair next to her, as charming as ever, his slender frame attired in the latest fashion.

The second son of a wealthy Boston family, Norman Martin had made it his goal to pursue his own fortune, and frequently regaled Amber with tales of his youthful exploits in that pursuit. He never let it be forgotten that he came from a family of means, and that he intended to be as influential as his father. Though Amber thought him a bit of a snob, he was pleasant company most of the time.

Smiling fondly at him, Amber was oddly grateful to Martin for distracting her from thoughts of Nick Windsor. She chatted with him aimlessly, laughing and waving her fan over his sweaty face to cool him, laughing again when he declared her an angel from heaven.

Blue eyes crinkled at the corners as he regarded her with open admiration. "How is it some handsome swain has not whisked you away, lovely flower? Even with the admitted distraction of the war, I can't imagine you still being unwed."

"Personal preference, I'm afraid," Amber said. "I've not yet met the man who intrigues me enough to care about him."

"Intrigue? Is that what it takes to win your heart?" Martin asked lightly, and laughed when she nodded and agreed.

"Partly. Of course, there will have to be something

else to make me fall in love, but I don't want to marry for convenience or gain. Only love will do, I'm afraid."

"You've read too many romances, m'dear," Martin observed, and his mouth stretched into a wide grin. "Have you considered that love may come *after* marriage?"

"Not for a moment," she replied promptly. "I'd rather die an old maid than marry someone who doesn't turn me inside out with love for him."

"I see." Martin's smile wavered slightly, and his blue eyes drifted over Amber's lovely face in a close inspection that made her shift uneasily. "You know, m'dear," he said quickly, "that I will always be here for you. As a friend, of course, if not as an *intriguing* suitor."

"Of course. You are a dear friend, and my papa relies on you greatly." Pausing, Amber looked out over the river for a moment. "What is your opinion of Nicholas Windsor, Mr. Martin?" she blurted, not realizing she was going to ask the question until the words were out of her mouth.

"Nicholas Windsor?" Martin repeated slowly. He raked a hand through his rich brown hair, appearing startled by the question. He had a boyish face and certain charm that appealed to the fairer sex, along with his reputation for being a man who had connections in the business world and a great deal of money to spend on those who took his fancy. Norman Martin was not a man accustomed to answering questions about *other* men. "Nicholas Windsor," he said again, then shrugged. "He's an excellent worker, of course, and very dedicated to his position. I think he could go far in the company, for a man of his character."

"What do you mean—a man of his character?"

"Well, you know. He's a firebrand, a hotheaded southerner who'll let his grudges rule his decisions. Not that he's in a position to make important decisions that may affect the company, but if Henri decides that the man will suit as an executive, as he has intimated, I'm afraid we may have problems. S.W. and C. deals with a lot of northern clients, you know, and we can't allow politics to interfere with good business judgment."

Amber's fan waved slowly, stirring tendrils of honey-gold hair at her temples. A faint frown knit her brow, and she sucked on her bottom lip, a habit she'd acquired as a child when she was troubled by something.

"So," she finally said, "you think that he may alienate important customers?"

"Eventually. If he's allowed to deal with them in more than the normal channels. Now, taking care of the invoices and seeing that the warehouses are in order seems to fit his capabilities to a fare-the-well. Any larger tasks would be taking a risk, I'm afraid. Why do you ask, m'dear?"

"Oh, no reason. His sister is dear to me, that's all."

"Oh," Martin said with a lifted brow, "that's your interest? Why didn't you say so? I would not have been so blunt."

"Wouldn't you?" Amber teased. "Did you think I was asking because I wanted him promoted?"

"I never underestimate a woman when it comes to men who have a way with the ladies," Martin said solemnly. "And Windsor has more than his share of feminine attention, it seems."

For some reason, Amber felt a wave of irritation. "Does he?" she asked sharply. "What do you mean by that?"

Shrugging carelessly, Martin watched her expressive face as he said slowly, "Not much, only that there seems to be an endless procession of available women at his doorstep. Unusual, considering that the man prefers living in a hovel to decent lodgings, and that he's a miser when it comes to money. Gambles, probably, which would explain why he rarely has any money to spend on necessities."

The ivory and lace fan flipped faster, stirring up a strong breeze that lifted damp strands of her hair from her brow. Amber stared past Norman Martin, lush lashes lowering to hide the gilt gleam in her eyes.

"Do you think it possible that he is suffering deprivation? I mean, so many people were hurt during the war, and—"

"M'dear," Martin broke in, "I think you're becoming entirely too involved with this friend's brother and his situation. The government has set up a Federal commission to provide relief for those who have no money or food. I've seen former planters stand in that line," he said on a note of satisfaction that made Amber look at him oddly. "High-born gentlemen stand there with their pride in their hands for a sack of meal or two, and it's not enough that—" He broke off and cleared his throat. "Well, I suppose it's hard for them. It's hard for everyone. If Nick Windsor is suffering, it's not because he doesn't get paid enough. He does well. I gave him a good salary to begin with, and your father doubled it when he saw what Windsor had done in the warehouses."

"Perhaps he's earned it."

"Most definitely," Martin agreed promptly. "Those warehouses were in chaos until Windsor arrived. He works from early morning until late at night getting them in order, and after he sacked most of the lazy bums who let them get into such a mess, he hired men who are willing to work. They're even working today."

"Is that where Nick is? Working?"

"Probably. His choice. Henri certainly made it plain that any man who wanted could attend his little celebration today." Martin's gaze shifted to the tables of food and the crowd of hungry people. "Waste of time and money, if you ask me. These folks are more interested in free food than work."

"Thank heavens Papa is a bit more charitable than some," Amber said so sharply that Martin's head jerked around.

He flushed. "I didn't mean it the way it sounded. I

merely thought it would be wiser to put more money in their pockets than it is to provide fancy food and fireworks."

Rising to her feet, Amber took a deep breath to ease her irritation. "You're probably right, Mr. Martin. But Papa is a great believer in recreation being as good for the soul as food. It's simply a difference of opinion, I suppose."

Martin had risen to his feet too, and he nodded with a chagrined expression. "Please don't be angry at me, m'dear. I did not mean to attack Henri's philanthropy. God knows, I sometimes think he goes overboard, like allowing all those displaced soldiers in his house, but I also think he's one of the kindest, most charitable men I've ever had the privilege of knowing."

It was said so earnestly, and with such a pleading tone, that Amber's anger dissipated. Of course, it was easy to understand how her father's actions could be misconstrued if viewed in a purely practical light, so she did understand Martin's viewpoint.

"I'm not angry, Mr. Martin, but—"

"Norman. Call me Norman. We've known each other long enough to at least be on a first-name basis, haven't we? Please? I'll think you're angry at me if you don't agree."

Laughing, Amber agreed. "All right. Norman. Maybe it's the heat that's made me so testy today. I think I'll seek a cooler spot for a while, so if you see my father, would you tell him?"

"Would you like an escort? I've got enough muscle to keep anyone from hurting you, though I admit that Roger beats any man I've ever seen when it comes to sheer bulk."

"Thank you for the offer, but I've got a few errands to tend, and I can manage them at the same time."

For reasons she didn't quite understand, Amber soon found herself at her father's warehouses. It was quiet, and in the tall shade of the vast building, cooler. Nothing stirred, and she wondered if Martin had been mistaken when he'd said people were working today.

Moving cautiously down the steep stairs between the outside corridor and the entrance to the main warehouse, Amber picked her way down the staircase and through the door. The heavy oak creaked slightly as she swung it open, sounding overloud in the eerie stillness. Dust filled the air, slightly hazy and warm and smelling of spices and grains and myriad other items that comprised the stock.

Amber paused at the end of a long aisle where the shelves towered above her. It was quiet, and she decided that everyone must have stopped working for the day. A vague disappointment filled her that she hadn't seen Nick, and as she turned to leave, she acknowledged the fact that she'd come to the warehouses particularly to see him. She'd hoped he might be at the picnic, but if he did, indeed, have a legion of lovely ladies at his beck and call, she supposed he would have better things to do.

Moving back down the aisle toward the exit, Amber heard a faint sound almost at the exact moment that a hard hand grasped her shoulder and spun her around. She swallowed a sudden scream, recognizing the harsh, raspy voice that demanded to know what she was doing.

"Dammit, don't you have any sense?" Nick said angrily. "This place is practically deserted, and anyone could be hiding in the shadows."

"So I see," Amber replied much more calmly than she felt. To cover her nervousness, she smoothed her muslin skirts with one hand and idly flicked her fan, spreading it in a clicking glide.

Glaring at her, Nick took a step back, his hand falling from her shoulder. "Idiot. With all the freed slaves running around Memphis, as well as former soldiers who don't have anything better to do with their time than insult ladies, I'd think that your father would keep a better eye on you. You certainly need a keeper."

"Are you applying for the position?" Amber asked coolly.

Nick swore softly. His dark eyes narrowed to glittering slits that made Amber take a cautious step back. "If I was," he grated, "I'd probably put you over my knee like a child and paddle your backside until you begged for mercy."

"I don't think even you are big enough for that, Mr. Windsor," Amber snapped. Her face flushed and she clenched her teeth together in growing annoyance and embarrassment. To be treated as a wayward child was not exactly the emotion she had thought she inspired in Nick Windsor, and his threat made her angrier than she should have been. Part of her acknowledged that fact even as another part reacted to it.

"Don't you?" he asked softly, taking a step toward her, backing her up against the high shelves. "Don't push me. You may find out that I'm big enough to do any damn thing I please."

"Such as terrorize your employer's daughter?"

"Such as keep my employer's daughter from getting into more trouble than she even knows is out there." Nick's mouth thinned into a flat line. He was so close, Amber could see the faint specks of reflected light in the jet irises of his eyes, the calculating glint that warned her not to go too far.

"I see. I suppose this is where I fall to my knees and say how sorry I am that I've annoyed you by being here? Sorry. Lying is not one of my better traits," Amber said with a light shrug that hid her growing turmoil. Did he have to stand so close? She could feel the animal heat of him at this distance, the masculine intrusion almost stifling even in the vast warehouse.

As if he sensed the reason for her agitation, Nick stepped closer, and when she made some small sound in the back of her throat, he leaned forward with that predatory grace that intrigued her as much as it alarmed her, putting both hands on the shelf behind her, trap-

ping her between his arms. Amber drew in a sharp
breath and looked up into his harsh face.

"What are you doing?" she demanded shakily.

"I think you know."

Before she could respond, his dark head lowered and
his mouth was covering hers, harsh, demanding, drawing
a response from her in spite of her determination not to
allow it. His mouth was hot and wild, tasting of pungent
tobacco, and Amber moaned. Without thinking, she put
her arms around his neck and held on, drowning in the
taste and feel of him. Her expensive fan dropped to the
dusty warehouse floor unnoticed. The pressure of his
lips forced her mouth open, and he plundered the velvet
depths with his tongue, forcing a response.

Holding her tightly against him, Nick circled one arm
behind her and lifted her up and closer, cradling her
hips against the hard, aching ridge of him so that Amber
felt his arousal. That made her heartbeat escalate to a
shattering speed that threatened to pound out of control, and she almost sobbed.

Inclining his head to a different slant, Nick increased
the pressure of his mouth. Kissing her with all the fiery
sensuality that she had known he possessed since first
meeting him, he met her every move until the sexual
tension between them had risen so sharply Amber
sagged against him. He held her, lifting his head slightly
to stare down at her with a burning, narrowed gaze.

She was shuddering, struggling for breath, her pupils
dilated with need and confusion. An aching emptiness
throbbed with wild abandon inside her, and she reached
for him when he released her abruptly and took a step
back.

"Damn you," he muttered hoarsely, his hands clenching into fists as he stared back at her.

Amber couldn't respond. She felt such a conflict of
emotions that she couldn't do anything but shiver and
stare at him. She vaguely knew that he was angry with
her, but the reason escaped her. Her breath came in

hort, harsh gulps of air, and her lips were parted and quivering.

"What . . . what's the matter?" she managed to ask, her voice sounding like a faulty pipe organ. She flushed slightly. He was still staring at her, not taking the hand she held out. She allowed it to drop to her side and struggled to regain control.

"I don't need this," Nick rasped, and his hands flashed out to grab her wrists and jerk her back to him. "I don't need this kind of complication."

She wanted to ask what he meant, but he was kissing her again, his mouth urgent and greedy, devouring her as if she could be consumed in that embrace. Her head tilted back and she felt her hair fall loose from the ribbons that held it up. Nick's hands were on her, his touch searing through the thin muslin of her gown, caressing her breasts, cradling them in his palms, his thumbs rubbing across the tightly beaded nipples until they ached. She was aching everywhere, an insistent throbbing that demanded she ease it, but she wasn't certain how. It was obvious that Nick knew what to do, and she sensed what that entailed. At the moment, she had lost all sense of what was right and wrong. All she wanted was an end to the burning need.

Faintly shocked by the masculine weight of him against her and how he used it to his advantage, Amber shifted slightly to accommodate him as he pressed closer. Wood shelves dug into her back but she ignored the dull pressure. The weight of Nick's hard body insinuating itself between her thighs was shocking and complete. Her legs spread slightly as he edged closer, his lips stifling any protest she might have made.

When she gasped as his hand cupped her breast in that subtly teasing agony, Nick's tongue explored her mouth more deeply, making her shiver again. His other hand slid down her ribs to her hip, paused, then moved lower. The dress she wore did nothing to disguise the heat of his palm against her, and she thought suddenly

of the multitude of petticoats she'd left in her bedroom
It had been too hot to wear them, or her corset. Beneath the thin muslin, she wore only the scantiest of
undergarments and a single petticoat.

As his hand tightened on her small waist, Amber felt
him slowly draw up her skirts, until she felt the relatively
cooler air against her legs. Curling her hands into fists,
she shoved against his broad chest, feeling bare skin
beneath her hands as she encountered the area where
his white shirt gaped open. His skin was hot, slick beneath her hands, and she was momentarily distracted.

That moment's distraction gave Nick time enough to
slide his palm beneath her petticoat. Amber jerked in
reaction to the touch of his hand on her thigh. His fingers skimmed the quivering expanse in a heated slide
that made her throat go dry and her pulses pound, and
she moaned again, the sound soft and caught in her
throat.

The sounds she made registered with Nick and he
smiled with wicked satisfaction. He kissed her again,
hard and deep, feeling her helpless surrender beneath
the movement of his hands on her. Damn, but she felt
good, so good he was losing all sense of reality. He
wanted her, and he wanted her now, here, even on the
dusty warehouse floor where anyone could stumble over
them. It didn't make sense, and he knew it in the portion of his brain that held logic, but the sharp press of
desire made everything else fade into oblivion at the
moment.

She was so finely made, slender and fragile and delicate and all the things that made women so different
and exciting, and Nick wanted to tell her how exquisite
he thought she was. He wanted to take her to a big bed
with clean sheets and a locked door, to strip away all her
clothes and pretensions and hold her in his arms and
bury himself inside her heated warmth until neither of
them could move. That's what he wanted.

None of it was possible. He knew that. Yet he

couldn't deny himself this small taste of her. Life had a
way of denying him anything fine, and he didn't see why
he should be begrudged just this brief satisfaction. The
shabbiness of his room and the long hours he spent
working could be forgotten when he held Amber in his
arms, and Nick tried not to think of what it would be
like when he let her go again. He'd deal with the sleep-
less nights later.

He'd deal with his frustrated desire later too, and the
knowledge that Amber Jenné stood for everything he
despised. Now, he just wanted a little bit more of
her. . . .

"Nick," she whimpered, pushing feebly at him.
"Stop."

He ignored that; in his experience, women usually
protested they weren't ready when they were. Any
woman who had her arms around his neck and her lush,
quivering flesh pressed against his hand couldn't be
taken seriously. Besides, he wasn't going to do what his
body was urging him to do. He was only going to do this
. . . and this . . .

Gasping, Amber's head tilted back as his mouth
found the rigid peak of her breast and his fingers slid
beneath the waistband of her pantalettes. His hand
spread over the mound of her soft belly, inching lower
as he sucked strongly on her engorged nipple. The barrier of muslin kept him from tasting her as he wanted to
do, and he groaned deep in his throat. This was getting
too close to real torture. He had to stop or he wouldn't
be able to. The combination of silken flesh and expensive perfume was deadly, and he knew it.

Wrenching his mouth away from her, Nick regretfully
removed his hand from her belly and smoothed her
skirts back over her legs. He was breathing hard, and
aching with such a painful erection that he couldn't
move for a moment. He leaned against her, resting his
forehead against the top of her head. She smelled clean

and sweet, and the silken fibers of her hair tickled hi.
nose.

Amber was trembling, her breath coming in shor
gasps, and when he lifted his head and looked down a
her face, he saw confusion mixed with desire in her ho
gaze.

Cupping her rounded chin in his palm, he kissed the
soft flesh just above the dark curve of his hand. Placing
tiny kisses over her creamy cheeks, he moved to her
mouth again, keeping his kiss light and sweet. Then his
hand dropped away and he stepped back.

"Get out of here," he said softly, "before I lose any
claim I thought I had on control. *Now*," he added with
such emphasis that she blinked. Her golden gaze focused slowly, then she flushed a bright pink.

"Yes. Yes, I will. Where is my fan? I dropped it, I
think, and . . . and I don't see it. . . ."

Her voice trailed into indistinct mutters, and Nick
swore mentally and glanced down at the floor. He spied
the fan a few feet away, scooped it up and pressed it
into her palm.

"Where's Roger?" he asked abruptly, and saw some
of her confusion fade into realization.

"Roger's at the picnic, where I'm supposed to be."

"I suggest you go back."

Smoothing her skirts with a trembling hand, Amber
said lightly, "Alone? I thought it was too dangerous for
me to wander around unescorted. Isn't that what you
said?"

"Yes, that's what I said. It is dangerous. You could
run into a man like me."

Her gaze flew back to his, and he felt her immediate
response. Before he could say anything, she shrugged
again, her slender shoulders lifting briefly.

"At least you're not boring, Mr. Windsor."

Nick felt a spurt of amusement at her attempt to be
worldly and nonchalant. "No, I'm not boring."

She raked her spread fingers through the loose tousle

of her hair and combed it into a semblance of order again, her eyes not quite meeting his. "Thank you for the lesson."

"Lesson?"

"Yes. I now know *not* to walk about without an escort again."

"Good." His shrug matched hers for nonchalance. "I aim to please."

"Do you? I doubt it. I think you aim to do exactly what you please without regard for anyone else."

"You're very astute. After all, I didn't say *who* I aimed to please, did I?"

Nick's mocking words made her flush angrily, and she gave him a stiff nod as she turned toward the exit. He watched her go, and when she had gone through the door to the stairs, he followed at a discreet distance. He'd meant it when he said she had to be careful, but he had no intention of allowing himself within fifty feet of her again. Not alone. No, never alone. Miss Amber Jenné was pure poison, and he knew it. If he let himself become any more involved with her than he had, he was in for the worst time of his life.

It certainly didn't help his savage mood any when he saw her traipse down to the picnic ground again and give Norman Martin her hand. Standing back under the lilac trees scattered along the river bluff, Nick was painfully aware of the distance between them. Amber's world hadn't been shattered by the war, while his had. She was still whole and relatively unaffected, while he knew his own shortcomings.

He may want Amber Jenné in his bed, but that was all it would ever be. He didn't want any part of her world or her father's. Even if he tried to remember the dreams he'd once had, they were gone now. He supposed they'd been like a great many other men's dreams, of home and family and long, leisurely days spent riding in his own fields and seeing to details, but he couldn't recall what the hell they were now. All that remained was the

burning desire to leave the South behind, to leave every
thing behind that had once been good in his life and wa:
now tarnished.

The hot sun beat down on his head, and the swee
scent of jasmine and honeysuckle filled the air as Nick
climbed back up the steep bluff to the warehouse and
went inside.

CHAPTER
6

AUGUST'S heat was being relieved by the promise of a storm. Lightning flashed against sullen clouds, and a distant rumble rolled beyond the river in Arkansas. Amber stood at the window of the new house her father had purchased in self-defense against the growing roster of residents on Adams Street. Leala was delighted with it, though it had been run-down and needed complete refurbishing.

Amber had taken on that task, needing something to take her mind off Nick Windsor. The outside had been painted, and the inside cleaned and painted as well. Rotten boards had been replaced, and the floors sanded and polished. Everywhere she looked there was the smell of fresh paint and hard work. And she was tired, though a strange restlessness filled her that she attributed to the approaching storm.

Some of the rooms had been furnished already, and she was waiting for goods to be delivered from the warehouse to finish off the rest. After that, it would be a simple matter of rearranging things, and the house would be ready for occupancy.

Moving from room to room, Amber paused to note down what was needed. In one of the upstairs bedrooms, a thick carpet covered the floor, and the room held a wide double bed as well as a small daybed for the

use of children. The linens had not been brought for
the daybed, and there was no mosquito netting for the
double bed.

She flicked back a damp strand of hair and read over
her list again, moving to the hallway when she heard a
voice call out from downstairs. It would be the men with
the rest of the furniture and supplies, and she leaned
over the upstairs railing to direct them.

"Up here, please, with the bedroom things. All the
kitchen items, leave downstairs."

Withdrawing, Amber moved back to the bedroom to
check for the rungs that would hold the mosquito netting. The frame was in place, but the knobs that would
hold the netting were missing. She sighed and jotted
down the omission on her notepad.

A quickening breeze filtered through the open window, and she moved across the room to close it against
the rain that might pour in. Black clouds rolled across
the river in an impressive display. Spellbound, she stood
and watched.

She didn't move until she heard the delivery men
bringing up the furniture her father had sent over, and
she turned to direct them. Beds were simple and sturdy,
nothing fancy. Nor were the chairs. Washstands, bowls
and pitchers, straight-back chairs soon were placed in
the rooms. There were only last minute touches to finish
up the furnishing.

"Miss Amber," Rufus said, wiping his sweaty brow
and grinning at her, "if we's through, we's goin'."

"You're through, Rufus," Amber said as she turned.
"And tell Mr. Jenné you did a splendid job."

"Yas'm, I will. Thank you, ma'am."

Amber smiled. "How's young Henry working out?"

Rufus grinned. Henry was his ten-year-old son, who
had begun running errands for SW&C to earn extra
money. "He's workin' out jus' fine. He's little, but he kin
run fast, an' he lissens good."

"He's a fine young man, Rufus. I know you're proud of him."

"Yas'm, I shore am. He'll be awaitin' on me now. The man's gonna brung up a paper fer you ter sign in a minute, but we's goin' on."

Amber's mind had already shifted to the furniture arrangement she needed. "Yes," she murmured distractedly, "that will be fine. Have him come up here. This chair is too big for this corner, I'm afraid. . . . Don't look at me like that, Rufus. I'll have someone else help. You go on. I know you've been working hard all day and want to get home."

Grinning, the former slave Henri Jenné had hired bobbed his head and disappeared downstairs with his helpers behind him. Amber smiled. It was Friday, and they were obviously in a hurry to collect their pay and spend the next two days at home. Or near home, anyway. She'd heard how the Negroes stayed mostly to themselves in shanties near the river, and on the weekends and at night there would be singing and dancing in the dirt streets. For most of them it was the only form of recreation they had, besides the sad overindulgence in whiskey. Rotgut, Henri said with a tight shake of his head, and the men who sold it to them should be shot.

"Worse than hurting a child, I say," he'd muttered on more than one occasion. "They live such drab lives, and then to be drunk on swill that hogs couldn't stomach—well, the white men who sell it to them are no better than criminals."

Amber agreed, but there was little she could do about it.

By the time she had the chair rearranged against a far wall, she was perspiring again, and she moved to open the window to cool off. Rain still smelled strong in the air, and the wind felt good against her hot skin. Thunder growled more loudly, rattling the house and thick windowpanes.

Pushing her hair up off the nape of her neck, Amber

stood in front of the window with her eyes closed, revel
ing in the brisk air that pressed her dress against he
body. There were no petticoats at all to slow her dow
today, only the thin cotton dress over her bare skir
Shocking, Leala had said, but practical. When there wa
work to be done, it wouldn't do to be hindered by bulk
petticoats, though she had no intention of leaving th
house to go back home without them.

A bolt of lightning cracked loudly, followed by a
boom of thunder that shook the very timbers of th
house. Amber had never been frightened of storms, bu
felt a strange excitement instead. It was as if the energ
charged up in the clouds and lightning charged her a
well, and left her feeling restless.

She heard the rain come, a veritable cloudburst tha
broke free of the clouds and dumped on the city, drown
ing out the noise from carriages and passersby below. I
drummed on the roof in a noisy rattle like rocks on tin
Striking the glass, it spattered inside to wet the window
sill and floor and the front of Amber's dress. She didn'
move, but let it cool her.

When she heard a sound behind her, she turne
slowly, as if in a dream, eyes hazy with the satisfaction o
feeling cool for the first time in days. Then her breath
caught and she felt the pulsing excitement of the storm
escalate into a whirlwind of anticipation.

Nick Windsor stood in the open doorway of the bed
room, a sheaf of paper in one hand, his shirt wet and
plastered to his broad chest like a second skin, outlining
the smooth perfection of his muscles. The paper was
damp and limp, and he gave it an impatient flick tha
drew Amber's gaze from the enticing span of his chest
to the paper, then his face.

A low throbbing began deep inside her at the way he
was staring at her, and she was suddenly, acutely, aware
that her dress was probably clinging to her with the
same transparency of his shirt. That brief thought was

verified when he muttered a low oath and flung the paper aside, crossing the room to her in three long strides.

"Dammit," he growled, "do you have to stand there looking like that?"

Amber didn't try to be coy and protest, but looked up at him as he reached out for her, moving into his arms as if she had every right to be there. His hand closed with careless cruelty in the damp wealth of her hair, pulling her head back for his kiss.

Amber's scalp tingled under the burning pressure of his grip, and his lips ground into her mouth. It hurt, and she could taste the anger in it as he crushed her to him, but it didn't matter. The months of frustrated need swelled in her in a surging tide that drowned out everything else but his touch. His hard body was a bruising force against her as he held her, but Amber didn't care.

His damp skin beneath her searching fingers was warm, and he smelled of wind and rain, arousing and male. Holding her, the tight peaks of her breasts crushed against his bare skin with only the wet material of her gown covering them, Amber felt his heartbeat thundering against her. She was more aware of Nick at this moment than she had ever been of anything in her life, of his male need and hunger and the abrasive pressure of her breasts against his chest, his hand tangled in her hair and the taste of his mouth burning into hers.

Nick made a rough sound in the back of his throat as he touched her everyplace he could reach, the satiny feel of her skin under his fingertips shaping to his palm and hand as if he had longed to touch her just that way forever. Amber spread her fingers over his muscled arms, feeling the taut stretch of them beneath her palms as he tightened his hold on her. A pounding heat grew in her, engulfing her in a fiery need that made her open herself to him. It was insanity, this driving ache that made her nudge closer and closer, wanting not even thin air between them.

"God," he muttered once, his voice harsh and grating against her open mouth, "this is crazy."

His words so closely paralleled what she was feeling that Amber didn't bother to respond. Nor did she try to pull away or stop him from unbuttoning the bodice of her dress. The buttons were loosed one by one, his fingers flicking them open with an easy dexterity a ladies' maid would have envied. While he was unbuttoning her gown, he was kissing her, his mouth moving from her lips to her ear, trailing heat in its wake.

She turned her head, tasting the salty tang of his skin beneath her tongue, rasping it over the faint stubble of beard that shadowed his strong jaw.

The glide of his muscles shifted slightly, and he was pushing her across the room toward the bed against the far wall. Amber realized it dimly, but couldn't stop him or herself. Then she was lying back on the mattress with Nick leaning over her, his arms braced on each side of her, his dark face fierce with passion.

As his weight slowly descended on her, he cursed softly in a litany of self-damnation even while kissing the bare skin of her shoulder and throat and the swell of her breast. His hand moved the bodice aside, and cool air washed over her bare breasts in a stinging tide just before his mouth covered a nipple. Amber arched beneath him, crying out at the unexpected warmth and spearing pleasure. Nick's hands shifted to the hem of her dress, and he was jerking it upward, his hand skimming over her thighs in a heated rush, tugging roughly at the fabric to remove it.

Amber curved her hands into Nick's shoulders, pulling at the damp material of his shirt until he shrugged out of it. The golden curve of muscled shoulders flexed with his movements, and he lifted himself to his knees to tug impatiently at the wet garment and fling it aside. Amber stared up at him, her throat closing with aching admiration for his male beauty. He was perfectly made, she thought, with his dark skin and hard bands of muscle, the perfect symmetry of bone and muscle that shouted of a healthy male animal.

Turning back to her, Nick paused, his hands closing into tight fists on his thighs as he gazed down at her. She was suddenly aware that her bodice was open and her skirts up around her waist. Her pantalettes were thin and clung to her thighs in an almost invisible weave of cotton. Amber made an awkward attempt to cover herself.

"No," he said hoarsely, one hand moving to catch her wrist in a firm grip, "don't. *God.* Don't. Just . . . just lie there and let me look for a minute. I've thought of you like this so many times—" His words broke off, and he swallowed, his jaw tightening visibly.

She shivered, and the dark direction of his gaze focused on her face. Outside the room thunder rolled in a crashing boom like cannon, and Nick's head turned slightly toward the window, his entire body tensing. Amber lay quietly, saw his stomach muscles contract as if he'd been hit, and wondered what he was thinking. She was startled when he swore suddenly and curled in a smooth motion to rise from the bed. His feet hit the floor with a thud.

"I'm a bastard," he growled, not looking at her. "Dammit, you don't even know what's happening to you, but I know better than this . . . I know better."

Bewildered, still flushed with passion and not following his abrupt switch from desire to anger, Amber sat up, her palm holding the drooping bodice of her gown over one breast, leaving the other bare. Nick flicked a glance toward her and groaned again.

"Cover yourself."

"But you said—"

"*Jesus!* Can't you hear? Put something over you, before I forget every bit of common sense I ever had and take you, Amber. I'm at the end of my self-control, and so help me God, if you don't cover those enticing breasts of yours, I'm going to push you back on that

mattress and forget your father and my job and right
and wrong and everything else and put myself inside you
until tomorrow. Or next week. Hell, I don't care." He
put a hand over his face, and she saw that his fist was
clenched with strain. "You don't even know what you're
doing, for God's sake."

Feeling awkward and embarrassed, and oddly angry,
Amber did as he said, her movements stiff. She sat up
and pulled her bodice closed and drew her knees up,
smoothing her skirt over her legs.

"In spite of your deplorable language, I knew what I
was doing," she said coolly, though she was burning to
cry out at him, let him know that he'd hurt her.

His head jerked and he looked at her. "Did you?
Maybe." A faint, sulky smile twisted his mouth for a
moment. He looked strangely sad. He bent and picked
up his shirt from the floor. Without putting it on, he
walked to the window and stared out at the rain. Amber
saw him tense when the roll of thunder growled and
boomed again.

"It sounds like cannon, doesn't it?" she said, and he
turned to stare at her.

"Yes."

"And that upsets you."

"No, it reminds me why I'm here in Memphis. It certainly has nothing to do with you, though you're the
prettiest distraction I've come across."

"Distraction." Amber felt a flash of heat shoot
through her. "Just what do you mean by that, Nick
Windsor? What is it you're trying to accomplish? Why
do you feel like you have to be alone to do it?"

His jaw clenched and he tossed his damp shirt over
one shoulder, crossing the room to stand by the bed and
look down at her. "I don't have to be alone, but I don't
need any ties, either. I've never made any bones about
the fact that I'm not staying, Amber. When I have
enough money saved, I'm leaving for Texas. Memphis is

only a . . . a way station for me. I want out of Tennessee."

"Why—because you can't have your way? Because your sister married a man you don't like and your side lost the war? That's the coward's way out, Nick Windsor, whether you want to admit it or not."

Furious, he glared at her, his black eyes narrowed and glittering. "Is it?" he asked tightly. "Since you know so much about it, why don't you tell me what I'm supposed to do. Do I go back to Clover Hill and live cozily with Alex Steele just like he never turned traitor and burned my house? Is that what you think I should do?"

Tears burned the back of her eyes, but Amber refused to let them fall. "No, not exactly. Alex *is* married to your sister now, and you might as well face it. I think you should put the war behind you, forget that he fought on the other side."

"That's easy for a Yankee to say." Nick's mouth thinned. "You won't hear many southerners say it, though."

"I may have been born in New York, Nick, but I've lived most of my life in the South. I don't feel like a Yankee."

"Or a Rebel," he mocked.

"No," she said truthfully. "I have sympathy for both sides, but I guess I'm more like Papa than I realized. I can see the waste of war, the horror, but not the necessity."

He flashed her a hot glance, then looked away. His voice was strained. "Your father's not exactly a southerner, either."

"No, he isn't. How would you classify him, Nick? A Yankee? But he was born in France."

"He grew up in New York," Nick pointed out.

"And that makes him a Yankee in your book?"

His jaw tightened. "Yes."

"Using that logic, you must regard me as a Confederate then, as I was brought up in New Orleans."

"Dammit, Amber, don't twist my words around."

"It's not your words that are twisted, Nick. It's your logic." She managed a light shrug, but was well aware of his furious eyes on her. "You speak very fluently about *sides,* and who's on which one, but I think you forget that it's not so easy to just pigeonhole people."

"You're right about that. People have a way of moving from hole to hole," he mocked. When Amber made an impatient sound, he took a step forward and grabbed her arm. "Look, dammit, you may find it easy to switch sides whenever the wind doesn't blow in the direction you like, but I don't. And I don't like being told I should be like the rest of you turncoats and preach loyalty with one side of my mouth and profit with the other."

Amber rose to her knees, put her face close to Nick's and said in the sugary tone of frustrated rage, "Your language leaves a lot to be desired, Nick. And don't be mad at the world because you got a slap on the wrist. So what if your house burned and you have to work elsewhere for a living? Do you expect everyone to feel sorry for you?"

The calculated cruelty of her words did not have the effect she'd intended. An opaque glitter chilled Nick's eyes, and his hand shot out to cup her chin in a harsh grip, fingers biting into her tender skin until she winced.

"Stay away from me, Miss Jenné. I may want to take you to bed, but I don't want to listen to platitudes from someone whose most trying moment has been when a new Paris bonnet is the wrong color." Releasing her with a contemptuous shove, Nick stalked from the room.

Amber listened to his boots thud against the stairs, then heard the distant slamming of the door. Another volley of thunder rolled across the river, and she fell back on the bed and put one arm over her eyes to stem the tide of tears.

* * *

Nick shrugged into his shirt on the way out of the house, not caring what anyone thought at the moment. Rain beat down on his head, wetting him thoroughly, cooling off his raw temper. Curse the woman, he thought with every long stride. Why did she have to be so desirable that he wanted her even when he knew she would never fit into his life? And why did she have to be so wretchedly perceptive?

So what if your sister married someone you don't like and your side lost the war . . . ?

It had taken all his self-control not to shake her until her teeth rattled. He wondered if she realized it, then thought that she probably didn't care. It seemed no one had ever denied her anything in her entire life, and he supposed that not caring which side won the war was an excellent way to keep from being denied anything.

He should have stuck to his original intention and kept going. After leaving Clover Hill, he had come back to Memphis to gather his few belongings and do just that, but then he'd met Norman Martin and accepted the position at SW&C. For a while it had looked as if things might work out, but now he knew better. Now he knew that if he stayed, he was going to get too involved with Amber Jenné. It was inevitable, whether he wanted to admit it or not. For all his determination, she got to him quicker than any woman ever had in his entire life.

It had gotten so bad that he couldn't even work up a decent interest in any of the women he'd met, women who would be glad to lie down with him in some cozy corner for a few hours and meet his sexual needs with enthusiasm and energy. Worse, it wasn't as if he hadn't tried, but images of Amber with her cloud of honey hair and golden eyes rose before him, destroying whatever desire he might have worked up.

"Well," he muttered, squishing through a puddle of water at the corner of Main and Exchange and ignoring his drenched boots, "that is about to change."

Altering direction, he made for the Pinch Gut district,

where smoky bars and loose women awaited those who
sought the sordid amusements to be found there. It
wasn't Nick's normal inclination to go there. He usually
steered clear of the place, not particularly liking the
whiskey or diversions, but this afternoon it seemed like
just the thing to take his mind off Amber. This afternoon he intended to drink a little, play some cards. And
take whatever offer was extended.

With that intention in mind, Nick walked quickly
down the crowded streets. The closer to Pinch Gut he
drew, the rougher the crowd. Even before the war it had
been bad in this section of town, and now, with the
influx of soldiers and swindlers looking to make a profit
from others' misfortune, it was worse than ever. Martial
law had done nothing to stem the tide of lawlessness.

Prostitutes and beggars elbowed one another along
Smoky Row on the east side of Auction Square, where
once slaves had been sold along with other goods. Back
during those times, the constant fires to ward off mosquitoes had left a thick haze in the air.

Pinch Gut looked as shabby and disreputable as ever,
living up to its name. Just north of Memphis at the
mouth of the Bayou Gayoso, the area had long been
inhabited by rough rivermen and their crude structures
built from leaky boats and whatever else they could find.
These men squatted along the riverbanks in their shanties, and their families had such a starved, diseased look
to them, with their belts drawn in tight, that the name
Pinch Gut had become common.

Houses of prostitution abounded, more now than before the war, it seemed. Nick passed them without a
glance as he headed for a tavern. The rain had only
aggravated the stench from the bayou, and the heat
seemed to simmer it into a stew of noxious fumes.

He pushed his way into a crowded tavern that smelled
of stale sweat and smoke, through men who were just as
wet as he was. Dropping into an empty chair at a table
in the corner, he ignored the music of banjo and tam-

bourine provided by an old black man and his grandson and ordered an entire bottle of whiskey. The proprietor looked at him closely.

"Money up front."

He dug into his pocket, muttering under his breath at the uncomfortable feel of wet clothes and unsatisfied arousal. Nick slammed his money to the table, keeping his hand over it. He met the man's hard stare with an equally hard stare.

"After I get my bottle."

It was provided grudgingly, and Nick splashed a liberal amount into a dingy glass he didn't dare inspect too closely. It burned going down, warming him. He had another, and began to feel better. It had been a while since he'd indulged himself. He was used to saving every cent, not spending it idly.

As his clothes dried and the whiskey warmed him, he took note of a card game going on at the next table. He sat and watched the players for a while, then rose from his chair and crossed to the table when one of them left.

When he sat down, giving a swift glance to the hard men playing, he felt a hand at his back. Without turning, he knew it was one of the women from the bar. Her hand caressed the back of his neck, toying with his still damp hair, and her voice was husky.

"Buyin' drinks for lonely ladies tonight, handsome?"

Nick shoved his ante to the center of the table. "Maybe. If the lonely lady doesn't stand behind me while I play cards."

A throaty laugh slid into the smoky air, and the woman shifted to one side. "That can be arranged."

Nick glanced up, appraising her. She was skinny, too skinny, but that was good. He certainly didn't need any reminders of Amber tonight.

"Pour us both a drink, honey." He turned back to his cards and for the first time felt that maybe luck was smiling on him. He wasn't a novice, and he knew the rough rivermen would try to cheat him if they could, but he was used to that, too. Any man who'd ever played cards with General Forrest and held his own could hold his own with these men.

A roll of thunder rattled the frame building, but Nick paid no attention. He concentrated on his cards and pushed all thoughts of Amber Jenné to the furthest recesses of his mind.

Amber was back at home on Adams Avenue when her father returned from the warehouse. She greeted him with a vague smile that made him look at her closely.

"You are not well, *petite*?"

"I'm fine," she lied, wondering how early she could go to bed without causing comment. They were in her father's private parlor, the only refuge in a house filled with boarders.

Sinking into his comfortable chair, Henri reached for the tobacco humidor on the near table and continued to regard Amber thoughtfully. "Is Leala's house completed?" he asked as he drew out a cigar and slid it through his fingers. "I saw the final invoice on Martin's desk."

"Yes. I accepted the last delivery today." She paused, then cleared her throat. "I forgot to sign for it, though. The paper is still at the house."

Henri lit the cigar, puffing slowly, thick smoke wreathing his head. "No matter. It will still be there. I, for one, will be glad to have my house to myself again, though I have this feeling that Leala will consider this house open to more even after we move these out." He wiped a hand over his furrowed brow. "I'm beginning to think she will put the Freedmen's Bureau out of business with her efforts."

A faint smile curved her mouth, and putting aside the book she'd been trying to read, Amber rose from the chair. "That is entirely possible. The bureau does seem overloaded. There are a great many refugees, you know, and with things so bad now, there are likely to be more."

"Well, the bureau was set up with good intentions to feed all the poor, black and white, but it seems to be floundering. A pity the government has decided to allow unscrupulous scalawags to ruin the South. That radical Republican Thaddeus Stevens in particular seems hell-bent on the South's destruction."

"Is it true that he suggested taking all the private as well as public lands of the seceded states and distribut-ing them to ex-slaves? I understand he made a speech saying that the Rebels' political hold would not be bro-ken until they were, and that each Negro head of family should be given forty acres and a hut, money gifts, and a pension. Doesn't he realize that unity between the states cannot be achieved with more hatred?"

"Apparently not. He called Lincoln a tenderhearted proponent of the Rebels, and adheres to President Johnson's harsher policies. I'm certain Lincoln never meant for some of this to happen."

Fingering the window curtains fluttering at the press of a damp breeze, Amber murmured, "I'm told that Lincoln intended to pay the planters for their slaves, a recompense, so to speak, for those freed. That would have gone a long way toward helping rebuild. As it is, the thieves have come in to buy up land for a fraction of what it's worth, taking it away from those who can't pay the taxes." Amber bent her arms in front of her, looking out the window at the rain-slick yard behind the house. Leaves dripped rain, but the worst of the storm was over. She wondered where Nick was, then shoved thoughts of him from her mind.

He'd made it plain that afternoon how he felt. He wanted her in bed, but in no other way. And though her body ached for him, she knew that wasn't all she wanted. The initial attraction had intrigued her, but there was an unexplainable link to him that had nothing to do with passion. She wished she knew why she felt that way, why she wanted to hold him against her and wipe away all his pain and hostility; but she didn't. All she knew was that she loved Nick Windsor in spite of his animosity.

The silent admission jolted her, and she turned sharply away from the window to find her father's puzzled gaze resting on her. Inhaling deeply to hide her agitation, Amber wondered if he'd asked her a question that she hadn't even heard.

"I'm sorry," she said when Henri continued to stare at her, "but I was thinking of something else. Did you ask me a question?"

"*Oui,*" he murmured, "but it's not important. I merely asked if Roger had returned from the auction."

"Auction? I don't know. I've been so busy with the house, and he's been running so many errands for everyone, that I haven't had time to do more than wave at him in passing. Do you need him?"

"Not tonight. In the morning, though, I wish for him to go with me. There has been trouble lately, and he's a wonderful deterrent."

"Trouble?"

"Some of the rivermen and riffraff along the bluffs have decided they don't like the Negro shanties. Rumblings have been heard that men intend to disguise themselves and wipe out the section one night. It's been rather tense at times, and Roger knows both sides well enough to negotiate, should it come to violence."

"Violence?" Amber felt a spurt of irritation. "The war's been over less than six months, and men are already thinking of more violence? Hasn't there been enough?"

"Hostilities run high, *ma petite,* you know that. Some men cannot forgive or forget." His gray gaze settled on her flushed face. "Even Nick Windsor carries a grudge on his shoulders like a banner. If he weren't so effective, I would be cautious of his employment."

"But Nick has never said anything against the Negroes," Amber pointed out, "only the Yankees."

"I know. Most planters don't hold grudges against their former slaves. So many of them were slowly being brought around to see that slavery was a vile institution even before the war, that if not for politics, the entire conflict could have been avoided." Henri shifted position, puffing on his cigar as he stretched his feet out on the small stool in front of his chair. "The intelligent men, men of breeding and education, were beginning to see that their way of life could not depend upon such a volatile issue. I have learned that Nick's father had already planned to free his slaves by the time war was declared, slowly releasing those able to fend for themselves. Many more planters were doing the same."

Amber made a frustrated sound. "All of it could have been avoided."

"Yes." Henri lapsed into silence for a moment, then murmured, "But now we are faced with a situation that has released much more than underlying hostilities. Men have come home to find their lives destroyed, and the resentment and anger will be directed at the outward cause. Those men who have never been overtly prejudiced before, will be now. It may come to brutal retaliation between the factions."

"Factions?"

"Yes. Black against white, brother against brother, neighbor against neighbor, just as it has been for over four years. Only this time there will be no declared hostilities. This time it will be an undeclared war."

Frowning, Amber wondered if her father weren't overreacting. Undeclared war? Between whom? She couldn't follow his line of thought logically. It didn't seem possible, not after all that had happened.

"I hope you're wrong," she said, and he nodded.

"So do I."

Lamplight fell across her father's face in a soft glow that shimmered slightly from the breeze whisking through the open window, and Amber felt a spurt of love for him. Henri Jenné tried so hard to be fair, tried so hard to remain neutral and see both sides of an issue, that at times she felt it tore him in two.

Moving to his side, Amber knelt by his chair and put her arms around his knees as she had as a child, smiling up at him. "This will all pass, Papa. One day, all this will be behind us."

His hand fell to the bright, burnished wealth of her hair, and he stroked it gently, letting the silky strands slide through his fingers. "Yes," he agreed softly, "it will be behind us one day, I'm sure of it."

Resting her cheek against his knee, Amber closed her eyes, letting her father's comforting touch ease some of her tension. He was always there for her, always understood.

She was still sitting at Henri's knee when Celia knocked on the parlor door, the sound a sharp tattoo of urgency. Amber's head jerked up as the little maid swung open the door and burst into the parlor, her eyes wide and frightened.

"Monsieur," she began in rapid French, words tumbling over one another in a spate Amber could barely follow. Fortunately, Henri had no such trouble, and he pushed Amber gently aside and rose to his feet.

"Shh, calm down, Celia. I will come. Tell Roger to wait for me."

"What is it?" Amber demanded as she rose to her feet. "What's happened?"

"It's Nick Windsor. There's been trouble downtown, and he's in jail along with a bunch of rivermen and gamblers. A riot of some sort, Roger told Celia." His mouth was set in a grim line. "I only hope I can help him. There was a shooting and—" He halted, seeing Amber's white face and frightened eyes.

"I'm going with you."

"No, *petite,* you cannot. Stay here. The Memphis City Jail is no place for a woman."

"I'm going." Amber's tone left no room for refusal. "If he's hurt, I want to be there."

Recognizing the steel beneath that honeyed tone, Henri gave a helpless shrug. "Then hurry. I need to talk to the commissioner before they charge him with something, and at least find out what he did or didn't do."

Amber didn't bother replying. She ran for her shawl, her heart pounding with anxiety. Nick and shooting and a riot—dear lord, why should she even care so much?

But the truth of the matter was that she did, and just the thought of Nick hurt and lying in that crowded, filthy jail made her entire soul cringe with terror.

CHAPTER
7

JACKKNIFING his long legs, Nick rose smoothly to a standing position, looking around him at the crowded cell. It stank of sweat and other smells he'd hoped he never encounter again, not after the Yankee prison camp. He stepped gingerly over a man stretched out on his back, his mouth open in a buzzing snore, and made his way to the front of the cell.

"Guard!" he shouted over the loud rumble. "Guard!"

"Waste of time," someone commented, and Nick looked down at the man speaking. "Even if he wanted ta come—which I can tell ya he don't—he wouldn't be able to hear ya over all this noise."

Nick thought about it a minute, then realized that the man was right. He nodded, and his gaze narrowed slightly. "Don't I know you?"

Grinning, the man tilted back his head so that lamplight from the corridor outside the cell fell across his face, and Nick gave a start of surprise.

"Beaver Thornton . . ."

"Yeah, that's me. We keep runnin' inta each other, don't we? First Chickamauga, then ridin' with Forrest." Beaver shrugged when Nick knelt beside him and asked what he was doing there. "Same as you. Cain't quite seem ta git the hang of goin' around and not shootin' somebody that makes me mad."

Nick's mouth thinned slightly and his eyes cooled. "It wasn't quite like that."

"Yeah. I hear ya. Anytime there's some shootin', it ain't never quite like that."

Nick raked a hand through his hair and thought for a moment, then decided it wasn't worth getting mad about. "Maybe you're right, Beaver. Tell me—were you with Forrest when it was over?"

Beaver nodded. "Yep. Stayed with him right to the end. He was plumb mad that you ended up in a prison camp, ya know. Said you was one of the best, Cap'n, and he needed ya."

"Did he." Nick lifted his head and stared across the corridor at the blank wall. "I always thought he was one of the best."

"He were. Still is."

"Not in prison, I hear, like some of them."

"Naw, ain't no damn Yankee prison that'll hold Forrest anyway. He got—what'dya call it?—exemption. Yeah, that's it. Exemption, because he was followin' orders, they say." Beaver chuckled dryly. "So was a helluva lot of the rest of us, and those Yanks are madder'n hell that we ain't all lyin' in some stinkin' prison somewhere."

"So I hear."

Stretching his legs out in front of him, Beaver winced slightly from some injury or discomfort, locked his hands behind his head and winked at Nick. "Get comfy, Cap'n. Yore in here fer a spell, I'll bet. None of them po-lice seem ta be in the mood ta let enny of us Rebels out of jail much. I'd swear that all of the Yanks up north came down here ta work, 'cause they don't seem ta be much of nobody else with jobs."

Though doubtful of that analysis, it did seem to Nick that no one in authority wished to hear his explanation or even talk to him. Rubbing his jaw, Nick slid down to the nasty floor next to Beaver Thornton and passed the time with him, talking about those who'd made it and those who hadn't.

They were still talking when a guard sauntered down the corridor, growling at the prisoners to shut up. He halted in front of Nick's cell and peered in.

"Windsor? There a Windsor in here?"

Rising, Nick said, "Yeah, right here."

Keys jangled, and Nick felt Beaver's surprise, then wariness directed toward him. As the cell door swung open, Beaver grabbed his pants leg.

"Be careful, Cap'n," he muttered. "They can git right rough at times."

"Thanks. I will."

The guard grabbed Nick's arm as soon as he stepped through the door and swung him around, slamming him up against the bars. He held him there with a club in the middle of his back while he secured his wrists behind him, then yanked him upright.

"Come on, Reb. There's some folks out here who want to talk to you."

Biting back his temper, Nick kept quiet as the guard half walked, half dragged him down the corridor to a crowded room where more prisoners waited. The din was deafening, and Nick didn't recognize anyone as he looked around. His guard held him tightly by the arm, jerking him along until they stood against a wall.

"Stand here," he said shortly. "And don't even think about moving. There're guys here who'd like nothing better than to shoot another Reb."

"I'll keep that in mind," Nick retorted, then winced as the guard shoved a club into his ribs with a solid *thwack*. He grunted in pain and doubled up. When the guard moved away, Nick leaned back against the wall and tried to catch his breath as he surveyed the room with growing apprehension. This didn't look good at all. What had started out as a minor argument over cards had grown into a full-scale riot between rivermen and gamblers.

"Great," he muttered as he realized that this would probably be the only chance he got to declare his innocence. After all, it hadn't been *his* fight; he'd just been dragged into it by an overeager combatant before he could get out of the way. What should have been a barroom brawl had turned into a war between Yankee and Rebel, with insults and fists being thrown freely.

He had no idea who had fired the first shot, or if anyone had been hurt. Someone had brought a whiskey bottle down on top of his head before he could get out the back door, and he vaguely recalled feminine arms around him as he hit the floor. After that, everything was a blur, with whistles blowing and men shouting and the strong smell of musky perfume surrounding him.

Naomi, probably, the whore who'd helped him drink his whiskey and lose his money at cards. Not that he cared so much about her at this point. He never carried more money than he could afford to lose, especially not to the Pinch Gut district. Life there was as short as tempers most of the time, and everyone had that "pinch-gut" look to them.

It occurred to him to wonder what had happened to the girl and why she'd tried to protect him. He remembered that, her bending over him and shouting at the men who were dragging him away, hanging on to him as if her life depended on it. A hard, mirthless smile tugged at one side of his mouth. So much for finding entertainment and a woman for the night. He should have known better. He'd learned that lesson as a youth, and had thought himself beyond being goaded into stupidity. Just went to show you what a woman could provoke a man to do, he guessed, and shifted his shoulders to a more comfortable position against the brick wall.

As Nick shifted, turning slightly so that he faced the door of the jail, two things happened at once—Amber Jenné came in through the doors with her father in tow, and the protective whore who'd tried to keep him from being arrested flung herself at him.

"Nick!" the girl cried, pressing close, her arms going around him. She stood on her toes and whispered quickly, "I have your money, lover, and will get you out of here as soon as I find the right guard to bribe."

Startled by both unexpected events, Nick couldn't think of anything to say to Naomi, and shook his head with a slight frown. His money?

How had she gotten it? he wondered. Then he remembered her hands on him as she bent over him, and guessed that she'd been doing what seemed important at the moment—rolling him. Of course, she had come down to get him out, but he had no idea how she intended to accomplish that when there had been a shooting and he was involved.

"Naomi," he began, edging away and wishing his hands weren't tied behind him. But she leaned into him and kissed him full on the mouth, her lips smothering anything he wanted to say. He tried to jerk away, aware that Amber had halted and was staring at him with wide, accusing eyes, but it was impossible.

Damn, he thought with a mental groan, just what he needed. Another complication. As if he didn't have enough.

Wresting his mouth from under the eager girl's, he said sharply, "Stop it. Not here. Look, if you've got my money, use it for yourself. It won't do any good now, for God's sake. I don't want to be accused of trying to bribe a—"

"No, no, lover, listen. I know one of these guards, and if I can just find him before they call your name—"

"Excuse me," Henri Jenné said gravely, and Naomi whirled around to stare up at him as he continued calmly, "but I believe that bribing an official will only cause more trouble. If you will allow me, miss, I believe I can help."

"Who're you?" the girl asked tartly, raking him with a narrow stare. Her glance shifted to Amber, who stood just behind her father. Even with the veil she wore tied down to keep out the mosquitoes, Amber's shocked expression was evident. Naomi scowled.

"His employer." Henri looked at Nick. "Are you directly involved? Have you been arraigned?"

"No, all I did was make the mistake of being there." Nick looked past Henri to Amber, but she refused to look back at him. His mouth thinned and he felt a hot flare of anger.

"Then my attorney can take care of this. I'll see to it," Henri said, looking from Nick to the frowsy girl again. Her uncombed hair, unwashed face, and the cheap, gaudy garments she wore made her identity obvious, but there was no condemnation on Jenné's face, only polite attention.

"You don't have to do this, sir," Nick said stiffly, and Henri shook his head.

"*Au contraire*, I do. Do you think I want my best supervisor sitting up here when he could be working? Not a chance."

Before Nick could say anything, Henri moved away, leaving him with Amber and Naomi. Both women seemed to detest one another on sight, and Amber was making an obvious effort to ignore the other girl. Naomi, on the other hand, was examining Amber in minute detail.

"Bet that there dress came from New York," she said after a moment, and Amber gave her a frosty stare.

"No, the dress style is French."

"Yore bonnet's got yards of netting on it to keep out the mosquitoes, right?"

"Yes," came the cool reply.

"Yeah, I had me one, but it's not too handy in my line of business." A saucy grin accompanied this statement, and Amber stiffened while Nick groaned inwardly.

Nothing else was said as the women eyed one another in open hostility. Amber managed to look cool and regal in her fury, while Naomi simmered with ill-concealed resentment. Nick's jaw tightened in irritation at being caught between two women eyeing one another like sulky cats, and he tried to ignore them.

His attention shifted to Henri Jenné, who stood in earnest conversation with a uniformed officer. Whatever Henri was saying must have finally decided the officer, because he came over to Nick at last and yanked him around, making no effort to be gentle as he undid his bonds.

"Released into your custody until tomorrow morning, Mr. Jenné," the officer growled, and it was apparent that he didn't like the situation at all. "See that you don't let him out of your sight until he shows up back here for a hearing, or the judge may put all three of us under the jail for a good long while."

"I understand perfectly, Officer Mahoney," Henri said with a slight smile. "I would not jeopardize any of us by even thinking of doing anything else."

Nick clenched his teeth tightly together to keep from saying what was on his mind, that this entire affair was a farce from the beginning, and that he hadn't done anything. But he didn't. It would be a waste of breath, and he knew it. No one was inclined to listen, much less believe him. Except, perhaps, Henri Jenné, who had come out late at night to help him.

As the four of them left the crowded police station and stepped out into the night air, Nick breathed deeply. He paused beneath the misty glow of a street lamp and turned to Jenné.

"Sir, I deeply appreciate this. I'll reimburse you for any expense you may have undertaken, and—"

"Nick," Henri interrupted, "please do not insult me. This was my choice, and I came of my own free will." His eyes flicked to Amber's veiled face and back to Nick. Clearing his throat, Henri continued, "I ask only that you come home with me this evening, so that I can honor my promise to Mahoney. He's a good man, though a bit abrupt, and I would appreciate your agreement."

Nick felt Naomi stiffen at his side, heard her muttered imprecation, and felt caught in the middle again. Henri Jenné deserved his cooperation, but he had no desire to go home with him and endure Amber's glacial disapproval. Nor did he want to go home with Naomi, as she obviously intended. What he really wanted was to go to his own rooms alone and get some rest. That, of course, was impossible. He could not deny Jenné his simple request.

"Of course, sir. If you'll excuse me a moment . . ." Turning, Nick grabbed Naomi's elbow and pulled her to one side. He saw the protest forming on her sulky mouth, and quickly stilled it. "Look, I appreciate your efforts, but as you can see, I have to go with him. Keep the money you found in my pockets for your trouble, and—"

"Bastard!" Naomi flashed, giving him a hard shove. "I may be for sale, but *I* get to choose when and where! You were nice to me, and I just wanted to be nice back." She fumbled in the bodice of her worn dress and started to withdraw the wad of bills she'd stuffed there.

Chagrined, Nick put a hand over her grubby fingers. "Don't. Let me make you a gift of it, please. I meant no insult, and I really do appreciate your helping me."

The girl paused, caught between need and hurt pride, and finally gave him a grudging nod. "All right. I'll keep it, but I just want you to know that I would have come to get you out even if I didn't have your money. You didn't do anything, and I hate those damned Yankee carpetbaggers who're tryin' to run everything into the ground."

"I know." Curling a finger under her chin, Nick lifted her face and smiled at her. "Thanks, all right?"

"All right." The girl gave him a cheeky grin. "And watch where you go at night, lover. I might not be there to help you out next time."

"Want me to see you to your door?" Nick asked when she started to turn away, and Naomi laughed.

"Why? What can happen to me that hasn't already? I'm a lot safer out here than you, sweetheart." With that, she turned, lifting her head and sweeping Amber with a cool glance, then sauntered down the street, her skirts twitching provocatively with every step.

When Nick turned, he caught Amber looking at him with an expression he couldn't interpret due to the shadows and her veil. He started to say something, then realized that anything he said at this point could only be taken the wrong way. Shrugging, he turned to Henri.

"Where would you like me to stay, sir?"

"Come home with me. With an entire house full of boarders, I'm certain we can squeeze in one more."

It didn't promise to be a wonderful night, not with Amber's stiff silence and his own frustration goading him. And he kept remembering the stunned, stricken look in those golden eyes, the quick flare of pain that he'd recognized when she saw Naomi's arms around his neck. It didn't help any to know that he didn't owe her any explanations. Nor did it help to be in her company, even at her father's request. Nick wanted to refuse, but knew he couldn't.

Roger waited at the curb with the Jenné carriage, and Nick paused to let Amber and Henri precede him. As she passed, Amber flashed Nick a tight, wounded glance that told him how upset she was. He shrugged helplessly. No point in dwelling on it. She'd either get over it or she wouldn't, and anyway, why should he care?

Amber was wondering the same thing. Why should she care what Nick Windsor did, or that he'd managed to find solace in the company of a shopworn girl with a dirty face and too-familiar manner?

But the truth was, she did care. When she'd seen Nick, then the girl, her heart had plummeted to her toes. It had been all she could do to keep from bursting into tears in front of everyone. But Amber wasn't her father's daughter for nothing, and she had no intention of allowing Nick Windsor to know he'd hurt her. After all, he'd made it plain that he preferred the company of Pinch Gut prostitutes to hers, and her face flamed when she thought of the intimacy between them earlier. Perhaps he considered her a clumsy substitute for the women who plied their trade along the riverfront.

Amber sat stiffly in the carriage, trying not to accidentally touch Nick, who sat across from her, their legs close in the narrow space. Just being in proximity to him made her quiver, and she carefully kept her hands in her lap, clenched together. Averting her gaze, she stared out the windows as if the wet, dark streets of Memphis were the most fascinating sight she'd ever seen.

The carriage lurched forward, and after a moment of thick silence, Henri said pleasantly, "We can discuss what happened when we get home. I'm certain you'll wish to clean up and have something to eat first. Jail food cannot be that plentiful or nourishing."

"Actually," Nick muttered, "I don't remember being offered any food. I was only there six hours or so. Guess they figured we weren't hungry."

"I suppose not," Amber said in a honeyed tone that made Nick look at her carefully. "After all, you *were* arrested in a tavern, were you not? And what my father is trying to tactfully say, Mr. Windsor, is that you smell to high heaven and need a bath before you spend even one night in our house." She heard her father's choked exclamation but ignored it.

Nick stretched like a dangerous cat, and Amber's nerves quivered when she heard the menace in his raspy drawl.

"Is that what he meant? Maybe I should sleep in the stable, then."

Amber's gaze shifted to his. The glow of the street lamps splashed misty light through the windows as they passed under them, and she recognized the furious glitter in his eyes.

"The stable would be most appropriate, I think," she

said sweetly, "since you seem to behave like a mule lately. In fact, Mr. Windsor, I—"

"Amber," Henri cut in smoothly, "I'm certain we still have room in the house. We would hardly treat Nick any differently than we would the other boarders, now would we?"

His gentle squeeze on her arm silenced her, and Amber shrugged lightly. "No, I suppose not."

When the carriage rolled to a halt in the narrow lane behind the Adams Street residence, Amber was the first to alight, taking Roger's proffered hand and stalking up the walkway without looking back. She had no intention of making any arrangements for Nick Windsor. Let her father do it. Or Leala. Or Celia. Or even Roger. Anyone but her. She didn't want to acknowledge his existence at this moment. Right now all she wanted to do was forget him, forget how he'd pushed her away that afternoon and gone straight into the arms of another woman.

Celia swung open the door just as Amber reached the top step, and she brushed past the maid with a terse explanation that the others were coming.

"Did you find Monsieur Windsor?" Celia asked, peering out into the night. It was apparent she'd been sleeping, and she pulled her wrapper more tightly around her. "I do not see him."

"With any luck," Amber said shortly, "he's had the good sense to go home. Is everyone else in bed?"

"*Oui*, long ago. Except for your aunt, and she awaits Monsieur Henri in his study."

"Wonderful. They can spend a long night discussing Nick Windsor and his wretched fate, then. I'm going to bed."

What Celia replied to that went unheard as Amber took the stairs to her room two at a time. She lifted her skirts high to keep from tripping over them, and when she finally reached the sanctity of her bedroom, she shut the door firmly behind her and leaned against it. Visions of Nick in that woman's arms kept returning to haunt her, and she recalled the surprise on his face, but no sign of distaste.

Damn him!

Amber spent several minutes pacing the floor of her room, turning up the small gas lamp on the wall and moving to stare out her bedroom window at the dark, damp night. Already, with the end of the rain, it was growing humid again. The sultry August night left her feeling restless and unsettled, and she could hear the sleepy mutters of birds in the trees. It was probably only a few hours until dawn.

Clenching and unclenching her hands, Amber moved to her bureau and began to unlace the ribbons that held on her hat. The netting caught in a hairpin, and she jerked it free with an impatient motion, then peeled away her gloves. She did it with angry efficiency, trying to blot out the images of Nick and Naomi, trying to forget that she had lain willingly in his arms only that afternoon and that he had pushed her away.

She unfastened her sleeves, then struggled to unbutton the long row of tiny pearl buttons on her bodice. She was so irritable that she yanked too hard and one of the buttons popped off, skittering across the smooth oak floor. Gritting her teeth, Amber knelt down and began to search for it.

A soft Persian rug lay in the middle of the room, but she'd heard the unmistakable sound of the button on bare wood, and knew it had probably bounced under the bureau. Amber squinted into the dark shadows under the bureau in an effort to spot the shiny pearl button.

"Damn, damn, damn," she muttered irritably, and stretched out on the floor to feel under the low-slung piece of heavy furniture with one hand. Her fingers encountered something small and slick, but when she pulled it out, it was only a hairpin, so she tried again. With all her concentration focused on the button, it was easy to miss the opening of her bedroom door.

Amber wasn't aware that anyone had come into her room until she had triumphantly secured the button in one hand and was sitting back on her heels. The first indication was Nick Windsor's lazy drawl.

"Do you always say your bedtime prayers in that position?"

Gasping, she whirled around, her heart thudding. Nick was leaning back against her bedroom door, looking as if he belonged there instead of out in the stable or down on the riverfront. Amber felt a flash of outrage punctuate her surprise.

"What the devil are you doing here?" she demanded, rising to her feet and smoothing her skirts with one hand while clenching the button in the other.

"I thought we might need to talk."

"You thought wrong." Amber put the button in a small china dish on her bureau. "I can't imagine what you might have to say that would interest me."

"Amber, about that girl—"

"Please," she snapped, her agitation obvious despite her resolve to stay calm, "don't bother to explain. I'm certain I don't want to hear anything you might have to say about your choice of . . . companions."

His mouth flattened into a thin line, and the black eyes narrowed even more as he stared at her coolly. "Amber, she was trying to help. I'd never met her before tonight. Or last night, since it's tomorrow by now."

"And that's supposed to make it better? Somehow, it falls short of the mark, far short. Now get out of my room before my father discovers that you've been bold enough to come in here in the first place."

"I doubt he'll notice. He's involved in a deep discussion with your aunt about the growing number of boarders—God, do you have every displaced Rebel in the South here?"

"Aunt Leala is up this late?"

"She said we woke her, and since she was up . . ." Nick shrugged.

"Yes, that sounds like her." Amber tried not to let him see how his presence upset her. Her hands were shaking and she had to struggle to keep the tremor out of her voice. "You might keep that in mind if you run into any of the boarders, by the way. My father and aunt play no favorites in misfortune, and expect all their boarders to be polite. Even to Yankees."

"So I've heard."

"And you still work for him. I'm astonished, Mr. Windsor. I'd thought someone with such high principles as yours would not stoop to working for a man who refuses to ally himself with the Noble Cause of the South."

Nick moved with that frightening swiftness Amber had forgotten, crossing to her in two strides and giving her no time to get out of his way. His hands curled around her wrists.

"Don't play games with me now, Amber. I'm in no mood."

"Really?" she asked shakily, tilting back her head. She watched his eyes narrow at her action: his thick, spiky lashes drifted half over the velvety black depths of his eyes to hide his expression. His hair was damp, as if he'd wet it, and tiny beads of moisture clung like diamond drops to some of his eyelashes and along the rough beard stubble darkening his jaw. It was obvious he'd made the effort to wash. She tried to pull away but couldn't.

"Let go of me, if you please, Mr. Windsor."

"Not until I've said what I came up here to say."

"And if I don't care to listen?"

"That wasn't one of your choices, Miss Smart-Mouth. I'm not exactly the villain you'd like to paint me."

"No? Can't tell it by me at this moment." She gave a pointed glance at his grip on her, but he wasn't at all moved.

If not for his fingers tightening on her arms, Amber might have thought him merely annoyed. Now she realized he was deadly angry, and that any chance word might set him off.

For some reason, instead of making her cautious, this made her bolder, and she found herself smiling sweetly, her tone as sugary as an entire field of Louisiana cane.

"Well, well, Mr. Windsor, I think that maybe you've grown more lax than you used to be. How quaint. Does this mean that now you're all for God and Union and Country . . . stop that. You're hurting me. . . ."

"Am I? Too bad." His grip tightened even more.

"What is it you want from me?" Amber demanded, trying to jerk away and growing more furious by the moment when he only eased his grip and didn't release her.

"What do I want?" he echoed roughly, and with a quick flex of his arms brought her up hard against him, one arm moving to mold her to his solid frame. Amber could feel the hot urgency in his body, and her own responded in spite of her anger. "Damn you, Amber Jenné, you know what I want," he growled, and before she could move, his mouth ground down on hers with a fierce possessiveness that made her quiver with longing.

This was what she'd wanted from him, this hot, eager capture of her mouth, the uncontrollable passion she'd sensed in him from the beginning. He'd almost lost control the last time, but had pulled away from her before yielding to it. She wanted to hold him tightly this time, until he couldn't let go of her.

"Curse you," Nick muttered, wrenching his mouth from hers for a moment, "curse you for doing this to me." His hand closed in the silky wealth of her hair, pulling her head back to bare her throat to his kisses.

Amber's eyes closed, and she moaned deep in the back of her throat. "Nick . . . please—"

"I told you what would happen if you didn't stay away from me, didn't I?" he said with a rough sound. "Why did you come down there tonight?"

Shuddering at the bold caress of his hand on her hip,

Amber murmured, "I had to see you, to know you were all right."

"So, now you know I'm all right."

Her eyes opened and she gazed at him from beneath the curved fan of her lashes, her lips parted and still swollen and wet from his kiss.

"Yes," she whispered softly, "now I know you're all right."

His face altered slightly, becoming harder, more intent, and just before he kissed her again, he said, "No, you don't know anything, not yet. . . ."

Amber's fingers clenched into the fold of his shirt, and she closed her eyes as she clung to him. It wasn't until he wrenched his mouth from hers and swore softly that she realized she'd been holding her breath. Her eyes opened slowly and she stared at him in confusion as he released her and backed away.

Putting a hand over his face, Nick shook his head. "Damn, you make me crazy, woman, crazier than— look, this won't work. I just wanted to explain to you about tonight, not take you to bed in your father's house. Amber, you're poison to me, pure poison. I can't think right when you come around me, so do us both a favor and stay away, all right? *Just stay away from me.*"

Amber couldn't move, couldn't offer even a protest when he yanked open her bedroom door and left, shutting it firmly behind him. But she knew, then, that Nick Windsor wanted her in spite of himself, and somehow that eased her earlier pangs of rejection. A faint smile curved her mouth, and she gazed at the closed door with a feeling of satisfaction.

He might not have known it, but Nick Windsor had just given her a good reason to put herself in his path at every opportunity.

CHAPTER
8

AUGUST faded into September, still hot and sul‑
try, with blistering days and muggy nights when insect
droned on and on, irritating those who tried to sit out‑
side to escape the heat. Nick sat out on the front porch
steps of the boardinghouse where he had his room
smoking his cigar because it wasn't allowed inside, and
swatting at mosquitoes as big as mockingbirds.

In the distance the sound of a riverboat whistle bel‑
lowed through the early evening air, packed to the ex‑
tremes again, he was certain. River traffic had picked
up, and the boat lines were getting rich. The tragedy of
the *Sultana* in late April hadn't seemed to deter them
from overloading the vessels, and he remembered how
the laboring boilers of the packet had exploded, killing
hundreds of people, many of them mustered-out Yan‑
kee and Rebel soldiers going home.

He stretched his long legs out in front of him and
watched the sun set in a hazy red ball on the flat Arkan‑
sas side of the river. He should be working, but things
were so well-organized now, he'd almost done himself
out of a job. The hours were shorter, and Henri Jenné
was so pleased with Nick that he'd offered him a promo‑
tion to the office.

So far, Nick had declined. He didn't want to be indis‑

pensable to Jenné, not when he wasn't certain he was staying.

The incident in Pinch Gut was almost forgotten, except by Nick, who realized how quickly he could lose everything he'd managed to build. Henri Jenné had quietly taken care of the charges against him, and the two men who had been killed were buried. A riverman was charged with their murder, all over a game of cards.

Nick had managed to stay away from Amber since that night, steering clear of her whenever she tried to corner him. He wanted her, oh, he wanted her. But he knew better. She wasn't for him, not Henri Jenné's daughter, with her expensive perfume and clothes, her idle hands and the bright expectation that life was good and kind. He knew better than that, too.

It almost made him laugh sometimes, when he thought about how he'd once viewed life with the same placid expectation. Nothing would change, he'd thought; he'd inherit Clover Hill one day and be a planter, like his father. Well, it hadn't turned out that way, and now he had other goals, goals that didn't include Amber Jenné.

There were times he was furious with himself for thinking about her, for letting her invade his waking thoughts at all. But he couldn't avoid his dreams, and there were nights he woke up in a hot sweat, visions of Amber and her tawny hair and eyes slowly fading from his mind. Those were the nights he hated most, spent alone in his shabby room looking out over the river, thinking of the days when he'd slept in a big bed with clean white sheets, of the days when he would have been able to offer a decent life to a woman like Amber.

Just the sight of her made his chest tighten, made his throat ache with a surge of hot need for her, to feel her under him, her lips parting eagerly beneath his, her hands clawing at his back with urgent demands. He knew she'd be like that in bed, knew she'd meet a man's desire with untrammeled passion, and he hated the thought it would be someone else.

He'd seen Norman Martin's obvious desire for her, and knew that Jenné's partner was bent on having Amber. The slender, dapper businessman made every effort to court her, and Nick had seen the barely concealed frustration in Martin's eyes when she treated him more like a friend than a serious suitor. He could understand Martin's frustration, because it so closely paralleled his own, for different reasons.

It ate at him that Martin could freely court Amber, could offer her a future, while he couldn't. There were moments when he felt like quitting his job, when he thought that if he had to listen to Martin's attempts to flatter Amber one more time, he would lose his temper and say or do something he shouldn't.

Then there were the times he wished Amber would treat *him* like a friend; he thought he could deal with the raw need he felt for her if she didn't look at him with an open invitation. But she seemed to melt like butter in the sun every time he touched her, and he didn't dare get near her again. All his iron self-control vanished somewhere when he was alone with her. Despite his best intentions, he always seemed to be taking her into his arms and kissing her. Even now, just thinking about her made him want to do a lot more than be her friend, and he shifted uncomfortably on the top step of the cracked stone stairs leading to the house. There were times memories of her came unbidden, conjured up by the sweet fragrance of a magnolia blossom, or honeysuckle vines. Then he'd recall the sweet, feminine scent she wore, and how soft her skin was, like the velvety furring of a rose petal. The tight ache would knot in his belly then, and he'd throw himself even harder into work to keep from thinking of her.

Sometimes, in the afternoons, he walked down to Pinch Gut. He'd seen enough poverty and despair there to make him want to help. At first he'd met with resis-

ance, but after a few times, some of the people he
topped and spoke to began to speak back. He rarely
arried much money, but he did have a line of credit at
ne of the grocers on Market Street. There was a world
f difference in that grocer and the drays that delivered
resh milk and vegetables to the wealthier homes on
Poplar Street. Maybe he didn't help much, but the little
e did made a big difference in some lives.

Some of the children he'd fed slowly lost that
pinched, wan look they all seemed to have. It amazed
him how much difference a decent diet could make,
especially when some of the children had never eaten
anything but fish and cornmeal.

Nick chewed on the end of his cigar, then put it out
against the stone stoop. Crossing his arms over his
drawn-up legs, he watched idly as a carriage rolled down
Vance, then came to a halt in front of the boarding-
house. When the driver swung down, Nick recognized
Roger and came to slow attention as the huge black
man stepped to the carriage door and opened it.

He knew before she stepped out that it would be Amber, and that she was looking for him. Rising slowly to
his feet, he moved down the steps to meet her. She
stepped from the carriage in a froth of lacy gauze and
femininity, and he felt as if someone had punched him
in the stomach.

Without taking his eyes off her, he said, "Roger, what
in God's name are you doing bringing her down here?"

Shrugging his massive shoulders, Roger said placidly,
"She wanted to come, Mr. Nick."

"And you always do what she wants." Nick said it
flatly, without censure. It was no secret that Roger
adored his mistress with the distant adoration of a man
admiring a pretty, frivolous butterfly. He followed her
everywhere, was at her beck and call.

"Don't be an old grouch, Nick," Amber said lightly,
but there was a determined glint in her eyes as she
looked up at him. He drew in a deep breath, then real-

ized what a mistake that was as her soft fragrance filled his senses.

Reaction hit him gut-deep, and he felt the almost painful tightening of his groin in response to her. His voice was rough when he demanded, "What do you want?"

"To see you. Why else would I come down here?" Her glance shifted to the boardinghouse, and Nick's jaw clenched.

"All right. You've seen me. Now go back home. This isn't your part of town."

"Or yours. Why do you live here when you make enough money to have decent lodgings?" Her delicate brow arched when he made an impatient sound. "That's not why I came," she said quickly, "so before you start being rude, let's step inside where I can talk to you."

"No."

Not batting an eyelash, Amber turned to Roger and said, "I won't be too long, Roger, if you don't mind running that errand for me."

Without pausing to look at Nick, Amber brushed past him and stepped daintily up the weed-strewn sidewalk to the front steps, lifting her skirts in one small gloved hand as she mounted them to the front door. By now, one of the other boarders had come out onto the porch, and he leaned forward politely to open the door for her. Amber gave him a sweet smile and sailed inside, leaving Nick still standing on the sidewalk with his mouth set and angry and his big hands clenched into fists.

"Might as well go talk to her, Mr. Nick," Roger observed as he stepped up into the driver's box again. "She's not going to leave until you do. She's a stubborn woman, Miss Amber is, and if she intends to talk to you —she'll talk come hell or high water."

Barely flicking him a glance, Nick nodded. "You're right, but she may not like what I say back."

As he strode angrily up the sidewalk, he heard Roger chuckle softly, then cluck at the elegant chestnuts that pulled the carriage. It rolled away from the curb as Nick yanked open the front door and entered the boarding-house.

He found Amber in the front parlor, discussing the hot weather with the landlady. Her ivory and lace fan moved slowly as she accepted Mrs. Rule's offer of a seat on the worn blue brocade settee.

"Thank you, ma'am. You can't imagine what a trying day it's been for me." Amber's eyes shifted to where Nick stood framed in the doorway glowering at her. "Oh, there you are. Do come in. Mrs. Rule was just going to fetch us some lemonade. Would you like a glass?"

"No."

"Is that all you can say after I came to visit you?" Her head tilted to one side, and if it hadn't been for the militant gleam in her eye, Nick might have been fooled into thinking she was teasing him.

He took two steps forward, which put him in the middle of the parlor. "No, and I can add that you don't play the part of a sweet southern belle that well, Miss Jenné. You come across as a rather spoiled debutante, but that's about it."

"Oh, then I'll have to work on it, won't I?" Her laugh was light and tinkly, but he still wasn't fooled.

Mrs. Rule, obviously feeling she was in the way, murmured that she'd be back with the lemonade, and left the parlor. Nick put his hands behind his back to keep from touching Amber. He wasn't certain if he wanted to kiss her or strangle her, but either option could be fatal.

"What on earth did you say to Mrs. Rule to get an offer of lemonade from her?" he asked mildly. "I've lived here for months and haven't so much as been offered drinking water."

"Perhaps if you smiled once in a while, you might get much more than that."

"She's not my type." He had the minor reward of seeing her cheeks flush.

"That's *not* what I meant, you vile fiend, and you know it."

Shrugging, he said, "How would I know that? If I recall correctly, you've also accused me of similar actions with another female."

"And rightly so, I'm certain!" Amber snapped, then inhaled deeply, blowing out the breath in a long sigh. "I didn't come here to fight with you, Nick, believe it or not. If you'd just—"

"Why *did* you come?" he cut in, moving so that the fading light from the windows fell on her face but kept him in shadow. "It's not exactly the thing to do, you know, visiting a man in his rooms."

"You're one to talk." Her brow lifted when he muttered a curse. "I see that you recall your two visits to my bedroom."

"One visit. One was a bedroom belonging to someone else." He flicked a glance at the open parlor door. "And if you want your reputation in shreds, this is the way to do it. What will Memphis society have to say about your being here?"

"Who's going to tell them? Mrs. Rule? Roger? *You*?"

"Maybe."

Her smile returned and she began to peel off her gloves. "Well then, since my reputation is already ruined, why don't we go where we can have real privacy? I have something of an urgent nature to discuss with you."

"Look, Amber," Nick began angrily, his brows lowering as he glared at her, but Mrs. Rule chose that moment to come back in with a tray, and he lapsed into silence. He waited impatiently while she chatted aimlessly with Amber, then he crossed to shut the door behind her after she left. When he turned back to the settee, Amber was holding out a glass of lemonade.

"Here. Might as well drink some of this so she won't have her feelings hurt. I have the notion you'll be charged for it, anyway."

"Probably. I don't give a damn. What is so important that you're bold enough—or dumb enough—to come here?"

A faint frown knit Amber's brow, and she waited until he took the glass of lemonade before saying, "I think someone is trying to kill my father."

Whatever Nick had expected, it wasn't that. He stared at her for a long moment before asking, "Why?"

"Because lately there have been several unexplained accidents involving him. It's the oddest thing—for a man like my father, who has never been overfond of firearms—to begin to carry one. And also, last week, when he was entering the offices, a stone gargoyle from atop the building suddenly fell to the ground, barely missing him."

"That, I remember," Nick said. "But it was an accident, Amber. The grouting around the base of the statue had dislodged, and it was loose. It just fell."

"So I heard." Amber looked down at her untouched glass of lemonade, the frown still in place. "But that's not all. I heard him talking to someone, and he said that if anything happened to him, he had his will already written." Sudden tears quivered on her lashes, and Nick shifted uncomfortably as she lifted a hand to wipe them away. "My father's never worried about his will before, Nick. Though of course, being the man he is, he's seen to those details. Somehow, this time, he seemed upset, and as if . . . as if he thought he was going to die soon."

"Well," Nick said slowly, still unwilling to believe what she was saying, "he is getting on in years, Amber. Perhaps he's only looking out for your future."

She looked up angrily. "Don't be stupid. Do you think I can't tell the difference between natural concern and this? I've known him far too long."

Setting his lemonade on the small table in front of the settee, Nick said impatiently, "If you really think that, go to the authorities."

Amber gave a very unladylike snort. "Do you think that would do any good? They'd only question Papa, and of course he would say it was all nonsense."

"Then maybe it is."

Clenching her hands into fists, she glared at him. "Don't you start that, Nick Windsor. I expect you to do something."

He felt a wave of astonishment. "Me? Do something? Just what do you expect—that I should be his body-guard?"

"Well—yes." Her chin rose defiantly at his derisive laugh. "Are you frightened, Nick?"

"Of what? So far, you haven't convinced me there's anything to be frightened of." She looked so upset that he felt a twinge of regret, and his voice softened. "Look, sugar, I know you love your father, and I'm certain you think what you're doing is right, but don't you think you're going a bit too far with this?"

"No," she said stubbornly, "I don't. And what's more, Aunt Leala agrees with me, too."

"Well, *there's* the clincher," Nick muttered. "Aunt Leala. I didn't think she saw anything but homeless waifs and soldiers. What has she noticed?"

"A dead dog."

If Nick was the kind of man to roll his eyes, he would have done so. Instead he shook his head impatiently and asked, "Do you mind explaining what a dead dog has to do with this?"

"Not at all. It was a mutt that Pensée—our cook—has been feeding the table scraps, and one evening when Papa came in late and she'd held his dinner for him, he decided not to eat. Well, it was so late, and she was afraid it wouldn't keep, so Celia set it outside for the stray dog. The next morning, the food was gone and the dog was found dead at the edge of the yard."

"Maybe a carriage ran over it."

"No, there were no marks. No blood. Nothing."

"Then," Nick half snarled, "maybe it died of old age,

or any one of a hundred other things. Dammit, Amber, I think you've just got an overactive imagination because you're bored. Why don't you go throw an expensive party or buy some new clothes or something else you like to do? This could be—"

He stopped abruptly when she shot to her feet and knocked over the glass of lemonade, her lovely face contorted in rage. "Don't you dare make light of me, Nick Windsor," she said through gritted teeth, "not when I came to you with something so important to me! I trust you, and now you act as if I'm some brainless ninny who can't do anything but eat bonbons and sew pretty seams."

"Well?" he asked coolly. "Am I that far from the mark?" If looks could kill, he thought wryly, he'd drop dead on Mrs. Rule's faded parlor rug. As it was, Amber glared at him until he could almost feel her golden eyes boring into him. "All right," he added when she began to jerk on her neat white cotton gloves again, "I'll look around. Will that satisfy you?"

"Don't bother." Her voice was much cooler than the burn of those eyes, and Nick fought the urge to agree.

"No, I said I would. You came to me for help, and I'll at least make sure he's not in any danger." His voice hardened slightly. "Contrary to popular opinion, I *do* care about something other than myself."

She flashed him a glance. "Oh, so that got to you, did it? I'm glad. I was beginning to think you're so hardhearted you truly don't care what people think of you."

"I don't. It's your opinion that matters," Nick said carelessly, and watched her eyes widen. She stopped buttoning her gloves and looked at him for a long moment.

"Is that true? That my opinion matters, I mean?"

"Yes, but maybe not for the reason you want it to. Look, Amber, I like your father a lot. I even like you, but—"

"Don't throw me any more crumbs," she muttered,

"you're turning my head with extravagant compliments."

"But," he continued, as if she hadn't spoken, "nothing will come of it. It'd be a waste of time for us to get involved, and don't bother pretending that's not one of the reasons you came here to see me. If you'd really wanted to talk about just your father, you'd have seen me at the warehouse. I've only been home an hour or two."

"How do you know I didn't go there first?"

"Did you?"

She tossed her head, and golden curls shimmered with the movement. "No. You're right. I did come here for more than one reason. I wanted to see where you live, and I knew you'd never invite me."

Nick looked around at the shabby parlor with faded rug and curtains. "Do you blame me? This isn't exactly the kind of place a man invites a woman he wants to impress."

Amber took a step closer, her voice low and husky. "Do you want to impress me, Nick?"

He swore silently, and clenched his hands behind him. "No, not like you think I mean."

She reached out to toy with a button on his shirt, her gaze riveted on his chest. "How do you mean it, then?"

Capturing her hand in one of his, Nick said gently, "Amber, honey, I want to impress you with something a lot more intimate than settees and carpets, but you're my boss's daughter. I don't own a plantation or a warehouse, or even my own horse anymore. All I have in this world is a Navy Colt that I took from a Yankee guard at the prison camp where they kept me, and a little bit of money stashed away for my future. That future doesn't include close ties, do you understand?"

She looked up at him. "No, of course I don't understand. Did you really think I would? I can't conceive of a human being actually *choosing* to be alone when there's someone who cares about him."

"Don't." His voice was rough, ragged. "I don't want anyone to care about me, dammit, and I don't want to care about anyone else." His grip tightened on her small, delicate hand. "It's too hard to lose the people you care about, Amber, but you wouldn't know that. You can't know it. Things have always come easy for you, and you don't have any idea how it feels to watch everyone and everything you love vanish right in front of your eyes."

"Don't patronize me," she said stiffly, blinking rapidly to hold back tears. "I may not have lost everything dear, but do you think me so devoid of human emotions and empathy that I can't feel for someone who has? My father and aunt aren't the only members of my family who have generous tendencies, you know. I may not do what they do, but I do have my charities—damn you, Nick Windsor, don't look at me like that!" Her small foot stamped against the wet carpet with a squishy sound, and she grabbed his shirt front. "I *can* understand how you feel, even if I've never had the same loss! What do I have to do—lose someone dear to be in your league?"

"Amber, sugar," he half groaned, "you don't know how it can change a man. Maybe that's what I want to say."

"That you're changed?" Amber's gaze fastened on his face as he tried to disengage her insistent fingers from his shirt. "I didn't know you before, so why should I care that you've changed?"

He managed to uncurl her fingers, then set her gently back. "*I* care. That's what matters."

Watching, he saw Amber reach for and regain control, and felt a wave of admiration for her. He also felt an aching pain that began deep in his belly and curled upward through every part of his body, lodging in his throat. He wanted things to be different. He wanted to be able to care about her, but he knew that if he did, he would risk a lot more this time than he ever had before.

There was something about Amber Jenné that lured him as inexorably and disastrously as a moth to a candle, and he had to struggle to resist the appeal in her eyes.

"Why?" he asked with husky frustration. "Why do you think we could ever be together?"

Tugging at the fringe of her gloves, Amber flashed him a quick upward glance through her lashes. "Because we both feel the same attraction, and you know it. Sometimes that's enough, but I don't think that's all there is to what's between us. If it was, you would have already done what we've almost done twice before, then gone on your way without thinking about it. I know it's different for me, so I'm assuming that you feel the same."

"Mighty tall assumption," Nick drawled, watching her through half-lidded eyes. "Did it ever occur to you, sugar, that I mean exactly what I said?"

"Not for a moment. Oh, you mean part of it, yes, but not the part where you said you don't want to care about anyone ever again." She looked up from her feigned concentration on her gloves and met his half-angry, half-amused gaze. "I don't intend to let you get away with it. You think I'm not right for you. I think we'd be good together. I always go after what I want, Nick Windsor, and I want a chance to prove to you that you're wrong."

"Dammit, woman," he growled, "you're a bold piece of goods to be talking to a man like that."

"Do you think so? Well, if I waited on you to make the first move, I'd die an old maid. I'll be here tomorrow to fetch you for a picnic, and we can discuss how we're going to keep my father from being killed then. Eleven o'clock, Nick. Be ready. Roger will drive us."

"I have no intention of doing any damned foolish thing like that," Nick said angrily, "and don't bother showing up here. I'll be at work."

"On Saturday? You can skip a day without the roof falling in. Be ready. Roger hates to be kept waiting."

"I'm not going, Amber," Nick said shortly, "and that's that."

Without bothering to protest, Amber moved swiftly to him and rose on her toes to press a quick kiss to his cheek. "Eleven," she said sweetly, and sidestepped him as he tried to grab her.

Nick followed her to the door, leaning against the peeling paint of the doorjamb as he watched her get back into the elegant carriage. She was determined, but so was he.

"I'm not going," he said aloud, softly, almost smiling when she leaned from the carriage to waggle her fingers at him as it rolled away from the curb. "I'm not going."

CHAPTER
9

BROWN water moved in a wide, sluggish ribbon below the high bluffs of Memphis. Sitting on the river bluff with her arms hooked around her bent legs, Amber tried to relax. She was finally alone with Nick Windsor, despite his reluctance. The spot she'd chosen for their picnic was remote, hidden on three sides by bushes, bordered on the other side by the river. The scent of jasmine and honeysuckle mingled with the lemony fragrance of magnolia blossoms, heavy in the still air.

As she wiggled her bare toes, she remembered her aunt's comments.

"I cannot believe that you would be so bold!" Aunt Leala had scolded when Amber informed her plainly that she had every intention of dragging Nick Windsor on a picnic, whether he liked it or not. "The man will be angry, *petite,* and an angry man never listens well. Especially a man of his reputation."

Her aunt had heard about him, from men who'd ridden with him or against him, and knew that Nick had a fierce reputation during the war when he'd ridden with Forrest.

One of the advantages—or disadvantages—in living in a house filled with displaced soldiers, was the constant gossip. When it was learned that Nick Windsor was working for their benefactor, one grizzled soldier with only one arm had drawled that he'd like to get a close look at the man who'd deviled Sherman's heels for so long.

"Sometimes Windsor rode ahead of Forrest's command as scout, an' I heared that he took out 'most near ever'one of a Yank troop camped on a bluff. Lookin' fer somebody, he said, but he never said who."

Amber had heard the men talk too, and had a feeling she knew who Nick had been looking for. She recalled that night at Clover Hill with aching clarity, the fury and rage on Nick's face as he'd confronted Alexander Steele. But he hadn't tried to kill him, not really.

"He'll listen," Amber said calmly to Leala. "And he'll help us keep Papa from harm."

"That's not the only reason you're doing this," Leala muttered shrewdly, and her words still rang in Amber's head as she sat on the river bluff with Nick Windsor and glanced surreptitiously at his stormy face.

In the end, it had taken Roger to help persuade Nick to leave the warehouse and come along, as well as her father. Both men had not wanted Amber to be denied what she wanted, though for different reasons. Roger knew the truth, whereas Henri Jenné simply wanted Amber to enjoy a lazy afternoon with a man he knew worked too hard.

"Go on, Windsor," he'd said jovially, "you might as well give in. When Amber has her mind made up, there's very little mere mortals can do to change it."

Furious, Nick had tried to politely refuse, but to no avail. Now he sat on the edge of a quilt, and his expression made Amber think of stone gargoyles. Breathing in air rich with the smells of the river and honeysuckle vines, she wiggled her toes. She noticed that he kept his gaze averted from her bare feet. She propped her chin in her palm.

"Do you really think it was an accident, Nick?"

His dark head turned slightly, black hair glinting with

blue lights in the warm afternoon sunshine. "What was an accident?"

"The gargoyle falling," she said impatiently. "I think it was deliberately loosened, and that someone tried to push it over on Papa."

"*I* think," he said with that cold deliberation that masked his fury, "that you've got an overactive imagination as well as a raging need to have your backside paddled until you can't sit down."

"Do you?" She tilted her head to one side, smiling sweetly. "You've mentioned that before, I believe."

"Yes," he growled, "and no one has taken me seriously. Your father should lock you in your room, at the very least."

"Is that what you'll do to your children when they misbehave? Lock them in their rooms or spank them?"

"I doubt I'll ever have children, so that remains a moot point." Nick reached abruptly for the wicker basket which emitted a delicious aroma from beneath embroidered linen. "Let's eat, so I can go back to work."

"Don't you like children?"

Exasperation lined his mouth with brackets as he ground out, "That has nothing to do with it. I won't have children."

"Oh." She leaned close, her tone confidential. "Was it a war wound?"

Nick glared at her. "Dammit, Amber, that's a hell of a thing to ask!"

"Well—was it? Just for future reference. There must be *some* reason why you say you won't have children. . . ."

"Leave it alone," he snarled, and she shrugged.

It wasn't easy to ignore his thunderous scowl, but she managed. Instead of looking at him, she fumbled under the napkin over the basket for a moment, then drew out two slender sticks. "Here," she said calmly, "have some candy. It might sweeten your temper enough so that I can stand your company."

"I doubt it."

She made a face, thrusting the peppermint stick into his unwilling hand. "So do I, but I'm eternally optimistic, I'm afraid. A lifelong fault of mine."

"Along with some others I could name," Nick muttered, but he took the peppermint stick and chewed on the end of it.

Smiling slightly, Amber lay back on the quilt and gazed up at the bright, polished blue of the sky. Clouds scudded lazily over the burning expanse, and a breeze gently tossed the still-green branches of the trees around them. Mid-September had a bittersweet feel to it, with the warmth of summer lingering, but the cooler nights promising the chill of winter was not far away.

With a soft sigh Amber closed her eyes under the press of sunlight warming her. She felt Nick stir restlessly beside her and heard him mutter. She fought a smile. He was certainly surly about his enforced participation in the picnic, and she hoped she could coax some genuine response from him before the afternoon was over.

"Are you enjoying your candy?" she asked lazily, not really expecting him to reply.

After a moment he said reflectively, "I used to think about candy a lot when I was lying out in the woods at night with nothing around me but men and mules. It was the little things I missed the most, I think."

"Little things? What kind of little things?"

"You know, candy and clean sheets, and a night spent without someone trying to blow my head off. Little things." He grew quiet again, as if he'd revealed too much of himself.

Without opening her eyes, Amber murmured, "Would you like to try some of the goose liver pâté Pensée put in the basket? There are other goodies, I'm certain."

"Wonderful. While most of the South eats salt meat

and cornmeal, you bring along a basket of pâté and champagne. I'm really impressed, all right."

His caustic comments snapped her eyes open, and she sat up abruptly. "I believe that the Jenné family is doing a great deal to help those less fortunate, Mr. Windsor. What, may I ask, have *you* done to alleviate the misfortunes of your fellows?"

"Not eaten pâté and drank champagne, for starters." His eyes smoldered with hot, dark lights. "I always knew you were spoiled, but this only proves it."

Amber gave a light shrug, lowering her lashes to hide the hurt his words gave her. "Maybe I am, but at least I'm not rude."

"No, just pampered, petted, and protected to the point of slavishness."

"Do you intend to fight with me all afternoon, Nick?" she asked sweetly. "I'd rather not. I wanted you to enjoy the day, as well as help me."

"Help you." He shook his head. "You don't want my help. You just want someone to dance attendance on you, like the other men in your life. Well, I won't do it. I'm not a puppet whose strings you can yank every time the impulse hits you. I'm a man, Amber, not one of your lapdogs."

Angry now, Amber glared at him. "Are you implying that my father is a lapdog?"

"No, just foolish where you're concerned."

"You've no right to say that."

"You, sugar, have no right to *do* it."

Staring at him, Amber saw the barely repressed anger in his eyes, and knew she'd pushed him too far by maneuvering him into coming with her. He was right—she should have known better. She should have known that Nick Windsor was not a man who would take to being manipulated, but she'd wanted to be alone with him so badly, she'd allowed herself to believe otherwise.

"You're right, Nick," she said quietly. "And I'm sorry I've forced you into this picnic. I was wrong."

He gazed at her warily, one leg drawn up and his forearm draped over his knee, his shirt open to reveal the strong column of his throat, brown and masculine and so beautiful it made her heart ache with longing for him.

Shifting slightly with that easy flex of muscle that sent out signals of danger and sensual appeal at the same time, Nick looked away from her.

"All right. Apology accepted."

"Truce?"

Still wary, he shrugged again. "I don't know. Never had much luck with truces before. Seemed like any truce was just a cease-fire to let the other side get reinforcements."

"All right, then, how about amnesty?"

"Amnesty?" The slight tug of a smile quivered at one side of his mouth. "What would you know about amnesty? You're one of those people who insist on unconditional surrender. Your father should have named you Sherman instead of Amber."

"Would you like me better then?"

Shaking his head, he said with a definite smile, "No." At her fleeting wince, he added, "I'm not certain I could like you any more than I do now. I already like you too much, and that's not good." He regarded her closely as he finished the last of his peppermint stick.

Amber couldn't help smiling. "There's where your theory falls apart, Nick. You don't know what it might be like if we were together, so you don't know if it's good or not."

There was an intensity in his gaze as he looked at her, and Amber held her breath when he reached out to cup her chin in his palm. "You're the most maddening woman," he murmured huskily just before he leaned forward to brush her lips with his.

This time he wasn't rough and urgent like the other times; this time, he was almost gentle. His mouth was warm, rich with the taste of tobacco and candy, his tongue slow and sweet as it raked against hers in coaxing exploration. Amber's arms lifted to wind around his neck almost without conscious thought, and she greeted the intrusion of his tongue in her mouth with tentative touches of her own. His lean, hard body shuddered at the touch, and she felt a surge of pleasure that she could affect him like he did her.

It was arousing, knowing that with her inexperienced kisses and caresses she could make this dangerous man respond so quickly and eagerly. When his hands shifted to caress the small of her back, Amber arched into him, her breasts pressing into his chest. Nick took quick advantage of it, his hand closing around the lush swell of her breast.

Easily controlling her instinctive jerk of surprise, Nick lengthened his caress, his fingers teasing the taut bead of her nipple into stinging response. Amber moaned as arrows of desire shot through her body. A throbbing pulse began to beat in the center of her body, making her writhe and ache. She felt empty, and wanted Nick to help ease the ache.

Instead of easing it, his kisses and lavish caresses only intensified it, until Amber's breath came in short, hot gasps for air and she trembled helplessly. There was something so primitive, so satisfying, about being beneath the warm sun and alone in this man's arms.

The heat of his body burned her even through his shirt and her thin shirtwaist, so that when he unbuttoned her blouse and it fell open, the cool air felt almost icy against her fevered skin. Amber's tension was washed away on the tide of his heated need, and her head fell back helplessly under the assault of his mouth, tongue, and hands.

Trailing kisses over the exposed arch of her throat, Nick took small, stinging bites, then returned to her mouth when she cried out softly. Capturing her lips in a searing kiss, he rotated his thumb over her nipple. Shivering, the ache grew hotter and heavier in her lower body, until she squirmed with it, her hips twisting beneath the long leg he'd thrown over her thighs. His head lifted and he stared down at her.

Hot lights glittered in his eyes, and his voice was rough and low. "This is crazy."

Her fingers tightened in the folds of shirt stretched tautly across his shoulders. "Yes."

"God." It was a tortured sound, and he muttered through his teeth just before he kissed her again, "Are you sure you want to keep this up?"

In a dazed voice she whispered against his mouth, "Yes."

"Amber, I can't lie to you—I won't fall in love or marry you. Do you understand?"

Amber heard him, and knew in some remote part of her that she must be insane to want a man who couldn't love her back. But she did. God help her, she did. And she didn't care at the moment what he said, only that he let her love him.

"I understand," she murmured when he drew back to look at her. Her hands stroked him. "Kiss me, Nick."

Nick kept kissing her, slowly drawing her blouse off and away, his head bent and his body contorted to keep from breaking contact. Shivering, Amber took his face between her palms. She kissed him gently, sweetly, and heard him groan.

His arms bent as if his weight was too heavy to hold him any longer, and he buried his face in the tumble of silken hair that had come loose somehow and was fanned out over the quilt. With fistfuls of her hair clutched in his hands, he said in a rough growl, "Keep that up, and you'll get a lot more than you bargained for, sugar."

"How do you know?" she whispered against the underside of his jaw, her tongue flicking out to graze along his skin. She felt his involuntary jerk and smiled. "You don't really know how much I want, do you, Nick?"

"I'm beginning to—look, I can't just keep kissing you

until I go crazy, you know. You've had me so tied up in knots these past months that it's a wonder I'm still sane. In fact, in light of what we're doing now, maybe I'm not sane."

"Good."

The river breeze was cool and gentle as he slowly sat back to gaze down at her breasts, barely concealed by the thin silk chemise. His gaze lifted to her face.

"Nick," she whispered, staring up at him, inhaling the rich, hot scent of him, male and arousing and vaguely intimidating. "Nick, make love to me."

He curled his lean fingers around her wrists and drew her bare arms up and over her head, pressing them down into the cushiony softness of quilt and thick grass. His dark gaze searched her face. "Do you know what you're asking for, Amber?" His grip shifted to a caress. "Do you?"

"Yes." She stared boldly back at him. "I know what I'm asking for—you. All of you, as close to me as I can get you, because I can't bear being apart."

A look of pain flickered on his taut features for a moment, and his black gaze was suddenly opaque and distant. Levering his lean body away from her, he looked up and past Amber.

"Don't," he said in a hoarse whisper. "Don't care too much."

He closed his eyes briefly, opening them when Amber slid her fingers into the gaping edges of his shirt to caress him boldly. Staring at her from beneath the straight fringe of his lashes, he held his breath. His stomach muscles contracted, and she felt the quivering in his arms as he still leaned over her, resting his weight on his palms.

Slowly bending, Nick touched the tip of his tongue to her parted lips, opening them with a gentle intrusion that grew hotter and wilder. Heat and sweetness spread through her with the taste of candy on his tongue, mixed with the heady flavor of desire. Amber's movements were awkward and clumsy, but as eager as his as she accepted the penetration of his tongue.

Emboldened by his ragged breathing and the growing ferocity of his kisses, Amber reached down between their bodies with a curious hand, finding and shaping the length and dimension of his arousal. He groaned aloud and stopped kissing her, his breath coming fast as he panted for control.

She gasped when he lowered his weight on her and she felt the rigid press of his erection against her through her skirts. Then there was no more time to wonder if she was making the right decision, no more time for anything but Nick as he made a rough sound in the back of his throat and covered her mouth with his. He kissed her, deeply, with the slow purpose of a man who knows that he isn't going to stop at just kisses.

Sunlight warmed them as Nick removed the filmy scrap of chemise, kissing each portion bared until she couldn't think. His lips lit fiery trails down her throat, over delicate collarbones, to the heated valley between her breasts. Then, in a lingering kiss, he covered her bare nipple with his mouth, making her arch upward at the shock of the contact. Why hadn't she remembered how it felt, that contradiction of heat and chill, the warmth of his mouth and the whisk of cool air across her skin when he lifted his head?

With the heated skin and burning caresses tormenting her, Amber tried to catch her breath and couldn't. It was hard, with him over her, his ebony eyes alight with desire, his legs spread so that his trousers were taut across his thighs, revealing his arousal. Her breath clotted in her throat, making her voice sound hoarse as she tugged at the waistband of his trousers until he paused and lifted his head.

"Off," she said thickly, her fingers catching at the small buttons. "It's not fair for me to be the only one without my clothes on."

"Since you insist . . ." Curling into a sitting position,

Nick rose to his feet and unbuttoned his pants. When his boots and pants were gone, tossed carelessly to the side, Amber gazed at him with open admiration, feeling a strange warmth invade her.

Nick knelt beside her, and her gaze lowered to the dark mystery of his body. She flushed. He was so much bolder than she'd thought he'd be, so much . . . Swallowing painfully, she looked back up at his face, half afraid he'd be laughing at her.

A faintly amused smile curved his mouth, but his eyes were hard and bright with passion. "Not disappointed, are you?" he asked in that raspy, husky voice that sent shivers from her head to toes.

"No, just—surprised."

"Don't you like surprises?"

"I'm beginning to—what are you doing?"

"Taking off the rest of your clothes, sugar. Hold still. I want to look at you like you're looking at me."

With everything gone, his hand smoothed over her flat belly to come to rest on the silky fleece between her legs, and Amber sucked in a sharp breath and stiffened. Nick looked up at her through half-lidded eyes.

Amber reached for him, wanting him to kiss her again. She was shivering in spite of the sun's heat. His fingers moved slightly, exploring the crevices of her body with a light, shattering touch that made her quiver. His thumb dragged across the sensitive folds until she bit her lip against the taut expectation that rose in her, higher and higher. When he bent to take her nipple in his mouth, she exploded into a thousand starbursts. Curling her fingers into his hair, Amber arched up toward the source of pleasure, sobbing his name.

Slowly relaxing as the waves of intense pleasure receded, she opened her eyes as he looked up at her and smiled. This was so outside the realm of her experience that she could only go by instinct. She had no idea what was normal and what wasn't, or even if any of it was normal. All she knew was that she loved Nick and wanted him, and that anything they did together *felt* right.

He began kissing her again, leaning over her, his lips hot and wild as he penetrated her mouth with his tongue. Caressing her breasts with both hands, he coaxed more cries of pleasure and need from her, until the fire rose hot and high again. She twisted beneath him, reaching for him, touching him boldly, stroking her fingers up and down the length of him with a passion to match his.

"*Jesus,* sugar," he murmured, beads of sweat dotting his brow and upper lip, "I don't think I can hold back much longer."

"Then don't."

He made an inarticulate sound, and spreading her thighs with his knees, wedged his body into the willing cradle. He kissed her again when she gasped slightly at the first small intrusion of his body between her legs. His palms cupped her buttocks.

"Relax, sugar," he muttered thickly, "just relax. It's only me, and I wouldn't hurt you for anything. God. You feel so good, so right . . . so damned right, when everything else in my life is so wrong."

Dimly aware of the texture of his voice, his need, and the blurring pain in his voice, Amber couldn't focus on anything but her struggle to maintain control. He was sliding his erection up and down against that bright, burning center he'd caressed with his fingers only moments before, an erotic glide that made her bite her lower lip between her teeth to still her cries. It felt as if the fire had reignited there, and shooting sparks spiraled up and spread outward in rivers of flame through her belly to every nerve ending in her body. She shuddered, grabbed at him, and felt him catch her hands and hold them at her sides while he moved his big body.

Her body recognized the intent if not the motion, and adjusted to take him without her conscious decision. The hard slide of him pressed against her intimately as she shifted, and he sucked in a deep breath when Amber's thighs parted for him. At the first sharp jolt of pain, Amber cried out involuntarily.

"Easy, sugar," he murmured, "easy. I'll wait until you're ready for me." Cupping her buttocks in his palms again, he held her still.

He was shaking, his muscles quivering with the strain of holding back, and Amber shuddered again. It was an unfamiliar invasion, sharp and aching, but when he remained still for a moment, the pain began to ease. She wiggled slightly, and he lifted his head, panting.

"Don't. Just—don't." A crooked smile flickered on his mouth as he tried to catch his breath. "Wait a minute, sweetheart. It's been a long time for me, too."

Looking up, Amber could see the tousled mane of his hair and the curve of his broad shoulders gleaming in the afternoon sun. He bent his head so that she couldn't see his face; it was hidden, all his thoughts, the naked hunger she'd glimpsed so briefly.

"Nick," she whispered, "please." She wasn't quite sure what she meant, except that she felt as if he was withdrawing from her and she wanted his closeness, all of him, his body and mind and soul, to be with her at this moment.

He lifted his head and gave her a tortured glance before he shut his eyes, thick lashes lowering to hide them as he began to move again, slowly. Passion stretched the skin tight across his high cheekbones. His body rocked forward again, stretching her until she dug her fingers into his muscled forearms to stop him.

"That hurts," she half moaned, panting. "Stop . . ."

"Hush, sugar," he muttered, "you don't know what you want."

Maybe he was right; maybe she didn't know. All that was certain at this point was that the incredible tension had somehow turned into pain, and he didn't seem to notice. His face was fiercely concentrated, his breathing ragged. She hadn't expected the pain. Not like this, this earing knife thrust that pierced her heated desire like a ash of cold water.

Nick controlled her frantic movements easily, his mouth taking hers again as he kissed her long and hard, his weight holding her down when she tried to squirm free.

"Easy," he growled when she pushed at him, his brows drawing together in a puzzled frown. "Why are you changing your mind now?"

"Because . . . it . . . hurts."

The puzzled expression slowly altered into one of shock, and when he eased himself deeper into her, Amber saw realization dawn on him. His gaze caught hers.

"Damn. You're a virgin?"

"Yes," she said softly. "What did you think?"

"It's probably better that I don't say," he murmured wryly. His quick glance was frustrated and condemning.

Amber drew in a shaky breath. "So—I'm not one anymore."

He looked startled. Then Nick rested his forehead against hers and laughed softly. "Ever a woman of mystery and surprise, aren't you?"

Amber wasn't certain if he was angry or pleased, but then it didn't matter anymore. He began kissing her again, gently at first, then with a rising urgency that she could feel. His hands moved over her body with tantalizing caresses that made her moan, and the heat she'd felt earlier returned to coil deep inside her. She could feel the strong thud of his heart, could feel the heat of his body just inside hers, and the fires merged into a steady flame.

Bending his head downward, Nick began to kiss her breasts, his tongue tracing wet paths over the ivory and pink flesh, lavishing attention on the beaded nipples that tightened at the flick of his tongue. When she moaned again, her hips moving in restless circles under him, he pressed forward, this time in a swift lunge. Amber gasped, but the pain dissolved when he remained still.

Then, slowly, he began to move again, withdrawing little only to thrust forward again, his body moving in slow rhythm. The erotic friction of him inside her erased the last of her discomfort, and Amber's hands clutched at his broad, smooth back. He muttered something unintelligible in her ear, his breath coming faster and faster as he moved against her.

There was an indescribable tension inside her, different than the tension he'd created with his hands. His hard-muscled body rocked against her with stronger strokes. Amber whimpered. Nick groaned harshly when she arched into his thrusts and cried out, and in the next instant he withdrew.

Shoving her deep into the quilt with rough, almost frantic motions, he shuddered. Dazed, lost in her own release, it took Amber a moment to realize what he'd done. He pinned her shoulders down with his hands, convulsing in short, hard spasms against her belly. Holding her tightly in his embrace, he shuddered again, another moan escaping between his clenched teeth. His body was rigid, and sweat misted his skin.

"Nick?" she queried softly when he didn't move for several minutes. His head was buried in the curve of her shoulder and neck, and she could feel his breath feathering over her skin. "Are you all right?"

"I don't know," came the muffled response, and he lifted his head. Tawny strands of her hair clung to his face, and he pulled it away. A faint smile curved the hard line of his mouth. "I should be asking you that question."

"So ask."

"Are you all right?"

Snuggling closer, she lifted up slightly to press a kiss to the column of his throat. "I'm absolutely wonderful."

"Little lady," Nick said, "I certainly agree with that."

Amber said contentedly, "Well, I'm glad to see that

ou don't have an incapacitating war wound. I was be-
nning to wonder."

For a moment there was only silence. Then Nick be-
an to laugh, deep rumbles of full-throated amusement.
mber realized it was the first time she had heard him
augh without reserve.

CHAPTER
10

LATE afternoon sunlight spread molten fire on the chipped surface of the river, reflecting orange and crimson brilliance. A breeze blew off the water, and Amber shivered in spite of the fact that she was dressed again and Nick had drawn the quilt up around her shoulders. Neither of them seemed in a hurry to return. The river bank was remote, private, and a sweet-scented haven from the world.

Hesitant to say anything for fear of breaking the languid spell cast by their lovemaking, Amber hugged her knees to her chest and gazed out over the river. She reached out and plucked a fragrant honeysuckle blossom from a trailing vine, and pinched off the stem. Aware of Nick's distracted attention, she licked the end of the tiny blossom where a drop of nectar quivered.

"Umm. Sweet."

Nick smiled faintly but didn't say anything. Amber plucked another one and held it out to him. "Want one?"

He shook his head. "No."

She waited, hoping he would say the words she wanted to hear, but he seemed content to stretch out like a lazy cat on the blanket. His shirt was open and his bare chest gleamed a dull bronze that drew her eye again and again. Resting on his side, propped up on one

:lbow, Nick had retreated back into himself, frustrating
1er.

Finally she turned to him and asked, "Do you think
5omeone might be trying to hurt my father?"

Nick shrugged. "I don't know." He tickled her arm
with a stem of grass that he'd plucked. "It doesn't seem
likely, but if you think he's in danger, I'll check it out.
Don't know what you think I can do, though."

"Everyone knows that you were a scout for Forrest
during the war, and that you were supposed to be as
light as a cat on your feet. They even called you a cat, I
think."

Nick shrugged. "They called me a lot of things. Cat
would have been one of the nicer ones, but I think
you've gotten me mixed up with someone else."

"Oh. Well, listening to all those soldiers around our
house can be confusing at times." She gave him a curious look. "What did you do that made you so famous?
Or maybe I should say—*infamous*?"

His face shuttered closed to her and he shrugged
again. "I don't know that I was infamous. I was just a
man doing his job, that's all."

"Not from what I heard, but if you don't want to talk
about it, that's all right."

"Looking for a hero, sugar?" he drawled, but his
mouth was twisted, giving him a sulky expression. "Forget it. I'm not interested in that particular honor. Too
damned convenient a term to be used freely."

Puzzled, she tilted her head to one side to look at
him. "What do you mean by that?"

This time his shrug was impatient. "Nothing. Forget
it. It's not worth explaining. Guess we'd better go soon,
or the mosquitoes will be out and eating us alive."

Amber curled her bare toes into the grass. "I hate to
go back. This has been a magical afternoon."

"Magical?" A faint smile curved the sulky line of his
mouth into humor. "I've a notion your father would call
it something else. You should have told me."

"Told you?" It was her turn to shrug carelessly. "[don't know what you're talking about."

"Sure you do." His gaze narrowed fractionally. "If I' known you were, ah, *inexperienced,* I never would hav gone so far."

Her chin lifted slightly and her tone was sugary an soft. "Oh? How delightful of you to tell me that now Why, in one little sentence, you've managed to cheape what we just shared to a mere autumn interlude. I sup pose that you are accustomed to more *experienced* women, but one has to start somewhere. You were jus my first—experiment."

The black eyes turned icy, and Nick's voice was a lo growl when he jerked her to him, his fingers biting int her upper arms. "Dammit, Amber, don't even talk lik that. I didn't mean it the way it sounded, and you kno it. I just think you should have told me, and let m decide before it was too late."

She kept her gaze steady as she pulled away. "Wha makes you think you have a right to decide something like that for me? You don't. It was my decision."

"Not when it involves me, and it did involve me."

Nick drew her to him again, his voice softer. "Sweet heart, you gave me a wonderful gift this afternoon. whether you realize it or not. I just wanted to be worthy of it, and I don't think I am." He kept his dark, liquid gaze on her face as he stroked her.

"Again, that's for me to decide." Some of her hurt eased at the frustration evident in his expression, and she knew he was struggling with his own demons. "Don't worry—no strings were attached."

"I'm not worried about strings." Nick pushed a hand through his hair and leaned back on his palm, bending a leg at the knee and staring at her solemnly. "I'm wor ried about you."

"Why?"

For a moment he didn't answer, just gazed at her silently. Then, his voice still soft, he said, "You just plow ight over anyone who opposes you, without stopping to hink about the consequences. Sometimes, people don't ike being told no, and when you ignore them, they hink of ways to get even."

"Are we talking about you?"

He grimaced. "No, not exactly. If I hadn't wanted to come on this damned picnic, no one could have made me. I was fighting myself more than you, I guess. I knew what would happen if I let myself get too close to you for any length of time." His hand reached out to lift a soft strand of her hair, and the fading sunlight cast it into shades of spun gold and shadow. He dragged the ends of her hair over his mouth, then shrugged. "I can't give you what you need or want. All I can give you is— magical afternoons."

Amber felt a sharp pain pierce her heart, but she did not cry out. She'd not expected he would feel instantaneous love after the intimacy they'd shared, but it was obvious it hadn't meant to him what it had to her.

"I see," she said after a moment, and saw his gaze sharpen. "I don't recall asking you for anything yet. Except your help in finding out if my father is in danger, and that should be given without reservation."

"I said I'd help."

"Don't get testy. I know you did. I meant that I wasn't aware you expected to be *paid* for your . . . your services."

He looked at her, his eyes smoldering. "That's the damnedest piece of nonsense I've ever heard. What the hell do you mean by that?" Grabbing her hand when she would have risen, he snarled, "If it's guilt or regret that you're expecting, you're looking at the wrong man, Amber. I warned you, and I don't regret what happened between us. I've wanted you since the first time I laid eyes on you, and God knows I've tried to ignore it. You just wouldn't listen."

Amber snatched her hand away. "I don't expect you to feel guilty or regretful. Heavens, I'd feel terrible if you did. All I expect is that you will keep your word and try to help me find out if someone intends my father harm."

"I've said at least three times in the last five minute that I have every intention of doing that."

"Then why are we fighting?"

"Because," Nick grated, "you expect me to love you and cherish you or something like that, and I can't. told you I can't. Don't look at me with those big eye like a pitiful kitten's and say you didn't expect anything I know you did. If I wasn't such a fool and weak where you're concerned, I'd have run like hell when you showed up on my doorstep. I'm responsible, all right." He swore softly under his breath.

"You're not alone. I'm every bit as responsible as you In fact, more so. I wanted you. I thought you might wan me back. It's not your fault that I was mistaken."

"Dammit, Amber . . ." His words were a groan, and she succeeded this time in standing up, fumbling blindly for her shoes as she tried to tug at her skirt hem to free it from beneath his hand.

He held it fast, giving it a hard jerk that brought her tumbling into his lap. His arms went around her immediately, and his mouth found hers as she struggled angrily against him. It was a punishing kiss, wordless, urgent, and needy, and Amber found herself yielding to it.

When he set her back, her lips were swollen and moist, and she stared at him with wide eyes. Her hurt and anger had dissolved under the force of his kiss, and she took a deep breath. Nick Windsor was a walking contradiction, whether he realized it or not. He said he wanted no ties, that he didn't want to care about anyone, but looking at him now, Amber knew that he was lying to himself.

Oh yes, Nick was definitely full of contradictions.

"I'll marry you," he said abruptly, not looking at her but staring out at the broad muddy river.

Amber stared at him in silent shock. His face was hard and impassive, showing no emotion at all. Her heart sank and she forced out a response.

"Thank you for being so noble, but such a sacrifice is not at all necessary. My father will not come after you with a loaded shotgun or a squad of vigilantes." She hoped her hurt didn't betray her, but it was impossible to keep her voice light and carefree when he sat there looking like a cornered tiger.

His head turned toward her; the familiar lines bracketed his mouth in the fading light. "Believe it or not, Miss Jenné," he drawled icily, "I still have some honor left. I've ruined you. I'll marry you."

"And make me regret it the rest of my life?" She shook her head. "No, thank you. I prefer a willing husband, not a resentful one."

"And if you're pregnant?" His voice was short, hard. "It's been known to happen."

"I'm certain of that." She began to get angry. "If I find that I am—*enceinte*—I will do what must be done then. I wouldn't be the first bride with a loose wedding gown."

"No," Nick said bitterly, "I suppose not. Well, I offered to do the right thing."

"Oh, and don't think I don't appreciate it." Her voice was tart when she saw his relief. "I think it's time we leave."

Uncurling his long body in a smooth motion, he rose to his feet, bringing her up with him. His hand remained on her arm, and when she glanced up at him, he looked uncertain and wary.

"Amber, I promise this won't happen again," he said, pushing a hand through his dark hair and looking away from her.

"*Au contraire,* Nick Windsor," she said sweetly, enjoying the startled look in his eyes, "I have every intention of this happening again. Don't make promises you can't keep."

He stared after her in astonishment as she picked he way across the grass, shoes in hand. Grabbing up the picnic basket they'd barely touched, he followed her to the carriage waiting just beyond the hedges. He'd secured the horse to a tree limb, and now he unfastened the snaffle hook that held it as Amber waited for him to help her up into the carriage. His frequent, frowning glances were decidedly wary.

It wasn't until they'd pulled up in front of the SW&C offices that Amber spoke, and then it was only to ask him to have Roger come out to drive her home.

"Thank you for a lovely afternoon," she said before he could say what was obviously on the tip of his tongue. "I'll wait for you to contact me about my father."

For a moment it looked as if he was about to say something she didn't want to hear, but the office door opened and Roger strode out, his smiling gaze flitting from Amber to Nick and back.

"Afternoon, Mr. Nick," he said easily, and Nick gave a faint shrug and got down from the carriage, handing him the reins.

"Afternoon, Roger. See her safely home before she gets into any trouble."

Roger looked faintly amused at Nick's sharp tone, and his gaze shifted back to Amber. She met his discerning look with an uplifted brow that she knew didn't fool him for a moment, but Roger wouldn't say anything. He might *think* it, but he'd never say it. Not to or about her.

The carriage rolled away from the curb, turning around in the middle of the street, and Amber had a glimpse of Nick as it made the turn onto Beale. He was still standing in front of the SW&C warehouses, staring after the carriage as if he didn't know quite what to do. Amber felt a spurt of satisfaction. He'd change his mind about ties and love before long. She'd see to it.

"Miss Amber," Roger said when the carriage stopped

on Adams and he reached up to help her down, "you know I want what's best for you, don't you?"

"Yes, of course I do. Why?"

"'Cause sometimes folks want things that's not good for them, and the good Lord says no. You might try remembering that when you want something that's not good for you."

She smiled and gave Roger's heavily-muscled arm a pat. "I will, Roger, thank you. If the good Lord decides to say no to something that's not good for me, I'll certainly listen."

Roger frowned. "It's not enough to just listen. You need to pay attention."

"I'll keep that in mind. Is Papa home yet?"

"No, ma'am, he's still at the office. He might be there awhile, talking with Mr. Martin about new contracts for pig-iron production."

"Pig iron again? Are they still arguing about that?"

A faint grin made Roger's white teeth gleam in his dark face. "Yes, ma'am, they certainly are. I think Mr. Henri is winning, though."

"Well, I would expect so." Amber stepped lightly up the walkway to the house. It looked almost deserted now that Leala's boarders had moved, except for a few who still lingered in the basement rooms. Those were men who had yet to be coaxed into moving, and Henri's patience was growing thin.

Still, the house was quiet when she went in, and she felt a wave of gratitude. She had to think, had to remember everything that had been said or done that day, and she couldn't do it with a lot of distractions. She wanted to remember every word Nick had said, recall his every move.

Shivering, Amber wondered if love was supposed to be this complicated. And painful.

Nick stared after her carriage for several long moments, not quite certain what to do. Damnedest woman he'd ever seen, he thought harshly, then half grinned when he recalled her final words to him. She was a blunt as a mallet sometimes; she'd made it plain she didn't intend to let go easy.

The rising sense of shame and chagrin he'd felt after the flush of passion had faded began to return, and he balled his hand into a fist. He'd lied like a fiend when he told her he had no guilt or regret. God, how he'd lied. What was he supposed to do now? He'd offered to marry her. *God.* What a farce that would be. But what else could he do?

After all, she'd been a virgin before today, and if it was *his* sister that some man had done that way, why—

Stiffening, Nick's brain seemed to bog down. He thought of Jessamy, and how furious he'd been when she'd fallen in love with Alex Steele. He'd wanted to kill Steele, and if he'd run into him right after he found out about them, he probably would have.

And now he'd done almost the same thing to an innocent girl; shame hit him so hard he felt beads of sweat pop out on his forehead.

No, he told himself, *this isn't the same thing.*

A carriage rumbled noisily past, and he moved blindly toward the door of the offices. It *was* the same thing, and he knew it. Alex Steele had at least married Jess; Nick couldn't deny the relief that had gone through him when Amber refused his reluctant offer. Alex and Jess were in love. He wanted Amber, but he wasn't at all certain that he loved her. He wasn't certain he even knew what love was.

Love. Nick's mouth turned down in a faintly bitter twist. *Love.* From what he'd seen, the kind of love he wanted was damn scarce between most men and women; he wanted what his parents had had for one another, that deep, lasting commitment and mutual respect. His eyes closed briefly and he felt like a fool for standing on South Main in the twilight and arguing with himself.

Shoving his hands hard into his pockets, Nick entered the quiet office building. It was dark inside; the evening lamps had not yet been lit: Even Dyer, who was always there, like an office fixture, was gone. Nick was glad. The small, dapper man watched him so closely, he frequently felt like a criminal suspected of thievery. He wasn't certain at whose order Dyer watched him, but he didn't like it.

Too restless to go home, Nick decided to go over the ledgers again. He'd discovered a discrepancy that he wanted to check.

Before he reached the office where he stored the ledgers, he heard the hum of voices and paused, surprised. Who could be here this late in the afternoon on a Saturday? Normally, the offices shut down until Monday morning, with only a guard left to secure them against some of the riffraff that roamed the city streets.

Curious, he stepped quietly down the hallway, acutely feeling the absence of his pistol. After four years of wearing it constantly, it still felt strange not to have it at his side. One of the advantages of civilization, he'd been told, was living without the worry of imminent danger or death. He'd laughed at that, having seen enough brawls and knifings in the poorer section of the city to equate them with the niceties of war on an equal scale. In war, he'd retorted, one just recognized the enemy more easily. Civilization had a way of disguising them.

Pausing outside the half-open door of Norman Martin's office at the far end of the wide corridor, Nick heard the raised voices rumbling in disagreement. Martin sounded furious, while Henri Jenné was making an obvious effort to be calm.

"Norman, Norman," Henri was saying in a level tone, "don't be foolish. This could be the chance of a lifetime. Think—with the war over, reconstruction is already in full swing. Beyond the Mississippi, folks are finding new lives in unsettled lands, and you know what that means.

Construction. Lots of it. This is the new wave of progress, I can just feel it."

"New wave?" Martin's voice was sharp and sardonic. "It's a fluke, Henri. Pig-iron production has fallen from over eleven hundred thousand long tons in 'sixty-four to less than a thousand this year. Over a million men who were in the military have rejoined the working force. With the rising influx of immigrants, who do you think is going to absorb all this? The wartime speculation in wholesale prices collapsed early this year, and we can't afford to invest so heavily in something that won't fly."

Henri's voice betrayed rising impatience as he said, "Have you ever heard of Andrew Carnegie?"

"Of course," Martin snapped. "Who hasn't? The man has invested heavily in railroads, sleeping cars, or some such thing that's supposed to be the latest in progress. He also has oil lands in Pennsylvania."

"Right." Henri's voice was calmer, but Nick could hear the growing excitement in it. "Have some vision, Norman. Carnegie has resigned from the Pennsylvania Railroad and founded the Keystone Bridge Company, as well as organized the Superior Rail Mill and Blast Furnaces. Now he is establishing the Union Iron Mills. I've been in contact with him, and I think he's on the right track with this. Pig iron can't help but play an important part in the future, and I want to invest in it. As my limited partner, you have a right to voice your opinion, but as owner and major stockholder, I have the last word. I don't want a power fight, Norman, really I don't. But I see the future riding on gleaming sheets of iron as well as rails for the railroad. It would be stupid not to invest."

"And I say it would be stupid to risk our money on such risky ventures," Martin returned testily.

Nick frowned, leaning against the wall and feeling only vaguely guilty for eavesdropping. It was a fascinating discussion, and one he had engaged in a time or two with Henri himself. He agreed with the older man.

Henri Jenné said wearily, "Norman, I disagree. And though I know you disapprove, I intend to make more investments. I'm sorry you feel this way, and hope you don't take it personally."

"Have you consulted the other stockholders?"

"Yes, and we take a vote next week. I'm certain that they agree, Norman. But you must remember that it is my company. My wife left me an ailing business, and I've labored hard over the past twenty years to build it to what it is now. You've worked hard too, I know, but you're still relatively new at this. Let an old man show you some new tricks."

"Tricks won't save the business when it goes down the river with the next load of worthless pig iron," Norman said in a snarl that made Nick stiffen. He heard the menace in the man's voice, and didn't understand it. It wasn't as if Martin was the owner, or was even going to lose his own money. From what he knew of the company structure, Martin had come in on sweat equity, and stayed to help Henri Jenné reorganize. It was family money that had started the business, and family money that kept it going in lean times. What was the matter with Norman Martin? Couldn't he see the possibilities?

Stepping away from the wall, Nick went down the corridor to the office where the ledgers were kept, frowning. He'd thought a man as astute as Norman Martin was said to be would leap at the opportunity to invest in something that was so obviously on the rise. The conversation he'd just heard contradicted that. It didn't fit, and he wondered why.

Nick turned up the gas lamp in the small office where glass cases held stacks of ledgers, all neatly labeled. It required a key to open the cases, and he reached into his pocket for it before he remembered that he'd left it in his warehouse desk. Damn. He'd been so mad at being maneuvered into taking Amber on a picnic that he'd just tossed his key into his desk drawer and stormed out.

Careless of him. These ledgers were important, and not just anyone could flip through them.

By the time he went to his warehouse desk and retrieved his key, then walked back down the echoing halls to the office, he didn't feel like working. It was growing late, and he realized that he hadn't eaten much all day. His stomach growled a reminder at him, and he thought of the heavy-laden wicker basket Amber had brought that they'd both ignored. He'd had peppermint candy and a bite or two of roll, and that was about it. Food hadn't been his priority this afternoon.

With that memory still vivid in his mind, he didn't notice the faint noises coming from the office until he was standing in the doorway. Then he halted, recognizing Norman Martin at the wide, flat desk in the center of the room. Martin was poring over a ledger, painstakingly entering notes with a pen, his expression so intent that he didn't notice Nick for a moment.

Nick cleared his throat and Martin's head jerked up. There was a guilty look about him that made Nick glance at the ledger on the desk, catching a glimpse of it just before Martin shut it with a leisurely hand and smiled.

"Windsor. Didn't expect to see you here."

"Mr. Martin. I didn't expect to be here." He shrugged, trying to dispel the notion that Martin was furious at being seen there. "Just thought I'd catch up on a little work in my spare time. There were some discrepancies."

Martin's brow lifted. "Were there? You'd better find them and correct them, then. Or are you here just to impress Henri?"

It was a jarring note, and Nick leaned one arm against the doorjamb. "I don't see that Henri's here for me to impress."

"Did you and Amber have a nice picnic?" Martin snapped, and this time Nick *knew* what was wrong.

"Nice enough," he replied coolly.

"I'll bet." Martin pushed a hand through his brown hair, his blue eyes regarding Nick icily. "You've come a long way in the past few months, Windsor. Really impressed Henri with your hard work and initiative."

"Have I? Thought I was just doing my job. That's why you hired me, isn't it?"

"You might keep that in mind—that *I* hired you." Martin slid the heavy ledger book from the desk and walked back to the glass shelves with it, putting it inside and relocking the doors. He turned back to look at Nick, sliding the key into his vest pocket. "I hired you, and I can fire you. Simple as that."

"You got a problem with me, Mr. Martin? If you do, spit it out. I'm no mind reader."

"Yeah, Windsor, I've got a problem with you." Martin took a few steps closer, fury emanating from his slender, muscular frame. "I don't like the cozy way you keep company with Amber Jenné. And I don't like the way you suck up to her father, either."

"Suck up? What the hell do you mean by that?" Nick felt his temper rise, and straightened his lean body warily as Martin came a bit closer.

"You know—attach yourself to him like a leech, ready and eager to be the next executive."

"Got something against a man doing better for himself?"

"No, just not at my expense."

"Don't see how I can do that," Nick said with a light shrug, "when you're the president of S.W. and C. I'm just a lackey, a paid clerk, so to speak."

"Try remembering that. If I keep hearing Henri say 'Nick said this, and Nick said that,' I might forget that you're only a clerk and think you're after my job."

Nick looked at him for a moment. "Every man for himself, Martin. Maybe you should remember that. Along with the fact that I don't want your damned job. I just want enough money to leave town, remember? I told you that on the head end."

"Yeah, and you're the one who seems to have forgotten it. And you've forgotten your place, too. You're nothing. You live in a run-down boardinghouse and don't have a pot to piss in, and you go sniffing around Amber as if you had a chance with her. Stay away from her, you hear me?"

Angry now, Nick said softly, "In the first place, I don't need you to tell me where my *place* is, and in the second, if I want to see Amber, I will. If I don't want to see her, I won't. Nothing you say affects that decision at all."

"Maybe S.W. and C. isn't a big enough company for both of us," Martin said harshly.

"You firing me?"

"Now that you mention it, it sounds like a damned good idea. Clean out your desk. I'll have your final paycheck ready tomorrow morning."

Nick's eyes narrowed. Martin didn't look right. His face was a peculiar shade of gray, his eyes a little wild.

"Mr. Martin, you may have hired me," Nick said after a short pause, "but it'll take more than you to fire me. If Henri Jenné tells me to clean out my desk, I'm gone. But I won't leave here when you've made it pretty obvious you're mad about something that has nothing to do with business."

"Such as?" Martin snapped.

"Such as Amber Jenné. She's the real reason you're mad, and if you think I'll stand in your way with her, you're wrong. I never had any intention of getting mixed up with her," Nick said with a slight twinge at how things had changed, "but I'm damned if I'll let you tell me what to do."

Martin hesitated and some of the color returned to his face. Running the fountain pen idly through his fingers, he regarded Nick closely, then gave a deprecating laugh. "Look, I guess I overreacted, Windsor. I've been working too hard lately, and when I heard you went on a picnic with Amber, well—I guess it's common knowledge that we've been unofficially engaged for a year now, and I lost my head. Thought you were trying to cut in on me."

Nick stiffened at Martin's words, but said, "You thought wrong."

"Maybe you're right. All that other—you're just doing your job. Don't take offense."

Nick didn't say anything. He didn't believe Norman Martin for a moment. It wasn't overwork that had made him threaten him, it was fear. After four years in intimate quarters with fear, he could recognize the emotion in an instant. The moment he'd mentioned going to Henri, Martin had backed down. Amber had been a convenient excuse, just more fuel to fire his anger.

"Look," Martin said, still smiling, managing to look half ashamed, "forget this, all right? I went too far. You're a good man, Windsor, and you deserve Henri's trust. You've earned it. I never meant to denigrate your work."

When Nick didn't say anything, Martin crossed to him and put a hand on his shoulder, looking surprised at Nick's quick jerk away. He smiled uncertainly this time. "Nothing personal, old man. I just get odd notions at times. This is forgotten as far as I'm concerned."

"Fine." Nick took a step back. "I'll be in early tomorrow."

"Good, good. Wish there were two of you. We need a good man in New Orleans." He gave Nick a speculative glance. "Don't suppose you'd be interested in taking on that job, getting it going and then hiring a man to take your place?"

"I'll think about it. This is the first I've heard of it."

"Of course. Henri and I have been kicking it around for a few weeks, but neither of us thought of letting you train a man for the job. You'd be perfect for the task."

"Like I said, I'll think about it. I'd have to know more."

Norman Martin walked Nick to the front door of the

offices, making an obvious effort to be disarming. Nick had the distinct feeling that he was up to something, and that it tied in with the ledgers. He made up his mind to check on it at the first chance. He didn't like being made a dupe for anyone, and he sensed that Martin would use him if he could. He just didn't know why or how.

CHAPTER
11

"WHAT do you know about Norman Martin?" Nick asked, keeping his distance from Amber. She perched prettily on the edge of his desk, idly toying with a letter opener.

Shrugging, she said lightly, "Not much. He went into business with Papa about five years ago. Papa says he's a hard worker—if a bit impetuous—and they get along well."

"How well do you get along with him?"

Startled, she flashed him a quick glance. "Me? I don't know. Well enough, I suppose."

"Well enough to marry him?" Nick couldn't help asking, folding his arms over his chest and leaning back against the far wall. His gaze rested on Amber coolly, and he saw her cheeks grow pink.

"No, but I can imagine where you got that notion. Have you been talking to Norman?"

"Yes, I've been talking to *Norman*," he mocked, then swore silently at his lack of control. He shrugged. "You were one of many subjects he felt it necessary to warn me about."

"I was?" Her eyes widened, capturing light from the tall windows and shining like liquid gold. "Norman Martin has never said anything definite, but I've gotten the idea that he would like to—well, court me."

"He'd more than like to, sugar. He's decided that you're his private property and he as much as told me to back off."

This time her flush was indignant. "Why, he has no right to do that! None at all. Of course, you're not going to listen to him."

"If I wanted to see you socially, Amber," Nick said, ignoring the sudden flash in her eyes, "nothing Martin said would keep me away."

"I see."

He had the feeling she did, and gave a silent sigh. Dammit, he'd let her get under his skin. He couldn't stop thinking about her, and for more reasons than the obvious. He wanted her, yes. No doubt about that. He couldn't sleep at night for wanting her, closing his eyes and seeing her exquisite face lit with passion for him, her cat's eyes glowing up at him when he kissed her, and her breasts—creamy pale, rose-tipped in the most delicious of hues—*Christ.* He was making himself crazy just thinking about it, and her sitting across the room perched on the edge of his desk and swinging one foot like she hadn't a care in the world didn't help. She probably hadn't even thought of that afternoon since it had happened, while he was driven insane every time she walked near him or he happened to catch a whiff of her perfume.

Snapping her fingers, Amber said for what was obviously not the first time, "Nick? Nick, are you listening to me?"

He ground his teeth. "No, not really. Sorry. What'd you say?"

She looked exasperated. "Nothing, except that Norman Martin has invited himself over to our house this evening, specifically to talk with me. Do you suppose he wants something?"

"Yes—you."

Nick's blunt reply took her aback apparently, for she gave a visible start. "Why do you say that?"

"Has he ever suggested that the two of you would make a good couple?" Nick asked sarcastically, and saw from her quick flush that he had. "That's why I say that. The man wants you, and he wants you badly. I'm surprised he hasn't appeared on your doorstep with a forty-carat diamond ring in his hand."

"Forty carat? That's rather large for an engagement ring, I think. Too gaudy. I prefer something in the, oh, ten-carat range."

"I'll bet you would," he said, levering his body away from the wall with a surge of restless anger.

"Oh Nick, don't be so grim. Don't you recognize a joke when you hear one?"

"Maybe not. Not where Martin is concerned anyway, not anymore. The man has been giving me hell all week, in such subtle little ways that I'm supposed to be too stupid to notice." His mouth flattened into a grim line. "I have noticed, and I don't like it worth a damn."

Amber regarded him with that remote gaze that could infuriate and entice him at the same time. "Perhaps you're reading things into your disagreement with him that aren't there. I know I asked you to investigate my suspicions that someone is trying to harm Papa, but I never meant Nor—Mr. Martin."

"Oh, you have someone specific in mind? Why didn't you tell me, so that I don't have to waste time figuring it out?"

"You're impossible." Amber's foot swung faster, and her hands knotted into small fists around the letter opener. Nick crossed to his desk and took it from her, laying it aside.

"Just so you aren't tempted to throw it at me," he muttered, and saw her eyes light with anger.

"Where did you go to school, anyway," she asked briskly, "Harvard? You're awfully good at figuring out my next moves."

He grinned in spite of his irritation with her. "As a matter of fact, I did go to Harvard." When her eyes widened with shock, he added, "And Yale, and West Point, and Virginia Academy—get the point?"

"You . . . you attended all those schools?"

"Yeah, for a short time, anyway." He shrugged. "I had more on my mind than education then."

"You were—"

"Sent down," he finished for her, "from every one of them."

"Why?"

"Fighting, usually. Sometimes a woman. Sometimes plain old cussedness. Believe it or not, I used to be ornery."

"Why is it I have no trouble believing that?" Her smile was faintly wry. "It's hard for me to reconcile a brash young man with the serious man I always see now."

"Is it? It shouldn't be. I've never been very good at following direction."

"You're good now."

"Desperate. There's a difference, Amber, a big difference."

"Yes," she said slowly, "I'm beginning to understand that."

"Are you?" He shook his head with a smile. "I doubt it. You haven't ever had to understand the unpleasant."

"Would you please stop trying to fit me into this cubbyhole you've made for me?" she flashed irritably. "I'm not a hothouse plant that has to be coddled and tended like you seem to think, nor am I the spoiled little rich girl that you'd like to make me."

"Right," Nick drawled sarcastically, "you're just a sweet, hardworking girl with no money or rich papa—"

"Stop it!" Amber surged to her feet, her small hands knotting into fists at her sides as she glared at Nick. "I can't help it if my father has money or if he's been generous with it. And I can't help it," she added in a tortured tone, "if you've lost everything you've always known. All I know to do is go on, Nick. Why can't you see that?"

"What do you think I'm doing?" Raking a hand through his hair, he turned away from her. It was galling that she could see that much of him, and he resented the fact that he couldn't hide his bitterness. "I am going on, Amber. I'm doing all I know to do, too."

"So why can't you forgive me for doing the same?" She came up behind him and put a light hand on the bunched muscles of his arm. "I can only make my own choices, Nick, not others'. If Norman Martin has other plans, they're his, not mine. If my father's money upsets you, it's his, not mine. My choice is to be with you, no matter what you have or don't have. Is that so wrong?"

Whirling, he glared at her. "Tell me why. I don't have the least idea why you'd want to be with me. I have nothing. I probably will never have anything but my pride, and that's damned inconvenient at times."

"Yes," she agreed quietly, "it is. I can't tell you why I love you, only that I do. Isn't that enough?"

Almost groaning, he shook his head. "No, it's not enough. It won't be enough if I can't feed you what you want to eat or dress you in the clothes you like to wear or—"

"You think I'm that selfish?" she cut in angrily. "Is that how I appear to you—greedy and self-indulgent?"

Frustrated, both with himself and her, Nick didn't answer. He moved to stand behind his desk, not trusting himself to be so close to her.

"No," he said evenly, "that's not how I see you. But it doesn't matter. The world will see things differently, and I don't want it said that I was after your money."

"How noble. I'm impressed. And here I thought your emotional range was composed of only irritation and rage. It's heartening to find that you can be noble as well."

"Isn't it?" His dark brow lifted mockingly. "Sort of reaffirms your faith in humanity, doesn't it?"

"Damn you, Nick Windsor," Amber said in a trembling whisper. "You deserve to be alone."

"That's what I've been trying to tell you, sugar."

When she left his office, her spine rigid and her chin lifted in that defiant tilt that usually made him smile, Nick sagged against the edge of his desk, his head down. Another one of these confrontations, and he'd forget everything he knew he should remember. He couldn't stand hurting her, though he knew that if he did what he wanted to—what his *heart* wanted him to do—he'd be making the biggest mistake of both their lives. It was madness to think he could ever fit into her world again, not anymore. That was all behind him.

Maybe Martin was the better man for her. He had a gentlemanly reputation with the ladies and Jenné trusted him. That ought to mean something. Norman Martin could give Amber the kind of life she was used to, the kind of life she deserved. *He* couldn't, even if he had money again. There was something in him that had died during the war, something he'd never get back. He wasn't willing to risk being vulnerable again. Watching loved ones die had left him crippled. He wouldn't allow himself to be hurt again. Ever.

Straightening, Nick stared down at the open ledger on his desk without really seeing it. He had work to do, and he needed to forget Amber, forget everything that interfered with his future.

Amber fought angry tears as she climbed into her carriage and told Roger to take her home. After leaving Nick alone for over a month, she'd thought he would be glad to see her. It was more than apparent that he wasn't, that he was even farther from her now than ever before. Frustration made her angry, but love made her desperate.

If she didn't know the battles he fought with himself, she'd have given up by now. But she did know, much more than he'd told her. Jessamy had revealed a lot inadvertently. She could see the pain Nick used as armor, and knew his struggle might never lead him to her. It was a chance she was willing to take, just to be with him.

But the cost was proving heavier than she'd ever thought possible. . . .

"Miss Amber," Roger said as the carriage halted in front of her house, "I heard that Mr. Martin would be visiting you this evening."

Surprised, Amber glanced at him. Roger rarely made comments on her personal life. "Yes," she said, "that's correct."

"And I heard," Roger continued, looking directly at her, "that he favors you a lot."

"I've heard the same." She accepted his hand down, and puzzled, looked up at his broad, stolid face. "Is there something you're trying to say, Roger?"

"Yes, ma'am, there is. Be careful."

"Careful?" She was astonished. "Careful of what?"

"Not what, Miss Amber—who."

"Roger, what are you trying to say?"

"That Mr. Martin wants you powerful bad, and I don't think he much minds how he goes about it."

Half exasperated with his oblique words, but intrigued, Amber shook her head irritably. "You aren't making any sense. What on earth would Norman Martin do that would be terrible?"

"I didn't say it would be terrible, but I think you'll find out what it is before anybody. Just be careful, Miss Amber, and don't take everything at face value."

No matter what else she asked or said, Roger would not elaborate. He simply shrugged his massive shoulders and told her she'd know soon enough. Thoroughly exasperated, Amber went into the house without looking back at him.

"Just like everyone to be so darn *mysterious*," she muttered. "I wonder why I bother asking questions."

Her temper had eased only a little by the time Norman Martin arrived that evening, and in spite of herself, she couldn't help but recall Nick's words as well as Roger's warnings. Martin must have sensed her uneasiness, because he took her hand in his and smiled warmly.

"Miss Jenné—Amber—I see that you're not yourself this evening. Have I come at a bad time?"

Glancing at her father, who stood by the mantel with a drink in one hand, Amber shook her head and managed a smile. "Of course not, Norman. Papa and I were expecting you."

His smile widened. "My primary purpose of visiting is not, I fear, to see your esteemed father, though I do enjoy his company. I came specifically to see you."

"So I was told." Amber shifted slightly, removing her hand from his grasp. "There's not a thing I can tell you about the business, I'm afraid," she said lightly. "You'll have to talk to Papa if it's important."

"On the contrary, this is vitally important, and I cannot imagine talking to Henri about it." Martin seemed amused, and the look he gave Henri Jenné was conspiratorial. Amber's unease grew by leaps and bounds.

"Brandy?" she asked to cover her nervousness, and stepped to the inlaid cherry liquor cabinet. Crystal decanters clinked with a brittle sound as she uncorked two before she found the good French brandy her father imported. The potent fragrance wafted up as she poured two fingers into a small snifter and turned to hand it to Martin. He was right behind her, and she gave a small start of surprise. "Oh—"

"Here, let me pour you some," he interrupted smoothly, and reached for the decanter. He smiled at her as he poured. "Now, let's make a toast before I say what I came to say."

Amber glanced uncertainly at her father. Henri was looking at the contents of his glass as if they were the most fascinating he'd ever seen, and she sighed. Of course. He would not interfere in any way, even to let her know what he preferred her to do. Or not do. That was her father.

Martin was lifting his glass and Amber did the same, forcing a smile. "To our futures," he said, his gaze on her, making Amber squirm, "and the future of Southern Warehouses and Company—may we all live happily ever after."

Amber laughed. "Happily ever after, Norman? I'll certainly drink to that!"

Martin was grinning, and Henri smiled at them as he lifted his glass in a silent salute. The brandy burned a path down Amber's throat and warmed her stomach, and she was glad she'd only taken a sip. It was potent stuff, and she had a notoriously light head for drinking.

When Henri emptied his snifter and set it on the table near his easy chair, Amber saw with dismay that he intended to leave the parlor. She sought frantically for a reason to make him stay, but nothing came to mind. She watched silently as he murmured a good evening and something about two young people needing to be alone, then departed.

As soon as the carved oak doors closed behind him, Martin took Amber's brandy snifter from her hands and set it aside. "Here," he said, "let me hold your hands for a moment. They're actually cold, sweetheart. It's still warm, so I can only assume that you're nervous. Am I right?"

"How astute you are," Amber said faintly as he took both her hands between his palms and held them. "Why all the drama?"

"Drama? Hmm. I'd thought of it more in the light of suspense or romance."

"Had you?" Amber flicked him a glance, and saw that behind his smiling facade, he was completely serious. She sensed that he was about to steer the conversation in a direction she wanted to avoid, as she had known he would the moment he'd arrived and looked at her so keenly. Amber had no intention of being caught in that uncomfortable trap.

"How about a mystery instead?" she teased, pulling away from him with a gentle tug. She reached for her glass and lifted it, watching him over the rim. "Or even a tragedy? Let's see what we could call it—I know, 'Adams Avenue Annihilation,' something on the order of *Hamlet,* or *Macbeth.* Just think what fun we could have with it."

"Amber," Martin began tightly, though the smile never wavered on his handsome face, "this is really serious."

"Serious? My, then it's definitely a tragedy. Something vile and modern, maybe, involving a tale of star-crossed lovers and murder most foul— Norman? What's the matter?"

His face had altered subtly, the attentive smile becoming a grimace. Quickly recovering, Martin said, "Nothing, only I do detest such melodramas. Those should be relegated to the vicinity of the Orpheum Theater, I'm afraid."

"Then I take it you don't read Poe or Dickens."

"You take it correctly."

"A pity. You should. Those authors have every element of human emotion in their works."

"Amber, I didn't come here tonight to talk to you about your favorite authors."

She tilted her head to one side, gazing at him for a moment. His face was flushed with color, his neat brown hair plastered to his head without a single strand in disorder. He reminded her of a solemn puppet.

"All right," she said with grim resignation, "why did you come?"

She wasn't surprised to hear him say, "To beg you to do me the honor of becoming my wife.

"I know this is sudden," he continued, "but I've longed to talk to you since you reached eighteen. I just never felt it was the right time."

"What's changed, if you don't mind me asking?"

He seemed startled by her question, but smiled at her. "My circumstances have recently improved to the point where I feel I could support you in the style you deserve. You are a woman who should wear silks and satins, wrap yourself in furs and expensive French perfume—why are you looking at me like that?"

"Oh, you just . . . just reminded me of something someone said not long ago, that's all." Amber felt suddenly hot and cold at the same time, and wondered if her distress showed. She hoped not. Nick Windsor's words had been brought back with a sharp clarity.

Martin's handsome face creased in a frown, but he only said, "Not another marriage proposal, I hope."

Amber's laugh was short. "No, far from it. Far from it."

"Miss Jenné—Amber—I know I cannot hope to expect the love from you that I feel, but if you could find it in your heart to consider my proposal and think of—"

"Martin, please. This is so sudden, as you said, that I find myself quite at a loss. I'd not considered marriage, and for you to flatter me with such a declaration is more than I can think on at the moment. Do you suppose I could have some time to think about it?"

"Then you will consider it?"

Amber felt suddenly panicked. "I said, just give me time to think, please."

"Of course." Without warning he swept her into his embrace and kissed her, and Amber stiffened. His mouth was wet and warm and covered her lips until she couldn't breathe. She pushed against him with both hands, but Martin held her fast. The evidence of his arousal nudging against her had the opposite effect than it had with Nick, and she began to struggle more frantically.

"Let me go!" she gasped, shoving at him, but he held her firmly. His mouth scoured her lips with frantic urgency as she tried to get away. Her hair came loose from its pins and fell down her back in a tangle, and he wound his hands in it to hold her still.

"You know you want this," Martin muttered, tightening his grip until she cried out angrily. "You'd never waste yourself on some worthless bum like Windsor. It'd be a crime—"

"Norman! Mr. Martin. *Let me go.*"

Finally perceiving that her movements weren't those he desired, Martin stopped kissing her and lifted his head. His blue eyes were cold and hard with desire, and he was breathing heavily. "One day, sweetheart," he murmured, "you'll ask for more."

Repulsed, Amber could only break away from his hold and back off. She bumped into the liquor cabinet and stopped.

"I'd like for you to go now," she choked out. "Please."

"When will you give me your answer?"

"My answer?"

He smiled. "You'll be the queen of Memphis, Amber, as my wife. We'll have enough money to do anything we want, and our social position will make every old tabby who's ever said the least little thing fade into nothing. We'll have the entire town at our feet."

She stared at him in stunned disbelief. After what he had just done, did he truly think she would seriously consider any proposal of marriage?

"Mr. Martin, you have not behaved like a gentleman," she managed to say. "I don't believe that I owe you any explanation."

His eyes narrowed slightly. "You're angry because of a kiss? It's not as if you hadn't invited it, you know, looking at me like that and wearing that gown."

Amber glanced down at her plain cotton gown. It fit her tightly across the bodice, not revealing any more of her bare skin than a dress she'd wear to church. The tiny puffed sleeves left more of her arms bare than her décolletage, and she looked back up at Martin furiously.

"Leave, Mr. Martin. Before I call Roger to escort you out."

Disbelief was mirrored on his face, but he shrugged. "All right. I've upset you, and I'm sorry. I'm a man, Amber, and I only reacted as any man would to a beautiful woman."

"I sincerely hope most men are gentleman enough to show more restraint," she said coldly, rubbing her hands over her bare arms in a nervous, furious gesture. "You've leaped on me like a mere schoolboy," she added. "I don't appreciate it."

"I can only say that I was overwhelmed by your beauty," Martin said stiffly.

"Why this time, and not the countless others that you've been in my 'overwhelming' presence?"

Ignoring her tart tone, Martin stepped to the parlor door and paused to look back at her. "Because I've only recently known I was in love with you. That's the best—and only—excuse I can offer."

When the door had shut behind him, Amber wondered if she'd overreacted to his kiss. Maybe he hadn't meant to be so pushy.

"And maybe," she muttered after several minutes of thought, "donkeys can fly."

Norman Martin had done exactly what he'd wanted to do, and she knew it. What puzzled her was *why*. Why had he decided she was the love of his life, when he'd always been too busy for her before? Not that she'd cared, but it was an odd coincidence that now, after she'd fallen in love with Nick Windsor, Norman Martin had declared himself in love with her.

Amber came to a swift decision. She intended to confront Nick and find out once and for all how he really felt about her. It was time he quit hiding behind protestations of North versus South. And it was time she discovered just how deeply she felt about him, too.

After several moments of thought, she hit on the perfect plan. She hoped.

* * *

The warehouse smelled dusty and empty. Amber in
haled a deep breath for courage, and pushed open the
door to the section where Mr. Dyer had said she could
find Nick. She was taking a big chance and she knew it
What if he didn't want to see her? What if he laughed a
her, or rejected her? Well, she'd been over and over this
a hundred times in her imagination, and nothing could
be worse than not knowing the truth.

"Here goes nothing," she muttered softly as she
stepped through the door.

She found Nick at his desk in the farthest section of
the warehouse, frowning down at neat rows of figures
He looked restless, shoving a hand through his hair a
few times and muttering under his breath. When he fi
nally looked up, she pasted a bright smile on her face.

"What are you doing here?" he asked before she
could speak.

"I thought I'd cheer up your day. Any objections?"

"A few."

"Alphabetize them for me." She perched on the edge
of his desk, accidentally scattering a small tray of pencils
across the floor. She shot to her feet again. Her dismay
must have shown on her face, because Nick grinned.

"You don't shop alone, I hope. I can just see you in a
china store picking out a new pattern from the broken
remains."

"Roger usually goes with me." Amber managed an
other bright smile. "I came to steal you away for a
while."

Gesturing at the paper-strewn desk, Nick lifted a
brow and said, "I've got a lot of work to do, in case you
didn't notice."

"I noticed." She shrugged. "It'll still be here when
you're through eating lunch."

"That's what bothers me." Nick rose to his feet.
"Look, I know you're here for a reason, so spit it out.
You didn't come just to visit me."

She drew an imaginary line on the polished square of
esk that was visible between two stacks of paper, drag-
ing her finger over the surface. "You're wrong. I came
ıst to visit you."

"I'm flattered. But still busy. It'll keep, I imagine."

"No, Nick, it won't." She looked up at him through
eiled lashes. "Aren't you even curious as to the rea-
on?"

"God help me, I know I'll regret asking this, but all
ight—why did you come?"

"Walk with me and I'll tell you," Amber teased, and
Nick smiled slightly. His dark eyes thinned as he raked
er with a bold stare, and she gave a small twirl, warmed
y his admiring appraisal. "Like it?" Rose-colored vel-
et whisked around her ankles, and the collar of the lacy
louse grazed her chin.

"What's not to like? You'd look good in a tow sack,
ut in a Paris original, you're the best."

"I detect sarcasm," Amber said with a loud sigh.
What's the matter now?"

"Amber, what *are* you doing here? I'm trying to
vork." Nick gestured at the acres of cargo stored in the
varehouse. "If I don't work, I might get fired, and if I
et fired—"

"I know. You won't get to Texas." Amber took his
and and held it for a moment, smiling at him. "Don't
•e a grouch. It's time for lunch, and I thought we could
o on another picnic."

Silence fell, charged with a sudden awareness of what
ad occurred at the last picnic they'd shared. Amber
aw it in his eyes, in the swift, startled glance he gave
ier, and wondered if he would be quick to reject her
gain. Then his shoulders relaxed, and she drew in an
insteady breath of relief.

"In November?" Nick shook his head, a rueful smile
urving his mouth. "I suppose you ordered sunshine and
varm breezes for this."

"Yes, but I didn't get them, so we're going to have a picnic indoors."

"Indoors."

"Come on. This will be fun."

"I'll bet the lions said the same thing to the Christians," Nick muttered, but he allowed her to drag him along.

Amber felt that peculiar lightness that always infused her when she was with Nick. His impenetrable masculinity drew her like a magnet, yet held her at bay at the same time. She could tease him, laugh with him, even be angry and fight with him, but there was a part of him she could never touch, and it intrigued her.

Even now, when he was smiling at her indulgently and letting her coax him into doing something he didn't want to do, he held out on her. There was a wariness in his eyes that warned her away, but only succeeded in luring her closer. He was so contained, so self-controlled. There were times she felt as if she would never truly reach him.

When she showed him the spot where she'd arranged their private picnic, he was amused, and the expression in his dark eyes warmed her for a moment.

"This it? Not bad," he commented, looking at the elegant blanket spread in a remote corner of the dusty warehouse. Gas lamps shed faint light. The rich fragrance of stored spices permeated the air. A silver-branched candelabra had been lit, and an array of delicacies temptingly arranged on the blanket.

"*Not bad?*" Amber echoed, then laughed. "You love it and you know it. Every man likes being pampered and today it's your turn." She held her breath when he regarded her efforts for a long moment, then shrugged.

"Just don't tell the fellas, all right? I don't want to listen to their remarks the rest of my days."

"They'd only be jealous. Here," Amber said, patting a pillow on the spread. "Sit here."

Nick sprawled on the spread with the pillow behind

is back and locked his hands behind his head. He
watched Amber through half-closed eyes as she arranged their picnic on elegant china plates, shaking his
head and smiling.

"You went to a lot of trouble."

"No," she said honestly, "Roger went to a lot of trouble. I just thought of it. He arranged most of it."

"Then maybe I should kiss him instead of you."

Her eyes danced with laughter. "Do that. It'd be great
fun to watch him make Irish stew of you."

"I always knew women were the more vicious of the
species."

"You're probably just kidding, but it's true. Ever seen
two women who wore the same gown to a social? It can
get pretty mean, I'll tell you."

"What makes you think I was kidding? I've always
thought it was too bad that a man couldn't bottle some
of that and use it to his advantage."

"You already have enough weapons," Amber said,
her breath stalling when he leaned close. She could feel
the impact of him on her senses, feel the heat emanating from his powerful, lean body, making her feel light-
headed and heavy at the same time. His eyes looked
almost drowsy, and there was a curious intensity in his
gaze that mesmerized her.

"Tell me something else, Miss Jenné. Tell me how it is
you manage to turn me inside out whenever I'm with
you."

Amber looked away, trying to keep a tight hold on
her reaction to him. She pushed a strand of pale hair
from her eyes with a quick, feminine gesture that made
him smile; she glanced back and returned his smile.

"I don't know. Maybe I'm just lucky."

"I think you plan it."

Her heart raced. "Maybe I do. God knows, I've tried
hard enough."

"You make it look so easy." He sat up and ran a hand
over her arm. Sliding his fingers through hers, he pulled

her toward him. "You know," he said softly, tracing
finger over the curve of her eyebrow to her cheek, "th
could be dangerous. There's no one else in this part c
the warehouse. Or did you already know that?"

Amber swallowed. It was hard to breathe with him s
close, his hand touching her lightly and his breath feath
ering over her skin in a heated caress.

"I already . . . knew . . . that everyone would b
. . . at lunch."

"Schemer." He kissed her, his lips lightly brushin
over her mouth. "Diabolical schemer." His hand sprea
over the soft skin of her neck, fingers tunneling into th
cluster of hair she'd pinned there, loosing it to fall ove
her shoulders. "You should be properly scolded," h
murmured against her ear, sending shudders throug
her at the whisper of his breath. Her head fell back.

"Yes," she whispered, shivering when his tongu
touched the gentle whorls of her ear. It was a deliciou
sensation, the warm, wet probing of his tongue and th
heated whisk of his breath that sent every nerve she ha
into spirals of appreciation. He kissed her ear, the
lifted her heavy hair and kissed the back of her neck
Her arms lifted, curving behind his neck to hold him
Suddenly she felt him stiffen in her embrace.

He drew back, swearing under his breath.

"God. What's the matter with me? I know better tha
this." He closed his hands into fists. "I shouldn't even b
here alone with you." Sitting back, he regarded her wit
smoldering eyes as she struggled for composure.

She cleared her throat and busied herself with puttin
food on china plates. "Chicken?" she said, holding out
plate.

He gave her a startled look, then a faint smile curve
his mouth. "Yes." He took the plate. Amber plopped
hefty piece of fried chicken on it. It had been sliced an
breaded, then fried to a golden brown, and smelle
warmly delicious. Nick eyed it, then looked up at her

"How did you know I haven't had any good fried chicken since . . . in a long time?"

"I'm a good guesser. Pensée is usually not as good with it as Aunt Leala, and she always wants to cover it with some kind of fancy sauce, but I think she did well."

"She did, indeed. Delilah—she was our cook—used to fry up so much chicken I'd make myself sick trying to eat it all."

Amber knelt on the satin spread beside him and piled more food on his plate, then sat back on her heels. "Tell me about the Clover Hill you remember."

He scowled and shook his head. "It's gone. There's no point in talking about it."

"It's gone, perhaps, but not forgotten. The house must have been large, and I understand that the front lawn was carpeted with red clover every spring and summer."

Nick shrugged, staring down at his plate. After a moment he cleared his throat. "There were wild roses that climbed over the fences, falling in clusters of blooms every year. I used to pick them for my mother. One year I got a good handful of this shiny green plant that I thought was pretty, and kind of wrapped it around the roses." A faint smile curved his mouth, and he looked up at Amber. "It was poison ivy, but she never said anything. She just took my little bouquet and told me how thoughtful I was, then sent me to Celine to have her give me a botany lesson and treat my hands with kerosene and camphor. I got to wear cotton gloves, too."

Amber laughed. "How old were you?"

"Maybe five. I remember it well, because I thought it was a treat. My brothers cried because they didn't get any gloves like mine."

"Did you share?"

"Of course not. I was the one who picked the ivy, so I got to wear the gloves. I did tell them they could get gloves of their own if they picked a pretty bouquet for

Mama, but they weren't as smart as me. They picked clover and violets, and all they got was a thank-you."

"Aren't you the clever one."

"Smart as a whip." He grinned at her. "When it started itching, though, I sure didn't feel smart."

Amber laughed. "Eat your chicken, Mr. Scholar. I'm impressed already."

"You don't sound it. You sound irritated, like most women get when a man plays with his food."

"It's a waste."

"So it is, sugar, so it is." He glanced up at her, and the sultry passion in his dark eyes made her heart thump so hard she was certain he could hear it. Or feel it.

Amber swallowed, then said as lightly as possible, "We are talking about food, aren't we?"

"Aren't we?"

"Maybe," she said in a rush, "I should tell you why I came to find you today."

Nick leaned back again, watching her intently as he tore off a strip of chicken and chewed it slowly. "Go ahead. You've fattened me up for the slaughter—have at it."

"It's nothing like that. I mean, not anything dangerous or terribly involved." She smiled nervously. "I thought maybe you'd trade me a truth or two."

"Trade? Am I dealing with a merchant?"

"I didn't mean it like that. I meant—darn it, Nick, you always make me say things I don't mean. I meant that I want you to tell me the truth about something very important.".

"Which is?" He set his plate down on the spread. She leaned forward and popped an orange wedge into his mouth, trying to appear calmer than she felt. His eyes were dark and unfathomable; Amber squirmed under his steady regard and looked away.

"Which is—how do you really feel about me?"

"Dammit, Amber, are we back to that again?" He raked a hand through his hair in the gesture she'd come to recognize as a stall for time. "I told you—I was wrong. I should have had more restraint than I did. I shouldn't have made love to you when I knew . . . I knew I wouldn't be staying. It doesn't matter how I feel about you, can't you see that?"

"No. I can't see anything like that. Did you expect that I would?" She flicked a crumb from her skirt, then glanced up at him with a frown. "You care more about me than you'll admit, and I know that."

"So?" His jaw thrust out belligerently. "I never said I didn't care about you. I just said—"

"That you didn't want to marry me," she finished before he could. "I know."

"If you know, sweetheart, why are we having this discussion?"

"Because you care about me. Don't bother to deny it, as I can see you are about to do." She shrugged helplessly. "And don't ask me why I'm demeaning myself to come here and . . . and seek you out. I'm not sure. All I know for certain is that you're too hard-headed and stubborn to take back what you said."

"Has it occurred to you," he asked in a dangerous tone, "that I *meant* what I said?"

"Of course it has. Many times. And maybe you did, in a way, but if you'll recall, you also said you care about me. I have no intention of allowing your pride to get in our way. I'm willing to wait until you think you have enough money to make a difference, though as I've told you—"

"Don't finish that." Nick stared at her in bleak exasperation. "I find it baffling that you would use the word *stubborn* in reference to me, yet ignore it when applied to yourself."

She shrugged. "I never said I was fair. Just that I love you."

"*Love.*" He said the word as if it was foul. "There's a lot done in the name of love that belongs in the gutter."

Startled, Amber stared at him and saw the disillusion

in his eyes. "Yes," she said slowly, "I suppose there is. Do we have to add to it?"

"Amber." The word was a groan. "You're tearing me apart. Have some mercy."

"Not until you do."

Rising to her knees, she leaned forward and put a hand on his chest. His eyes met hers, and he slowly covered her hand with his. Her heart thumped, and she managed a tentative smile at the burning intensity she recognized in his eyes. Lord, she could lose herself so easily in that dark gaze. . . .

Slowly, with obvious reluctance, Nick drew her close, until she half lay across his broad chest. His face was close, so close she could count each individual eyelash; his mouth—that erotic curve of moody temptation— nibbled on her fingertips and made her breath catch. Amber felt herself falling again, falling under the spell he cast so easily. And he didn't even try. That was the worst injustice.

She closed her eyes when he turned her hand over and kissed her palm, his lips warm and inviting against her quivering flesh. When his mouth moved up to her wrist, the movement pulling her closer to him, Amber spread her other hand on his chest for balance and yielded to the silent seduction of her senses.

There was a kind of quiet desperation in his movements as he cupped the back of her head with his broad palm and gently forced her head down until her mouth was a half inch from his lips.

"Damn you," he said hoarsely. "You don't play fair at all."

"All's fair," she murmured, the tip of her tongue flicking out to touch his mouth, "in love and war."

Spotty candlelight wavered, throwing splotches of rosy light over his sardonic expression, then he was kissing her, his mouth hot and hard and driving out every coherent thought for several moments. Somehow—Amber wasn't quite certain how—Nick's hands had shifted beneath her shirtwaist, loosening the hem of the blouse and pulling it up so that his hard, callused palms glided over her in an erotic stroke that made her shiver.

She wriggled appreciatively when his palms cupped her silk-covered breasts, thumbs brushing over excited tips in a lingering caress. He made a rough sound in the back of his throat. When he lifted his head, she saw the desire glittering in his hard, jet eyes.

"Nick . . ."

His name came out in a breathy whisper, sounding like a moan or a plea, or a caress. One muscled arm curved around her back to press her against him, and he was rolling over, pinning her beneath his weight. He lifted his body, palms against the satin spread, and stared down at her.

"I can't fight this . . . I don't want . . . dammit, Amber. Why are you doing this?"

"Because I love you."

He groaned softly and closed his eyes. She saw the muscles in his throat work for a moment, then he opened his eyes and gave her a tortured smile.

"I deserve to be shot. God knows, I hope someone does it soon and puts me out of my misery, but I can't deny that I want you."

Slowly lowering his body, he kissed her again. She put her arms around his neck and held on, opening her mouth for him, dueling lightly with her tongue. He tasted sweet and tangy, and she remembered the orange wedge she'd popped into his mouth. A faint whimper escaped her when his hand returned to her breast and tested the taut nipple with a flick of one finger.

His legs tightened convulsively where he straddled her, and he shifted so that his thighs were between hers. Amber felt the hard proof of his arousal nudging against her, and twisted impatiently to free herself of her heavy skirt and petticoats. As if sensing the reason for her awkward motion, Nick reached down to draw up her skirt, his hand sliding up her leg to the open crotch o her fine cotton drawers.

When he touched her, she trembled, and he muttered something soft and soothing as he began to stroke the tender folds of flesh between her thighs. Amber's arms tightened around his neck.

Nick felt it, that fine trembling that told him she was as eager as he was. Damn. He knew better. He was allowing her to manipulate him, but for the life of him he couldn't resist her silent, welcoming offer. He'd dreamed of her like this so many nights, lying shaking and willing in his arms, her mouth half open and her gold eyes glazed with desire for him.

Bending his head, he circled the silken thrust of a nipple with his tongue, wetting the material of her chemise and making the peak tighten to a rosy bud. He sat up and pulled down the chemise, freeing her breasts. With a move that was slow and almost reverent, he cupped both creamy globes in his palms, gazing down at the contrast of his dark hands on her pale skin. He felt like an intruder on something sacred, and immediately resented the thought.

She was a woman, and he was a man, just as God intended. And he wanted her, wanted to fit himself inside her and hear her pleasure moans in his ear. Slowly deliberately, he bent to tease a nipple with his tongue, sucking it gently into his mouth when she writhed. He trailed kisses between her breasts, then down her narrow torso to the small indentation of her navel. He felt her jerk with surprise and smiled.

"Nick . . . my skirts . . ."

"I have no intention of undressing you in here," he said softly, and had the brief thought that he should stop while he still could. That thought was banished by her hand on him, and he closed his eyes and held his breath as she explored the rigid outline of his body through his snug pants.

He tried to hold back, wanted to prolong the anticipation, but Amber's inexperienced, eager movements hurled him into a heated rush. He fumbled with the buttons on his pants, his mouth covering her lips to stifle her moans of pleasure as his other hand found an erotic rhythm between her thighs. Then he replaced his hand with his body, and heard her soft gasp.

Beyond control now, Nick thrust into her with a hot, delicious slide that made both of them shudder. His body reacted before he thought; he began to move in the swift, shattering cadence of sex, thrusting into Amber with mind-rending fervor.

She responded with an excited whimper that only heightened his own excitement. Accepting his rough kiss with ravenous lips, she arched upward, meeting him thrust for thrust, her body closing around him and hurling him toward release. Nick managed to resist that compelling force until he felt her contractions tighten around him. Then he surrendered with a hoarse mutter.

Drained, Nick sagged against her, aware that he'd lost control once again. When he moved as if to roll away, Amber's arms tightened around him and he stayed, relishing the comfort of her embrace, the slight nuzzling of her lips against his throat and the underside of his jaw. He rested his weight on his elbows and forearms, cradled in her thighs.

He was cognizant of the fact that he'd compromised both of them by giving in to desire instead of common sense, but it was done. Again. He levered his torso up and gazed down at her with a faint, half smile of self-reproach.

"We're both crazy, you know."

"Mm." Amber opened her eyes, golden and lazy and replete with satisfaction. "I agree. Maybe they'll lock us up together."

Nick made an exasperated sound in the back of his throat, but stared at her with amusement. "I doubt it."

Dragging her fingertip from his jaw down the column

of his throat to where his shirt gaped open at the neck, Amber said in the same lugubrious tone, "Too bad."

He grabbed her hand when it trailed down his chest to the open waist of his trousers, wedging between their bodies. "It will be more than too bad if someone decides to come back here and check on us. Come on, sugar—get up."

She allowed him to help her back into her chemise and blouse, tucking the hem into the waistband of her rose skirt, then smoothing it over her legs. She caught his hand when he began to retreat. "No. Not yet. Just one more kiss."

"Amber." He gave an impatient groan. "Just how much do you want from me?"

Her eyes opened wider. "I told you."

"Nothing's changed." He looked away from her. "Nothing. I said I'd marry you, but—"

"But you won't love me." Her voice was mocking.

He gave her a sharp glance and saw the quick, downward drift of her lashes, hiding her eyes from him. He shrugged.

"Yes. I won't love you."

"How safe. And cowardly."

"If you want love and marriage so badly," he snapped, goaded into retaliation, "marry Norman Martin. He certainly hangs around you often enough!"

Amber grew still. Her eyes reflected shock, then pain, and her voice was hoarse. "Maybe I will, Nick. That should ease your conscience a great deal."

He raked a hand through his hair, and his jaw set against the surge of pure fury that scoured him at even the thought. "I didn't mean that."

"No, Nick," she said quietly, "I think you meant every word. I've just now realized that you're not at all the man I thought you were."

He glared at her when she rose in a graceful twist of her body and began to gather up the dishes. Damn her for making him feel like the worst kind of a heel, when she was the one who'd started this. He rose to his feet and buttoned his pants silently, then bent to help her retrieve the dishes.

She stopped him. "No. I'll get them. I wouldn't want you to strain yourself."

His temper exploded. Grabbing her by the upper arms, he yanked her to him, forcing his words out between clenched teeth. "Amber, I didn't ask you to come here. I didn't ask you to love me. All I've ever asked you is to leave me in peace. Why won't you do that? Do you think all you have to do is snap your pretty fingers and you'll get just what you want?" He gave her a shake that made her thick mane of burnished hair fall over her shoulder and into her eyes. "It doesn't work that way, sugar. Not with me. God knows, I'm as weak as any man who has something thrown at him time and again, and I'm not proud of it, but I won't let you force me into something I know won't work."

Her face drained of color, then two bright crimson spots burned on her cheeks as she stared at him. It made him think of a painted porcelain doll. He groaned silently.

"Dammit, Amber, I know I'm a bastard, but—"

"No." She pulled away from him, lifting one hand to stop him. "You're quite right. I should have listened to you. I'm sorry I didn't. I've always been hard-headed. One of my many faults, I've been told."

"Amber honey—"

"Don't, Nick. Just—Just let me leave with what dignity I've got left."

A familiar throbbing began low in his belly, rising until he thought he would choke on it. He watched her silently, wanting to offer comfort but not knowing how. Everything he did or said was wrong; part of him embraced that fact as heartily as part of him rejected it. He didn't want to love her. God. He didn't want to see her hurt, either.

His hands curled into fists as he watched her graceful

movements, the female elegance of her making his insides twist into knots. He didn't dare let himself be drawn into the web she'd fashioned for him. He knew too well the pain of disillusionment and lost love.

Amber turned to face him, flinging back a heavy strand of tawny hair that curled over her shoulder and teased the thrust of her breast. He swallowed hard.

"If you want to see me again, Nick," she said clearly, "you will have to come for me. I won't make myself available again."

He didn't say anything. He couldn't say anything. He stood in silent misery as she walked away from him.

CHAPTER
12

"MISS Jenné is not to be bothered." Martin eyed Nick across his desk. He lifted an elegant, expensively clad foot and raked a match across the sole of his gleaming demiboots, keeping eye contact with Nick the entire time. "You're becoming a vast inconvenience, Mr. Windsor."

Nick found it vaguely amusing; the man's efforts to intimidate him were laughable, at best. He'd always been much more intimidated by drawn sabers and loaded rifles than he had words, anyway. Even those intimidations had ceased to have the same impact after a while. It was taken in course, and so was Norman Martin.

"I'll keep that in mind," Nick said in reply to Martin's blunt warning. "After all, I'd hate to bother her when you're so dead set on doing it."

"What's that supposed to mean, Windsor?"

"I'm not the man who's been showing up on her doorstep six nights out of seven, Mr. Martin. You are."

It was true, and the knowledge burned Nick to the core. He wasn't quite certain why. He'd walked away from Amber, hadn't he? Told her, basically, to go find another man? Yeah, but he hadn't really meant Norman Martin. Something about the dapper, handsome president of SW&C made him edgy.

Martin stared at him belligerently, snarling, "Damn you, Windsor, you're getting entirely too cocky. I know you had your sights set on Amber, but I'd better not see you anywhere near her again. Got it?"

"We've had this discussion before."

With a last, heated glance, Nick pivoted on his heel. He needed to leave Martin's office before he plowed a fist into that smirking face. His entire body quivered with the effort to hold back. He headed for the front door, through for the day. If he ran into Martin again, he might not be able to keep from hitting him.

It was frustrating, knowing that Martin was up to something devious but not being able to figure out what. If the answer was in the ledgers Nick had seen him perusing, the man was damn careful. After hours of investigation, Nick had not been able to find a single error that pointed to manipulation of accounts.

He could suspect Martin of clever juggling with the books, but proving it was a different matter. And until he had proof, he didn't want to go to Henri Jenné.

"Going out, Mr. Windsor?" a soft voice asked, and Nick halted to look down at Dyer.

"Yes."

"Shall I take your messages?"

Nick's eyes narrowed. He didn't like David Dyer, didn't like him at all. The man reminded him of a weasel.

"No. I'm not expecting any messages."

Dyer smiled. "Be careful, sir," he said obliquely, and Nick gave him a faint smile.

"I always am, Dyer. Maybe you should remember that."

A cool wind hit Nick as he stepped outside the offices, and lowering clouds promised rain. November had come in with brisk winds and wet weather. It was gloomy, which matched his mood perfectly.

Since their "picnic" in the warehouse, Nick had seen Amber only from a distance. He'd made it his main objective to stay away from her, knowing how vulnerable he was. It didn't ease his mood any to notice that after the first few times, she made an obvious effort to avoid him, too.

Until today, Norman Martin had seemed a complacent winner. A faint frown creased Nick's brow. Why the sudden warning from him? It didn't make sense. Martin would know that he and Amber had not spoken more than a half-dozen words in the past week. Why the sudden insecurity?

And why, Nick asked himself bitterly, did he care? He should take the money he'd saved and leave. He had enough to last him awhile, and if he took his time and spent little of it, he'd be able to afford a small bit of land. He could always add to it; buy more cattle, hoard the profits, buy land—

A knot formed in his throat. His dream was getting dusty. And worse—tarnished. He wasn't certain why, but the plan to leave Tennessee and go to Texas was beginning to lose its appeal.

Nick kicked at a pile of leaves skittering down the street, then crossed South Main and cut over to Beale. The rain hadn't deterred some of the Negroes, who gathered outside dingy storefronts along the street to talk and play their music. He paused once when he heard a familiar tune; hunching his shoulders against the bite of the wind, he listened to a haunting melody that brought to mind Saturday nights at Clover Hill.

Plaintive and sweet, a poignant tune drifted into the wet autumn night, sung by a half-dozen throats. It was a Negro hymn, a spiritual, and it held a touching beauty that made his eyes water.

As he stood there listening to lyrics of hope and love, a wave of homesickness so intense it was crippling washed over him. He thought of his family. He hadn't seen them in almost eight months. He hadn't wanted to, but now, for some reason, he felt the need to see his mother and Celine and Bryce. Even Jess. He turned away, then jerked when a man stumbled into him, reeling.

"Got a match?"

Nick smelled the sharp, sweet scent of bad liquor. "Yeah." He lit a match, held it up, and was startled by the face illuminated by the small spear of flame. "Moses —is that you?"

Staggering, the former slave from Clover Hill peered up into Nick's face with a puzzled expression. "Do I knows you?"

Nick's throat tightened. "Yes," he said gruffly. "I used to ride on your back when I was a kid. You called me Careless most of the time."

The old man's eyes widened and he gave a wheezing cough. "It cain't be . . . Mastuh Nick?"

"It is. Moses, what are you doing here?"

"Livin', mostly. Dancin' some. Drinkin' a lot." Moses laughed hoarsely. Ragged sleeves flapped around bony wrists when he waved a hand to encompass the street. "This is my home now, Mastuh Nick."

"Your . . . but where do you sleep?"

"Inside a doorway, if I'm lucky. 'Neath some bushes if I ain't." He shrugged. "I works some when I can."

"But Moses, there are places that would take you in and feed you, give you some work—"

"Naw suh, not an old man like me. I ain't good for nuthin' no mo'. I cain't tote loads, and my eyes ain't so good no mo'." He coughed until he doubled up, then straightened. "I had me a li'l shack, but some folks came down and burned it."

Nick thought of the pitiful shanties he'd seen, worse even than the dilapidated shacks of the Irish on the river bluffs.

"You go home to Clover Hill," he said in an angry rush, "and Miss Abigail will see to you. Dempsey's there, and Celine. Old Billy is making everyone miserable, as usual, but he'll give you a warm blanket and a bed."

"I cain't do that, Mastuh Nick."

"Why?"

"That road's too long, suh. Just too long for old bones."

Another wheezy cough made Moses shake like a windblown leaf. Nick shrugged out of his overcoat and draped it over the old man in spite of his protests. Then he stuffed a wad of money into the gnarled, work-worn hand.

"It's not too long when you ride a train, Moses. Now take this and go home. Go home, do you hear?"

Tears welled up in rheumy eyes, and a wordless message passed between old man and young. Moses reached out, and Nick put his hand in the old man's grasp.

"I'se goin' home, Mastuh Nick. Thanks be to God, I'se goin' home."

"Good. Tell my mother to send me word when you get there so I'll know you're safe."

"I will."

Nick looked up and past the old man, slowly realizing that the song had ended and another one had begun. He wondered if he would ever go home, then knew that it would never matter as much to him as it did to Moses.

"'Bye, Careless," Moses said softly, and Nick gave him a half-startled glance, then grinned.

"Don't go getting too cocky, Moses. You've still got to deal with Old Billy."

Rolling his eyes, Moses nodded. "I 'lows as how he'll give me a time, but it's got to be better than this."

"God knows, you're right."

Nick watched the old man walk away, his steps still unsteady and feeble. He hoped he made it home. It would be nice to have a homecoming. It hit him then, how much he wanted to go home. Not to Clover Hill; that was gone for him. But the longing for a home hit him so hard and quick it was almost like a physical blow, and he sagged against a wall. There had to be something more out there for him. There had to be.

Wheeling, Nick walked away from the singers, walking blindly in the growing dusk. Purple shadows faded into indigo, and he still walked without a definite direction. He should have been surprised when he realized he was on Adams Street and the Jenné home was in front of him, but he wasn't. He'd walked the ten or twelve blocks as if guided by an unseen hand, and he acknowledged with a sense of chagrin the part of him that refused to admit the obvious.

A street lamp glowed in the still night, the gas flame flickering inside the pale globe and shedding misty patches of light on the quiet avenue. The two-story house was aglow with light, and Nick tried to envision Amber inside, sitting in front of the fire with a book. A faint smile curved sardonically. More than likely she was pursuing a much more active project. She wasn't really the type to sit and sew a fancy scene on linen, or knit a pair of warm socks. It left his imagination a variety of images to use, none of which involved anything domestic.

He was still standing in the shadows just beyond the street lamp when Norman Martin arrived in a rented hack. Martin got out and spoke to the driver, then the hack rolled away from the curb.

Nick tensed, and felt foolish for waiting in the dark like a spurned lover. If he had any sense, he'd get out of there before Martin noticed him. That would be the crowning indignity.

Yet he lingered, watching as Martin was admitted to the house, the open door throwing a warped square of light across the dead brown grass of the yard. He recognized Celia, saw her reach for Martin's hat and overcoat.

Then the door shut and he was left out in the cold to stare at the house and wonder why he was such a fool.

Nick wasn't sure how long he stood there. He'd

turned to leave when the sound of the front door opening caught his attention. He stepped back into the shadows beyond the street light and watched.

Norman Martin stepped briskly down the walkway to the street, pulling a smart bowler atop his pomaded hair. His three-piece suit was the latest from New York, complete with vest and spats. Quite the dandy, Norman Martin. Nick followed him, keeping just far enough behind to avoid being noticed.

There was no motive save curiosity at first; then Martin went into the Pinch Gut district, keeping to the shadows thrown by the crumbling brick walls of the buildings. That definitely stirred Nick's curiosity. Why would a man like Martin take his life into his hands to go there? It didn't make sense. Most well-heeled gentlemen wouldn't set foot in Pinch Gut. Too many footpads and cutthroats lurked there, as well as the brawls between the Irish and the Negroes. Those were growing more frequent, and elicited a great deal of concern from city officials.

Nick hesitated, watching as Martin pushed open a door and went inside a two-story brick building. The building wasn't unknown to him; his curiosity evolved into full-scale, hard suspicion. He waited several minutes, then crossed the street and went inside.

Restless, Amber frowned out at the rain. It had been raining for three days, and the streets were flooded. Some parts of the city were nothing but quagmires.

Just the day before, Henri Jenné had almost been run down by a wagon that careened around the corner out of control, barely missing him as he stood on the corner of South Main and Beale to wait for Roger. The street in front of the warehouse offices was so flooded, it was impossible to navigate.

A shiver traced icy fingers down Amber's spine as she thought of her father's narrow escape. Someone had to be making attempts on his life. She was as certain as sunrise about it. Yet Nick had done nothing.

Breaking her own rule, she'd gone to the warehouse to confront him earlier that day.

"What are you doing about it, Nick? I'm certain that was a deliberate attempt on Papa's life!"

Nick had given her a maddening stare, remote and unreadable, and said politely, "I'm doing what I can, Miss Jenné."

"It certainly doesn't seem that way!"

He'd glared at her, and a flash of temper glittered in his dark eyes. "Keep your drawers on. I'm doing what I can, for Christ's sake."

Angry and embarrassed, Amber had left his office without another word. He hadn't seemed to care. He was doing his best to stay as far away from her as possible, and it was so obvious it was humiliating. Even Henri had noticed, and that was the final insult.

"Have you had bad words with him, *ma petite*?" he'd asked, and Amber had shaken her head.

"No, not really. We just had a . . . a difference of opinion."

"Ah. *Vive la différence,*" he said, kissing his fingers with a Gallic gesture and a grin, and Amber had found it impossible not to smile at him.

Now, still prowling restlessly in the parlor, she was glad to see her father come in the front door, shaking rain from his hat with snarls of discomfort. She hid a smile as she went to him.

He looked up at her, his snarls subsiding. "*Chérie,* how glad I am to see you. You are the sunshine that brightens my rainy day."

"And you," she said, helping him remove his coat, "are an old flatterer."

"Old?"

She laughed at his look of comic dismay. "No, not old in years, only in wisdom."

"Ah, what a silver tongue you have, my sweet. No onder the men fight over you so."

Startled, Amber half turned, his coat still in her ands. "What do you mean by that?"

Henri put an arm around her shoulders, plucking the et coat from her hands to give it to Celia. The little aid flashed a smile as she took it and disappeared.

"Come help an *old* man dry out, and I will tell you ll." He steered her to the back parlor, his private re-eat. Once settled into his favorite chair with a glass of randy and a satisfied smile, Henri regarded his daugh-er's flushed face for a moment.

"Well?" she prompted impatiently. "Who was fight-g? And what was the true cause of it?"

"I can put little over on you, I see." Henri sipped his randy, then said, "It was, of course, Nick Windsor and orman Martin. They fell out today, and it took three en to pull Nick off poor Norman. Even then, I think e would have completed the beating if not for Roger. hank God we have Roger. The man is a diplomatic enius, for all his sheer size. Few men would think to rgue with him, but I saw a killing fever in that young an's eyes today that I'd not seen in a long, long time. ince the last war, I believe."

"Oh Papa, to you, the 'last war' refers to the one back n 1814."

"So?" Henri's gray brows rose dramatically. "I was a ixteen-year-old boy, 'tis true, but I fought bravely. Men id not have the modern weapons they have now. We ought with what we had, and they were crude." He assed a hand over his eyes. "I thought never to see uch bloodlust in a man's eyes again, and until today, ave not."

Amber couldn't help a shiver. It was easy to imagine Nick with death in his eyes. She'd seen the fine edge he valked at times, had seen him walk away from Alexan-er Steele when his eyes screamed *murder*. She looked t her father's troubled expression.

"What started the fight, Papa?"

"Chance words, I suppose. Neither man would com ment, but George Hopkins told me that it started be cause Martin said he intended to marry you." Henri shrugged. "I believe there was more than that, but Hop kins was afraid to elaborate. Dyer told me that Martin demanded to know why you visited Nick Windsor in his private office today."

"Did he?" Amber smoothed the folds of her skirt with one hand. "And what did Nick have to say to that?"

"According to Dyer—not the best of sources—Wind sor told Norman that it was none of his business, and that he had no intention of allowing anyone to say any thing about you behind your back. From there, the conversation rapidly deteriorated, I believe, with accu sations being tossed back and forth like bullets."

"Accusations?"

"Mismanagement of company funds, for starters." Henri sighed and rubbed at the crease between his brows. "That's when the first blow was struck. Norman hit Nick for saying that he thought him inept at manag ing certain ledger entries, or some such nonsense."

"Do you think so?"

"Think what?"

"That it's nonsense? I mean, Norman is not a clerk after all, but I understand that he won't allow anyone else to enter the figures for certain shipments."

Henri looked at her closely. "You've been keeping up I see. What else do you think?"

"I think that some errors have been made, and I'm not at all certain they're honest errors. Tell me, Papa— do you really think that the money you've lost on pig iron shipments is that much?"

An amazed expression settled on Henri's face. "Who have you been talking to?"

"Nick Windsor."

"Ah."

That one reply seemed to say a lot, and Amber kept her eyes on her father's face. She knew he wouldn't be pleased by her interference, but she couldn't think he could be that displeased, either.

"And how," Henri asked after a moment, "did you and Nick Windsor enter into such a discussion?"

"I asked questions, and he answered them."

"I see."

She was afraid he did, and sighed. "Papa, what is your true opinion of Nick?"

After a moment Henri said slowly, "I think he's an honest man, but one that won't allow himself to become deeply involved with anything or anyone. Not at the risk of himself, anyway."

"Meaning?"

"Meaning, *chère,* that you shouldn't let yourself get too attached to him."

"And you think I'm in danger of that?"

Henri sipped his brandy. "*Oui,* I think that you have already done so."

Amber flushed and looked away. Moving to the window looking out over the courtyard garden in the rear, she stared at the bare tree limbs clacking in the wind. Rain dripped from the eaves in a steady patter.

She turned restlessly. The day of the picnic seemed so far behind her now, and still Nick was no closer to her than before. Every one of her efforts had failed. He'd bought Norman Martin, but not because of her, not really. She'd only been a part of it, and she didn't know what he was thinking. Or wanting.

She'd even tried to make Nick jealous by allowing Norman Martin to court her, but that seemed to have failed as well. Miserably. Instead of bringing Nick to her, he avoided her even more. Now she had to deal with Martin, and she was angry at herself for being so insensitive. She didn't want to hurt Norman, but it was plain that she would have to be blunt or he'd think she really cared for him. She sighed heavily.

"Amber Elizabeth."

She turned with a start of surprise. Henri's voice wa gentle and sad. "Yes, Papa?"

"I've asked Nick to come here this evening. I need t speak with him about his accusations today. If you wisl to stay, you may, but I do not think he will speak freel in front of you."

Her mouth curved in an ironic smile. "That's a ver polite way of asking me to leave when he gets here Papa."

"Do you think so? *Bon.* Then I have succeeded. Don' worry. I have invited him to stay for dinner, and yo may see him then. Now, come here, *ma petite chou,* s that an old man may kiss his daughter."

Amber went to him and kissed his smooth cheek. Al her life she had been able to turn to her father with an problem, yet now when she needed him most, she foun it impossible. Why? Was it because she didn't want t admit just how far her love for Nick had taken her Some, perhaps, but not all. Henri would not condemr her for loving freely, nor for making unwise choices. Bu he would be hurt and disappointed, and she couldn' bear that.

"Je t'aime," she murmured, and Henri laughed.

"Your French accent is execrable," he teased, hugging her. "I should have taught you better."

Amber laughed with him. "I'm an American, remember? I was born in New York."

"And brought up in New Orleans, where only the barbaric speak English." Henri's smile widened when she made a sharp exclamation. "Excellent. Much better accent then, *chère.*"

"You scoundrel. I don't know why I love you so much."

"Neither do I. I'm just grateful." Giving her another hug, Henri glanced at the clock on the mantel. "Nick will be here soon."

"I can take a hint." When she reached the door, Amber turned and paused. "Tell the illustrious Mr. Windsor that I don't appreciate his avoiding me lately. He'll know what I mean."

As she shut the door behind her, she heard Henri say wryly, "I daresay he will."

CHAPTER
13

NICK watched Henri over the rim of the glass of excellent brandy he'd been offered. He knew what was coming. It stood to reason that Jenné would want to know why, in a moment of anger, he had made such grim accusations against Norman Martin. He'd berated himself bitterly for his lack of control, but what was done was done. He thought briefly about telling him about following Martin, then changed his mind.

He shifted position and glanced around the small back parlor where Jenné had greeted him. It was well-furnished and cozy. A gas lamp glowed on the wall behind a wide mahogany desk, and the gleaming floor boasted a thick Persian rug in the center. Damask wallpaper with an embossed pattern covered the walls from the chair rail to the high ceiling, and the rich sheen of wood below lent an elegant touch. Definitely a comfortable room.

"So, Nick," Henri was saying, waving him toward a stuffed chair near the fire, "tell me what's going on."

Nick's hand tightened on his glass, and he sat down and faced Henri before replying. With his long legs stretched out in front of him, he took a deep breath and met the older man's kind gaze.

"I have reason to believe, sir, that someone is stealing from you."

"Stealing from me?" Henri stared at him thought-fully. "What makes you think that?"

Nick fidgeted. "There are discrepancies in the books, and when I tried to check on them, the figures were altered. Someone knows that I'm suspicious and is covering their tracks."

"And you think that someone is Norman Martin."

No getting around that statement. Nick nodded. "Yes, I do."

"I see. Well, I know there is no love lost between you two, but I had not considered that it had come to this."

Leaning forward, Nick said slowly, "Mr. Jenné, I don't make accusations lightly. And I don't trust men who do. But there *is* something going on that's definitely wrong. I have no solid proof who's doing it, only my gut instincts. I'd like the freedom to investigate."

"Gut instincts." Henri frowned and relit his pipe. He gazed into the fire for a long moment, not speaking. The silence wasn't ominous, only thoughtful, and Nick waited. He knew that Henri was trying to absorb all the implications of what he'd said, and it was a tall order.

"Well," Henri said after a long moment, "why don't you see if you can come up with some proof, Nick? Norman Martin and I have been partners for a long time. He's never stolen from me, but I am not stupid enough to trust him implicitly. I've watched him, and know that he's not above cutting corners. I don't want to accuse him unjustly, and will not unless I have solid evidence. I'll trust you to come up with it, if you think he's guilty. But don't let anyone else know what you're doing. This must remain confidential."

"I understand." Nick looked down at the contents of his glass and swirled it thoughtfully. He thought about Martin. The man was definitely up to something; he'd seen enough to make him suspicious, but he decided not to say anything. Not yet. That could wait until he had more proof. There was something else he needed to know first, something that might make Jenné think he was overstepping his boundaries. He looked up at him.

"Mr. Jenné, I want to ask you a question that may seem a little strange at first."

A faint smile curved the older man's mouth. "Does it have anything to do with my daughter's belief that someone is trying to kill me?"

Startled, Nick nodded. "Yes. She doesn't think you've noticed. I've done some checking on my own, but I can't find any solid evidence, only a string of unusual circumstances." He shrugged. "Nothing has happened in the last few weeks to change my opinion."

"Amber is known for wild assumptions on unreliable information at times, but this is one of her most unnerving." Henri paused to clear his throat. "What's even more unusual is the fact that I've noticed some—well, *peculiar* events myself."

"Such as?"

"Such as the gargoyle falling, though I had ordered the grouting checked and repaired only two weeks before. Such as, the *bad* food that was served to me at my office, and even here at home. Such as, the stray bullet that barely missed me one morning on my way to work and was never explained. And yesterday, a carriage nearly ran me down on the corner."

"I see." Nick set his drink down on a table. "Have you discussed this with anyone else?"

"Officer Mahoney at the police station. Perhaps you recall him?"

"Yes." Nick kept his opinion to himself. Officer Mahoney had not impressed him as a man to confide in, but obviously Henri Jenné felt differently.

A lopsided smile twisted Henri's mouth. "I know you must feel other than kind toward Mahoney, but he's helped me in the past. He has some rough edges, but he's a good policeman. He believes in law and order."

Nick didn't reply, and Henri sipped at his drink as he said slowly, "For the first time in my life, Nick, I've

ken to carrying a firearm. *Me*, wearing a pistol in my
st pocket as if I was a common criminal of sorts. It's
diculous. I never felt the need for a weapon even in
e worst part of New York City. Now, in the gentle
outh, I feel the need."

"Whatever the South is," Nick replied, "it certainly
n't gentle. If it ever was, it's become a rough place to
ve, with the new influx of carpetbaggers and Yankee
coundrels. I don't know if you've noticed, but the Pinch
ut district is rougher than ever, with more killings ev-
ry day. The Irish and the Negroes hate one another.
ensions have gotten to the boiling point, and I'm will-
ig to bet something happens soon."

Henri looked alarmed. "Another brawl?"

"Or worse." Nick rubbed a hand over his jaw and
dmitted quietly, "It's gotten so bad that no one bothers
o look anymore when two men fight. Especially if one
f them happens to be a man of color."

"I'm glad to see that it bothers you," Henri said. "I've
nown too many men who profess hatred for the Ne-
roes, or the Irish, or the Italians, or anyone whose skin
r nationality is different. Prejudice causes grief."

"But it's a fact of life. We can't ignore it because we
on't agree with it."

Eyeing him shrewdly, Henri remarked, "Your com-
nents intrigue me, Nick. I'd thought you a man with
lenty of prejudices. Yet you talk as if you have none."

Nick met the old man's steady gaze. "I have my preju-
lices like everyone else. I just don't try to force them on
thers."

"I see. A noble sentiment, if a bit vague."

"Not noble, just cautious."

"At least you're honest. Are you as honest to yourself,
wonder?"

"What do you mean by that?"

"I understand you have an abhorrence for Yankees,
et you say you have no prejudice."

"Not all Yankees. One Yankee in particular," Nick

corrected. "I've no dislike for you, sir, and I've learne
to live with the rest. I've got no choice."

"And you have a choice about the one?"

Nick's mouth tightened. "I suppose you've been tal
ing to your daughter."

"You suppose correctly. Amber tells me that you
brother-in-law chose the other side, and that you ha
him for it."

"Not quite right. I hate him for burning my house an
turning my sister against her family."

"Did he? Somehow, I have the feeling that you're th
only one who's estranged."

A muscle leaped in Nick's jaw, and he struggled
hold his temper. "Sir, I don't feel that this is a matter
discuss with you or anyone else. It's a private affair."

"I understand." Henri set his half-empty glass on th
table beside his chair. "Dinner will be served in a fe
minutes, and I would like to ask you something befor
we go in, *s'il vous plaît*."

Nick sensed what was coming, and wasn't surprise
when Henri asked bluntly, "What are your intentior
toward my daughter?"

He inhaled deeply before saying, "Only honorable
sir. I don't wish to hurt her, or you, so I intend to re
main at a distance from now on."

"Do you?" Henri nodded thoughtfully. "I see. Why i
it that I have the feeling this is not what she wishes. No
you."

"Probably because it's true. I hold a great admiratio
for Amber, but nothing will ever come of it."

"Why?"

The old man's directness startled Nick. He floun
dered for a moment, not quite certain what he shoul
say. The truth would sound trite to this aristocratic gen
tleman, yet anything else would be an insult.

"Mr. Jenné, before the war, I would have courte
Amber as she should be courted, but now I canno
Surely you can see the reasons."

"I suppose." Henri's steady gaze was unnerving, and Nick shifted uneasily as Henri said slowly, "Now, you no longer feel—how do I say this—*worthy* of her? Or some such nonsense as that, anyway."

"It's not nonsense. I could never give her what she's used to having."

"And that is all that matters, heh?" Henri snorted. "I thought I'd reared my daughter to be more charitable than that. Money, with all its privileges, will not suffice for love. And I have seen her unhappy face these past months and know that she bears a great affection for you. Amber is most transparent in her emotions, a great gift. You should cultivate it, young man." He eyed Nick closely. "I find that I'm disappointed in you."

"Disappointed?" Nick shot to his feet, raking a hand through his hair. "Sir, I don't understand. How can you want me to court Amber? I have nothing left."

"There, you are wrong. You have your future." Henri's gray gaze remained steadily on Nick's face. "If you continue as you are now, you have a great future ahead of you. You're honest and dependable, and intelligent. You can do anything you wish to do. Not many men can say the same."

"This is impossible," Nick muttered.

"Nothing is impossible," Henri smiled wryly. "If Amber heard me, she would be angry, but I cannot bear the sight of her sad face much longer. Whatever is between you two, I wish that you would settle it. Ah well. In the end, it is not my wishes that matter, but yours and hers. My young friend, this is a subject that I find very difficult to discuss with you, and I do not want it to come between us. No matter what your decision, it will not interfere with our business together."

"I appreciate that, sir."

"Now, shall we go into dinner before Celia comes to fetch us? Pensée—our cook—becomes quite outraged when we are late."

* * *

Amber tried not to glance at Nick too often, but wa very much aware of him sitting across from her at th long dining room table. With all the boarders ensconce in the new house, the only diners were the three of them. Henri seemed preoccupied. Nick stared down a his plate. There was an undercurrent of tension tha made Amber more quiet than usual.

The clink of silverware and china dishes provided th only sounds, except for the slight hiss of the gas lamp overhead. Amber fidgeted, wondering what had bee discussed in her father's private parlor. She knew tha Henri had wanted to discover the real cause of the dis agreement between Nick and Norman, but there was wary expression on Nick's face that told her they' talked about much more than that. He would hardl look at her, save for a few surreptitious glances whe she first appeared in the dining room. He seemed deter mined to ignore her.

And she was just as determined he wouldn't.

"So," Amber said, her voice sounding overloud in th quiet room, "have you admitted yet that someone's try ing to kill you, Papa?"

Startled, Henri glanced up from the excellent souffle Penséc had prepared. "You are direct, as always, *m petite*," he murmured with a sigh. "*Oui*, we have decide that there may be someone who wishes to do me harm.

"I knew it." Amber glanced at Nick, who was pickin idly at his soufflé with a fork. "Now, maybe you can fin out who, Mr. Windsor."

He looked up at her then, and his black eye smoldered with irritation. "Yes, I suppose I can. Than you for pointing it out to me." He paused, then adde sarcastically, "Miss Jenné."

"Oh, I didn't mean it would be easy." Amber chewe on her bottom lip with rising annoyance. "Don't be s prickly, Nick. I only meant that it should be easier fo you now since Papa intends to cooperate."

"Should be."

Another silence fell, and Henri stared down at his plate as Amber glared at Nick. Her voice was sharp when she said, "Don't be obtuse. I hate it when you're obtuse. You know very well that someone is trying to kill Papa."

Nick's jaw tightened. For a moment he didn't say anything, just looked at Amber across the table. "Obtuse?" he finally said in a half snarl that made Henri look up in alarm. Nick's fork hit the plate with a loud clatter, and Amber stared at him as he rose to his feet. His voice was only slightly calmer when he said, "Miss Jenné, please step into the hall for a moment."

Henri made no protest, but watched silently as Amber rose to follow Nick from the dining room. She cast a quick glance at him, and he merely lifted a brow. Then Nick was pulling her through the door and into the hallway, his hands quick and hard on her arms.

"What do you think you're doing?" he said when he turned her to face him. "Your meddling will only make things worse. If you're trying to impress Papa, forget it."

"Impress—Nick Windsor, you are an insufferable ass." Amber jerked her arm from his grasp. "I've been worried. Just because you haven't actually *witnessed* an accident, doesn't mean that there's no danger. And you've done nothing that I can see."

"You said it—that *you* can see. Has it occurred to you that I may have been guarding him myself?" His voice was a low snarl, and her eyes widened.

"No. I just thought—"

"There's something new. You thinking."

"Don't be insulting."

"Why not? *You* are. I said I'd do my best, but you obviously don't consider that it's good enough."

She sighed. "Oh, it's not that, Nick, honestly it isn't. It's just that I've been so worried."

"So worried that you upset your father? It doesn't sound to me like you're worried, just impatient."

"That's not true—"

"Don't you think I've been trying to find out if someone hates him enough to want him dead? Don't you think I've stayed up nights and gone over every detail I can? I have. And I don't need you to tell me how to do it. If you think you can do so much better, do it yourself. Or ask your rich boyfriend."

"Rich boyfriend?" Amber echoed. "Who is that?"

"As if you didn't know. Who visits you every night, then brags the next day about making you his wife? Who the hell do you think? And while we're on the subject, you might inform your father that you've made your choice and it isn't me. He seems to be misinformed."

"So do you!" Angry, Amber glared up at him. "Or don't you bother *asking* someone the truth before you toss around accusations like peanuts?"

"Who am I supposed to ask? Martin? You?"

"You could try asking me, yes."

"We don't seem to be able to converse without shouting," Nick ground out, and Amber saw the warning flicker in his dark eyes that betrayed his rising temper.

"No," she said sweetly, "we don't. But that's not my fault."

"Dammit, Amber—"

"No, Nick, don't try and put the blame on me. You're the one who avoids me all the time. What are you so afraid of—that you might actually love me back?"

Nick drew in a deep breath and said evenly, "Don't hand me that. You know what I mean, all right, and it had better stop. Dammit, Amber, it was a cheap trick getting your father to talk to me."

"Why, you conceited jackass!" She shoved hard at him, and he let go of her arms and took a wary step back. "Who do you think you are? Do you think I'm so desperate for love that I'd ask my *father* to appeal to you? Damn you, Nick Windsor, I've never seen a more vain man in my life, and I thought I'd seen plenty!"

"I don't doubt that," he said coolly. "I've seen some of the company you keep."

"Which is supposed to mean?"

"Which means, Norman Martin."

"Jealous?" she murmured with a lifted brow. His mouth tightened into an angry slash.

"Jealous of Martin? Not a chance. He's as vain a man as I've ever met."

"And that bothers you."

"Dammit, Amber, he wants to marry you. He has money, if that's what you're after, but that's all I can see that he's got. Except an ego the size of Tennessee."

"Speaking of egos," she said sweetly, "yours doesn't seem to have suffered any major damage. Perhaps it was flattering to you to have me so openly declare my feelings, but I've never been that good at subterfuge. One of my weaker traits."

"Am I supposed to argue with that? Forget it. You've got as much guile in you as a kitten." His voice softened, and he shook his head. "Sugar, you're too damn honest about your feelings. Learn to hide things. If you don't—"

"If I don't, I'll end up like you? That's what I'm afraid of. I don't want to be like you, hiding behind excuses so that I never risk anything. You took risks with General Forrest, but you're too scared to risk anything now."

"This is different."

"I'll say. And you're a coward, Nick Windsor."

He clenched and unclenched his big hands and turned to look down the empty hallway. The gas lamps hissed softly. In the dim light, Nick's face reflected something she'd never seen before. He looked back at her after a moment, his eyes bleak.

"If you want a husband so badly, marry Martin."

Amber paled; her throat ached with hurt and anger. "That's the second time you've suggested that. Perhaps I should take your advice, you pigheaded Rebel."

"Maybe you should. And you're right—I am a Rebel.

And you are a Yankee. We're miles apart in life, Amber. You've no idea what it's been like for southerners, and you don't care. We'd end up fighting all the time if we were together. I've had enough of fighting to last me a lifetime."

"Is that what you think? That I don't know or care?" Amber shook her head. "Where do you think I've been during this war? I've been right here, and believe me, it hasn't been a bed of roses like you seem to think. Maybe I'm from the North, and maybe I *am* a Yankee, but I love the South. I've suffered some of the same deprivations, Nick, and I've done what I can to help. The color of a person's skin hasn't guided my actions, nor where they were born. I've just done the best I can. I've tried not to hate anyone, even when General Hurlburt ordered his troops to *requisition* all our supplies one month, leaving us with a lot of hungry people and no food. It didn't matter to him who my father was or who he hurt—but that was one man, and I don't hate half a continent for his actions. Why do you?"

"Because I'm a pigheaded Rebel."

"And you intend to carry a grudge for the rest of your life?"

"Probably." He raked a hand through his hair and gave her an exasperated look. "Why is it that you always make me sound like an immature brat?"

"Possibly because there are times you act like one."

Nick leaned one shoulder against the wall and looked down at her. "We always end up fighting, when we should be able to talk like normal people."

"Yes." Some of her anger cooled. A slight smile touched the corner of her mouth. "We should be. There's enough hate in the world. Let's not add to it."

"You're a dreamer, Amber Jenné, a beautiful dreamer. Do you think it's that easy for everyone? That all you have to do is wave some kind of magic wand and all the hate goes away?"

"No, I'm not that big a dreamer, but who says we can't start a new trend?"

"You're dangerous."

"Because I believe in peace and harmony?"   ·

"No, because you have a way of making others believe in it." He cupped her chin in his broad palm, and just the warmth of his touch made Amber quiver in response. "Remember," he said softly, "that most folks are a sight more comfortable with their own prejudices than someone else's."

"And you? Are you more comfortable with hate than love?"

"It hasn't come to that."

"No, you just won't admit that it has. Nick—" She put a hand on his arm when he withdrew. "Don't shut me out. Give me a chance to be part of your life."

His hand dropped away. "I can't. Not like you want."

Amber fought to keep from showing how much that hurt, and her voice was thankfully steady when she said, "All right. I suppose I'll have to finally accept that."

"It'd be easier on both of us."

"I hope you're right." She managed a careless smile. "Just in case you're curious—I've not yet accepted Norman's marriage proposal."

"It would be a good idea if you didn't."

Amber smiled. "Didn't? You just told me to marry him. I thought you were so hot on seeing me engaged to him."

"I was mad when I said that. He's not the man for you."

"Oh, and you consider yourself an expert on the right man for me. Thank you. I certainly appreciate your concern, but I have different ideas about it."

A crooked smile twisted his mouth, and there was an uncertain light in his dark eyes. "You usually do, but trust me on this one, Amber. Martin is not the man for you."

Frustration made her look away from him, and she

hoped the pain didn't show as she tried to keep her response light. "Can you tell me why? Just out of curiosity, of course. You seem to know who isn't the man for me, but don't have a clue as to who the right man is."

"For God's sake, I don't know why. I just don't like him. That's all." His eyes narrowed slightly. "You can't be dumb enough to believe Norman Martin's masquerade."

"Why not? I believed yours." Amber stepped just out of range when he reached for her. Pain and anger made her voice husky when she said, "You have no right to say anything to me about the friends I choose. You've made your choice. Now leave me to mine."

She didn't know why she said that, except that the frustrated look on his face eased some of her pain.

CHAPTER
14

🌹 "HE'S gone?" Amber just stared blankly at Norman Martin, not quite comprehending what he'd just said. "What do you mean?"

Martin looked faintly surprised. "Why, I mean that Windsor went to New Orleans. What did you think I meant?"

"Gone? To New Orleans? But when?" Amber felt suddenly cold inside, and she shivered in spite of the warm fire lit in the parlor grate. "Why would he go?"

"The company sent him." Martin stretched comfortably, his blue eyes regarding Amber for a long moment. "You seem upset. Did I misunderstand something? Are you and Mr. Windsor—"

"No," she said quickly, "you haven't misunderstood. I'm just surprised, that's all. Papa didn't mention it to me."

"Well, it was not exactly a sudden decision. We've been needing someone in our warehouses who can work miracles, and Windsor seems to have managed that well enough." The pale gaze turned shrewd. "He asked to go."

Amber cleared her throat. "Did he? I'm glad to see he has such ambition." Her hands were steady when she poured another cup of tea and held it out to Martin. "I suppose he'll be gone a few months?"

221

"A few—no, he's not coming back. Sorry. I thought you knew. I can see that this has distressed you."

"Nonsense." Amber forced a smile. "I was just wondering if he bothered to tell his family."

"I doubt it. He left in rather a hurry. Went on one of our barges, he was so determined to get there quickly. It was almost as if he was running away from something, but then, I've had that feeling about him before."

"Yes. Nicholas Windsor does give that impression, doesn't he?"

She never knew later what conversation followed Norman's disclosure that Nick had gone. She vaguely recalled his kind face and the understanding look he gave her when he left. He must have guessed how she felt; she'd never been that good at hiding her feelings.

Well, this was an answer of sorts. By leaving without even telling her good-bye, Nick had made it obvious he didn't want any part of her. Why did it have the power to hurt so badly?

A sudden thought struck her, and she stiffened. They'd quarreled, and she'd told him to leave her to her own choice, meaning Norman Martin. Surely he didn't think—but of course he did. She'd meant for him to think she wanted to marry Norman! And now he was gone without a word and she had to tell him, had to explain that she'd only wanted to prick him, that she hadn't meant it.

"What am I going to do?" Amber whispered wildly.

She ran to her writing desk, drew out a sheaf of paper and retrieved a pen from the drawer. She stared at the blank paper for a long time, then shook her head.

Impossible. She was no good at writing what she felt. Besides, she wanted to see him.

She put the pen and paper away, her decision made. It didn't take her long to make her plans.

Nick stood on the deck of the barge slugging through the rough waters of the Mississippi. Wind tore at his clothes, and he stood with his legs spread and braced for balance. Damn this slow-moving tub, he thought without rancor. And damn the circumstances that had put him here.

He'd not quite believed Martin at first, then had come the handwritten request from Henri Jenné transferring him to New Orleans by the next vessel leaving the Port of Memphis. He'd barely had time to consider the doubled pay raise before he found himself at the docks and on board an evil-smelling barge that stank of wet cotton and tar.

A caustic smile curled his mouth. Amber would probably tear up the note he'd written her, and he couldn't blame her. If it hadn't been such a golden opportunity to make extra money for a few weeks work, he'd have turned it down. It didn't help any to know that Martin had counted on the hefty bonus as an incentive to get him to leave immediately.

"You'll be retiring to Texas a wealthy man," Martin had said in a jovial manner that hadn't fooled Nick for a moment.

Nick had looked for Roger, but was unable to find him before he left. He'd ended up giving the note to Dyer to deliver to Amber. He'd barely made it down the slick cobblestones of the bluff, listening to the impatient ringing of the barge to signal its departure.

The captain, a burly man with an unkempt beard and eyebrows like a grizzly, had stared at him sourly and mumbled something about company men before he'd had Nick shown to his cabin. Cabin was an elegant word for the tiny space that Nick couldn't even stretch out in. It was stuffy and cramped, and he spent most of his time above deck, standing at the low rail of the lumbering barge and watching the river wash past only a few feet below him.

"Hurry up and wait," he muttered, staring across the moon-drenched river. The heavy barge would take at least a week to get to New Orleans, and he was beginning to wish he'd passed up the offer and stayed in Memphis. Even the torture of being so near Amber was better than the long hours of nothing to do but think about her.

Amber Jenné was a temptation he hadn't been able to resist, and a complication he couldn't resolve. She was more of a threat to him than any Yankee had ever been, because she alone involved his emotions. He'd thought he was past that at last, that he could stuff all his feelings behind him and forget that he had any. Yet Amber, with her saucy persistence, had managed to get to him where no one else had.

Clenching his fist and scraping it over the slick rail, Nick made plans to complete his business in record time, surprising Norman Martin and everyone else. He'd be back in Memphis before the middle of December, if things went according to schedule.

"Are you certain you want to do that?" Henri asked. His brow lifted. "After all, *chère,* the trip is long, and—"

"And I want to go." Amber gazed out the window at the gray day, watching the wind push leaves across streets and lawns. "It will be warmer in New Orleans, if a bit wet."

Henri gave her a sharp look before saying slowly, "All right. I'll be glad to make the arrangements, but I still think it unwise for you to go visiting friends now."

"Why now?" Amber said with an edge to her voice, turning to look at Henri.

The old man's chin set in that obstinate thrust that made Amber groan inwardly. "I know why you go—to find him."

"If you're talking about Nick Windsor, he's not lost, the way I hear it." Amber turned back to the window, feeling her father's gaze boring a hole between her shoulder blades. "I'll take the train. It's faster."

Henri was silent for a long moment before saying, "If

I allow you to go, you will take Roger with you. I'll feel better knowing that he can protect you."

"I'm quite certain I won't need protection, and if I come back at once, I won't need Roger." She didn't tell her father that Roger must stay to protect him from danger, but she knew that he had guessed.

"I see," Henri murmured wryly. "Well, then, since you are so determined, you may go with your aunt Leala when she leaves tomorrow morning on the *City of New Orleans*. She will be your chaperone."

"Aunt Leala is going to New Orleans?"

"*Oui*. She goes to get our old house ready for selling. I told her that others could do it, but she insists that she has things still there she wants to go through instead of allowing strangers to do so." A faint smile curved his mouth. "My sister has always been stubborn, too."

Amber hesitated. "What will she say about my going to New Orleans with her?"

"Probably that you are quite mad."

"And what do you think, Papa?"

Henri's disapproval was evident in his voice. "If Nick wanted to see you, *ma petite*, he would have at least written you."

"Why are you so certain Nick is the reason I'm going? If you'll only recall, I've said many times that I missed my friends in New Orleans."

"Not in the past few months," Henri said dryly, "not since Nick Windsor came to Memphis."

"Pooh," Amber said unconvincingly. "That's not true."

"Close enough." Sighing, Henri added softly, "I want no hard feelings between us, but I cannot give my permission unless you promise to stay with your aunt."

"Of course. I will be delighted," Amber said promptly.

Henri looked at her skeptically, but nodded. There had always been trust between them, and neither would like to see it destroyed now. He sighed. "Go, child, but I only hope you are not going to make—"

"A fool of myself again?" Amber asked tartly when Henri halted in mid-sentence.

"No, a mistake. Though I like young Windsor, I'm not certain I much care for the idea of my daughter making herself too available to him." Henri rose from his chair and Amber turned toward him. "If he cared for you, he would not behave as if he did not," Henri said gruffly.

Amber wanted to fling herself into her father's arms and sob out her uncertainty and anguish. She held back with an effort, not wanting him to know how close he was to the truth.

"We . . . had words," she said lamely. "It's not all his fault that things are bad between us. I—get mad easy."

"I wish I was as certain of pig-iron prices as I was of that," Henri said with a trace of humor that made Amber smile. "You have a sharp, impetuous tongue, and I know that well enough."

"So says my doting father."

Henri held his arms out wide, and Amber stepped into them with a gush of love welling up for him. He understood. He might not have approved, but he would not try to stop her from at least seeing Nick. It was more than she'd hoped for from him.

"Be careful, *chère*," he said hoarsely, rubbing his jaw on her bright, burnished hair. "Do not ask for more pain."

Amber thought it an unnecessary warning. She knew very well that she invited more pain for herself, but she could not stop now. Not until she knew for certain that Nick Windsor did not love her at all.

But once she and her aunt were on the train heading south to New Orleans, Amber began to wonder if she should have listened to her father. His advice was given out of love. He knew too much about her, knew how distressed she'd been by Nick's abrupt departure. Apparently, she was much more transparent than she thought.

Worse, she'd begun to see images of Nick everywhere she looked, his lean frame slouching lazily against a wall or sprawled in a chair, or lounging at a desk in the offices.

There was no escaping the tormenting memories of his hands on her, his insolent mouth touching her lips, her breasts, sparking fires in her that still smoldered and waited. It was agony thinking of him like that, agony at night when she lay in her lonely bed and longed for him to hold her.

"Dear God," she moaned softly, burying her face in her palms and aching with desperation. She was doing the right thing—she had to be.

"Are you ill?" Leala asked, giving her a sharp look, and Amber sat up straight.

"No. Just tired. I'll be all right. Really I will."

"Hmmph." Leala didn't look convinced. "I have a feeling there's more behind your reason to go with me than going through a dusty attic, but I won't ask. Just don't expect me to turn a blind eye, Amber Elizabeth. I don't have many reservations about some things, but watching someone I love grab at heartache with both hands isn't easy to take."

"I know." Amber's throat tightened. "I intend to visit with my friends while I'm in New Orleans."

Leala Jenné gave her a long, searching look. "Be certain you are properly chaperoned. I will not have it said that you are loose."

Amber's lips twitched. "This, from my modern, free-thinking aunt Leala?"

"I have the luxury of free-thinking because I have no expectations in life. I do as I please, but it has cost me more than you can dream. Everything in life has a price, *ma petite*. Try and remember that. Do not be so impetuous that you forget you must still live in this world."

Her aunt's words made Amber wonder if there was

more behind her decision to remain unmarried than she'd ever said, but Leala had turned to stare out the window, and Amber didn't ask. Yes, she knew well enough that there were prices to pay for what one received in life. She just hoped that it wasn't so high she regretted it.

When she finally stood in front of the lacy iron door that was the last barrier between her and Nick, Amber began to remember all the reasons she should have stayed in Memphis. He hadn't wanted her here—why would he be glad to see her?

Streetlights flickered hazily across the narrow, cobbled street. She could hear strains of music and laughter through some of the doors flung open along the avenue. New Orleans hadn't changed in the years since she'd lived here, not so much that she didn't recognize the shadier part of town. She'd come alone, escaping the maid Leala had assigned to her like a bodyguard. Amber glanced down and saw that the hansom cab she'd rented still waited. Just in case.

Just in case he slams the door in my face . . .

"Nothing ventured," she muttered as she rapped sharply on the edge of the door, "nothing gained."

Footsteps sounded inside the second-floor room, and she sucked in a deep breath as the handle turned and opened. Nick stood framed in the open door, his brow lifting in surprise, the dark eyes lighting with a glad gleam before narrowing.

"Amber. What in the hell are you doing here? Is everything all right?"

"Are you going to invite a lady in, or do you want me to explain out here?" she asked, her voice husky with fear that he would send her away.

"God—I didn't mean . . . come in." The door opened wider and he stepped aside, casting a quick glance around the room as she entered. He waved a deprecatory hand. "It's not much, but it's cheap."

His obvious embarrassment endeared him to her. Amber saw the uncertainty in his gaze and the flash of masculine hunger that he couldn't hide. A wave of relief swept through her, making her knees quiver.

"It's perfect. At least you aren't wasting company money on fancy lodgings."

A faint smile curved the hard, insolent line of his mouth into humor. "Guess that's one way of looking at it. Not much of a place to entertain a lady, though, which brings me back to my question—what are you doing here, sugar?"

"Well, I—" She tripped over something—the edge of the rug, maybe. It didn't matter. All of a sudden she was in his strong embrace as he reached out to catch her, and explanations were forgotten as he kissed her.

It was a hard, demanding kiss, drawing out her resentments and pain and any emotion but need. She needed Nick, needed him to want her, to kiss her like this and make her body come alive again. This was the only time she felt complete, felt as if she were a part of the world, when she was with him. Anger, pain, or passion, Nick Windsor could make her feel *some*thing. Amber realized that what had been missing from her life was a real involvement. She'd just gone along on the fringes of everything for so long, nothing held any value for her. Until Nick.

Until this.

His hands were spreading over the small of her back, over the short jacket she wore, holding her so tightly against him she felt the warmth of his lean, sturdy body through several layers of clothes. She was engulfed, lost, drowning in sensuality and need and desire, and Nick didn't wait to ask, but began undressing her, his hands quick and certain on the many buttons and fastenings of her clothes.

Cool air whisked over her body as he removed each article of clothing and tossed it impatiently aside. Amber was vaguely aware of shivering as she stood pliantly in his arms. Then he lifted her up and carried her across the room to the bed.

Leaning over her, he began kissing her again, his mouth moving from her lips to her closed eyes, to her chin and down. She opened her eyes to look up at his familiar dark face. A surge of love for him almost choked her, and she was grateful when he kissed her again and smothered the confession.

She was acutely aware when he stopped kissing her for a moment and rose to his knees on the bed to strip away his clothes with feverish haste. She gave a wordless cry of abandonment, and he soothed her with more kisses, then the sweet luxury of his body.

She cried out again, but this time with the piercing pleasure that he gave her. Panting, she rose to meet his urgent thrusts with eager anticipation. Nick made a rough sound in the back of his throat, and her heart lurched. Their mating was wild and fierce and sweet all at the same time, caught up with the pure release of passion. Amber felt weightless, as if she'd been swept up in a tornado and spun through the air without something solid to hold to. She clung to his broad, muscular back, her hands digging into his slick skin to hold on, hearing his muttered love words in her ear as she moved mindlessly beneath him.

Nothing mattered but this, this connection between them, the closeness they shared and the sweet ecstasy he gave her. For now, it was enough.

When their passion was spent, he held her in a loose embrace, his breath feathering over her cheek as he rested his weight on his elbows and brushed at her hair.

"What are you doing here, love?" he asked softly, kissing the tip of her nose, then the corners of her mouth. His thumb brushed over her bottom lip in a light caress and she smiled.

"Looking for you."

"Looking for— Why?"

He sounded genuinely puzzled, and Amber opened

her eyes to look up at him. Spent passion had softened the harshness of his features, given him a subtle tenderness. His eyes were half hidden by the lazy droop of his spiky black lashes, and there was a sweet curve to the insolent, sensual line of his mouth. She was glad he hadn't flung her own words back in her face.

"Don't you know why?" she whispered, unable to resist reaching up to stroke back a sable strand of his hair.

Nick shrugged. "Not really. It'd be too much to hope that you might have come just because you missed me."

There was an undercurrent of sincerity in his teasing voice, and she reacted to it.

"But I did, Nick. And I had to explain."

"Explain what, love?"

"Why I said— Why did you leave without telling me?" she demanded irritably.

"Not enough time. The barge was about to leave. I wanted to, but I couldn't. I had hoped," he added with a faint trace of mockery, "that you would understand."

"I might have, if you'd been the one to tell me." She lapsed into silence, then murmured, "I couldn't stand it in Memphis without you."

"No one to fight with?"

She smiled and thumped a finger against the end of his nose. "No one mean enough to fight with since you left."

"I've got my own ideas about that," he said dryly, but his eyes crinkled with amusement. "So, you came, what —four hundred miles—just to see this ugly face?"

"Umm-hmm. No one ugly enough left—ow!"

"Don't say it." He laughed, digging his fingers into her rib cage and making her squirm. "I'll make you pay."

"Just tell me something."

"What?" He nuzzled the side of her neck and distracted her for a moment.

To stop him, she took his face between her palms.

"Why did you leave without at least sending me a note?" His surprise was genuine, she could see that.

"I did send you a note. Martin was in such a big hurry to get me down here—you didn't get my note, did you."

It was a statement, not a question, and she shook her head. "No, I didn't. I haven't heard from you since you left."

"I've written you three times." His expression was grim. "I don't guess you got the other two letters either, because I sent them to you in care of the office. I suppose Martin has his spies paid pretty well, to hold back your mail."

"Three letters? My my, you must have had a lot of explaining to do," Amber teased, suddenly grateful that he had actually tried to contact her. He cared, despite his protestations and insistence that he didn't.

Nick's arms tightened around her and he shifted so that his knee wedged between her thighs. He'd pulled a light quilt over them, and it slid as he dragged his palm over her thigh up to the curve of her waist.

"Explanations don't matter now," he said against the arch of her throat, pushing aside a tawny curl with his finger to kiss the ivory skin beneath. "You're here. That's what counts."

"You've certainly changed your mind," Amber said softly. "Is there a reason for this? I wasn't sure you'd let me in tonight, and now—"

"I missed you. I thought about you all the way down the damn Mississippi River, and I sure lord thought I'd never get here." He leaned back, and lamplight reflected in the depths of his dark eyes. "I only beat you here by two days, Amber. What did you do—take a slow train?"

"Not quite. It took a few days to complete the arrangements. My father's subtle way of giving me time to change my mind, I'm sure."

Nick looked startled. "He knows you're here?"

"Of course. You don't think I'd leave and not tell him

where I was going, do you?" She snuggled closer, rubbing a hand over the hard bands of muscle on his chest and stomach. "I came with my aunt Leala. She's getting our old house ready to sell. Papa's the one who made the arrangements for us, and saw to it that the office would give me your address. The telegraph is a wonderful invention, in case you've forgotten that it's so handy."

"Sugar, I cut enough telegraph wires during the war to make that transatlantic cable to Europe and back twice."

"It broke, you know."

"So I heard. They'll fix it, and then we'll have wire service to any spot in the entire world." He rubbed his jaw against her hair. "Progress. Kinda scary, isn't it?"

"Terrifying." She kissed his chest. "Next thing you know . . ." Her tongue flicked out to moisten a trail down his chest to the flat bands of muscle on his belly. ". . . we'll have a railroad . . ." She smiled when he sucked in a sharp breath. ". . . all the way to California." Her heavy hair fell across his thighs, and the quilt slid to the floor, unnoticed.

"Jeez—if you keep that up," Nick said with a groan, "we won't leave this room till we're too old to care."

"Good."

Amber looked up at him, saw the desire in his eyes, which she was sure was only mirroring her own, and smiled when he uttered a husky curse and rolled her over to pin her beneath him.

"Tease," he muttered, then laughed when the twist of her hips made a liar out of him. "Sweet . . . sultry . . . Amber." He kissed her between every word, and when she responded with eager kisses of her own, he took her again.

Their bodies took up the rhythm with perfect harmony, and it didn't matter what else went on in the world as they sought their own private paradise. Amber finally drifted into an exhausted, exhilarated sleep, and didn't even realize it.

"So what are we going to do today?" Amber asked, twisting a thick strand of hair around her finger as she smiled expectantly up at Nick. She'd arrived at his door only a few minutes before, and he didn't have the heart to tell her that he couldn't spend much time with her, though he knew he had to.

He groaned. "Amber, I've got to work. I wanted to be through with this by mid-December."

"Odd, that Norman would say you weren't coming back to Memphis. I wonder why."

"Don't be naive."

Amber looked up at the sharp tone of his voice, and he stifled the impulse to say what he really thought. Better let her figure that out for herself. He'd only sound jealous or spiteful.

"Business deals are always changing. I'm going to help out here for a while, then go back."

His gaze drifted over her slim form, the thin wrapper that she wore loosely thrown around her, leaving tempting displays of creamy skin open to his glance. He considered staying awhile longer, then knew he couldn't. If he gave in to what he wanted to do, he'd end up spending six months in New Orleans on a six-week job. That certainly wouldn't earn him any points.

"I'll probably work late, but if you come down to the offices later, I'll take some time for dinner."

She looked disappointed, and he smothered a smile. Damn. He'd better be careful. If he wasn't, he'd find himself married to this golden-eyed little temptress before Christmas. Maybe the old adage about absence making the heart grow fonder was true, because he'd sure as hell missed her on the interminable trip down the river; so much so that he'd wanted to go back for her.

Only his innate caution made him careful about reck-

ess promises. He couldn't say what he felt—what he'd
only just admitted to himself that he might feel. Love.
ust the word scared hell out of him. The thought of the
esponsibility it brought with it was worse than facing an
entire battalion of armed Yankees. No, he couldn't say
anything like that, couldn't make any promises.

"You know where to come," he settled for saying, and
leaned down to kiss the sad expression from her face.
Her response was so ardent that he felt his body's reac-
ion with wry dismay.

"Wear something easy to take off," he whispered, and
she laughed.

"I'll surprise you."

She did.

Nick greeted her at the front door that afternoon, and
saw that she was covered from neck to ankle. He
grinned at her, then escorted her into the executive of-
ices. After making the rounds of being introduced to
the office employees of SW&C, Amber followed Nick
nto the tiny cubicle that was his office. She perched on
the edge of his desk, drawing her heavy mantle closer
around her as she smiled lazily at him.

"What's for dinner?"

"I thought we'd go to a restaurant, if we don't take
too long," he said, still slightly preoccupied with the
rows of neat figures he'd been given to inspect. He
glanced up, saw the expectant expression on her face
and smiled. "Sorry. Where do you want to go?"

She stood up, giving him a peculiar look as she tugged
at the strings to her mantle and began to unbutton the
tiny rows of frogged fastenings. Mystified, he watched,
then reaction hit him in the belly and made his eyes
widen.

"What the—Amber, you crazy idiot!"

Laughing, she gazed at him with impish lights in her
eyes. "Well, you said wear something easy to remove."

"Yeah, but I didn't mean—*Christ!* You don't have on
enough to cover a flea, woman!"

"If it's not a *large* flea, I do."

She pirouetted, and he watched appreciatively as her slender legs performed a graceful step. Wearing nothing but white stockings, silk garters, a long chemise and shoes, she made him ache with need for her.

"How did you get out of the house like that?" he asked.

"I wore my cloak. My aunt's not *that* suspicious, though she has guessed where I'm really going when I say I'm visiting friends, I imagine. Poor Marie. My maid usually ends up lying her garters off for me." She fiddled with a lace bow at the low, scooped neck of her chemise, and gave him an innocent smile when his gaze focused on the swell of her breasts.

"I ought to tan your hide for this prank," he said thickly, but knew he wasn't making much of an impression on her. His lust had to be evident, and he couldn't even think straight as he came around the corner of his desk and reached out for her.

"Wait," she said, dancing just out of his reach, "I thought you wanted to go out to dinner."

"No," he said grimly, "not with you in that costume, what little there is of it. I'll send out. We'll eat here."

Amber lifted her arms and undid the pins in her hair, letting the rich, golden mass fall around her shoulders. He watched in helpless agony.

"We seem," he said slowly, "to spend our most intimate moments in the most public of places. I wonder if this trend will continue."

"That depends," she said archly, "on how long you think you have to spend most of your waking hours working."

"I'm beginning to rethink my goals." This time when he reached out for her, he caught her. Dragging her to him, he bent his head and kissed her, bending her slowly over his desk. Her breasts were creamy temptations barely veiled by lace, and she brought up her legs to wrap them around his waist in a blatant invitation.

"Did you lock the door?" she murmured, and he had
ɔ pause and think.

Releasing her slowly, his eyes narrowing in the dimly
t room, he stepped back and reached out with one
and to lock the door. Then he began unbuckling his
elt, keeping his eyes on her flushed, expectant face.

God, she was beautiful, with her hair tumbling
round her bare shoulders and gleaming with rich lus-
rous lights. Beneath the winged fan of her lashes, she
vatched him with gilt eyes full of emotion, and his con-
rol wavered. He wanted her; he needed her more than
e'd thought he could, and it was unnerving.

Her features were pure and perfect, a pristine angel
vith blazing wings, and he felt something deep inside
im begin to thaw. That frozen part of him that had
emained locked away for four long years shifted pain-
ully, and he closed his eyes against it.

CHAPTER
15

TWO weeks passed in a dreamy haze for Amber She eagerly met Nick every night, not caring about any thing but seeing him. She loved him so much, loved the way his dark eyes would light with pleasure, then turr smoky with passion when she managed to tease him from exhaustion into lovemaking.

Most of all she loved the moments of intimacy shared as they lay in one another's arms after making love and talked. She discovered a side of Nick she'd only sensed before, the glimpses of what he would have been had the war not changed him. There was a teasing tenderness in him that she saw when his guard was down.

It only made it more precious to her when he tried to cover up those lapses of control with a gruff comment or half-embarrassed surge of energy. She knew, without being told, that it was very difficult for Nick to relax the constant vigil he held on his softer emotions. And knowing that, she was willing to wait, though patience had never been one of her crowning virtues.

"Don't you get tired of meeting like this?" Nick asked with a frown one evening, and Amber laughed.

She snuggled close, tucking her hand into his open shirt and stroking his bare chest. "Not when I know you're the reward," she murmured, watching the tiny dark chest hairs curl around her fingertips.

"That can't be too exciting," he said, amused.

"It's not. It doesn't get exciting until you kiss me."

Nick turned slightly, his lashes drifting in a lazy droop over his eyes as he searched her face. Lifting one hand, he cradled her chin in his palm and rubbed his thumb over her lower lip.

"I don't know what I did to deserve you, sugar, but it had to be good."

Her laugh was throaty. "I'm glad you think so. Sure it wasn't something you're paying for now?"

His mouth found hers in a long, sweet kiss. "If it is, all my crimes should be so well-punished," he muttered against her mouth, and lifted her into his arms.

Amber put her arms around his neck as he carried her across the small room to the bed, knowing that dinner would be late again, as usual. No matter their good intentions, most nights found them snuggling in bed instead of going out to eat, and Nick often just went to the nearest café for their evening meal.

It suited both of them.

New Orleans was blessed with a warm autumn, and sometimes when Nick had gone to work Amber sat on the small balcony of the room in the Quarter and watched the interesting procession pass below. She never felt the first inclination to seek out some of her former acquaintances, nor spend much time in the Garden district where she'd lived before. She preferred remaining anonymous, devoting all her attention to Nick.

He was in love with her. She knew it, could sense it in spite of his reluctance to admit it. He revealed it in the way he touched her, held her against him with his heart still thundering after they'd made love, his face buried in her hair sometimes so that his breath feathered across her cheek. There was genuine emotion in those moments, in the unspoken love of his embrace, and she cherished each one of them.

The pleasant weather and nights of love lulled her into a false sense of security. She discovered it one

morning an hour after Nick had gone down to the ware
houses for work.

With the pride of accomplishment, she gazed around
her at the neatly made bed and swept floors, delighted
with how nice it looked.

"Wouldn't Aunt Leala be amazed?" she murmured
tucking a strand of loose hair behind one ear. Her hair
swung free, and she was wearing only a blouse and skirt
her feet bare. She looked, she knew, like one of the
poorer inhabitants of the Quarter, but she didn't care
She was happier than she'd ever been before.

When a knock sounded on the door, Amber was sur
prised. No one ever visited. She smoothed her rumpled
skirts, spared a moment's regret that she hadn't been
tidier in her appearance, and opened the door.

The young woman who stood on the small balcony
was garbed in the latest fashion. She looked exquisite
from the tip of the ostrich plume in her stylish bonnet to
the gleaming toes of the dainty kid pumps she wore on
her feet. Amber felt immediately at a disadvantage, and
hoped that this young woman was not someone she was
supposed to know.

"May I help you?" she managed to ask pleasantly
still barring the entrance and half hiding behind the
sturdy door. She was acutely aware of her bare feet and
lack of proper wear.

Raking her with a bold stare, the young woman
smiled slightly. "I don't think so. I was looking for
Nick."

Her voice was controlled, well-modulated, showing
only a hint of a southern accent. Amber felt even more
uncomfortable in the face of her poise. The fact that the
girl was very, very pretty didn't make her feel much better.

"Mr. Windsor is at his office. Have you asked for him
there?"

"No. I usually meet him at his lodgings, but this time

'm afraid business kept me for an extra fortnight." Her
lark head tilted to one side. "Are you his domestic?"

"Domes—no. No, I'm not." Irritation edged her
voice. This young woman seemed entirely too familiar.
'Are you a friend of Mr. Windsor's?"

A throaty laugh purred into the air between them,
and wide blue eyes assessed Amber with a speculative
gleam beneath thick, lush lashes.

"You could say that. We're very—close—friends."

The inference was not lost on Amber. For once she
could think of nothing to say.

Taking advantage of Amber's silence, the girl said,
'May I come in?" As she swept past Amber into the
small room, she glanced around, a knowing smile curving her mouth, then looked back at Amber. "Nick always seems to prefer shabby lodgings. I wonder why."

"I couldn't say." Amber shut the door and leaned
against it, her self-protective instincts finally roused.
'Perhaps you should tell me why you're here,
Miss . . ."

"Lesconflair. Léonie Lesconflair." The small smile
still smoothed her mouth, and she began drawing off
her gloves as she watched Amber. "Might I ask your
name, since we seem destined to be acquainted?"

"Amber Jenné."

"Ah, he does prefer women of French descent—tell
me, are you an ardent southerner, too?"

"No, I am not."

"How surprising. Nick always swore he would never
be closely involved with anyone who wasn't loyal to the
South." She surveyed Amber. "But then, you are a
pretty little thing, so perhaps he took that into consideration."

Amber glared at her, stifling the urge to fling something at the arrogant, exquisite woman. "I was not
aware that Ni—Mr. Windsor was expecting you."

"Oh, he never knows quite when or where I'll show
up." The smile flashed again, confident and bold and

making Amber want to scrape it off her face. "But then one can never seem to pin Nick down to anything definite either, can one?"

"That depends on what *one* may be trying to gain," Amber said in the same cold tone. "Just why are you here, Miss Lesconflair?"

Blue eyes widened with surprise. "Why, to be with Nick, of course. Oh. I can see he didn't tell you."

"Tell me that he was expecting you? No, your name has never come up, I'm afraid." Amber moved away from the door, stepping into a patch of sunlight streaming through a window. She felt its warmth, but was so cold inside, she could have been standing in a furnace and not been warmed.

"That is too bad of Nick," Léonie was saying with a sigh. "He never stops to think what his actions do to others." She tugged off a glove and draped it over the table Amber had just polished, then began to remove the other. "My baggage will not be here for another hour or so, so that gives you enough time to gather your things, Miss Jenné."

"What on earth makes you think I'm leaving?"

Léonie laughed, the sound rich and sultry. "Because if you don't, poor Nick will be forced to tell you to your face that he no longer desires your—company. It can be quite embarrassing, I assure you."

"Miss Lesconflair, I think you'd better explain why you seem to think he'd do any such thing."

The wide blue eyes narrowed fractionally, and the rich voice grew hard. "Why? Because he has done it before. This time will be no different. Nick and I are to be married, and though I cannot like his little . . . peccadilloes, I would rather he have them now than after the wedding. I'm an understanding woman, but I'm not so understanding as to permit such indelicate behavior when I am his wife."

Amber felt the world fall away from under her, and

she eyed the slim, arrogant beauty with growing apprehension.

"Nick has never intimated that he was to be married."

Léonie laughed harshly. "And did you think he would? No, then you would not have fallen so easily into bed with him, would you? I thought not. You look respectable enough in a way, though I think you should be more aware of appearances."

"I think you should offer more than just your word that Nick intends to marry you. After all, I've never heard of you, and his sister never mentioned you."

"Poor Jessamy. She is too caught up with her handsome Yankee husband to involve herself in Nick's affairs." The other glove was laid atop the table, and now Amber saw the diamond ring flashing on Léonie's left hand. She held up her hand. "Like it? It is a Windsor family heirloom. Before it belonged to Abigail, it was in the Fontaine family for years. . . . Oh, I see that you're upset."

"Miss Lesconflair," Amber said through clenched teeth, "a ring is not exactly proof."

"No, I suppose not." The girl's brow creased for a moment, then she brightened. "Would letters from him be proof? You are familiar with his handwriting?"

"Familiar enough." Amber watched with growing misery as Léonie Lesconflair pulled two letters from her reticule and held them out.

"These are the latest, and all I have with me, I'm afraid. I'm not in the habit of carrying around his letters, though I probably should for occasions like this." She made a small face to indicate her distaste. "Nick will have to curb his baser urges, I'm afraid, or we shall come to words. I hate to argue with him, and make it a point—the one on top was written two weeks ago, on his way to New Orleans," she said as Amber reached out for the letters. "He's a man of few words at times, but you will be convinced, I think."

As Amber unfolded the letter with remarkably steady

hands and began to read, she only half heard Léonie'
chatter about Nick and Clover Hill, and their spring
wedding. The letter was in his handwriting, and pain
fully clear:

> Sugar,
> I'm on my way to New Orleans for a few weeks. It
> won't take me long to complete the job—all I seem
> to think about is being with you. There's a lot I'd
> like to say, but I'm not much of a letter writer.
> Guess when I see you again, I'll show you how I
> feel.
>
> Nick

The second letter was much the same, written when
he was alone on the barge, and Amber read the few
words through a blur of tears. When she could lift her
head without risk of revealing her emotion, she handed
the letters back to Léonie.

"Well, I suppose that's pretty good proof. We both
seem to have been . . . misled."

"Yes, but I'm afraid I have the advantage. I know how
he is, whereas you seem to have been fooled by him. He
avoided you for a while, I bet, until you thought he did
not care. And he pretended to feel reluctance, but allowed you to coax him? Ah, I thought so. He is very
good at that. He should be on the stage."

"And I should be on the train." Amber somehow
found the poise to add, "I would appreciate your leaving
until I am able to gather my things, Miss Lesconflair.
I'm sure you understand."

"Of course." She gathered up her gloves and put
them on again, the brilliant diamond ring flashing in the
patch of sunlight warming the room. "Perhaps I will join
him at the office for lunch. That way, he will know what
has happened without my having to mention it. It's always so much easier that way."

"Oh, by all means, make it easy on him." Amber went

to the door, opened it and stood aside. "Good day, Miss Lesconflair."

"Good day, Miss Jenné." She paused in the open doorway. "If it is any consolation to you, I will see that he does not do this to any other foolish woman."

Amber's eyes flashed dangerously, and Léonie took an involuntary step back. "I would question who is the bigger fool, Miss Lesconflair, one who was fooled by his lies, or one who knows them and still lingers. Good day. *Good day*," she added fiercely when the woman opened her mouth as if to speak.

Nodding silently, Léonie Lesconflair left and Amber slammed the door shut behind her. In the space of a few minutes all her dreams had come crashing down around her. The shock was so great that she still didn't quite comprehend the enormity of Nick's deception.

The dazed, lost feeling did not leave her on the long trip back to Memphis.

Dark shadows shrouded downtown Memphis. The Pinch Gut district was noisy. Nick leaned against a brick wall and lit a thin cheroot, blowing smoke into the air as he waited. He was in a dangerous mood. The old feelings were back, sharp and strong, and he welcomed them.

He hadn't felt this on edge since the war, since he'd ridden with Forrest on midnight raids. The mood of bitter passion that had driven him since he'd returned to the Quarter to find Amber gone without a note or any hint of the reason had increased by the week until it was a hard, cold core inside of him. Not once since his return to Memphis had he been able to see or speak with Amber. Not once had she given any indication she'd spent weeks with him.

He was past wondering why. Now, the reason had ceased to matter so much. He'd accepted it, just one more disappointment in a world full of them. Women were as fickle as the fates of war. He should have kept

that in mind and not assumed things would be different.
Maybe then he'd have been more prepared for the way
it had turned out. He guessed she'd just gotten bored
with him, bored with being left alone so much. He'd
been a fool to think her vows of understanding were
real.

None of that mattered now. Now, he had a score to
settle.

Norman Martin had sent him to New Orleans on purpose, as Nick had suspected, but until a chance discussion with Henri Jenné, Nick had not known that the
older man had no inkling of it. He'd thought—as Martin
wanted him to—that Jenné had ordered his hasty departure from Memphis.

And that small discovery had started him thinking
about some of the other neat little lies Martin spouted
at times. Once again he'd taken to following Martin at
night.

It was cold, and a damp December wind was blowing
off the river. It chilled him to the bone, and Nick
hunched his shoulders against the cold. Damn. Martin
was up to something. He knew that much. He'd seen the
men he met with, and recognized a few of them. Bad
customers, men who wouldn't hesitate to kill someone
for pay. Yet no overt attempt had been made on Henri
Jenné's life lately. That suggested several possibilities.

Nick swore softly under his breath, pressing his shoulders against the brick wall and wondering why he hadn't
done this sooner. He ground his teeth together in frustration. Hadn't he learned *any*thing in his years of riding
with Forrest?

"Never let an enemy expect you, son," the wily general had said time and again. "Keep 'em off their guard,
and then you've got 'em where you want 'em."

Nick squinted against the curl of smoke from his cheroot, and stared at the door Martin had used. It swung
open and shut several times, but none of the patrons
was Martin.

After more than an hour passed, he was finally rewarded when Martin emerged. He wore a shabby coat—a smart move in this section of town where a man could get his throat cut for a nickel—and an oversize fedora that he kept pulled over his face, but Nick knew him at once. It was the same disguise he'd worn before.

Shoving away from the wall, Nick waited until Martin had turned south on Main Street before he followed at a distance. A hired hack stood at the corner of Main and Vance. Martin climbed in quickly and the carriage rolled away at a brisk pace.

Nick stayed where he was.

When the hack returned a half hour later, clopping slowly down the cobbled street and moving toward the stables, Nick stepped out and hailed the vehicle. The driver slowed to a halt and leaned out.

"Through for the night, mister. Walk up to Exchange if you want a cab."

"That's all right. You'll do."

"I told you—hey!"

Leaping up to the running board, Nick grabbed the driver by his collar. "Don't get excited. I just want to talk. A man by the name of Beaver Thornton told me you might be a good conversationalist." His grip tightened. "And don't reach for that pistol, either. Not unless you want to chew on the muzzle awhile."

The man's voice came out in a slight squeak. "I dunno what you're talkin' about."

Still keeping a tight grip, Nick reached behind the driver and took a heavy pistol from the curve of the footguard. "This one. Now be a good man. I only want some light conversation."

Lamplight fell across the driver's face as he shifted to loosen Nick's hold. His fleshy face was unshaven, pale eyes wide with fright. The horse began to toss its head nervously. The vehicle wobbled as Nick slung his body onto the seat next to the driver. He caught the strong smell of whiskey and grinned.

"Tell you what, my good fellow, you start answering a few questions for me, and I'll buy you a bottle of the best. Beaver said you like scotch."

"Won't do me no good if I ain't alive to enjoy it."

"That's true. But right now, I'm the man you gotta please. Let's start with your name. *Your name,*" he repeated with a flex of his wrist that brought the driver's head snapping around.

"Whitcomb. Dammit, you're breakin' my neck. . . ."

"I'll do more than that if you don't get a little more cooperative." Nick's smile was not calculated to inspire confidence. "All right, Whitcomb, suppose you tell me if you pick up that last gentleman fare very often."

"What gentlem—all right, all right, just don't choke me to death." When Nick loosened his hold, Whitcomb coughed once or twice and glared at him. "I pick him up a couple times a week."

"And how do you know when to pick him up?"

"He sends a boy to tell me."

"A boy. Describe him."

"Sheeit! Describe a—all right. Lemme think a minute. About ten years old, I guess, skinny. Black as soot. That good enough?"

"For now. Do you always wait here?"

"Wait here and drop him off here. Will you let up on the collar a bit? I can't breathe."

"Where do you take him from here?"

"Not far. Down Union a ways."

"Ever go anywhere else?"

Whitcomb muttered under his breath, and Nick's grip tightened again. "I asked you, Whitcomb, if you ever go anywhere else when you leave downtown."

"Look, mister, I don't wanna get involved in nothin'. I got a wife and kid."

"You're already involved, but it doesn't have to stay that way. I asked you if this guy ever has you take him anywhere else. Now I know he does. Where?"

"*Jeezus,* will ya let up? Yeah, he has me take him

another place sometimes." His eyes rolled, glimmering in the misty light of a street lamp. "Down to the shanties, all right? He goes there once in a while. And to a nice house over on Adams. Once in a while I take him way out on Poplar, to a vacant house." A shaking hand tugged at his collar. "That enough, mister?"

"Do you know him by name?"

"Naw, he's just a fare." Whitcomb tried to move, and Nick gathered another fistful of his grimy collar. Whitcomb blanched. "Look, mister, you don't have to buy me a bottle or nuthin' if you'll just let me go. I've told you all I know. He's a regular fare, and that's it."

"Tsk tsk, Whitcomb. You're too nervous to be driving a hack in this part of town. You ought to move to another section for a while. If you understand what I mean."

Whitcomb licked his lips. "Move . . . ? Yeah, I guess maybe I should do that."

"Excellent." Nick released Whitcomb's collar. "I hope I don't see you for a while."

"Goes double for me, mister." He lifted a shaking hand to his throat. "You got a grip like a bear."

"But I have a nice smile. Here. This ought to cover the price of a bottle. No, I insist," Nick added when Whitcomb tried to refuse the money. "It wouldn't be polite not to keep my word, would it? And I am always a man of my word, Whitcomb. Remember that."

"I'll remember it," Whitcomb grumbled, taking the bill Nick pressed into his hand. "And I don't know who told you that you had a nice smile, but they was wrong."

"Calling the lady a liar?" Nick asked pleasantly as he stepped down from the carriage. It swung with his movements, and Whitcomb picked up the reins again.

"No," he said, shaking his head. "Reckon you never showed her the one you just showed me."

"Reckon not," Nick said as Whitcomb slapped the reins against the horse's rump and sent it at a fast clip down the street. He leaned against the lamp post and stared into the murky gloom beyond. Martin was visiting the shanties, which meant many different things. One important thing leapt to mind—someone had been stirring up trouble between the Irish and the Negroes, and now he had a strong suspicion who. But why? What would Norman Martin have to gain by causing that kind of trouble?

It didn't make sense. It just didn't make sense.

Killing Henri Jenné made sense in a way, because Martin would stand to gain something. But this—he had to be wrong. There had to be another reason for a man like Martin to show himself in the part of town where dissent waited to erupt into violence. Now, he just had to figure out what it was.

He had to ask some questions, and he knew whom to ask.

"Mr. Windsor is here to see you," Celia announced, her mouth widening into a grin when Amber looked up with a gasp. "Ah, he is a very handsome man, *n'est ce pas*? And so wicked-looking, too—it's always the wicked ones who are most interesting, don't you think?"

"Really, Celia," Amber managed, rising from her chair, "you say the silliest things."

"Ah, but I am not the only one to notice. There is Amelia Collingwood, who has managed more than once to interest this so handsome Mr. Windsor, I hear."

Amber's heart constricted and her voice was cold. "I cannot think why you imagine that I care who does or does not interest Mr. Windsor."

"*Non?* Too bad. He has become quite the rage since getting back from New Orleans, I hear, *n'est ce pas*?"

"Send him away," Amber said, turning her face away from Celia's too-knowing eyes. "I have no intention of seeing him."

"This is not the first time he has come. Do you intend to send him away forever?"

"If I can."

Celia snorted. "I never thought you a coward. *Mademoiselle,*" she added politely when Amber gave her a sharp look.

"And I never thought you such an interfering nuisance. Now go, send him away."

"He'll just come back."

Amber thought about that. Perhaps it would be best to see him and tell him once and for all that she never wanted to speak with him again. That seemed to be the only way she'd ever get rid of him.

"Very well, Celia. I'll see him for a moment or two. But do not make any attempt to serve tea or welcome him. He won't be staying long."

She wasn't sure why, but nerves made her stomach lurch, and she took special pains with her appearance. Perhaps it was the memory of how she'd looked in New Orleans, when Léonie Lesconflair had come and shattered her world.

After combing her hair and fastening a new lace fichu at her throat with a large cameo pin, Amber cast a final glance in the mirror and arranged her skirts before going downstairs. Nick. Here, again. She closed her eyes, fighting the surge of weakness at knowing he was so close. So treacherously close. *God.* She wondered why he'd come. Surely he must know that she knew everything now.

Opening her eyes, she stared at her reflection in the mirror, glad to see that nothing showed on her pale face. Only her eyes reflected the misery she felt. She pinched her cheeks to give them color, then gathered her courage and went downstairs.

Nick looked oddly out of place in the fashionable front parlor, like a tiger in a tea room. Amber almost smiled at the thought of his lean, powerful frame perched on one of the dainty flowered sofas.

He turned away from the fireplace mantel where he'd been leaning, raking her with an appreciative glance before veiling his eyes with lowered lashes. He was still wearing an overcoat, and it swung slightly with his movements.

Amber's breath caught, and for a moment she couldn't move. Nick looked different; his face held a new cynicism, apparent in the set of his mouth and the more angular structure of his bones. It looked as if he'd lost weight. His hair was longer, brushing the collar of his overcoat, and she caught a glimpse of a gun belt beneath the garment, which set her pulses racing. He'd always seemed dangerous to her, predatory, but now he looked completely feral, with that taut expectation of trouble in his eyes.

"Sorry to bother you, Miss Jenné," he began politely, "I won't stay long."

Amber smiled. It was a forced smile, polite, even friendly, but with no hint of the raging turmoil inside her.

"I'll count on you to keep that promise, Mr. Windsor." She followed his conversational lead, and walked to the wing chair beside the fireplace. Turning, with one hand lying on the high back of the chair, she gestured at his gun. "You didn't need to come armed."

"One never knows."

Amber swallowed an angry comment and gave him a cold stare. "How may I help you?"

An amused smile pressed at the corners of Nick's mouth. "By answering a few questions for me."

"I hardly think you need to come to me for that. If you want answers to something, please interrogate someone else."

"But you're the one who is so concerned about her father, remember? And I've learned some new facts that might prove your theory."

"It's not a theory. Someone *was* trying to kill him. I suppose they gave up since he's now so well-guarded."

"I wouldn't count on it. Let's just say they may be biding their time."

Amber felt a spurt of disquiet. "I thought—I mean,

Roger watches Papa day and night, and there has been no hint of anything wrong."

"Which is just what someone wants us to think."

"Are you certain?"

"As certain as I can be. Are you willing to take a chance on my being wrong?"

She thought for a long moment, then sighed. "No."

"Then answer my questions. I don't want to ask Henri and get him alarmed again." He watched her with a dark, remote gaze that made her look away.

Damn him—standing there so cool and composed.

"Of course." She seated herself and arranged her skirts in a graceful fall before clasping her hands in her lap and looking up at him. "Fire away."

A mocking grin squared the hard line of his mouth. "You make it so easy. All right. Would you mind telling me if Martin makes it a habit to come here every night?"

Her brow rose delicately. "Really, Mr. Windsor, are you that concerned with my habits?"

"No. His." The dark slash of his brow crowded his eyes when she laughed. "You find that amusing?"

"Infinitely. I didn't think Norman was your type."

Nick's mouth twisted into a sardonic smile. "He's not. My *type,* as you refer to it, leans to the more feminine side."

Her eyes met his with a clash that she felt all the way to her toes. "So it's said."

"It is?"

Amber knew, even as she said it, that she sounded jealous, but she couldn't help it. "Yes, your female conquests are legion, I'm afraid."

She could cheerfully have bitten off her tongue the moment the words were out, because Nick gave her an arrogant grin that mocked her jealousy.

"Ah. Any particular conquest in mind?"

"No." Her voice dripped ice. "Though perhaps I should warn you that Amelia Collingwood's father is reputed to be quite efficient with dueling pistols, in case you truly have amorous inclinations in that direction."

"Amelia Collingwood? I'll keep that in mind. I have run into her a few times lately."

"I shudder to think where."

"Do you?" He moved with easy grace back to the mantel and stood with his shoulders pressed against the marble shelf as he regarded her with amusement dancing in his eyes. "My business takes me all over town, you know. Your father's freighting is local as well as distant, and so I seem to end up in various offices."

"I wasn't aware Amelia involved herself in business," Amber said dryly, wishing she hadn't started this discussion. Nick looked to be enjoying it too much.

"Oh, she's not directly involved, but maybe you recall that her father owns a dry goods store way out on Poplar . . ."

Amber stood up. She hid the nervous gesture of her hands in the folds of her skirt as she said with a trace of impatience, "Yes, I'm well aware of Collingwood's store. Not that it matters. Please continue, Mr. Windsor, with your questions."

"You forgot to give me an answer."

"Oh. Yes, Norman makes it a habit to visit here."

"Does he normally stay long?"

"Long enough." She tilted her head to one side, forgetting that she had arranged it in neat curls over her ears as she toyed with an errant strand. "Why do you want to know?"

"I have my reasons."

"Ah. I love mysteries." Her sarcasm was not lost on him, and he shrugged.

"What do you know of his outside interests? Does he ever discuss his activities with you?"

"Well, he belongs to a gentleman's club on Front Row, and he attends social functions—why do you want to know?"

"What kind of social functions? Do you know the name of the club?"

Beginning to feel edgy, Amber gave him a curious glance. "The usual—card parties, teas, a few dances. I think the name of his club is Grantham's."

"How long has he been visiting you at night? Does he ever mention where he goes when he leaves here?"

Exasperated, Amber snapped, "Weeks, and no! Would you mind telling me why you've grown so curious about him? Does this have anything at all to do with Papa?"

"I'm the one asking the questions," he reminded her coolly.

"And if you want more answers, you'd better come up with some of your own," she shot back. His brow lifted.

"Any chance of us having a conversation without a fight?"

"Slim."

"It beats me why I—" He halted abruptly.

"Why you what?"

"Why I bother," he said with a rueful grimace.

Her throat closed. He looked at her almost sadly, and there was such a faintly wistful expression on his face for a fleeting instant that her heart lurched. Maybe he had loved her after all. She held out her hand. "Nick," she said in a choked whisper that made his eyes narrow slightly, "can't we—"

"Don't say it." He cleared his throat and looked away from her for a long moment, and Amber's heart fell. She schooled her features back into a polite mask and hoped he hadn't guessed that she'd been about to make a fool of herself again.

"Don't say what?" She laughed. "I was only going to say, can't we act like civilized people? After all, you work for my father. We're bound to run into one another on occasion."

"True." His eyes caught and held her gaze. "I didn't come here just to ask questions."

"What other reason could you possibly have?"

"To give you a warning—stay away from Martin."

Surprised at the abrupt statement, she stared at him with widening eyes. He stood with his hands clasped behind his back, his legs apart and braced, and looked at her with a faint frown.

"Again?" she managed to say. "This is beginning to get monotonous, Nick. You've always been jealous of him, so I'm not surprised, but don't you ever weary of telling me to stay away from Norman?"

His mouth tightened. "On occasion. I mean it about Martin. He's dangerous."

"And you're not? You've hurt me more than he ever could."

"Have I? But at least you're alive."

"Some consolation." She was angry, angry because he stood there so cool and remote, and angry because she'd betrayed her true feelings. It was humiliating that he should know she still ached over him.

He gazed at her coolly, and that made Amber even more angry. He could pretend so well. He could hide everything he felt and gaze at her as if she was just a hysterical woman and he was a poor, put-upon male who must suffer her outrageous whims.

"You're too late," she said, hearing the words but not quite able to believe she was saying the lie until she saw the stunned surprise on his face. "Norman and I are engaged to be married."

"You little fool," he said hoarsely.

"Am I?" She shrugged. "Perhaps. More of a fool if I believe anything *you* have to say."

"Amber—" It came out as a groan, and Nick paused. Damn her. She stood there looking like a satisfied cat, knowing she had her paw on the mouse's tail. He felt a wave of fury rise up, almost choking him.

"I don't believe you," he said flatly, watching her shrug again and move away from him to stand by the wing chair. He tried to remember why it had once been important to him to be received in the front parlor instead of the back, but couldn't recall the reason. Not now. Not when she'd just managed to knock his feet out from under him. Again.

"It's true. We just haven't announced it yet. I imagine that Norman will do so any day now."

"Why?"

"Why?" She gave a nonchalant shrug. "Because it's customary to announce one's engagement—"

"No, I mean why *him*? Haven't you listened to a single thing I've told you?" Frustration lowered his voice to a rough growl that made her back away.

"Oh yes," she said softly, "I've listened. I heard you say that you would never love me. Then I heard you say you'd missed me, and that you . . . you cared. Well, what you didn't say and should have was that you cared only for yourself. By the way, how is Léonie?"

"Who?"

"Never mind, Nick," she said with heavy sarcasm, "I know the entire tale. It doesn't matter anymore."

"I'm glad, because I don't know what the hell you're talking about," he said flatly. "As usual."

"My marriage to Norman," she said, twisting the knife more deeply. "Remember?"

"Jeezus, are all woman so hard-headed?" Pain and anger drove him to incaution, and he grabbed her by the shoulders and pulled her roughly to him. "Dammit, Amber, I won't let you do this."

"You have no say in the matter." She glanced pointedly at his hands on her shoulders. "Let go of me before I scream."

He released her with a shove and stalked to the parlor door. Pausing with one hand on the knob, he looked back at her pale face fringed with the unruly mass of gold hair and shook his head.

"I hope you live long enough to regret this, sugar."

He was almost out the door when he heard her whisper, "I'm sure I will."

CHAPTER
16

IT was a week before Christmas. The weather had turned bitterly cold, and snow had spit from the low clouds but left little trace on the frozen, rutted streets. Only faint patches of white showed here and there.

A huge evergreen tree had been erected in the front parlor, decorated with red velvet bows and festoons of white rope garland. Sprigs of holly and spruce made the house smell spicy and festive, but Amber found little joy in the season.

She'd ruined her life, and she didn't know how to get things right again. There was a strained relationship with her father that she knew had to do with her engagement to Norman, yet Henri would not admit it. He claimed he had many business details on his mind, and wished her well, but remained remote.

Even Celia had evinced shock at the news of her engagement and voiced her disapproval.

"*Sacré bleu!* You are marrying the wrong man!" Horrified, she didn't mince words, and shook her finger in Amber's face. "Any fool can see that you love Monsieur Windsor, not that fancy man with cold eyes. Ah, why have you been so foolish?"

"I'm not being foolish," Amber had said miserably, but she knew Celia was right.

She'd let her temper paint her into another corner,

and now she was stuck with her decision. When Norman had heard with delight her promise to marry him, Amber had been too angry to care what he might think. She'd only wanted to show Nick Windsor that some man wanted her. By the time her temper had cooled, she'd found herself engaged to Norman and embarking on a series of elaborate wedding plans that seemed more fantasy than reality.

Once, she had tried to tell Norman that she hadn't meant her acceptance. He had barreled right over her protests and faint disclaimers with enthusiasm and plans and vows of undying love, so that she felt like the worst kind of villain for wanting to renege.

Now she was caught in a trap of her own making, and it didn't help to know that she was the only one anguishing about it. From the gossip, she'd heard that Nick had, indeed, begun seeing Amelia Collingwood. And Letty Winston, and Mary Ella Hunter, and—the list was endless. He seemed to have forgotten Léonie Lesconflair, and there had been no mention of his betrothed.

A noise in the hall caught her attention, and Amber turned from staring out the parlor window. It was her aunt, and Leala was chatting with Celia as the maid took her coat.

Amber met her in the hall, and Leala smiled crisply as she rubbed her hands together. "It's cold, *ma chère*. Where is the fire?"

"How are all your boarders?" Amber asked when they were seated in front of the fire and Celia had served hot, spiced tea and a plate of holiday treats.

"Fine. Some of them have found permanent jobs, but many of the others begin to despair. The economic situation is grim." She sipped at her hot tea, then looked up at Amber. "What is this news I hear of you?"

"News?" Amber fidgeted slightly, feeling herself flush like a green girl. "Do you mean about my engagement?"

"Your folly. *Mon Dieu, ma petite,* have you taken leave of your senses?"

Amber's chin lifted defiantly. "Norman Martin is a good, decent man."

"Have I said he is not?" Leala snorted. "*Non,* I have not. I merely say that he is not the man for you."

"Why does everyone think they know who the right man is for me?" Amber demanded, surging to her feet. She planted curled hands on her hips. "And just who is, might I ask, since Norman so obviously is not the right man for me?"

Leala stared at her with a petit four halfway to her mouth, her lips parted and her eyes wide with amazement. "Why, I have no idea, *petite.* I can only say who I think would make you unhappy, not who would make you happy."

"Then perhaps you should talk with Celia," Amber snapped, eyeing the maid who was peeking in the doorway. "*She* seems to know who I should choose!"

Obviously aggrieved, Leala put down her untouched pastry and eyed her niece for a long moment. "Perhaps she only wishes you to be happy."

Amber sank slowly back to the stuffed chair, her cheeks hot with embarrassment. "I apologize," she said stiffly, "for making an idiot of myself. I've been—on edge lately."

"So it would seem." Leala patted her knee comfortingly. "Why don't you take a little trip, *chère*? The south of France is nice this time of year."

Amber smothered a sigh. "Perhaps after Christmas."

"*Bon.* It will be good for you. Now, where is my brother? I have news for him."

"Good news, I hope."

Leala laughed. "The best. We have found another sponsor for my house, one who is willing to finance jobs, I think. I hope so. It is too grim not to be able to help those poor soldiers."

As she rose from the flowered settee, Amber said, "Papa is in his usual place."

"Ah. Of course. The very masculine refuge of his own parlor. He says all these flowers make him—what is the word?"

"Nauseous."

"*Oui.* That is the one. *Bon nuit, petite.*"

"*Bon nuit, tante,*" Amber murmured, but Leala was already at the door, bustling energetically down the hallway toward the back parlor, where Henri preferred to spend his evenings.

Left alone, Amber decided that a good night's sleep couldn't hurt anything. And possibly it would give her the strength to cope. She started for the door, and Celia stuck her head in the room.

"Your book came in the post today," the girl said. "I put it in the library."

"Book? What book?"

Celia shrugged. "I did not read it, but I think it must be a book you sent for. It's on the library table."

As she ducked back out of the room, Amber shook her head. Celia made no secret of the fact that she thought her mistress a fool for choosing Norman Martin over Nick. Perhaps she should have told them all the truth, but part of her was reluctant to reveal how she'd been so easily duped. And betrayed. And hurt.

The library was dark, with a single lamp burning on the far wall and casting only a faint glow. Amber crossed to the long table in the center of the room and reached for the package lying there.

A soft, scuffling sound caught her attention, and she looked up, her heart lurching when she recognized the shadow that disengaged itself from the others.

"Nick." Her voice came out in a rusty squeak, and she cleared her throat. "What are you doing here?"

He turned up the gas lamp, light flooding his face, casting it in a study of harsh angles and planes. Then he came toward her, and she stilled the impulse to run. He looked grim. His eyes flicked over her, and his lashes quickly lowered to hide the hungry glint she saw flicker in their depths. His voice was raspy and impatient.

"We need to talk."

"Talk? I can't imagine why." Amber was proud of how coolly she responded, when her heart was doing somersaults and her pulses were beating a mad tattoo.

"Now is not the time to play games, Amber." Nick took two long strides toward her, stopping only when she backed away. "Dammit, do you think I'm going to rape you or something? Stop acting so stupid and listen to me."

"Stupid! You come here uninvited and stand there and tell me I'm stupid. Please leave before I call Roger to throw you out."

"That should be interesting."

She pushed at an errant strand of hair that fell in front of her eyes. "I don't have to stand for—what are you doing?" Her voice rose as he moved toward her again, grabbing her hand.

"That your forty-carat engagement ring, sugar? It looks big enough to blind a man. Nothing short of ostentatious for you, I guess."

She flushed and belatedly remembered the ring on her finger. She pulled her hand away and lifted her chin. "What do you want? Surely, you didn't come here to congratulate me."

"Right." His mouth curved into a sulky line, and the look he gave her could have melted raw iron. "I told you —I want to talk to you."

"We don't have anything else to say."

Amber tried not to look at him. He looked so—predatory. Like a huge cat, all lithe and determined. And he moved like one too, his strides loose and graceful as he cut off her retreat.

"The hell we don't. No, you're going to listen. This is important. Amber, will you be still? I have to ask you something about Martin."

"Again? I'm tired of answering your questions. We were both wrong about him, Nick." She shoved his hands away when he tried to grab her arms. "He's just . . . a little brash, that's all. Maybe you don't want me, but Norman certainly does. And he makes no bones about it either, or excuses."

A sardonic smile curled Nick's mouth, and he folded his arms over his chest and leaned an elbow on a high-backed chair. "Is that right? I'm delighted for you. I'm certain you and the illustrious Mr. Martin will live happily ever after. If you don't mind him stirring up a bit of a rebellion, that is."

"What are you talking about? And don't try and tell me that Norman is behind those attempts on my father's life either, because he's not. He wasn't anywhere nearby when the food was tampered with, nor was he nearby when that carriage barely missed Papa. I overreacted, just like you said."

"Most of the time, I'd agree that you overreact, but this time I have to admit you were right." Nick's voice was soft, but his eyes flashed angrily at her. "Your father is still in danger, and you can believe that. Not only is he in danger, but your precious *Norman* has a few other irons in the fire that need cooling off."

"As usual, you're not making any sense." Amber tossed her head and tried to concentrate on something besides Nick. He looked so alien in the somber library, so—dangerous. In a room filled with dusty volumes and dead languages, he looked out of place and too large for life. "How did you get in without being announced, anyway?"

"Celia. At least *she* still likes me."

"She didn't have her heart broken by you. I did."

"Did you? You have a fast recovery rate, sweetheart. We can talk about that some other time. Right now, I want to know if your betrothed plans on taking you to the Christmas Ball at the Gayoso House."

"That's none of your business, thank you very much."

She took a step toward the door, but Nick moved so fast she never made it. He grabbed her shoulders and spun her around. Hot lights glittered in his dark eyes as he glared down at her.

"Don't play debutante with me, little lady. I'm not one of those puppets you prefer. I asked you a question, and I expect an answer. Straight and simple."

"You're hurting me." He let go of her and took a step back, and Amber drew in a calming breath. She'd forgotten how fast he could move, or how quickly he could anger. And in spite of herself, she saw that he was deadly serious. "This has something to do with Papa, right?"

"Right, sugar."

"Don't call me that." She moved to a lamp table and toyed with the lace cloth a moment, then turned to face him. "Yes, I'm going to the Christmas Ball at the Gayoso House with Norman. Why do you ask?"

"Can you get me an invitation?"

She stared at him. "What? You want to go with Norman and me to a—"

"No. Not in a hundred years. I just want an invitation."

She shrugged. "Get one from Papa. He has more influence than I do."

"I'd rather he not know I'm going to be there yet. You aren't worried I won't fit in, are you? Maybe I should tell you that I learned how to dance when I was still wearing diapers, and that I know all the proper social repartee. I can lie with the best of 'em, sweetheart."

"I've no doubt of *that*." Amber stared at him uncertainly. "And who do you intend to bring with you? Your betrothed?"

When he just stared at her, Amber shrugged lightly. "Or perhaps you prefer that charming creature who draped herself all over you the night Papa got you out of jail."

Nick shrugged. "She'd probably fit in with judges and

politicians, but I'm willing to bet she's got better sense. No, just a single invitation will do, thank you."

"Why do you want to come anyway? I thought you hated anyone who wasn't a blue-blooded southerner that spouts rebellion and states' rights and all that wonderful stuff."

"Can you get me an invitation, Amber?"

She looked away from him. It hurt to look at him too closely when she still—no, she couldn't even *think* that.

"Yes, I'll get you an invitation. I'll leave it with Mr. Dyer at the office."

"No, not at the office. Send it to my room by Roger. I trust him." His voice grew mocking and hard. "Private mail has a way of being violated at the offices of S.W. and C., I've learned."

Her gaze swung from the fire back to him. "Nick, what is going on? Do I need to know?"

"Honey, if you needed to know, I'd tell you. Just get me that invitation." He strode to the door, paused and turned back to look at her. "If I see you kissing Martin at that dance, I might cut in on you."

Her chin lifted. "I wouldn't advise it. Norman's terribly jealous."

Nick laughed. "If you're trying to discourage me, sugar, that's a damn poor way to do it."

The door shut behind him before she could think of a reply to that, and Amber stared at the closed door for a long moment before she moved. He'd done it again—turned her world upside down without even trying. Or maybe he had been trying. Surely, no one could ever set her pulses to racing like Nicholas Windsor could.

A guilty pang struck her as she thought of Norman. She should never have agreed to marry him. If she hadn't been so angry and hurt, she would have had enough sense to take back her hasty words and drop the subject. But she hadn't, and her pique had led her to accept Norman the day after her argument with Nick.

God. How much worse could this get? Even her father had been startled by Norman's announcement of their engagement, and the ring she wore on her left hand felt heavy and cumbersome. Like iron chains instead of a four-carat diamond in an exquisite setting. She flinched. Why did she do such stupid things? Nick had been right when he said she was stupid. She should never have—but it was too late for regrets now. She had, and she'd have to rectify it before it got any worse.

CHAPTER
17

LAMPS lined the curb in front of the Gayoso House at the corner of Main and Gayoso streets. Tall, elegant white columns soared above wooden sidewalks. The street was a hard, frozen rut for the well-sprung carriages that rolled toward the gaily lit hotel. Strains of music floated to the icy street each time the double doors swung open.

Shivering, Amber allowed Martin to help her down from his carriage. Hot bricks beneath her feet had kept her warm on the drive, but now the wind felt even colder than before.

"I think it's colder this year than it has been in a long while," Martin observed as he tucked her fur-lined hood around her face. He smiled, and Amber managed to smile back.

"Yes. It certainly seems colder," she agreed. She stifled the desire to ask if he couldn't offer any more personal comment than that. Why borrow trouble? She had enough already, and if Norman Martin wasn't exactly a scintillating conversationalist, he was trying very hard to be an attentive escort.

"Do you like my new carriage?" he asked, and without waiting for her reply, added, "It's the best of the line. I had it made in St. Louis. Only the best for you, m'dear."

"It's lovely, Norman."

"Did you notice the velvet cushions? And the squabs have an extra layer of padding." He cast a look back at the shiny, black-lacquered vehicle pulling away from the curb. "Only solid black horses, of course. That's all that would look right with it. You couldn't have noticed in the dark, but the horses are perfectly matched. No white on them anywhere. And my driver wears only black. Except for his white gloves, of course."

"Are you attempting to make some sort of statement?" Amber muttered as she held his arm and tried to keep her cloak from blowing open. "All black, no white."

"No. What do you mean by that?"

He looked surprised, and Amber sighed. "Nothing. It's just that black is so—well, colorless."

"That's the point." He smiled. "It's intended to be elegant, the first stare in fashion."

"I'm certain it is."

Amber noted with a feeling of relief that the door was being opened for them, and a rush of heat enveloped her as she stepped inside. Her nose felt icy. If not for her fur muff, her fingers would be frozen, she was sure.

A two-story vaulted ceiling dominated the lobby. It was no wonder the hotel was considered one of the wonders of Memphis and the South. It had all the latest conveniences, such as its own waterworks, gas works for the lamps and even cooking, its own sewer and drainage system, and indoor plumbing. There were hot showers, marble tubs and silver faucets, and the latest invention —flush toilets. Truly a marvel.

The food was said to be the best in the South, as the Gayoso House had its own bakeries and wine cellars, and boasted European cuisine. Amber could smell the tantalizing aromas of pastries being served by white-jacketed waiters in the lobby. Several patrons were sipping hot toddies under the light of cut-glass chandeliers.

A smiling porter ushered them toward the ballroom

on the second floor, and as they mounted the broad sweep of stairs, Amber looked back at the decorated lobby. It was ablaze with light. Guests mingled in noisy celebration, and a piano tinkled softly with Christmas music. Fragrant boughs of evergreen spiced the air, and sprays of holly and mistletoe clustered around groups of candles and lamps. It was a festive atmosphere, and she hoped she could absorb some of it.

As Martin helped her out of her cloak, his eyes widened appreciatively. Amber's gown was a dull, shimmering bronze that caught the glow of light. Small, puffed sleeves fell off the shoulder, and her low bodice revealed a hint of creamy skin and enticing shadows. A golden topaz pendant encircled her slender neck, resting between the two soft mounds that drew Martin's instant attention.

"Do you like my new gown?" she asked, trying to adopt a light tone but somehow failing.

"Like . . . like it? It's— You are the most beautiful thing I have ever seen."

There was no mistaking the sincerity in his tone this time, and Amber managed a smile. It *was* a lovely gown, and even though she'd lost weight, it still fit her well. Celia had fussed with it, pinning it, muttering in French, and taking up small tucks as she reproved her mistress for losing weight before she wore the new gown. Then the maid had dressed her hair in a cluster of curls atop her head, leaving several tendrils to flutter in front of her ears and over her forehead in gentle, drooping curls. Elbow-length gloves kept her arms warm, and Martin frowned as he noticed them.

"No one can see your ring, m'dear."

"I know, but the gloves will keep me warm. Besides, *I* know I have it."

"Yes, but I wanted everyone else to see how big a ring I can afford to give you." A faint note of displeasure made him sound peevish, and he shook his head. "Won't it fit over the glove?"

"Really, Norman, if it did, I would lose it. And besides, do you consider me your betrothed or a trophy?"

"Both." He smiled at her sharp exclamation. "Don't fuss at me, sweetheart. Any man would be proud to display you on his arm. I didn't mean it as an insult."

"I know."

That was the trouble. She did know he'd meant it as a compliment. But she didn't want to be *displayed*. She wanted to be loved. And she wanted to love.

Amber tried to concentrate on greeting people and making the appropriate reply when introduced.

Her smile didn't falter until she saw Nick.

He paused in the entrance, his dark gaze sweeping the room with a casual glance. Her breath caught. It was the first time she'd seen him in formal wear. In the black frock coat, high collar, and narrow tie, he was dressed like many of the other men. A red silk vest with gold threads skimmed his chest, tapering to his lean waist in a perfect fit.

Her throat closed. He'd been handsome before, but now—now, in a lavish setting of crystal chandeliers, brocade walls, and elegant people, he was devastating. His self-assurance and lean good looks always commanded attention, but dressed in expensive clothes and standing with negligent ease in the room, Nick made her think of a handsome young prince. All he needed was the white charger to complete the picture.

"What in the hell is *he* doing here?" Martin growled softly, and his hand tightened on Amber's arm.

"I imagine he's here for the same reason we are," she said coolly, trying to drill her pulses into a normal rhythm again. "It's Christmas."

"But this is an invitation-only affair, and I can't imagine Nicholas Windsor would know anyone of importance." Martin sounded disgruntled, and Amber almost laughed.

"If you'll recall, Norman, Mr. Windsor's family owns a large tract of land in Hardeman County."

"Not for long," he muttered, and she swung around to face him.

"What do you mean by that?" Her eyes narrowed when he looked away from her and shrugged.

"Taxes, of course. All the big plantation owners are losing their land to taxes."

"That's nonsense!" Amber said sharply. "Many of them have lost their land, that's true, but a great many of them are finding ways to keep their homes. The Windsors have paid their taxes for the year."

Martin regarded her for a long moment. "You sound very upset about it. Does it mean that much to you?"

"Jessamy Windsor is my friend. Of course it means a lot to me." Amber looked away from his penetrating stare, and her eyes happened to meet Nick's sardonic gaze across the crowded room.

His dark devil's brow lifted, and there was a saturnine glitter in his eyes that made her flush. She looked quickly away, and saw that Martin had noticed her disquiet.

"There are times, my sweet," he said softly, "that I wonder if you are truly *over* that preening coxcomb."

"Do you? Then let me set your mind at ease on that score. I am quite *over* him, as you say, and indeed—was never that caught up with him."

Martin laughed. "What an unconvincing little liar you are, Amber. But I appreciate your effort to spare my feelings." His hand smoothed her arm. As his fingers tightened around it, he steered her in the opposite direction from Nick Windsor, and she began to breathe more easily.

Though she'd secured his invitation, she had no idea why Nick was here or what he intended to do. She gratefully accepted the tall crystal glass of champagne that Martin pressed on her.

"Do you mind?" he murmured. "I see Judge Thompson over there, and I need to speak with him a few

minutes. Will you be all right if I leave you here with
Mrs. Whitten?"

"Quite all right, I assure you." She smiled to convince
him. It wasn't the complete truth. Mrs. Whitten was a
dead bore, and talked incessantly of her brilliant grand-
children and wealthy children until Amber wanted to
scream with exasperation. Only her rigid social training
kept her smiling and nodding at the appropriate times.
Her mind was busily engaged with keeping track of Nick
Windsor as he prowled the room.

It seemed that Norman was dead wrong when he'd
said not many of the guests knew Nick. From the way
people greeted him, it was obvious he was very well
known. And highly regarded. More than a few seemed
eager to draw him into their group, and she felt a wave
of irritation that he fit in so easily yet preferred not to.
Why? Did he really feel that—inadequate without his
money? Good heavens, the entire South was still reeling
from the effects of the war, and Nick should realize that
he was only one of thousands of displaced southerners.

Amber frowned. There had to be more to it. His ar-
guments were becoming stale, and she knew he had to
realize by now that he wasn't alone. It was just a convenient excuse to keep from committing himself to her,
and she'd better face it. Nick was alone because he
wanted it that way.

It was hard to convince herself of that when he allowed Mary Ella Hunter to drape herself over him like a
snug-fitting cloak, and smiled down at her as if she was a
fairy princess about to grant him three wishes. Amber
stifled the inclination to throw something large and le-
thal at him, and nodded politely when Mrs. Whitten
said that her four-year-old grandson was the most cun-
ning child alive.

"I'm certain he is, Mrs. Whitten. Most children are
quite special to their family."

The elderly woman gave a vigorous shake of her head
and put a hand on Amber's arm. "Oh no, everyone

agrees that he's quite brilliant. You must come see for yourself."

At that moment Amelia Collingwood swept across the room toward Nick, her white satin gown a splendid contrast to her dark lush beauty. Amber felt a wave of nausea when Amelia put a possessive hand on Nick's arm and he bent to hear what she was saying. The petite brunette coyly brushed her lips against his cheek as she whispered something to him, and Nick laughed aloud.

The nausea escalated into a raging attack of palsy, and Amber's hands and knees began to shake. Her champagne glass shook so badly the liquid sloshed over the rim and wet her gloves.

Damn him. The only reason he'd wanted that invitation was to come and meet other women. She knew it. There could be no other explanation. He certainly didn't seem to have any other purpose for standing leisurely in the center of the room and allowing lovely ladies to flirt with him. Amber was well-aware of how expert the flirtatious lovelies could be, too. She'd watched them with amusement over the past eight years, but now she was not at all amused. Now she was furious.

"My dear," Mrs. Whitten was saying insistently, and Amber reluctantly dragged her attention back to the dowager.

"What is it?" She didn't realize how sharp her voice was until Mrs. Whitten gave her a shocked look. Amber bit her lower lip and sighed. "I'm sorry. What were you saying?"

"Tuesday or Wednesday?"

Amber stared at her. She had no idea what the woman was talking about, so she said off the top of her head, "Tuesday."

"Excellent. Come to visit little Alva, and you can tell me if you think he is the most brilliant child you have seen."

Amber wanted to come up with a reasonable excuse,

but knew she was doomed. "Tuesday will be fine, Mrs. Whitten. Now, if you will excuse me, I see someone I simply *must* speak to."

She managed to escape, and headed straight for the door. She had no intention of remaining a moment longer than necessary, and Norman was not in sight. She had to get out of there; it was painful watching Nick be bombarded with available females.

Lifting her shimmering skirts with a gloved hand, Amber swept out into the wide hallway and paused. She had no idea where Norman could be. He'd still been in the ballroom the last time she'd seen him, but she'd been so busy looking at Nick that she hadn't seen Norman leave. Drat. Where could he be?

"Lose your lover?" a deep voice drawled in her ear. Amber turned slowly, steadying her breath as she looked up at Nick's dark, sardonic face.

"Why, Mr. Windsor, how can you tear yourself away from all your admirers? I declare, they'll be plumb devastated if you don't hurry right back."

Appreciation of her affected drawl and honeyed voice made his eyes crinkle at the corners. A smile kicked up one corner of his mouth.

"You can beat any of those gals at their own game, can't you, sugar?"

"I told you—"

"I know. Don't call you sugar." He shrugged and indicated the ballroom with a nod of his head. "Where's Papa? I thought I'd see him here tonight."

Amber shifted slightly and wished he weren't so close to her. She couldn't think straight when he was so near, all the memories so recent and painful.

"Papa's at home with a cold. He asked me to make his excuses for him."

"Did he?" Nick moved closer, and Amber backed away a step. "Don't worry. I won't attack you right here. Too public."

"A lady can never be too careful," Amber murmured

neasily. A faint scent of his shaving soap reached her, and her throat contracted painfully. She'd missed him. Now he was here and she should confess that she'd lied to him about Norman. The charade was becoming more than she could bear.

"That's what I've been trying to tell you," Nick was saying in a soft tone that drew her attention. "A lady can never be too careful with some people."

"Ah, back to square one, am I right? Another warning. You're becoming boring in your dotage, Mr. Windsor."

Nick chuckled. "I'm crushed. Seriously, Amber, you need to stay on your toes. I don't trust your lover."

"What do you think he's going to do?"

He shrugged. "I don't know."

Amber wavered between laughter and anger. She settled for, "What do you mean, you don't know?"

"I just know he's up to something no good, not what." He gave an impatient shake of his head when she started to walk away, and reached out to catch her hand. "Ugh," he muttered, "your gloves are wet."

"Champagne. Let go of me. This doesn't look right."

"Maybe we should be sitting on a quilt. We seem to do our best talking then."

His dark eyes met hers, and she saw the wary hunger in his gaze as he looked at her.

"You're beautiful tonight," he said softly, "but you always are. Waltz with me?"

"And disappoint your gallery of beauties? I'm not at all sure that would be fair."

"Didn't you once tell me that all's fair in love and war?"

"Which is this?"

"Truce."

"Ah," Amber said with a knowledgeable smile, "I seem to recall your telling me that truce was a time for the enemy to gather reinforcements."

"That's right. And here come yours, so I'm going to take the decision away from you."

Without waiting for her consent, Nick curved an arm behind her back and swept her into the ballroom and out onto the floor. The strains of the "Tennessee Waltz" filled the air, soft and lilting and lovely, and they swayed across the parquet tiles.

It was the first time she'd danced with him. Amber felt his muscled arm against her back and his warm body pressed close, and she tried not to show how it affected her. She inhaled the rich, spicy scent of his shaving soap and knew that every time she smelled that particular fragrance, she'd always think of Nick.

It was heaven and hell combined. She seemed to drift like a cloud over the floor, caught up in a pleasant dream of what might have been. Of what she had once hoped would be.

Nick looked down at her and knew he'd made a mistake. He should have stayed across the room instead of yielding to the impulse to go after her. Martin's reappearance had only triggered his need to hold her, and the dance was an easy excuse.

Just the sight of Amber, composed and serene and incomparably lovely in her shimmering, off-the-shoulder bronze gown, had done things to his resolve that he remembered far too well. She'd always had that effect on him. A tilt of her head, a flash of gilt eyes and a smile, and he was gone every time. An aching hunger filled him that he knew he'd never be able to ease.

Seeing Amber in this setting, in the world where she belonged but he no longer fit in, he was more aware than ever of the chasm between them. Lovely Amber Jenné, her saucy gold head held in an arrogant tilt and her cameo face as carefully remote as an untouchable princess, made him realize the total futility of what he'd thought—in a moment of insanity—he might be able to achieve. She wasn't for him. She lived in another world. He'd been a fool to think otherwise.

His arms tightened around her, and as they turned in the steps of the dance, he saw Martin glaring at them from across the room. He stifled the impulse to grin cockily at him. No point in setting him off too early.

"So what exactly are you doing here?" Amber asked, dragging his attention back to her.

"Trying to see if I can get your fiancé to bust something internal. He looks close."

Amber's eyes darted in Martin's direction, and Nick felt her resistance with a flash of surprise. "He does look unhappy," she said after a moment.

In reply, Nick danced her in another direction, so that Martin was hidden from view. "Are you taking on that responsibility?"

"What responsibility?"

"Of making Martin happy."

She looked up at him, gold eyes shadowed with something he didn't recognize. "Everyone is responsible for their own happiness. Perhaps people can make others unhappy, but I'm not sure it would be fair to ask someone to take on the burden of making me happy."

"I thought we were talking about Martin."

She flushed. "Well, we are. Indirectly, anyway."

"And how is the witty Mr. Martin as a lover?" he asked, and felt her stiffen in his arms. To cover her reaction—which he was certain would be fiery—he swept her past the orchestra.

"You . . . you—"

"Sore loser?" he prompted when she sputtered helplessly. "I guess I am."

Her head snapped back, and there was no mistaking the anguish in her eyes. "If I remember correctly, you were never in the running."

"Touché," he murmured wryly. He couldn't help it. The question came out before he could stop it. "So why did you run off and leave me in New Orleans, sugar?"

Her fingers dug into his shoulders, and he felt her

vibrate with the effort to remain calm. "I should think you wouldn't have to ask."

"But I am. Just to clear up an unanswered question. You know how I like to balance the ledger."

Tears misted the gold eyes glittering up at him, and for a moment Nick was nonplussed. Why would she be upset?

"Forget it," he muttered, unwilling to hurt her any more. If the memory of how she'd run out on him distressed her, then he could do without his answer.

They were near the side doors, and he saw his chance and took it. He didn't care who saw them as he danced her out the open French doors onto a small balcony. Huge potted plants screened the balcony from the lobby below, and before Amber could offer a protest, he pulled her hard against him.

He set his mouth over hers, feeling her hands come up in a reflex action as he plundered her mouth. His blood heated as he kissed her, remembering all the other times he'd felt her satiny skin beneath his hands. When her arms lifted and clung to his neck, he felt a surge of response so deep and quick he couldn't think for a moment. His blood turned to steam and he lifted his head, panting slightly.

"Come with me, Amber," he whispered hoarsely, his voice urgent and needy.

"Come . . . ?" She licked her lips, her tongue flicking out to test the swollen surface. "Where?"

"God—anywhere." He tried to think. His rooms were out of the question. So were hers. To take her upstairs would be treating her like a whore, and he couldn't stand that. Neither could he stand the thought of leaving her there with Martin.

But then it didn't matter, because as he looked down at her in growing frustration, he saw her blink as if just waking. A faint smile curled his mouth into bitter mockery when she jerked away from him. He'd delayed too long.

"No! I won't ever let you do that to me again, Nick Windsor, so don't even try it!" She inhaled sharply, and put her palms to her flushed cheeks. Her eyes—cat eyes —glittered with anger and emotion, and he steeled himself for her next words.

"You're despicable. I refuse to be drawn into your selfish schemes again."

"Selfish?" He shook his head. "What did I do that was so selfish, sugar?"

She was breathing in quick, tortured gasps, the bronze gown dipping dangerously low over her breasts. "Don't pretend you don't know. I suppose you have to make your . . . *conquests,* but I don't have to play your game. Go back to Léonie. If she'll still have you."

He grabbed her arm when she started to whirl away, frustration making his grip harsh. "Just who the hell is Léonie?"

"As if you didn't know! Did you think I'd never find out? I did. And I saw the letters—let go of me before I scream and draw a very large crowd, Mr. Windsor."

His hand fell away and he heard his own voice, cool and soft, say, "Whatever you want, sugar."

She stared up at him uncertainly. He recognized the conflict of emotion in her face, but remained silent. She wasn't making much sense to him, but she rarely did when she was angry. Her temper took over, and common sense didn't return until the storm faded.

Amber worried her bottom lip in a characteristic gesture that made him smile, and he ignored the warning in her eyes when he reached out for her again. His lean fingers closed over her arm above the elbow, digging into tender, soft skin that had a narcotic effect on him, drugging his caution as he pulled her close. He kissed her again, holding her against his body, but there was no response, as there had been before, and he released her with a sigh of regret.

She stared up at him a moment, mouth wet and quivering, then slapped him, hard, her gloved palm

crashing against his cheek. He grabbed her wrist before
she could repeat the action, hot temper making his body
rigid.

"I wouldn't."

Her eyes flashed muted gold sparks at him. "There
are few things you wouldn't do, Mr. Windsor."

He was about to ask her just what was making her so
blamed mad at him when Norman Martin strolled up,
his pale eyes cool with fury.

"Amber love, I see that you're all right. I was beginning to wonder."

Nick dropped her hand and took a step back, his gaze
flicking to Martin before it went back to her. She looked
as if she'd been sleepwalking, and he wished savagely
that Martin would do the world a favor and fall off a
bridge.

"Norman," Amber said, turning blindly toward him,
"please take me home. I—The champagne gave me a
headache."

Martin's pale eyes stabbed accusingly at Nick, but he
was the picture of a perfect gentleman as he said soothingly, "Of course, darling. Although I cannot leave myself, I will see to it that Hobbs sees you to your door so
that you are not . . . accosted by anyone else."

Nick's mouth curled in a mocking smile. "You're a
great actor, Martin."

Martin jerked, his eyes narrowing. "What the devil do
you mean by that, Windsor?"

Shrugging, Nick drawled, "Just what I said. You can
be anyone you want to be. For a little while." He
crossed his arms over his chest and regarded the man
through lowered lashes, watching his reaction. "What
do you do when the play's over?"

"I don't know what you're talking about. In the cups,
old man? I suggest you stagger back to your sleazy room
and sleep it off."

"Not a chance," Nick said softly, and saw the way
Martin grew tense. "Not a chance."

"I think it's time you and I had a long talk, Windsor," Martin said coolly. "But I have no intention of boring Amber with such tawdry business."

"Not unless you want her to hear the truth."

Amber looked from one man to the other, then said firmly, "I want to go home. *Now*."

Martin tucked her hand into the crook of his arm and elbow and led her away, and Nick watched them go without comment. He tried to stem the rising tide of frustration, and wondered again just why Amber was so mad at him. It went beyond the norm. There was betrayal and pain in her anger, not just the uncomplicated irritation of a woman who no longer found him appealing. No, there was something behind it, and he intended to find out what. After he nailed Martin's hide to a wall, that is. That came first.

When Amber left with Norman Martin, Nick pretended not to notice. He concentrated on the bevy of beauties who surrounded him, all atwitter at this latest addition to the social set. It seemed that an invitation to the Christmas Ball guaranteed one's entrance into society. If he hadn't needed to be there to keep an eye on Martin, he would have avoided it like the plague.

His hand closed involuntarily into a fist, and he heard a small gasp of delight.

"Are all southern men as gallant as you, Mr. Windsor?" a pert little brunette crooned softly, dragging his attention back to her as she clung to his arm. "You don't seem to want to let go of me."

His response was automatic, dredging up from the years of experience he'd had in verbal fencing before the war. "Why would any man want to let go of such a lovely woman, sugar?"

The brunette—he struggled to recall her name—giggled. "You are a flirt, sir."

Forcing a smile, Nick made an expected reply, his attention drifting again. His gaze moved along the far wall lined with tall palms and spectators, then jerked back when he recognized a familiar face. Dyer. What was he doing here? He stood beneath the fringed fronds of a palm and sipped at a drink as if he belonged there, and Nick frowned.

Dyer wasn't exactly the kind of man who would garner an invitation to the Christmas Ball. This nouveau society of Yankee carpetbaggers and eager entrepreneurs would hardly tolerate a lowly clerk in their midst. They were too busy trying to create an air of old world elegance to allow that. Few of the old Memphis citizens would attend this ball; they were either too poor or too proud or both. It was a slap in their aristocratic faces to watch the money being made by newcomers, and they snubbed them just as arrogantly as the newcomers snubbed men like Dyer.

Until now, it hadn't occurred to Nick that Dyer might be so heavily involved with Norman Martin. Now it was obvious. And it reinforced his belief that there would be trouble tonight.

Amber shivered in the night wind, but managed a faint smile when Martin tucked her inside the warm interior of his carriage.

"Thank you, Norman. I apologize for leaving so early, but—"

"Think nothing of it, m'dear. I would come with you, but I have to see a few men on business matters. Even parties are no excuse for shirking my work."

He leaned in, kissed her lightly on her cold, unresponsive lips, then withdrew and shut the door. Amber heard him give an order to the driver, and the carriage jerked into motion.

The sharp sound of hooves on frozen ground sounded loud in the night, and Amber reached out to wipe at the glass windowpane so she could see out. Street lamps cast brief ellipses of light over the buildings and walkways, and a theater marquee lit up the far end of the street in a brilliant display of colored lights.

Amber gazed at it idly as they drew near, eyeing the huge letters announcing the play, *Macbeth*, with the female lead being played by what the marquee proudly proclaimed as "The World-Famous Actress, Léonie Lesconflair."

The name jolted her, and Amber fumbled at the window to peer out, watching the marquee fade as the carriage passed it. *Léonie Lesconflair.* There could only be one. It was too unusual a name not to be the same woman Nick was to marry. Her heart fell. Knowing she was an actress explained a lot. Léonie had been so confident, so self-assured, but she would be if she was accustomed to stepping out on a stage.

Miserable, Amber huddled into a corner of the carriage. Nothing ever seemed to go right. Now that Léonie was in town, she would probably head straight for Nick again. Somehow, even knowing that he'd been faithless and betrayed her, didn't keep her from hurting at the thought of Nick with Léonie.

He deserved the slap she'd dealt him, for being a cheating dog, yet when she recalled the print of her hand on his lean, dark cheek, she couldn't help flinching. He'd looked—hurt. Not just angry, but actually hurt, as if she had somehow wronged him. There had been a quick flare of surprise and pain in his eyes before the temper rose, and she'd been shocked to see it. Why would he think he had any right to be hurt?

It was *she* who had the right, *she* who had been betrayed and lied to, and humiliated. Not Nick Windsor. Oh no, never Nick. He insulated himself too well with his wall of prejudice.

Once home, she went through the motions of getting ready for bed, moving mechanically through the house as if in a daze. Out of old habit, she left her discarded gown in a bronze puddle on the floor. But when she turned to get into bed, she paused to pick it up and hang it in the high armoire. The two weeks spent doing daily cleaning in New Orleans had at least left her with a good habit or two, she thought ruefully.

It wasn't until she was in her bed and tossing sleeplessly that Amber wondered why Nick hadn't brought his betrothed with him to the ball. And why didn't he admit that he at least knew her? He couldn't think his pretended ignorance would make her any less angry, could he?

Léonie Lesconflair. The beautiful brunette had made it quite clear she would take Nick under any conditions, and the knowledge made Amber wonder if she loved him less because she expected him to be faithful. But then, Nick had made *her* no promises, nor given her a ring. His only commitment had been with his body. And that wasn't enough for her.

CHAPTER
18

 NICK stood in the shadows of the empty alley and waited. He'd seen Dyer follow Martin. The man had slipped from the ballroom like a silent wraith. There had been no furtive conversation with Martin as he'd expected, no indication that the two men even knew one another. Beyond a brief, silent nod, they'd not exchanged a single acknowledgment.

Puzzled, Nick did his best to wait patiently. It had taken him more than one try to disengage himself from his clinging female companions, who had pouted charmingly when he'd left in a hurry. Only promises to return swiftly had gained his release.

Now he stood in the alley near the SW&C warehouses and tried to ignore the cold. He should be used to it. Hadn't he slept in icy trenches often enough? And endured cold rain that turned to sleet and froze men's feet to their tattered boots? Sure he had. And he'd learned not to notice after a while, because to notice would be inviting misery.

Shoving his hands deep in his pockets, Nick hunched his shoulders and concentrated on listening. Beyond the alley, small sounds blended together. Wagon wheels, shod horses, the rattle and whir of cargo being loaded below on the docks. Shouts and an occasional screech punctuated the night, and he could hears strains of music every now and then.

The familiar weight of his pistol felt good at his side, and he shifted slightly so that the butt was more easily accessible beneath his overcoat. He had no idea what was going to happen, only knew, from overhearing Norman Martin issue an order to the small boy who usually rented a hack for him, that tonight was the night.

"Tell the hack to pick me up in back of the Gayoso House at ten o'clock, Henry," Martin had said sternly. "And if you let anyone find out, I'll skin you alive, you hear?"

Shaking, the child's soft brown eyes had been terrified as he'd nodded. "Yassuh, I woan let no one heah me."

Young Henry, one of the dock laborer's sons, ran the more trivial errands for SW&C, providing extra income for the poor family. It enraged Nick that Martin would stoop to frightening a child for his purposes. Especially timid little Henry. But it had provided him with the information he needed, and now he was here and ready and waiting, and there was no sign of Norman Martin.

It was long past ten o'clock, and nothing moved in the alley or near the warehouse doors but a few rats, squealing and snarling in the dark. Nick watched them idly; the shiny glint of their eyes glittered whenever the shaft of light from a street lamp at the end of the alley washed over them.

It was a shadow blocking out the light that finally told him someone had stepped into the alley, and he pressed into the shadows until his back was against the brick wall. Footsteps echoed in the dark, and he saw the brief outline of a hack roll past the mouth of the alley, then disappear. Someone was saying something in a low, gruff tone, and there was a heavy thud.

It wasn't until he heard the creak of a side door that Nick began to guess what Martin intended.

Crazy bastard, he thought, how does he think he'll get away with it?

He'd begun to edge closer when he heard another voice. This one was higher, sharper, and he tensed. It was a female. Amber, maybe? Dammit, he didn't need to be worrying about her getting hurt during this.

Then he heard the voice rise stridently, and was relieved. Amber sweet-talked, snapped like an angry cat, and did everything but outright call a man what she was thinking when she was mad, but she did *not* get that strident note in her voice. It had to be someone else.

They disappeared into the depths of the warehouse, a faint light flickering as they walked. Bold, he thought, to carry a lantern with them as if no one would question their presence. Where was the night watchman?

That question was answered a few minutes later when Nick saw the crumpled figure half hidden behind a stack of crates.

A trail of open doors led him through the echoing corridors of the warehouse and up to the office, and Nick crept stealthily up the steps. When he reached the office where the ledgers were kept, he wasn't surprised to hear Martin's voice.

"Dammit, Léonie, you should have stayed at the theater like I told you."

A rustle of satin indicated a shrug, and the woman's light laugh was mocking. Nick stepped into the obscurity of another shadow, and caught a glimpse of them through the half-open doorway.

"Really, Norman—or should I say Kevin?—you are ever the worrier, aren't you?"

There was a quick, fierce oath before Martin said sharply, "I told you not to call me that."

"How can I help it? I've known you by that most of your life, me darlin'." There was a faintly malicious edge to her voice, and the hint of an Irish accent that made Nick curious. The woman had gone from a pure, cultured accent to a lilt in the space of a heartbeat.

Still swearing, Martin began to stack ledgers on the table in the middle of the room, his voice cutting. "If that's the way you want to play it, my fine Irish *cailín*, go ahead. But leave me out of it."

"Afraid your pretty, dumb little betrothed will find out the truth about you?"

Martin turned slowly, resting his hands atop a stack of ledgers. "If she does, I'll know who to come to. And if I do—"

"You won't do anything." Crisply, and with amusement evident in her tone, the woman stepped closer. "If you do, I'll have to show Miss Jenné a piece of paper that I've saved all these years. She might be interested in knowing that her husband-to-be is already married. And to the woman whom she thinks is to marry the man she really loves. God, that's rich."

Her laugh rang out as Martin swore viciously, and Nick saw her step close.

"Oh no, Kevin, my love—don't make threats you can't keep. If anything happens to me, a letter goes straight to Henri Jenné, as well as to the local authorities. You'll be arrested and hanged for murder, my handsome husband. Do they know that you're really Kevin Murphy, boy actor from County Killarney and darlin' of the London stage until you decided to try for the biggest masquerade ever? No, we know that no one even suspects."

Martin's voice was wary when he asked, "Why did you come to Memphis?"

"To share whatever it is you're getting from this business, and I can bet it's a pretty penny. Bookings have been slow lately, even for the 'World Famous Léonie Lesconflair.' "

"Mary Kate O'Shaugnessey," Martin said bitterly, "you think you're so damned clever, but I swear, if you mess this up for me, I'll see to it that you never appear in another play in your life."

"And how do you plan on that if you're running one step ahead of the law, me fine spalpeen?" She laughed cruelly. "You don't think I went all the way to New

Orleans to put on your little charade just for a few miserable dollars, do you? I can assure you that I didn't. I played my part well, Kevin, and I want more. I so quickly convinced that stricken little fool that her lover was to marry me that I should be given an award for it. She was easy, but if I hadn't done it, she wouldn't be marrying you. Now, with all Papa's money in your pocket, as well as ruling stock of the company, you should be generous."

"I've given you all I have."

"I know." Léonie shrugged prettily. "But you're about to have more, aren't you?"

"Not if I don't destroy some evidence of certain—shall we say—unauthorized withdrawals of company funds. That damned Nick Windsor is too close behind me. Even married to Amber, I should get rid of these ledgers."

"And you have a plan to do this without causing suspicion, I assume? Thus, this elaborate scheme tonight."

"Exactly, my sweet." There was a soft, silky menace to his words. "In fact, I've just discovered how easy it would be to get rid of two problems at once."

Nick heard the warning in Martin's voice, and wondered if Léonie was aware of the subtle shift in his attitude. Apparently she was, because she was suddenly pointing a small two-shot pistol at Martin.

"I wouldn't work up a headache thinking too hard," she said coolly. "It might be dangerous. Oh yes, darlin', I know you too well to trust you. You'd shoot your own mother for a few dollars, and I know that well enough."

"I don't know what you're talking about. Did you think I would actually harm you?"

Her laugh drifted lightly in the shadowed room, and the glow from the single gas lamp lit up her face. "If I was foolish enough to allow it, yes. Now—what were you saying?"

"That I'll split the profits with you, of course, but you

have to disappear. No more theatrical appearances in Memphis."

"Of course not. For a substantial fee, I'm willing to forget I ever knew you. By the way—what do you intend to do about your future wife's lover?"

Martin's mouth thinned into a harsh line. "Don't remind me of that, Léonie. It's not wise. For a while I thought I'd lost everything by going too slowly."

"And I saved it for you, darlin'. Remember that when you're tempted to get rid of me."

"Léonie, I'd never get rid of you," he said smoothly. "You come in too handy. Besides, you're very decorative."

"So is your fluffy little bride." Her voice lowered to a soft purr. "She looked very content playing at being a wife, so you should enjoy her."

"She'll pay for choosing Windsor first, by God, and she'll pay dearly. But so will Windsor." There was a faint bumping sound before Martin muttered, "Here, help me with this. It's got to be done right. There won't be any second chances."

Nick melted back into the shadows in an effort to see what Martin was doing. What he'd overheard explained a few things, including Amber's anger. So she thought he was to marry Léonie—what a farce! He didn't know if he was mad at her for not trusting him or at least asking him, or relieved that it could be easily explained to her once this was over.

Inside the office, Martin and Léonie were pouring kerosene over the ledgers. Nick recognized the pungent smell at the same time as it hit him what Martin intended to do. A fire would certainly destroy evidence of embezzlement, but how did he intend to get away with it? In light of his own accusations—and what he'd seen tonight—Martin couldn't hope for success.

Nick was so intent on what Martin was doing, he forgot about Dyer until he heard a faint scuffling noise behind him. He turned at the same time as Dyer brought an iron pipe crashing down, and barely managed to avoid being hit in the head as he instinctively ducked. Dyer yelled, a short sound that Nick cut off with a quick slam of the side of his palm against the smaller man's throat. It ended in a strangled gasp as Dyer dropped to the floor, but the ringing sound of the iron pipe being dropped alerted Martin to his presence.

Leaving Dyer gasping for breath, Nick slipped behind a heavy wooden desk and crouched down, sweating in spite of the chill. He slid his hand around the edge of his coat to tuck it behind the leather holster holding his gun. He watched tensely as Martin burst out of the office, then paused, looking around him.

The scant light threw long shadows and wavering illumination that fooled the eye, but Nick saw and recognized determination as well as fear on Martin's face. He wouldn't give up easy.

Martin stepped out cautiously. When he reached Dyer, he looked around before kneeling beside the choking man and asking dispassionately, "Are you alone?"

Dyer's tortured moans were incomprehensible, and Martin grew impatient. "Dammit, man, did you at least do what you were told?"

A short nod was answer enough, and Martin looked satisfied. "I don't know what the hell you were doing out here, but—"

"Isn't it obvious?" Léonie demanded, kneeling beside Dyer in a rustle of silk. "He's been hit by someone."

"Hit—yes, I suppose you're right. Dyer, who was it?"

"You fool, he can't talk. Mr. Dyer, just nod your head if we are correct, can you do that? You'll be all right in a few minutes, but time is of the essence right now."

Léonie's smile was falsely sweet, and Nick imagined she'd done an excellent job of playing his intended bride for Amber. It was a wonder he hadn't gotten a bullet in the head instead of abandoned.

He'd take care of that soon enough, but now he had

to stop Norman Martin—or Kevin Murphy, or whatever his name really was—from doing what he obviously intended. Kerosene and a match in this office so near a warehouse filled with dry goods and flammable stores would set the entire city on fire before it could be controlled.

"It couldn't have been the night watch," Martin was saying in a grumbling tone. "Dyer took care of him first. There must be someone else in here. Maybe he got someone to help him put the—"

Léonie touched Dyer lightly. "I think he's passed out. We can't ask him any questions."

"Is he still breathing?"

"Yes. What do you want to do?"

"Come on," Martin said urgently. "We've only got a few minutes before things start happening. I've got to be ready."

She stood up, looking down at the still gasping Dyer. "What about him?"

"Leave him," Martin said without hesitation. "One less witness to worry about later." Martin stepped back into the office before returning with the empty can of kerosene. "Let's get out of here. I've got to be back at the Gayoso House when this begins."

Nick waited until they were gone, footsteps retreating down the empty corridor, then he stepped out and knelt beside Dyer. He was breathing in shallow gasps, but he was alive.

After retrieving a few of the ledgers from the office, Nick returned to the unconscious man, grabbed him around the ankles and pulled him along. Whatever happened, he'd need Dyer to testify about Martin.

Cold air hit him as soon as he stepped into the alley, and the blast roused Dyer, who began to moan softly.

"Not now," Nick muttered, pausing to prop the man up against a wall. "Quiet," he said when Dyer finally opened his eyes. "If you make any noise, it's liable to be your last. Got that?"

A faint croak emerged, and Dyer grabbed frantically at Nick. There was such urgency in his gaze that Nick frowned. "Is there something you need to say?"

Dyer nodded vigorously, but only strangled gasps came from his bruised throat. Nick smiled grimly.

"It'll have to wait. You stay here until I get back. If you run into your buddy Martin again, you'll end up dead, I can tell you that. In case you haven't figured it out yet."

By the time Nick stashed the ledgers and made his way to the street, there was no sign of Martin or the lovely Léonie Lesconflair. He supposed Martin had returned to the Gayoso House, but as he walked up South Main, he saw him standing with a knot of men. Nick ducked out of sight and edged as close as possible.

"You all know what to do," Martin was saying, using a thick Irish accent that surprised Nick until he recognized some of the men. These were the Irish laborers, the rivermen, the workers who lived in the shanties clustered on the bluffs.

The men began to mutter, and one shouted, "Aye, we know what to do right enough!"

"Good," Martin said. "Remember—they've taken over what should be yours. They're going to take what belongs to your children next, and if you don't burn them out and stop them, they'll all end up with your jobs."

Nick knew what was coming next, and wasn't surprised to hear Martin say, "All those former slaves, they're the ones who've got your jobs, boys. And they'll keep on taking them until they take over everything. Are you going to stand for that?"

"No!" came the reply from over a hundred throats, sounding like a deep roar. When some of the men moved, Nick saw weapons in their hands as well as unlit torches.

He knew then what Martin intended. It would all be blamed on a riot between the Irish and the Negroes, the bursting of tensions. Martin had carefully orchestrated this entire scene to coincide with his own plans, and Nick wondered how he could stop it. He was only one man; he'd trusted no one, not needed anyone else in his life. Except Amber.

If he didn't stop Martin tonight, Amber would never know what kind of man she intended to marry until it was too late.

Nick moved blindly toward the police station, not knowing just what he'd say or if anyone would believe him. He only knew that he had to hurry or he'd be too late.

Officer Mahoney was behind the desk, and frowned when Nick burst in. "Still incitin' riots in the district, bucko?" Mahoney asked sarcastically.

In that moment Nick knew what he would say and how he would explain what was happening a few blocks away. "As a matter of fact, Mahoney, you might be interested in what I'm going to tell you . . ."

Amber sat up in bed, frowning. Something had awakened her. A low, rumbling noise like a freight train sounded in the distance. She blinked, then swung her legs over the side of the bed and went to her window. It was chilly, and she shivered as she struggled with the heavy window. It finally lifted with a rough sound.

A blast of cold air whipped inside, and she distinctly heard the noise now. It was the muted roar of anger; she'd heard it once before, when men had gotten into a brawl and Roger had not been able to whisk her away in time. It was a menacing, frightening sound, as it had been that day near Clover Hill.

Flickering lights bobbed like fireflies, and Amber saw the darting flames weaving through the streets. Torches.

She found her robe in the dark and ran down the shadowed hallway to her father's bedroom door. It was ajar, and she pushed it open and peered into an empty room. Dread welled up in her. He should be here nursing his cold. The bed gave evidence of hastily thrown back covers.

By the time Amber found Celia and learned that her father had received an urgent message from Norman Martin, the noise had grown louder. Quivering with fear, the little maid lapsed into a disjointed mixture of French and English that was more confusing than helpful.

"Calm yourself," Amber said sharply when Celia began to weep and moan about a revolution. "I'm certain this is no such thing. If you don't quiet, I'll slap you silly."

Shocked as much by her tone of voice as her words, Celia's eyes grew big and she murmured with a shiver, *"Oui, mademoiselle."*

"Good. Now, how long ago did Papa leave?"

"Perhaps a half hour. I do not know. I heard the noise when I went back to bed, and then I hid in the cellar because I was so frightened."

Amber wondered briefly what she should do, and wished that she knew where to find Nick. He might be furious with her, and she might dislike him, but she knew he would handle the situation.

Making her decision, Amber turned to Celia and said, "Do you know where to find Roger? Did he go with Papa?"

"Non, mademoiselle," Celia replied, moaning softly. "It is Thursday night, and Roger, he always goes to his meeting. . . ."

"Oh lord, I forgot. Then Papa is alone—Celia, go to Aunt Leala's house and get one of the men to find Roger. Have him meet me at the offices, do you understand?"

Celia paled. "You cannot mean to go out! That would be too dangerous. . . ."

"I mean just that. I have to find Papa before he gets hurt. He is so trusting, and—never mind. Just do what I said. And don't look at me like that. I know what I'm doing."

Amber prayed she was right about that as she ran upstairs to get dressed.

CHAPTER
19

TORCHLIGHT cast distorted images across the street. The crowd of angry men had grown to more than two hundred, by Nick's estimate. He suppressed the furious inclination to shoot Norman Martin at first sight. The man had incited a riot for his own purposes, and if something wasn't done, there would be serious repercussions before the night was over.

"Sweet Jaysus," Mahoney breathed beside him, and Nick flashed the Irish policeman a tight smile.

"I told you, Mahoney. Now do you believe me?"

"I do indeed, Windsor. And my apologies for callin' you a liar." Lifting a whistle to his mouth, Mahoney blew a loud, shrill call that brought more uniformed officers to his side. Within minutes, mounted policemen began streaming down the streets toward the bluffs.

Nick stepped back and out of the way as Mahoney called up all available policemen. He had business of his own, and he intended to handle Norman Martin personally.

The Gayoso House was still bright with lights and thronged with partygoers. No one seemed to have noticed that only two blocks away men were swarming toward the clusters of Negro shacks on the south river bluff. Even if they knew, Nick thought wryly, few would care. The plight of the Negroes hadn't touched many purse strings or hearts lately, even among the relocated northerners. Maybe especially among the northerners, who had no former servants among the unfortunate souls living in poverty.

Laughter mixed with the clink of glasses and tinkle of music in the lower lobby as Nick entered the hotel. He'd started toward the stairs leading to the mezzanine level when he caught a glimpse of Martin on the far side of the lobby. Switching direction, he pushed through the crowd just as Martin exited through the far doors.

"Damn," he muttered, and a doorman looked at him curiously as he stood at the curb.

"May I help you, sir?"

"I wish you could," Nick said as he stepped off the curb and looked up and down the street. There was no sign of Martin, and in the distance the noise from the riot was growing. It was easily heard now, and people were beginning to notice.

Nick took off in the direction of SW&C again, cursing under his breath. Martin must have stayed just long enough to create the impression that he was still at the party.

When he reached the alley between two of the warehouses where he'd left Dyer leaning against a brick wall, Nick saw that the man was gone. Not that he'd really expected him to stay. He'd just not had time to make sure of it. Dyer was only a small part of this, anyway.

The rumble of shouting men was loud now, and he could see dark shadows darting back and forth under blurred flames. A shot rang out, sounding much too close, and Nick began to run toward the open door of the warehouse. It sounded as if it had come from inside, when he'd expected gunfire from the rioters.

He'd just stepped inside the door, his pistol drawn, when a sixth sense warned him of danger. Ducking, Nick barely avoided being struck. He turned, swinging his arm up to catch his assailant under the chin, but the man was taller than he'd assumed. The edge of his palm caught the man on his collarbone, and he heard a quick grunt before he was grabbed.

Shoving backward, Nick managed to throw his attacker off balance enough to release his harsh grip. He feinted, dropping to one knee, then surged upward with a swift motion that made the man stagger as he caught him full in the midsection. They both went sprawling, Nick on top. The man's huge arms closed around him in a bear hug and he squeezed, crushing Nick's ribs in a viselike hold.

In the struggle, Nick recognized something familiar. "Roger?"

His attacker paused, still hugging Nick in a hold. "Mr. Nick?"

"Yes. What are you doing here?" The constricting embrace fell away and both men staggered to their feet and looked at one another in the skimpy light of a lamp overhead.

"Same as you, likely. Looking for Mr. Henri."

Startled, Nick swore softly. Martin was thorough, he gave him that.

"No, not quite. How do you know Henri's here?"

"'Cause Miss Leala sent me looking for him. Said he'd gotten a message to come here, there was trouble, but Miss Amber got upset about it."

"Amber. Wonderful. I know I shouldn't ask, but where is she?"

Roger's face looked troubled in the faint light. "Home, I hope, Mr. Nick. There's trouble outside, and he doesn't need to be out. That's one reason Miss Leala was able to find me—I went to check on them when I heard what was happening. I'm sure Miss Amber is home in bed."

"I wouldn't count on it. Look, do you think you can find Henri all right?"

"That's why I'm here," the huge man replied with a slight smile. "I'll find him."

"Do that. I've got someone else I need to find."

"If you mean Mr. Martin, he's upstairs."

"Up—Roger, we need to find Henri quick. Or we might be too late."

Roger didn't bother to ask questions. He must have seen from Nick's face what he meant. Both men started up the stairs, but were only halfway to the main hallway and the business offices when they heard a dull boom, followed by sharp crackling.

At first Nick was puzzled, then he caught the whiff of kerosene and knew what had happened. Martin must have left an entire trail of the flammable liquid. The warehouses and offices would go up like a bomb.

There was no need to say anything to Roger. The huge man burst into action, arms and legs pumping up and down as he took the stairs three at a time. Nick was barely able to keep up, and by the time they shoved open the door to the main floor, they were greeted by a wall of flames.

"Roger!" Nick shouted, grabbing him by his coat. "Don't do it!"

Roger calmly unhooked Nick's hand from the material of his coat and said, "I'm going to fetch Mister Henri. You'd better go find Martin. And make sure Miss Amber is safe."

Before Nick could stop him, Roger pulled his jacket over the lower half of his face and dashed through the flames. The heat was intense, and Nick watched helplessly, barely able to see Roger through the flames and thick smoke.

Another dull explosion jerked Nick into action, and he ran back down the closed stairwell. Smoke was thick on the lower level as well, and he was choking by the time he reached the cool air of the alley. Gasping and coughing, he leaned over with one hand on the brick wall as he struggled for breath.

His lungs ached, but a sense of urgency spurred him into motion. If Martin was still in the offices, he'd been caught by his own trap. Nick looked up when he heard

he sound of breaking glass. He saw a second-floor win-
low burst outward and flames shoot through in orange-
yellow arrows.

Nick pushed away from the wall, one hand still
against his burning chest. Then he heard a scream, high-
pitched and piercing, and his head jerked up. It sounded
ike a woman.

On the heels of that thought came another scream,
and he tried to pinpoint the origin. It had sounded as if
t came from inside the warehouse.

Amber screamed again. Flames ate greedily through
he walls and licked along the floor, forming a barrier
between her and the door. She reeled, still half stunned
rom the force of the explosion that had knocked her
hrough a door and into a blazing room.

"Help!" she screamed, then choked on thick smoke
hat filled her lungs, nose, and mouth.

"Amber, Amber—are you all right?"

It was Norman Martin, and she tried to focus on his
voice as she peered through billowing smoke. She didn't
know what had gone wrong. One moment she'd been
standing in the hallway as her father and Norman ar-
gued, the next, an explosion had shattered the world.

"Norman!" she screamed. "Where's Papa?"

"Safe," was the muffled reply, then, impatiently,
"Make a jump for it, Amber. I can't get to you."

"I can't." She stood, terrified, as the flames grew
higher and hotter.

"You've got to—I can't even see you. I'm at the door;
just follow the sound of my voice."

The smoke was oily and choking, and Amber wiped at
he tears streaming from her eyes, not daring to breathe
deeply. She focused her attention on the barely visible
doorway and Martin's upraised hand, then took a running leap through the searing flames.

Martin caught her, but the impact sent them both to
he floor. Amber's skirts were on fire, and he came up to

one knee and began beating at them with his hands as he rolled her over. Pain seared her legs and she gasped and cried out.

"Be still," Martin ordered, smothering the last of the flames with his coat. He was still kneeling over her when Nick saw them.

Martin's head jerked around, and Amber rose up on her elbows as Nick approached with long strides, fury creasing his features. Her heart skipped a beat when she saw him.

"You all right?" he asked tersely, barely glancing at Martin, who had risen to his feet in a clumsy surge.

"Yes, but Papa—"

"Where is he, Martin?"

Confused, Amber swung her gaze to Norman, who was glaring at Nick with hatred. "Nick," she began, "Norman saved me. Papa—"

"Quiet, Amber. There's no time. Where is he, Martin?"

Martin's jaw jutted belligerently. "Find him. I'm getting out of here."

"Norman!" Amber cried, unable to believe that he would be so callous. "You were with him, and—"

"Come on." Nick reached out and jerked her to him, his jaw tightening when she pulled back.

"No, I'm not going anywhere with you!" Tears stung the backs of her eyes. He looked so—different. His eyes were black, and his cheeks smeared with soot. She was suddenly afraid of him, and leaned away when he snarled a curse.

"Dammit, Amber, this is no time to play games. This building is liable to fall down around our heads any minute, and I need to get you out of here so I can—"

"I'm going with Norman."

Martin laughed. "Hear that, Windsor?"

"Maybe she wouldn't be so friendly if she knew that you'd lured Henri here to kill him," Nick grated, and Amber felt a cold chill despite the growing heat from

he flames. Smoke boiled down the hallway in increasing
louds, and she felt the pressing need to flee.

Backing away from both of them, she said, "I'm going
o find Papa. . . ."

Martin turned to look at her, and his face was grim.
No, you aren't. We're getting out of here, princess."

When Nick took a step toward them, Martin lifted his
rm and Amber saw the pistol in his hand. "Don't try it,
Vindsor," he said coolly. "You're right. There's no time
or this."

Nick flicked a glance at Amber and shrugged. "Right.
o get her out of here."

Martin grabbed Amber's arm and pulled her with
im, running down the hallway. She kept up with him as
est she could, with her skirts in burned tatters around
er ankles. She tried to recall what her father and Nor-
nan had been arguing about, but they had been too far
way for her to hear more than their raised voices.

Yet there had been such certainty in Nick's voice, and
look of furious betrayal as well as something else when
he'd allowed Norman to pull her with him. There had
een indecision in his eyes too, and frustration. If only
he could think clearly, had time to think. It was all
appening so fast.

"Come on, sweetheart," Norman rasped, yanking her
o hard she almost fell as he shoved open a door. A
last of fresh air hit her in the face at the same time as
he heard a muffled *boom*!

"What was that?" she almost screamed, clutching at
Iorman's sleeve. He grabbed her close.

"The same thing happened a while ago. Probably
hen Windsor opened a door. Causes a draft or some-
hing, and feeds the fire."

"Then, the fire behind us—"

"Yeah. Anything up there is probably a cinder by
ow."

Amber screamed and tried to pull free. "I've got to
nd them! Let me go—"

"Forget it. It's too late. By now the fire's spread al over the warehouse as well. Damn that Dyer . . ."

"Forget it?" Amber succeeded in pulling free. Anger and pain spurred her, and she screamed, "I will not How can you—"

Martin lashed out, the back of his hand catching her on her left cheek and sending her reeling. Lights exploded in front of her eyes, and she heard him say calmly, "You're hysterical. Don't make me do that again, sweetheart."

Shocked as much by the force of the blow as his barely recognizable voice, Amber didn't struggle as he half dragged her with him. Grief as well as shock rendered her immobile, and she was only vaguely aware of her surroundings.

It wasn't until she gulped in a breath of cold, fresh air that she realized she was outside, and that Norman Martin was shoving her inside a carriage. Shots were being fired, and she heard shouting and screams. She felt as if she'd somehow landed in Purgatory.

"Get in, dammit," Martin growled, and Amber resisted feebly. The carriage rocked. Nervous at the melee, the horses pranced and whinnied, making the carriage roll back and forth on the cobbled stones of the alley. Above them another window shattered, and glass sprayed out into the alley.

"Let me go," Amber said, regaining some of her momentum when Martin ducked the shower of glass. She managed to avoid his reach long enough to edge past the horses, but he caught her by the back of her dress before she could escape.

No match for Martin's greater strength, Amber found herself dumped into the bottom of the carriage, her head reeling. Dazed, she was aware of Martin giving someone orders; then the carriage lurched into a fast pace, wheels rattling on the uneven street.

Amber battled her fear, and wondered if mild-mannered Norman Martin had become unhinged by the

ight's events. Nick's warnings echoed in her memory,
nd she knew suddenly what he'd meant.

"Amber."

Looking up, the inside lantern reflected Martin's
alm face; she felt a wave of revulsion. "What?"

"Don't be angry with me, honey. I was so frightened
or you. I'd never hurt you deliberately, you must know
hat."

"Where are you taking me?" she asked dully. "And
hy won't you let me up?"

"I don't want you to hurt yourself. Honey, you were
o frantic back there, and I know you're worried about
our father, but it wouldn't do him any good if you died
rying to help him."

She lifted teary eyes to him and was almost fooled by
he sympathetic expression on his face. Almost. There
vas a part of her that could not forget the look on his
ace when Nick had accused him of trying to kill her
ather. And that same part of her brain told her that it
nust be true.

Looking down, Amber levered herself to a sitting po-
ition. Her back pressed against the seat, and Martin
fted her up to sit next to him.

"You do understand, don't you, Amber?" he asked
oftly.

She turned her head away to gaze out the window.
Yes," she lied. "I understand."

Relief colored his voice. "Good. Honey, I hope that
our father is all right. The fire pumper had arrived by
le time we left, and if anyone could help him, they
an."

She turned back to look at him. "If they knew he was
ere. But they don't. No one was there to tell them."

Martin blinked. "Well, there was a riot. I suppose
at's what started the fire. I heard that the Irish were
ying to wipe out the Negro shanties down by the
ver."

"Did you?" Amber looked at him with deliberate disbelief. "I find that hard to believe."

"That there's a riot? My God, didn't you see them?"

"Not that. That they started the fire. They weren't close to the warehouse or office when I got there, and Papa was there before me."

Martin dismissed her with a wave of his hand. "You're still irrational. Overset by fear and grief, I imagine. I'll have the doctor give you something to make you rest. When you wake, you'll feel much better."

"Don't you dare try anything like that," she said fiercely. "I'm not *over*set—I'm *up*set. You ran off and left my father and Nick Windsor to die without even trying to save them. How am I supposed to feel?" Her voice broke on the last word, and Martin looked at her gravely.

"I'll make you forget this," he said finally. "After we're married, I'll make it all up to you. In time, honey, this will—"

"No!" she shrieked, unable to remain calm any longer. "You will never make me forget this night, Norman Martin! And as far as marrying you, you can certainly forget about that."

"No," he said coldly, "I will *not* forget about marrying you. I've spent too long waiting as it is. You will marry me, Amber, and you will marry me soon."

She stared at him incredulously. There was a fire in his pale eyes that made them gleam, and with soot on his face and his hair mussed, he didn't at all resemble the man she thought she knew.

"I should have listened to Nick," she said in a whisper, and Martin laughed.

"That you should have, my sweet. But you didn't, and with any luck, the annoying Mr. Windsor won't be around to offer any more unwanted advice."

Amber looked away, sickened and terrified. He had changed from a kind, sensible man into a man capable of murder and kidnapping. She was truly all alone now

She tried to think, but the evening had robbed her of quick wit. All that came to mind was that she was in more danger than she'd ever been in before.

That feeling intensified when Martin signaled to the driver to stop. Amber shuddered with cold and apprehension, and when the door swung open, she took her chance and leaped.

Cursing, Martin caught the singed hem of her dress and jerked. Amber fell to her knees and sharp pain made her cry out. In an instant Martin was on top of her, lifting her up by her arms and standing her on her feet.

"Don't try that again," he said harshly. He put a hand behind her head and held it still so that she had to look into his pale blue eyes. The carriage lights shone in her eyes, and all she could see was the icy glitter in his as he said in slow, measured words, "It won't be too healthy for you if you get too hysterical, Amber honey. The doctor might recommend keeping you secluded for a long time."

"Is that a threat?" she forced out between cold, trembling lips.

"Call it anything you like. Just remember it."

He turned her around and marched her up the crumbled walkway to a house she didn't recognize. She had no idea where they were or how far away from town. The house looked dark and deserted, and tall brown weeds swayed eerily in the night wind. She choked back a desperate sob.

"Where are we?"

"Belongs to a former friend. He doesn't live here anymore, and I use it sometimes."

"For what?"

"Shut up, Amber. You ask too damned many questions."

Casting a hopeful glance over her shoulder, Amber saw that the carriage driver had started the horses up and was pulling away. There had been no exchange be-

tween the driver and Martin, nothing to indicate there
needed to be. Apparently, the driver was accustomed to
Martin's routine.

It was as cold inside the house as out, and Amber
stood shivering in the entrance hall as Martin fumbled
for a lamp and match. She heard the scratch and hiss of
the match, and saw the tiny flare as he held it to a lamp
and turned the knob. A slow, steady light began to grow,
and Amber looked around her.

A steep flight of stairs led to the second floor, and
two rooms opened off each side of the short, wide hallway. Martin took her into the first room on the right
and shoved her onto a chair.

"Don't move," he muttered.

When he moved to the fireplace and poured in some
coals, she moved to the edge of the chair. Her nerves
were stretched taut, and she quivered with readiness
should Martin be lax enough to ease his guard. He was
too close now, too vigilant, but he had to relax soon.

Martin stood up and turned around, gazing at Amber
with a speculative gleam in his eye that made her shift
nervously. She lifted her chin and stared back at him
with outward defiance, hoping to bluff her way free.

"You'll never get away with this, Norman. My father
will see that you hang if you force me to anything."

"Your father, my sweet, is charcoal by now." Martin's
mouth twisted. "Do you think everything that happened
tonight was by accident? Oh no, I've planned carefully.
To the last detail, as a matter of fact."

Amber swallowed a surge of pure terror and asked
coolly, "What do you mean?"

"That the *riot* being enacted is my doing." His satisfied smile made Amber shiver. "It took months of plan-
ning, but after you and your lover discovered that some
of those well-planned accidents were no accidents, I had
to think of something. So this is it. Took a little longer
than I wanted, due to your meddling, but I've succeeded
at last."

"You're crazy." Her words were a faint, horrified whisper that made him laugh.

"Am I? I don't think so." Martin moved to stand beside her, lifting a strand of her loose hair in his fist as he looked down at her pale face. "I have it all now, my sweet. Henri was balking at some of my plans, and sooner or later he was going to find out about the missing funds. If Nick Windsor hadn't started nosing into the ledgers, none of this would be necessary. But he did, and I had to think of something. As partner and president, it was easy enough. Dyer was only too eager to help, the silly fool, and fell in with me gladly enough. Then you had to involve Windsor. I thought for a while he wouldn't find out anything, but he's too damn persistent. And then you, my love, had to become involved with him." Martin shook his head, his pale eyes glittering in the flickering light. "A mistake. Windsor became more liability than asset. I had intended, you see, to pin the embezzlement on him. It would have worked if you hadn't gotten him so involved with your father. I knew then that Henri wouldn't believe me. So I came up with the idea of the riot to cover up the, ah, burning of company records. It was easy enough. There's a lot of natural tension between the Irish and the Negroes as it is, and not many people care if anyone burns down those shanties on the bluff. That would cover my tracks well enough, and then I had the brilliant notion of getting rid of any future problems at the same time. A simple message to Henri, an accident, the riot to blame the fire on, and voilà! The company—and the woman— is mine. With you as my wife, sweetheart, I have controlling interest in S.W. and C."

"I'll stop you," Amber said softly. "You'll never get away with this."

Martin smiled and cupped her chin in his palm. "Poor love. You've become unbalanced because of the death of your father. A tragedy, but think how generous I will look when I take care of you, marry you anyway, and see that you live the nice, comfortable life of an invalid. Of course, no one will see you but me, but as you will be a recluse, that will be considered normal."

His calm, unemotional recital frightened Amber more than anger would have. There was something terrifying about a man who could relate his misdeeds so tranquilly.

"I see," Amber said after a moment. "And if I choose not to be an invalid?"

"Ah, I don't quite trust you, me little darlin'. You aren't as cooperative as you should be. Maybe in a year or two, I will give you the opportunity, if you have proven yourself."

A year or two. Amber shivered with another chill, and looked away from him. If she let him see the hatred in her eyes, he would never let down his guard.

But Martin seemed to know how she felt, because his grip tightened briefly and he lifted her chin. "Look at me, sweeting. I know you'd like to tell me how you feel but don't dare. It's all right. In your position, I'd feel the same. Get used to the idea of our marriage. I do so hate stubborn women."

"How unfortunate," Amber murmured. He still held tightly to her chin, and she had to force the words out.

Laughing, Martin bent and brushed his lips across her mouth. Amber jerked as if burned, and his other hand splayed across the back of her head to hold her still.

"Get used to this, too," he said, winding his fingers in her hair to hold her as she tried to yank free. His other hand moved to caress the arched line of her throat, fingers sliding over her skin and making her shudder with revulsion. "You didn't mind Nick Windsor touching you like this, did you?" Martin asked savagely. "I know all about it. How do you think I felt when you met him in New Orleans, lived with the bastard like a common slut? I wanted to kill you both. And maybe I'll finish this one day. Once I've had enough of you."

"I'll die before I'll let you touch me," Amber burst

out. "I love Nick, and I'll never forget that you killed him!" Tears burned her eyes, but she refused to let them fall as she glared up at Martin. "He'll always be between us, Norman. You'll never be free of him."

Martin's eyes blazed and he tugged cruelly at her hair as he lifted her from the chair.

"Wrong, sweetheart. I'll see to it that you forget him. I won't have his ghost in my bed."

"And you'll never have me in your bed. Not willingly. I'll fight you until my last breath."

Martin was holding her close to him, and she saw the flare of fury in his eyes grow bright. His hold tightened, and he began dragging her from the front room.

"Maybe I won't wait. After all, you're no virgin. A few hours won't make any difference."

Amber fought him as best she could, slapping at him and twisting her body, but he countered her moves with brutal blows that stunned her. The hallway was dark with shadows as he half dragged her down it, and she began to sob hopelessly even while she kept fighting.

When Martin kicked open a door, Amber grabbed hold of the doorjamb with both hands. Cursing, he tried to pry her fingers loose while still holding her by the hair. Everything was a blur of motion, so that Amber didn't hear the soft words that made Martin drop her. She felt herself suddenly released and tried to scramble up, her hair hanging in her eyes.

"Stay there, sugar," a familiar raspy voice said, and her heart lurched. She pushed the hair from her eyes and looked up at the dark figure blocking the hallway. Even with the light behind him and his face in shadows, Amber recognized him.

"Nick . . ."

"Yeah. Just stay there. Martin and I have something to talk about."

Martin had whirled around at Nick's first word, but now he recovered enough to grab for Amber. Nick's pistol jabbed at him, and he paused.

"I wouldn't, Martin. This thing's liable to go off."

"And how would you explain murdering me?" Martin snarled. "The authorities would hang you before sunrise."

"I can't see how that would make any difference to a dead man." The muzzle of the pistol waggled slightly. "Move over there away from Amber. I don't like seeing you so close to her."

Martin hesitated, and Nick thumbed back the hammer with a slight, clicking sound that spurred Martin into action. He moved quickly aside.

"All right. Be careful with that damned thing."

"I'm always careful around guns and crooks, Martin. And by the way, Henri is still alive."

"Alive! Impossible! I—" Martin halted in mid-sentence, eyeing Nick narrowly. "You're lying."

"No, I'm not. You forgot about Roger."

"No, I didn't. Roger was at a meeting."

"And the minute he heard the noise you were stirring up with your friendly little riot, he left. You didn't count on loyalty between the races, did you? But Roger discounts the color of a man's skin when he feels loyalty. He has pride, Martin, and a lot more dignity than you'd ever know about. He went to warn Henri Jenné, and to protect him if necessary. If not for Roger, Henri would be dead. You'll hang for this."

Crossing his arms over his chest, Martin leaned back against the wall with a laugh. "Do you think so? I don't. After all, it was Dyer who lit the fire, not me. The bastard just tried to kill me too, that's all."

"And almost succeeded. You should have a little loyalty, Martin. If you hadn't tried to kill Dyer, he would have waited until you were ready tonight. As it is, you'll hang for it."

"You're really laughable, Windsor. Do you think anyone is going to believe you over me? And even if Henri is still alive, I didn't try to hurt him. Why, I even saved his daughter from being killed."

"You also tried to burn down the offices with him in them. Do you think he'll appreciate that?"

"It's your word against mine, and you're not very well received in Memphis. Even the authorities know that. A little matter of being arrested a few months ago in a Pinch Gut brawl will discredit you as far as they're concerned."

"Except that I've got a witness in my favor."

"If you're talking about that sleazy little whore Naomi, I'm afraid she's met with an unfortunate accident." Martin smiled at Nick's soft oath. "It was recent, not too long after your last visit to her." He glanced over at Amber as he said the last, a smug smile on his handsome face.

Amber ignored him, though she couldn't help a brief flash of pain at the thought of Nick with someone else. She inched her way up the wall until she was standing. "You seem to have forgotten about me, Norman. I have no intention of allowing you to get away with this."

His stare was cold. "I'll deal with you later."

Nick laughed, jerking Martin's attention back to him. "How do you expect to deal with me now? You seem at a disadvantage, in case you haven't noticed."

"Don't look now, Windsor," Martin said softly, "but we have a visitor."

"I'm not falling for that one."

Amber glanced down the hallway and her eyes widened. A shadowy figure stood outlined in the open doorway. She screamed a warning at Nick, and he threw himself to one side just as a shot rang out. It all happened so fast, she couldn't follow the sequence of events, but somehow Martin had her in a tight hold, his pistol jabbing into her rib cage, and Nick had disappeared into the shadows.

Martin swore harshly, dragging the struggling Amber along with him as he approached the figure. "Help me find the bastard," he snapped out, and a low laugh answered him.

"You can't seem to hang on to anything, can you?" a female voice asked coolly.

Amber stared in disbelief as Léonie Lesconflair stepped into the light. "You!"

Laughing, Léonie said, "You're very observant, my dear. I'm pleased that you remember me."

"But you—aren't you with Nick?"

"I regret to say I've never had the pleasure of meeting him. Not that it matters now." She flicked a glance at Martin. "Hurry up, Kevin. We need to get out of here. The fire is under control, and the police have subdued the riot. There are going to be lots of questions soon, and I don't want to have to answer them. Damn you for involving me in this."

Her cool voice penetrated Amber's terror, and she realized suddenly what a complete fool she'd been. The confused jumble of events took on a clear shape, and she snapped out of her daze.

Jerking free of Martin's grasp, she turned at the same time and dug her shoe heel into his instep, catching him by surprise. As he grabbed for her, howling with pain and fury, Amber ducked under his outstretched arm and ran. Shots rang out, and she heard Martin snap at Léonie not to shoot her, for God's sake.

Panting for breath, Amber fled down the hallway blindly. An arm snaked out as she passed a door, snatching her inside the room.

"Nick," she gasped out, knowing it had to be him.

"About time you got here," he said against her ear. "Now stay behind me and don't move until I tell you, all right?"

"Yes. Oh Nick, I'm so sorry I didn't believe you. I should never have—"

"Not now, sugar. Let's concentrate on getting out of here."

"Is my father really alive?"

"Yes. No more questions, Amber. Listen."

It had grown quiet and still, though her ears still rang

with the echo of the shots. Nothing moved, and she could hear her own and Nick's ragged breathing. Nick's sturdy body was pressed close to hers, warm and comforting and protecting, and Amber held back a sudden sob. She felt so foolish and responsible. She should have listened, should have allowed him to explain instead of never giving him a chance.

"If we get out of this," she whispered so softly he had to lean close to hear, "I'll never doubt you again."

He squeezed an arm around her and kissed her quickly and fiercely. "I'm sure I'll have to remind you of that."

Amber wanted to laugh through her tears. Instead she leaned closer into him. They crouched in the dark and waited, until Nick finally whispered, "Follow me."

Her heart pounded and her pulses raced with fear as she clung to his coattail. There was a window at the far end of the room, and Nick pushed it open, swearing softly when it screeched loudly.

"Hurry, sugar. And when you hit the ground, start running. Don't look back, and don't stop. Head toward the lights on the horizon. That's town."

"But what will you—"

"Run, Amber. Don't stop," he repeated. Grabbing her face between his palms, he kissed her again, then lifted her up and sat her on the windowsill. "It's a short drop. Roll when you hit the ground and you'll be all right."

"Nick—"

"I'm right behind you."

Amber heard footsteps in the hallway and knew there was no time. She swung her legs over the wide windowsill, took a deep breath, then dropped. She rolled when she hit the ground, her skirts flying around her in a mad tangle, then scrambled to her knees and began running. Her breath sounded like a steam engine in her ears as she fled, straining to hear Nick's steps behind her.

When the first shot rang out, Amber hesitated. At the

second and third shots, she stopped, whirling around. She couldn't lose him again. If something happened to Nick, she didn't know if she wanted to go on anyway.

High weeds whipped around her and she panted for breath. Her side ached and her throat hurt, and her knees were shaking so badly she could barely stumble along. As she neared the house, she heard harsh grunts and thuds, and knew that Martin had caught up with Nick.

There was no moonlight, only the fickle glow of lamplight shining through the windows of the house and onto the ground in feeble patches. She strained to see through the murky gloom.

Two figures battled fiercely, and she recognized Nick's taller, lean frame as he countered a blow from Norman Martin. There was the sickening thud of fists pounding into flesh, and the low curses of the men as they fought viciously.

Amber bit back a scream when Martin managed to knock Nick down, leaping on his prone figure and straddling him to pound at his face. She pressed her hands over her mouth, watching as Nick grabbed Martin's arm with one hand, using his other to slice down in a brutal chop. There was the loud, sickening sound of a bone snapping, and Martin screamed.

Then Amber saw a slight movement to one side, but there was no time for a warning before Léonie said coolly, "Hold still, Kevin. I can't miss at this range."

She leveled a small pistol at the two men, and Amber tried to run at her but felt as if she was only standing still. Her long skirts tangled around her legs and she couldn't move fast enough, would not have been able to stop that bullet if she'd been next to her.

The pistol report reverberated in the air in waves of sound that tore a wrenching scream from Amber. Her horrified glance went to the two men, and she saw as if in a dream a quick twist that freed Martin from Nick.

There was a grunt of pain, and Amber briefly closed her eyes with grief.

When she opened them, she saw Nick lying still and quiet, Martin suspended over him as if hung by a wire. Then, slowly, Norman Martin toppled to one side.

Léonie Lesconflair cried out and ran to him as he fell to the ground. "Kevin, oh Kevin—where are you hit?" She pulled his head into her lap, kneeling on the ground and rocking back and forth, crooning as if to an infant. "You'll be all right, me darlin' boy, you'll be all right. . . ."

Amber ran to Nick, who'd rolled to his feet and picked up his pistol and Léonie's. He stuck her pistol in his belt and reached out with his other arm to catch Amber as she flung herself at him.

"Nick, Nick, I thought you'd been shot."

"I told you," he said wearily, "to run and not look back."

"I know." She sniffed, wiping at her tears. "But I couldn't just leave you behind again."

"Woman, I wonder if you'll ever do what I tell you."

Amber tilted her head back and looked up at him in the gloomy light. "Probably not. Maybe if you *ask* me instead . . ."

Nick laughed, squeezing her tightly. "Just wait until I get you alone again."

A surge of love choked off any response, and Amber buried her face against his chest. There was no doubt in her anymore, no doubt that she loved Nick Windsor with all her heart and soul. If it took her the rest of her life, she intended to prove it to him. Maybe he'd never return it as freely, but she would learn to be patient.

She was quiet while Nick knelt beside Martin, and felt nothing when he closed the open, staring eyes with a gentle hand. Léonie looked tired and bewildered as she sat in the damp grass beside Martin's body.

"I guess I loved him after all," she said quietly, and Nick just watched her. Léonie shrugged. "He was a lousy husband, but we knew what each other was like. Ambition got in our way, and we forgot about the love. . . ."

Her voice trailed into silence. In the distance Amber could hear the sound of approaching horses.

"Miss Lesconflair," Nick said gently, "the police are here. They're going to want to question you."

Straightening her shoulders, Léonie met his gaze with a slight, mocking smile. "Then I'd best take my cue and find my mark, hadn't I?"

"Maybe the truth would be best." Nick lifted her to her feet and held her until a man Amber remembered as Officer Mahoney arrived.

"Everything all right, Windsor?" he asked with a curious glance at Amber.

"It is now. I think Miss Lesconflair—also known as Mrs. Kevin Murphy—has a few things to explain." Nick glanced over at Amber, and she heard him ask softly, "How's Henri?"

"Hurt but alive. He'll be right soon enough. We caught Dyer, too." Mahoney's grin flashed brightly in the dark night. "And you were right about Roger—he's one good man to have in a fight."

"As long as he's on your side."

Mahoney laughed, nodding. Then he turned to Léonie. "Come along, miss. We need to go downtown."

Shivering with reaction and cold, Amber waited silently as Nick walked toward her. His loose, easy stride was so dear, so familiar, that she felt the spurt of tears in her eyes, and couldn't hold them back.

"Aw, don't cry, sugar." Nick folded her into his embrace. "It's all over now."

"I know." She buried her face in his chest again, wrapping her arms around his lean, sturdy frame. Love and fear that she'd lose him after all kept her silent, and she held him tightly.

But then Nick glanced down at her and lifted her face

to his with his palm. "Sugar, in case I forget to tell you later—I love you."

Her mouth curved in a tremulous smile, and she quavered, "You won't forget. I'll see to it."

Setting his mouth over hers, Nick kissed her hungrily. When he lifted his head, they were both breathing heavily, and she recognized the flare of passion in his dark eyes.

"Sugar," he said huskily, "I have a feeling you won't have to remind me very often."

Epilogue

RED clover carpeted the sloping hills, and warm sunshine spilled over the fields as the carriage turned into the long drive past the ruins of Clover Hill. Amber tucked her hand into Nick's and smiled up at him.

He looked tense, and there was a bleak light in his eyes that she hadn't seen in a long time. "I'm sorry I let you talk me into this," he muttered, his jaw tight.

"It will be all right," she said softly.

He glanced down at her with a faint, wry smile. "Sure it will. It's just that there are so many memories here."

"All of them unhappy?"

He looked startled. "No."

"Then why not forget the unhappy ones and remember the best ones?" She snuggled close, listening to the carriage wheels rumble over the rutted road. "Besides, we're making new memories every day."

Nick grinned, and his dark eyes narrowed with amusement. "That's not all we're making."

Amber's hand moved to her stomach and she felt the slight kick of the new life growing there. A wash of contentment spread through her, and she glanced down at the plain gold wedding band on her left hand. She would have the rest of her life to love Nick and their children.

"Do you think your mother will be pleased?"

320

"If I know Mother, she'll be ecstatic. And Celine will make us all crazy fussing around you. She likes babies."

"Do you?"

"I've never known any before, except for my brothers and sister, and I was too young to care much then." He laughed at her quick frown. "Yes, sugar, I'm sure I'll like any babies you give me. We'll keep them, anyway."

As Amber smiled and settled against his shoulder, Nick looked back out the carriage window. The familiar rolling hills brought to mind many memories, and Amber was right—not all of them were painful. In fact, most of them were happy. He'd grown up here, spent his boyhood and youth here, and he guessed he'd never regret that.

There weren't many regrets in his life now anyway. He'd grown past all that. Life was too short and uncertain to waste time with hate or regret or indifference. He intended to spend every possible moment filling his life with love.

Amber had taught him that. She'd taught him with her determined, passionate zest that the only thing worse than loss was never having loved. All the bright tomorrows stretched ahead of him now, filled with Amber and their child, and probably a house full of children. He didn't care. He made enough money as the new president of SW&C to support them comfortably if not lavishly, and nothing else mattered.

The carriage rolled to a halt in front of the house, and Roger got down from the driver's seat to open the door. Nick got out first, glancing around, smiling when he saw Moses walking toward him with a wide grin.

"Reckon you knowed whar home is too, Careless," the old man said when he reached him.

Nick put a hand on his shoulder. "Reckon I did, Moses."

"Told Old Billy you'd be here." Moses's face was

creased in a broad smile of satisfaction. "Guess he'll
know who's smarter now."

Nick laughed. "I guess he will." A door opened, and
he turned toward the house, to see his mother and Celine.

Now that he'd come home to Clover Hill to bury the
sad memories and begin the new, he felt a sudden surge
of anticipation at his mother's joy.

It was everything he'd hoped it would be.

Abigail Windsor stepped off the front porch. She
folded her oldest son in her arms and wept with an
unusual show of emotion, exclaiming her happiness at
his homecoming.

"Nick, I always knew you'd come back," she said, and
laughed when he looked startled. "I didn't mean to live
here. I meant back from that dark place where you've
been since the war."

He smiled ruefully. "I guess I've been a jackass."

"Oui," Celine said before Abigail could reply, her
still-unlined face creasing into a smile. "You have been
a jackass of the first place, Mr. Nick, but we knew you'd
come to your senses. Jessamy always said you would."

Nick felt a pang of regret. "How is Jess?" he asked
carefully.

Abigail nodded in the direction of the house. "Why
don't you go ask her how she is? She and her new baby
are inside."

Nick's throat closed. "And Steele?"

Abigail watched him closely. "He is with them, of
course."

Hesitating, Nick felt Amber step aside and took a
deep breath. Without speaking, he opened the front
door and stepped into the small house. He heard Amber begin a conversation with his mother, and knew that
she intended he should do this on his own.

Jessamy Windsor Steele was lying on a small bed
across the room, and Alex stood warily as Nick ap-

proached. The two men eyed one another briefly, then Nick put out his hand.

"Congratulations, Alex. Boy or girl?"

Alex grinned and took his hand. "Boy."

Nick's gaze moved to his sister, and he saw the sheen of unshed tears in her eyes. He knelt beside the bed and with a gentle finger pushed aside the blanket covering the tiny form in her arms.

His voice was unaccountably husky when he asked, "What's his name?"

Jessamy laughed softly. "Nicholas Alexander Steele. Do you think he'll live up to it?"

For a moment Nick couldn't speak. Jess knew about unconditional love too, it seemed, and he was ashamed that it had taken him so long to arrive at the same conclusion.

His dark eyes met his sister's blue-gray gaze, and he smiled at her.

"If he's anything like his parents, I'm sure he'll live up to whatever life hands him."

Reaching out, Jess put her hand in Nick's, and they both smiled.

Later, when Nick went to the Maple Springs Cemetery where his father and brothers were buried, Amber asked softly, "Do you regret having to give up Clover Hill so that it will remain in your family?"

Holding her close, he shook his head. "No. There will always be *some* regret, of course, but it's not really mine. Bryce can have it. Or Jess and Alex." He smiled at her quick glance. "No, there's no more hatred. You changed that for me, my little Yankee gal."

Amber laughed, and stood on tiptoe to press a kiss to his cheek.

Nick's arm tightened around her waist. "I wish my father could have met you, Amber, and that my brothers had the same chance for love that I've found. But as for the past, I've laid it to rest. We've got the future ahead of us, sugar, and that's all I care about anymore."

A soft spring wind blew through the ancient cedars and pines in the cemetery, and seemed to whisper a song of hope and rebirth. The war was over.

Here is an excerpt from *The Island Harp* by Jeanne Williams—a breathtaking saga of 19th-century Scotland, it is also the moving tale of two star-crossed lovers: Captain Iain MacDonald, a man torn between passion and honor, and Mairi of the Isles, the fiercely proud peasant girl who has sworn to save the land and the Gaelic traditions that are in her blood. Together, they embark on an adventure of the spirit and of the heart, in this powerful novel that will live in your memory long after the last page is turned.

The Stones formed a Celtic cross, a long aisle leading to a circle from which radiated three single rows. Peat cuttings had cleared deposits five feet deep from between the aisle stones. There, with the shrouding mist obscuring anything more than an arms-length away, the three of them, old woman, maiden and girl, awaited the dawn.

It came with a burst of rose-gold rays slanting through the mist. Like a glimpse of a fairy world, Mairi saw the hazy purple hills of Harris and Uig, the waters of Loch Roag, drenched with light jubilant as a shout of angels before sinuous vapors, still glowing like living forms, hid that vista with their own magic, and the cuckoo called.

Had she seen a Shining One pace through the golden clouds, Mairi could not have been more entranced or reverent. Suffused with splendor, part of the radiance, she wished for Cridhe in order to add her song to the joy of larks and lapwings. It was one of those rare moments when matter lost its density, dissolved into particles of dancing light that might solidify into weird and beautiful shapes, engendering a new creation.

"We can go now." Gran's voice jarred Mairi. She wasn't ready to leave.

"Why don't you and Eileen have your rest at the byre?" she suggested. "I'll come in a bit."

Gran sighed. "These long tramps draw the bones right out of my legs. Give me your arm, Eileen child, and don't streak along like a plover!"

The mist hid them before the whisper of their steps faded. Drawn toward the center and the great stone that reared twice Mairi's height from the peat, she felt as if the filmy opalescence was alive but not in a frightening way. Advancing between the stones, she entered the circle and approached the central megalith, a squared pillar with a graceful bend as if the island's eternal wind had gradually flared it.

How had the island looked when the enormous stone was set in place either by forgotten spells or ingenious, equally mysterious methods? No peat then, no Black Moor. And according to ancient songs, there were birch trees, hazel and rowan, vast forests of them. So different it was now, yet blood of Mairi's blood, flesh of her flesh, had built this place of worship.

In spite of their brief lives, her people were like the rock underlying peat and thin soil. Perhaps that was all the message the Stones need hold for anyone.

She started forward, and as she did, Iain loomed out of the mist. "Is it you, Mairi?"

Her heart stopped. "Yes."

Was he real or an apparition? No, the dark stubble on his face did not grow on the scar. His gaze probed her as no phantasm's could, scanned her as if to discover the tiniest wisp of reaction. What should she say? What could she do?

"You haven't been to us," she said into the weighted silence. "I—I was afraid some ill had befallen you."

"Is it ill to know the truth? That I am disgusting, even to a woman eager to wed my uncle's money?" The wound twisted his mouth. Through his slurring words, she smelled whiskey on his breath.

"Iain—"

He said judiciously, head tilted to one side, "You look substantial enough, Mairi, but if you're really standing there why don't you shrink as my uncle's choice did?"

"You've been drinking, Iain."

"I wouldn't have married the lady, in spite of my uncle's urging. He's hot for another heir in case I'm killed. But it was educational to watch her try to overcome her disgust. So I visited a whore. She kept her eyes closed, and not from ecstasy."

Mairi did then what she'd wanted to do ever since he returned that spring, took his face in her two hands and reached on tiptoe to sweep the scar with her lips, press her mouth against it as if the kiss could heal. His breath sucked in. His arms closed around her, crushing her to the hard length of his body. Their lips sought each other's.

Trembling, they sank to the earth but as his hands found her breasts, as she cried out in gladness, he tore his mouth away, shoved her from him as he started to rise. "My God, Mairi! Get up, girl. Get away from here!"

"I love you, Iain."

"And I love you." He buried his face in his hands. "Run away, child, before I do what your Clanna would rightly kill me for."

"Iain, I am no child." Rising on one arm, she drew him down to her. "Oh, Iain, love me, make me your woman!"

His kiss was flame and worship. His hands sent honey sweetness through her, a melting, rushing flood that swept her into a boundless sea. Then there was pain but he moved in her so gently that her sundered tissues cleaved to him, she herself, with a cry of triumph, thrust till he filled her in a wild throbbing that left them drained, light and floating.

"Mairi," he sighed at last against her hair. "Oh, my darling! I'd rather lose my battered soul than hurt you but see what I've done—"

She smiled at him, rich with the feel of him within her, his essence spilling all rose and gold and lovely as the mists. She caressed his seamed cheek, smoothed his black hair with her hands.

"See what I've done," she challenged tenderly. "My man, my laddie, you had no chance at all."

He stared at her in wonder, then traced the contours of her face and throat, said with a rueful, husky laugh, "If I didn't know better, Mairi MacLeod, I'd swear you seduced me."

"If I did, I'm not sorry." At his troubled look, she added fiercely, "Sorry I'll never be!"

He kissed her and it seemed she had always known the rough sweetness of his mouth, the clean male scent of him with its tinge of sea salt, the embrace that while it filled her with fresh hunger gave her an inexpressibly safe and protected feeling. Perfect peace. That's what it was with him after the loving. But that peace changed.

Could it happen again? In spite of the aching where he'd entered her, she ran her hands beneath his shirt and stroked the back of his neck, savored the joy of touching him, learning the muscles of his shoulders, following the bones.

He grinned. "Little witch! So fast you've learned! You tempt me to carry you off to Inverness or Edinburgh, keep you for myself for always."

"I wouldn't go. Not even for you, Iain . . ."

The Island Harp by Jeanne Williams—coming from St. Martin's Paperbacks in May 1993!

Heading for a new life in California across
the untracked mountains of the West,
beautiful Anna Jensen is kidnapped by a
brazen and savagely handsome Indian who
calls himself "Bear." The half-breed son of a
wealthy rancher, he is a dangerous man with
a dangerous mission. Though he and Anna
are born enemies, they find that together
they will awaken a reckless desire that can
never be denied...

SECRETS OF A
MIDNIGHT MOON
Jane Bonander

IN THE BESTSELLING TRADITION OF
BRENDA JOYCE

She was a pawn in one man's quest for power.
A man who stole her legacy and ignited
a passion deep within her...

BLOOD RED ROSES

KATHERINE DEAUXVILLE

"A DAZZLING DEBUT...
A love story to make a medieval
romance reader's heart beat faster!"
—ROMANTIC TIMES